Cover Art: Dorothy Wilkinson

Town Book Press
255 East Broad Street
Westfield, NJ 07090

Town Book Press is an imprint of The Town Book Store of Westfield, Inc., and independent bookstore established in 1934.

Printed in the United States of America

First Trade Printing: September 1999

10 9 8 7 6 5 4 3

Library of Congress Cataloging-in-Publication Data
Callahan, Billy, 1970-
Muckraker: based on a true story / by Billy Callahan.
    p.   cm.
Summary: Sixteen-year-old Ashley is worried because a story that he has written for his school newspaper, revealing extensive drug activity in a local park, may expose his older brother, but then he fears for his own safety.

ISBN 1-892657-06-6 (trade paper)

[1. Drug abuse Fiction.   2. Journalism Fiction.   3. Newspapers Fiction.
4. Brothers Fiction.   5. High Schools Fiction. 6. Schools Fiction.]
I. Title.
PZ7.C1294Mu   1999
[Fic]-dc21
                                                99-29501
                                                CIP

For Jeff

Muckraker

Based on a true story

by Billy Callahan

The cops in this town
are bored. What's say we
all kick this round to
sparks every Mischief Night, huh?

Billy C   10·31·04

Town Book Press
Westfield, NJ

1

HI'S EYE   *vol. 58, No. 7*   *Westfield High School*
p.2 Student Editorial   *October 21, 1992*

Student Recounts Dangerous Halloween
by Ashley Munroe

I had loved every Halloween until this one, several years ago.

I used to live for the decoration, the animation, even the feeling of anticipation, which started as far back as September's first hint of autumn, lasting through that empty drab feeling when the morning sun would shed an unwelcome light in my room after an evening of trick-or-treating. Halloween always took on an invitingly strange appeal, the night when allowance blended with the sneaky and freaky.

Tonight I was trick-or-treating with my best friend—two boys dressed as drab scarecrows, though trying to present different appearances. He was more of the country bumpkin—hiking boots, big dungaree overalls, hay protruding from a wide, floppy black hat. His mother had carefully painted his nose black and his cheeks red. I wore a lame straw hat, a flannel shirt, black jeans, and tennis sneakers. I recently saw a picture of the way I looked that year. I never realized how utterly ridiculous my appearance truly was until I found the photo. Still, it was an easy costume that didn't require an annoying rubber mask that smelled like a tire store.

We had just started making our rounds back toward home. My plastic pumpkin candy holder—a jolly orange face with jutting cheeks handed down to me from my brother and for days after each Halloween smelled like ambrosia when I put my nose inside the hole on top—was jiggling in time with my steps. Now it was getting heavier by the house and the load was wearing me out. Plus, it was nearing bedtime. I was nine years old and my friend was eight, and it was now the latest either of us had ever been out at night alone.

A car was gliding up the street behind us. We were walking on a sidewalk of Sinclair Place and the engine's noise simmered down as it neared. I turned my head, and under a brim of hay, I saw a midnight blue sedan. I remember the muffler sounding like it could drop at any moment. The passenger-side window was rolled down.

"Kids are out late," a man's voice said to us. "What's goin' on?"

"We're okay," I said back. "We're going home."

"Look awful young. You live far?"

"No." If the guy wanted me home, I was now planning to get there faster than before. His bugging me was starting to ruin the close of my night.

"Why don't you lemme drive you home."

It wasn't as much a request as a demand, and I suddenly remembered this hook-nosed policeman who'd given a talk to my third-grade class on safety earlier that same week. His message, which seemed to resound in my brain like flashing electric neon, was the same one I'd seen printed on classroom posters: "Don't Take Rides From Strangers."

"No thanks," I replied as politely as I could. I leaned over to wave him off, and as soon as I saw him I realized something was wrong. I wish I could tell you how I knew this, but the truth is, I just knew. Maybe it was his eyes—two beady pupils in an intense glare. His brow seemed to be in a hard frown and the darkness in the car caused the whites of his eyes to glow spookily.

I straightened and looked at my friend. The wide floppy hat brim caused him to tilt his head and jut his chin to see me. He caught the alarm in my expression and looked from me to the car. We turned and started walking on.

A few seconds later it became apparent that the steady ticking of that weakening engine wasn't going away. The man maintained the movement of his car alongside us. I guessed he was about college-aged, but I could have been wrong. Age is distorted when you're nine. I checked the guy again from the side and he was still staring right at me. It was like all I could see in that car were the whites of his eyes. I will never forget how they bored into mine. I pulled my face away.

"Don't stare at him," I whispered tightly to my friend.

The guy's voice rang out to us from the car with an annoying impulsiveness.

"Just lemme take you home. Don't be stupid. It's late."

"We're fine," I nearly whimpered. "We're walking. We—"

The car sped ahead and skidded at an angle ten feet in front of us. The way the sedan rocked from the sudden halt made the danger real and evident. The engine ticked to a high steady hum as the sedan was set in park. My friend and I both stood rigid as the guy stepped out and watched us over the roof. He waved us over.

"Come on over here, both of you. Got tons of dolls and baseballs I wanna get rid of."

He moved toward the front of his car just as we started past it. Out of the sedan and under the lamp, he looked older than college-age. He was wearing a long black trench coat and sneakers without socks. I thought from his strange appearance that he was coming from some gym. It figured, since he had said he had a lot of baseballs. Still, I was confused. I wondered why he wanted to throw dolls our way. I wondered why he was hurrying over empty-handed if he did. Perplexity painted my face until he spread the flaps of his coat, fully revealing himself to us.

I only glimpsed him, but it was enough to catch every grotesque detail. He wasn't in a completely erotic state, and it wasn't the boldly unwarranted surprise that freaked me out so badly. It was the look on his face—focused on my friend. His eyes seemed to gloss over and his bottom lip was draped lazily. A barely audible sick moan drifted from his mouth and the sound was enough to start us running.

We dashed past him and sprinted up Sinclair, candy from my pumpkin falling behind our hustling steps. The man could have chased us down easily, but he stayed where he was. After crossing Lawrence Avenue, my friend and I, having heard the slam of a car door, paused and looked back. The car was in the same place, the man now sitting hidden behind its headlights. For a second I stared, confounded by why this guy would get his jollies from doing that to boys. Then I looked at my friend, amazed. With his painted face and hay wig, he had been mistaken for a girl. I remembered the disturbing way the man had looked at him.

Suddenly another strange thing happened. Down the street, the headlights blinked off and the car started coming forward like an evil shadow. For a second I still couldn't believe what I was seeing. The sedan's pace now accelerated as if barreling for us.

My friend flinched in alarm and took off up the nearest driveway. I shifted my feet and start stumbling terror-struck after him. Behind, I felt like the last gazelle running from a charging lion. Both of us, however, were disappointed to find a six-foot steel gate at the back of the premises. It was so dark that we could not move quickly without placing our hands protectively in front of our faces. I dropped my pumpkin to the ground with a thud and moved along the shrubbery against the gate, making small wounded-animal noises. My friend quickly covered my mouth and told me to "can it!" We crouched silently in the darkness. Now that I was still I noticed my heart drumming painfully against my chest.

The sedan came slowly into view. There was a telltale scraping of tires on pebbles and a beam of street light streaked over the outline of the lightless car as it passed at walking pace, the man barely visible to me. My friend's breathing stopped for a second when the brake lights flashed, sending the area into an eerie crimson glow. The muffler rumbled madly as the sedan jolted to a stop. The guy knew we were there watching. For one horrible second the whites of those eyes reappeared and seemed to spot us in our frozen trance. Suddenly the engine roared and the car lunged ahead to the corner of Elm Street and, without pausing, screeched right, disappearing around Franklin School. My friend and I gathered ourselves and made for home by way of back yards. We never saw the midnight blue sedan again.

For years I would see that face, remember the whites of those eyes glaring at me from the darkness of that blue sedan. They would be under my bed, in my closet, in bushes all over my neighborhood after dark, always behind me. They would further disquiet my nightmares. The midnight vehicle would follow me home from school, ride alongside me on roads after sunset, always a lightless chassis floating dark and silent on the shadowy asphalt.

The possibility of those eyes still haunting our town kindles a small paranoid itch in my skin every fall. Westfield Police files indicate several similar incidents each year between the nights of October 30th and 31st. The police view these events as minor, since they believe that the victim of a flasher is very rarely in any form of physical danger. The danger for my friend and I that night, however, did not necessarily have to be physical to frighten me beyond any scared feeling that I have ever had.

So take care this Halloween. You just never know who will be out.

2

My anonymous trick-or-treating partner that night was my neighborhood best friend, Blake Spencer, the single most famously colorful character in my entire life. That Halloween night with little Blake really did haunt me. For every ensuing year, I took very little pleasure in finding a costume or accumulating candy, because my only persistent Halloween memory was candy spilling out of my dropped pumpkin and me cowering against a fence, unable to react or protect myself. Hence, I hadn't had much interest in the holiday at all.

But that, along with my life as I knew it, was all about to change.

No town is immune to social deviance, even a prominent, affluent, suburban town like Westfield, New Jersey. Always known to locals for its high taxes and steep real estate values, Westfield boasts winding roads and long avenues of tall Victorian homes with huge wraparound porches and sided with gable rooms sprouting cone roofs whose points are dwarfed by tall oak and elm trees. In recent years, some Colonial houses have been given an oft-times tacky facelift with tall pillars that only serve to contrast the face. This is your basic white-collar town, always expanding with families of professionals driving shiny sport utility vehicles and whose children attend a high-rated school system.

Being a 16-year-old sophomore at a big school like Westfield High was too much like being a number. I always wanted to have a voice, no matter how small it was. So I started writing for our school paper, the *Hi's Eye*. It originated in ninth grade on a hunch that journalism class would be a cinch, but I really began to like the creative way it allowed me to tell stories to all my friends. I was, however, a bit of an extremist, but I liked it better that way. It was an insanely addictive feeling and I wondered if I could stop on account of my own safety. It honestly was not my nature to toil with my own nature, but I came to discover that I was exceptionally good at it. I just never dreamed it would go like it did.

I had never sought out adventure, nor had I taken risks, until I began to write. Sports, starting with little league soccer and up to JV wrestling, provided the only real interaction I had with most kids beyond class. I had always been pretty innocent, studious, never seeing much beyond the realms of English, math, science, and the neighboring streets of Westfield.

One person changed that. His name was Steven Durant, a seventeen-year-old from Roselle Park who had been stabbed two weeks before. No matter what anybody said or still says, I knew I had good reason. No, I didn't do the stabbing—I did the worrying. It was my town, and the park where I played when I was little, and I saw what was becoming of it, saw what was being allowed, never understanding why. Let me take you to the day it became most vitally apparent to me.

Orange and yellow leaves at the pinnacle of the tallest trees basked in the last rays of setting Sunday sun as I pedaled back home through town on my old Redline dirt bike, a hand-me-down from my brother, Tyler. He was actually my mission at the moment. I had ridden my bike to the Rialto, where he ripped movie tickets and swept floors for a paycheck, only to find out that he had left early, around four. It was nearing six, and I guessed he was over at Jenn Dolan's. I really needed to talk to him. I needed to ask him how in the world his car ended up halfway on our neighbor's lawn last night.

Tyler was a senior at Westfield High and just two months shy of his eighteenth birthday. His college of choice was Bucknell University, and by all accounts, his grades seemed to indicate that he would be there at this time next year. He missed the honor roll only once in high school. He wasn't the type of kid who would allow the Wymer's to wake up to his Grand Am angled haphazardly on their grass.

I zipped my jacket as high as it would go and passed through the picturesque park in the middle of Westfield. Two fountains spurted high streams of white water in the air, the slapping, spraying sound a pleasant comfort. The park was named after some Indian, Mindowaskin, who hung out in this town hundreds of years ago. The town had placed a copper sign engraved with its history on the side of the park facing the police station.

The scent of fall leaves saturated the air. Up ahead, the Presbyterian Church's tall, lighted steeple stood visible through the thinning elm trees. A leaf blower hummed a high tone from a nearby yard. Whenever it stopped the evening seemed quieter all around.

I could hear the laughing and calling before I even saw them.

"Ashley!"

My head snapped left to the sound. It came from the usual bunch of kids congregating at the stream bridge to smoke whatever they could put to their lips. The evening air seemed to carry their yells and laughs more sharply. I did know a couple of them. They were sort of a tough burnout breed from school who wore ripped jeans, cut-off shirts, and scowls on their faces when they weren't stoned. Incidentally, *burnout*, I've since learned, describes a breed of tough punk who burns marijuana out until there's none left. I bet you never knew that. That's why I'm here.

An odd-looking guy was waving to me from the bunch. I had a feeling who it was but I wasn't sure, so I swiveled my handlebars and aimed toward the group. The park lamps were blinking on. Jerry Corcoran. In my mind, I was remembering the way he used to look— normal, plain. I had known him since the first day of junior high. Everybody called him Coors for short. I felt dumb, having to wave back from the squatted position of my brother's dirt bike. Other kids I knew distantly from school watched me glide up. I stared back coyly, feeling the ironic brush of familiarity.

I set my bike against the side of the small bridge and checked the police station through the trees clumped on the nearby island. The overgrowth was enough to keep us shaded from the immediate view of the precinct just across the road.

Coors had been busy burning matches one after another and writing his name on the cement arches with the blackened ends. He was up to the R. There were signs that Coors obviously wasn't the first artist. Names and messages covered the concrete. Written in black magic marker on the side of the cement wall, catching my eye, was *SW+GS 4ever*. I tried to remember if I knew those initials. Really I wanted to etch in two extra initials: BS. I swear, *4ever* always carries this phony naïve quality to it. How wonderful if it ever held true. More than likely though, the ink lasts longer than the relationship. So after the breakup, what do SW and GS do when they see it in passing? Time to get a thicker marker.

I knew Coors well in junior high, back when he didn't have a grudge against normality. The year before this, he'd pierced his left ear twice and shaved the entire back of his head. What hair he left on his scalp he'd since colored three different shades, once blue. Now, he had taken to wearing army boots, even to gym. It seemed he was searching for his identity and finding it in a crazy confused conglomerate.

Coors extended a fist from his black heavy metal jacket. Though I represented his opposite, he always did like me.

"Ashley?" he said.

I tapped on his fist, then squeezed my hands in my jeans pockets and shrugged as casually as I could.

"Hey, Coors."

"You looked like you'd had enough Wednesday night." He burned another match, a fire of boredom. "It's usually not like that. That was pretty rough."

I had also wandered into Mindowaskin on Wednesday night. Coors was right about it being rough. I had no intention of hanging out here ever again. It was only out of curiosity, but once was enough for me. I could be friendly with anybody, but I certainly didn't fit in with this crowd. I'd always run with the mainline "popular" group, the clique. My upbringing was not one that would stand me in the middle of a dopefest as much as it would the gallery of a golf tournament. Besides that, I wasn't hard or macho like most here. I've never shaved my head, or grown my hair to my shoulders and beyond, as was the custom of the late-night Mindowaskin type. I have light blond hair that I've always kept cut to a couple inches in length. I never wore leather jackets or graffiti on my clothes. I didn't smoke and I had yet to know what drunk felt like. I was plain vanilla.

I always knew Tyler was different. He was a lot wilder than I, but that really doesn't say much. To define it more clearly, my brother always seemed to be on the cusp between straight and reckless. I was comfortable with my nature, he was at odds with his. My brother wanted to break out of the shell in which my parents had raised him. It was never more obvious to me than when I saw him stride a few paces over the footbridge, not a very big bridge at all, and push me with affectionate smile.

"What are *you* doin' here?"

It seemed like a fitting question, for both of us.

I tried to answer him, but couldn't get through slight surprise at seeing him *here*. Before I could issue a reply, some guy I recognized from his grade but didn't know personally smacked his palm on my brother's chest and held it there. Tyler's eyes appeared befuddled until he saw his lighter drop back into his hands.

"Bang Zoom?" the kid asked.

Tyler nodded with a wink. The quiet grin he gave the kid immediately put me at a stand of naiveté. My brother stuffed his lighter in his shirt pocket. It was a silver flip lighter he fashioned with pride. He swept his hand against my shoulder and looked at me in an oddly guilty manner.

"Mom huntin' me?"

I shook my head. "No. I am. Why? You in trouble?"

"Kinda," Tyler replied sheepishly. He and I do share the same shape to our eyes, if not the same color. His eyes cut sharply and smoothly in his face, only they're dark, gleam like marble, whereas mine are green and are said to sparkle as though I'm in a state of amusement. Our eyebrows are the Munroe trademark—tiny angles forging an air of intensity.

I spied him with an erudite smile. "About your car?"

Tyler and I crossed back over the stream's footbridge, away from the skaterats. He stood under the lamppost and described to me how he was ready to call the cops this morning. His Grand Am, he figured, had been entered by someone during the night, placed in neutral, and rolled off the street where it ended up on the Wymer's lawn. He watched me with gazing glossy eyes while his arms casually waved the story along. "I'm just like—" He stopped to show me the surprised face he made upon seeing his car this morning. "Nothing was stolen, thank God," he finished.

I meshed my lips thoughtfully, quite resolved.

My brother then stuck a dangling cigarette in his lips and leaned against the lamppost. A hand went to his hip and he slouched pensively, staring blindly into the dirt as though reading something on it. His dark bangs were drawn away from his forehead. Tyler's hair colored him the odd ball in my family. Unlike my parents and I, who are blond, his is deep brown. His dark eyes returned to mine.

"I'm ticked, Ash."

Dayle Tanner had been listening in. Now he shook his head at my brother's dangling nic stick and huffed from a smile, "You're a walking smoke stack. I never see you without a butt, Munroe."

Kids here appeared to know Tyler comfortably. I wondered about that.

"Yeah," he replied. His tone was easy, withdrawn. "Everyone dies from something. *I* control *my* fate."

The last time I'd seen Dayle Tanner was in the cafeteria, walking through the food lines with a proctor. He'd threatened Mr. Parker, his math teacher, after refusing to go to the office. His subsequent proctor was Mrs. Cultrik, a drop-dead blonde who dressed like a business exec. Guys in school had a pitiful thing for her. To see her giving Dayle all of her attention that day made me wonder if Dayle was very dumb to get an in-school suspension or very smart.

Dayle Tanner always gave me the creeps, long before I had any trouble with him. He went to the same grade school as Tyler and me, and even though he was okay with my brother, he never seemed to notice me, except to be an occasional jerk. He had been the only kid under sixth grade with long hair in the back. And it wasn't just long; it was curly long, so that it waved ominously from side to side when he marched in his tough strut. Even though he was a senior, he had braces, but for a very good reason. His jaw had to be restructured after a bad sophomore-year fight, one in which he came out the better. The fight left him with some scars that only further emphasized his rat-like eyes. They were slanted and squinty, making him appear frowning and sarcastic. I usually avoided him.

I glanced over Dayle to watch Jerry Corcoran approaching my brother. Coors signaled to him with a toss of his head and they walked onto the little footbridge. I didn't feel like being alone next to Dayle Tanner, so I followed and sat on the crest of the waist-high bridge wall, hanging my legs over and swinging my feet against the cement like I was riding a wide motorcycle seat. Coors and Tyler didn't mind. In fact, they used me as a shield from the police station. They stood close, focusing their attentions on a crumpled plastic sandwich baggy stuffed at the bottom with what looked like tiny dried leaves and dashes of oregano. It didn't take a genius to see what was happening, and Tyler really didn't care about me watching him pass a few folded bills to Coors in exchange for that sandwich baggy. He rolled it up with a sweeping glance of the territory, pulled up a flap of shirt, and jammed it crumpled into his dirty jeans pocket. Then he winked at me. That was the oddest part of the whole thing.

I couldn't say anything. Any tinge of adolescence was gone forever in my brother's eyes now. I tried to reason that it was normal and a passing thing. I didn't want to ask anything that might sound stupid and wimpy, so I stared over at my bike, at the old blue inspection sticker down the shaft. It expired in 1985. I tried to concentrate on that, on something youthful. I remembered bicycle inspection every spring at Franklin School. The cops would get all serious with us, and we'd line up on the playground with our bikes, hoping they'd pass. Thinking back, how bad could it have been? I never saw one bicycle with a red rejection sticker in my life. It was definitely a great way to miss school in the morning. But what tests do they use with which to pass a bicycle? It's not like some mechanic in a welder's mask would shout over to men in lab robes with notepads, "Okay, men! Flame test! Check. Brake test! Check. Chain guard! Check. Pressure gauge: 120 over 30. Looks good! Test the bell! Good ringability?" Then the men in lab coats would turn their heads to me. "We'll mark you good on these points, son." A brand new sticker color would be slapped on my bike. Honestly, though, it was insane. For days leading up to this, we'd be nervous that the cops would snare us off the street for riding unlicensed, unregistered bicycles.

"Wrong move for him," someone said behind me. "If he shows, I dunno."

Baseball Benton Crossey, an athletic-looking kid in my grade whose dark hair was shine-hardened from gel, appeared for all he was worth to be glaring at me. He had an olive-skinned face and was wearing a grim, unfriendly look above hunched shoulders I came to take as wannabe tough. Big testosterone head, I thought. Either there was something he didn't like about me or he was just cautiously defensive with his macho glare. Whatever it was, I could see right through it, but that doesn't mean it didn't ruffle me all the same.

"You're gonna see a very funny look on his face," he was softly warning Guido Delisi, a kid in our grade who looked and acted like Benton. Guido always followed Benton around to sponge off his identity.

For a few feared seconds, I thought Benton was talking about me. But I was relieved to hear his problem was with some kid named Joey. From what I could understand, Joey had bullied Benton's little brother at a party the night before. It seemed this visit was a first time for Benton, purposed by seeking this Joey.

I was just plain afraid of Benton Crossey. Cocky, hot-attitude sneer on his face, way too built for a sophomore. Wasn't always that way. I knew him in sixth and seventh grade when he was kind of a loner, before he got big. Most of his sudden size came from nature, some had to have been artificially inspired. Whichever, his focus for weight training was obviously baseball. He'd started at first base for Westfield the spring before, achieving third team all-county as a freshman.

Baseball Benton stood calmly, spitting every few seconds. I saw he had a swollen lower lip. He shook his head, asking Guido how Joey could be so stupid. Benton routinely neglects to use sharp consonants. "Tha's incre-ble," he said for the third time.

Dayle Tanner, however, leaned toward Crossey, squinting oddly at him, showing his braces. "Aw, you do that stuff? You're nasty."

Benton only scowled at him, making an irritated noise with his mouth.

"Bro, shut your mouth." He spit again, and from it I noticed what I had previously thought was a swollen lip was really chewing tobacco wedged against his lower gums. From the huge amber gobs he'd been spitting I should have given him, a baseball player, that much credit.

"I swear," Dayle still chided, "if vomit ever had a flavor, that'd be it."

Two kids zipped up the asphalt paths on skateboards toward us, swerving their bodies, heads stationary like pros. They pulled up, the taller kid, John Kohleran, also in Tyler's grade, gently holding something in his fingers. Dayle laughed when he saw it was a small joint.

"You gonna fillet that?" he asked. John shrugged and nodded wordlessly.

I nudged Tyler. "*Fillet* that?"

Gel-haired Benton with the try-to-be hard look lost some of his toughness just then. His mouth betrayed him, lips curling into a grin, laughter puffing through his nostrils. It's funny how slight comedy can turn the direction of emotion one way or the other.

"I will after this," John answered to Dayle. "Watch."

John handed the pot stick to Dayle and attempted to spin his skateboard under his feet in front of us. He'd begin his routines by patting the pavement with his foot, sending himself rolling. Suddenly he'd jump, flipping his board crazily with one foot, only to end up sprawled on the grass. Undaunted, he'd get right back up and do it again.

John and Dayle always hung out together, like some intrusive mixture of intimidation. Blond-haired and holding a surfer-dude appearance, John looked a lot less frightening than Dayle and was more approachable. I really didn't have any problem with John Kohleran until I saw him slap his girlfriend, Varsity Carnoustie, in the hall at school. Varsity, properly named Jennifer, had earned herself a harrowing reputation prior to choosing stagnancy with Kohleran, and it was quite plain to me that John was having a tough time dealing with her past.

John finally gave up his painful routine and bummed a light from a junior-high kid, stopping once to look all around. When he was sure he was safe in his distance, he brought both hands to his face and scratched the lighter to the two-inch joint. His blond bangs glowed from the flame. A deep inhalation—he let his arms fall as he watched the pavement for a few seconds. Finally he exhaled.

"Just hung with The Landlord," he croaked to Dayle.

Tanner stuck his hands in his pockets and rocked on his heels, nodding. "Is he gonna throw down on Wednesday night?"

"Think so," John replied.

A group of ducks swam around the island nearest to us and Coors backed away to chuck his cigarette butt at them. My brother Tyler did the same. I rested a hand on the bridge and stared down for a few seconds at both pieces of litter floating in the lamp light on clear water like the ultimate uninvited guests. As it seemed to be with Tyler, they didn't belong where they were. The four mallards, two with shiny green heads, paddled gamely nearer, mistaking the cigarettes for food. One duck raised up and beats its wings rapidly, slamming them into the water with its head and neck erect, cleaning itself. Coors doubled over and snatched a stick, callously hurling it like a propeller at the ducks, separating them in a splash. The mallards spread their wings and walked on the surface of the pond back over to the island, leaving tiny trails of wake. One of the retreated birds near the island tipped itself over to dunk its head under water in search of food on the pond's bottom; the way it paddled its feet and wiggled its butt in the air seemed a proper and fitting gesture.

John's twig of reefer was being smoked down almost to nothing. Behind me I could hear Dayle chuckling. "Friggin' Kohleran. Always wants to fillet at sunset."

John took a suck of what was left, held his breath, and amazingly raised his eyebrows as well as the stem at me. For a second I felt like I was out of myself. I couldn't believe what was happening so quickly, but I took the thing between my thumb and forefinger like he did. I hate to admit how accepted I felt by him. The little piece of rolled paper, the width of my thumb now, felt warm and crinkled. I suddenly felt dangerous, criminal. If the cops decided to converge on us now, I'd be the red-handed fool. Still I inspected the stem closely, whiffing the spicy aroma and watching smoke trail thinner and thinner from the black dot. I lifted my eyes to everyone around, checking side-to-side before my brother's fingers left his pocket and closed themselves around the teeny joint. I surrendered it like nothing.

Tyler twisted to face John. "Want it?"

John's lips curled and he shook his head, coughing. He was finished filleting.

Right in front of me, Tyler raised the stub to his lips and sucked so hard his eyes squeezed. Then he turned and snapped the little roach over the cement railing, arching it into the stream. I listened to my brother cough and watched the joint fade into the dark stream, hoping for a sizzle.

I walked over to the side of the big pond and stared at the precinct house. White caravans and cop cars sat alongside the small road, and even with the fading light, I could see big blue letters on the side: WESTFIELD POLICE. The distance to the cop shop? From the very spot where I stood I could have thrown a Frisbee and hit the front door.

"How is it that cops never show?"

My question took everyone by surprise. It was John Kohleran who sauntered over to me, eyeing the precinct. He huffed.

"These sorry cops don't do jack," he spat, "even in their friggin' back yard, dude. This is nothin'. Stick around 'til tonight, dude. We burn big time, some nights 'til like, three in the morning. Then we try to find homes to sleep in."

There was common laughter until Benton Crossey straightened, vaulting his eyebrows ahead. Everyone seemed to come to life. My head whirled to the left, my fears confirmed when a kid I knew, Joe Apel, came striding down the ever-darkening path, ignorant of the impending peril.

Benton swaggered intently toward Joe. We all watched as he did so.

"Wrong night for you," I heard him utter calmly, true to his form.

Joey's eyes twisted in confusion as Baseball Benton backed away and pulled apart his jacket at the snaps.

"What's your problem wih' my brother?"

Joe Apel had hazel-green eyes that seemed pleading, a feature accentuated at this point. His face jutted forward. He frowned. "Huh?"

Crossey yelled, "Corey! My brother! Last night you're in his face! Why?"

The confusion left Joey Apel's countenance. Red patches formed on his cheeks, his eyes blinking, surprised, cornered. Sudden sweat on his forehead gleamed under the street lamp. Although scrappy, tough, able to handle himself, Joey was a size medium to Benton's large. He seemed torn between running or bravely and stupidly getting this over with. He decided the latter.

"Had nothin' to do with you," said Joey.

Every kid in the area watched this exchange knowingly, adding an impression of seriousness. Benton stepped closer and rolled his face into Joey's. Apel stood there, and it was as though you could feel his pulse. He tried to stand tough, but the change in his pants pockets was jingling.

Benton pointed his hands at his own chest proudly.

"Stupid, bro. You know I can break you in a million friggin' pieces." He held himself with unavoidable confidence, chin in the air. The brass of his language frightened me. His face was right against Joey's now—a standard show of brute intimidation—though the smaller kid seemed more fazed by the stench of Benton's chewing tobacco. Crossey finally backed away a few inches.

"Gen'lmen," he said, pointing lazily. "Get the police if you don't want your friend hurt."

Tyler instinctively stepped in front of me. I felt myself breathing hard. The whole time I probably didn't blink once. Just as Joey opened his mouth, I felt my teeth clench, wanting to say the right words for him— "You're right. I'm sorry. Where's Corey? I'll go apologize. Anything you say."

Instead he frowned and pushed off. "Dude, just get *outta* my face."

It was odd how quickly it ended. I'd never seen anybody punched in the face except on TV. This was different. There was no sound of a sharp smack, no one hurdling into a ten-foot stumble. It was over before I expected, and if I turned my head I would have missed it. The only noise was the rapid rustling of Benton's jacket. He didn't even feign a punch; he simply crashed a straight right on the left side of Joey Apel's jaw line. Quick moans surrendered from those around, some stepping back from the shocking intrusion on their night. Joey fell away to the ground where he rolled on his stomach and put his face in a folded arm. His shirt was slightly turned up from the fall, exposing his lower back. I wished I could have done something for him—such a clean punch—but Benton shifted and kicked Joey's waist, evoking a sick, squealing groan from the depths of Joey's diaphragm. That was the scariest part. Benton didn't *want* it to be over. I thought he'd made his point, but he seemed to need more. Guido Delisi circled near, making sure no one jumped in. Joey's only movement of defense was curling into a ball.

That's all his friends needed to see. John and another guy passively stepped in Crossey's path and talked him down slowly, methodically, attempting to steer his glare away from the injured heap on the grass. Benton swatted them away.

I had righted my bike, swung a leg over, and was pedaling back toward the obscurity of town.

I trotted through the kitchen door when I got home, a little tired from my ride. My mother, wearing a hand towel over her shoulder, smashed hard-boiled eggs in a special slice gadget to make egg salad. I was hungry enough for it to actually look good to me.

"Close the door," Mom said. "You want to heat all of Westfield?"

For a moment I stood there, taking it all in. She looked so relaxed, so much the stuff I'd been used to my whole life. Distinct contrast to where I'd just been. Quick reality check.

I looked out the kitchen window at our darkened back yard, reminded of the time difference. Mom had me change the clocks to one hour back the night before and this evening was tinged with a definite shift in brightness, or lack thereof. It's always an oddly inviting adjustment when you think about it. "Remember," she'd told me, "fall back." I'd gone into every room clock, car clock, VCR clock, computer clock, radio clock, and microwave clock until I had properly ushered in autumn. I never realized how many clocks were around the house until I had to change them.

I leaned on the counter and chewed a piece of wheat bread. Mom squashed the eggs together with mayonnaise in a silver bowl. She paused, wiping hands on her shoulder towel. The towel stayed draped where it was and she went back to scooping.

"Did you see your brother?"

I thought about how Tyler looked while he stood next to Jerry Corcoran—huddled close, faces tilted down at their hands. I pictured his eyes shut tight from that futile drag.

"Yeah, I did."

Mom continued to mix. "Working hard?"

I stared at the counter for a few seconds. "Yup."

3

It was the morning of Monday, October 26, and I had a lot to think about as I sat with my chin in my right hand and gazed out Mrs. Spencer's car window. The world was bright with sunlight blazing the bright colors of the fall leaves to life. I wished I could have reveled in it more, only I was bothered by a big decision I had to make by nightfall to Mr. Kellogg, the faculty advisor for the school paper. I was certain of my decision, and that's what bothered me.

I usually went every morning with Blake, whether it was my mom or his who drove. This morning Mrs. Spencer had the disrupting privilege. Still tasting Crest toothpaste, I sat in the back seat of their Acura and watched the backs of Blake and Mrs. Spencer's heads.

"I'm going to start regulating your time on the phone at night," Mrs. Spencer was telling Blake.

There followed a few seconds of anxious silence. It seemed they were going to resume a prior argument. Sure enough, Blake Spencer spoke up in his defensive quipping tone.

"What the *heck*, Mom! No one in our class passed. The teacher doesn't know Jack *or* Jill."

"That's no excuse."

Blake shook his head angrily. "Mom, I'm telling you, the lady doesn't like me. It's ridiculous. Spanish is the only class I don't fool around in, yet the teacher hates me more than any other."

I glanced at the top half of Mrs. Spencer's face reflecting in the rear-view mirror. She was younger than most of my friends' parents; a tall, very attractive woman who drank a lot of wine and usually overdressed herself for her job—a local lawyer's secretary. This morning a large, white fabric barrette held her straight brown hair in a thickly styled ponytail. She had added a little definition to her arched eyebrows and her lipstick was bright. Her blue suit made her look cutthroat and imperial. I couldn't deal with the strong scent of her perfume this early. Although beautiful and in her late thirties, she was kind of a flaky woman, habitually contradicting herself. It seemed the only things I was hearing her say to Blake lately were reprimands.

The woman sighed. "Blake, you had just better learn to get along with her."

Blake turned to stare at his mother with disbelief. "Mom, listen to what she does. Every time I ask a question, she just turns away and points to someone else raising their hand."

"Then you should raise your hand, too."

"I *do*, Mom! Every time. And every time she calls on me she acts disgusted with my question."

A strong wave of Mrs. Spencer's perfume floated by me again. I blinked when our eyes met in the mirror. I wondered if she wanted me to validate this. Frowning at her son skeptically, she shut her eyes until her head faced the road again.

"Is that why you walked out in the middle of class last week?" she asked.

Blake's head swiveled sharply to smile up at her. "How'd you know?"

"Answer the question."

"Well—that, and other reasons."

Mrs. Spencer put fingers to her forehead. "My gosh, Blake."

Blake Spencer was my down-the-street neighbor and sole best friend since first grade. Most all of my childhood memories involve him in some way. Even though he was always failing to pull me into crazy things I was too scared to do, he tolerated my passivity. In fact, at times he seemed proud to be my best friend, and I loved him like a little brother. Oftentimes I even treated him like one. It was hard to squash the desire to tease him. He looked like such the proverbial little boy, and he fanned the flame of that fact in his mannerisms.

Blake now turned to look back at me. I raised my chin off my fist.

"You've heard about Ms. Rocha," he said, indicating his mother. "Ashley, tell my mom how much a retard Ms. Rocha is."

I just couldn't help laughing at him. He had this pleading look to his face that seemed to anticipate my sympathy, but I was short on it then.

"Leave Ashley out of this, young man," said Mrs. Spencer. "This is between you, your father, and me. You're not a quitter and you're staying in that class like everyone else."

Blake rested an elbow on the windowsill and jammed his head onto his hand. "Where'd that straw-haired hag get her teaching credentials, female prison? She's probably retained so much water it's clotting her brain."

"Blake—"

"Mom, you have no idea. She nearly put Kelly Manzo to tears by dumping her test in the garbage because she did it in pencil. No shit, Mom."

"Watch your mouth, mister!" Mrs. Spencer snapped.

The silence in the Acura was suddenly thick. Blake giggled softly with his head crouched into his shoulders. "Sorry."

Mrs. Spencer lifted her face in the mirror. "Ashley, please don't ever get his habits."

Blake glanced back at me again in a small manner and I tightened my lips to keep from smiling at his sinister-sounding laughter.

Blake looked like a conservative boyish version of Andy Gibb, and that's the out-and-out best way I can describe it. It kept bugging me for years whom his countenance reminded me of until I saw the cover of an Andy Gibb album on VH-1. Blake had straight dirty-blond hair and kept the same style since the day I met him—a perfect side part culminating in a wave of bangs bouncing over his forehead. Nary a blade had ever touched his face, and there was no indication one would be doing so for many years. His chin was devoid of even the tiniest hint of peach fuzz. His teeth were bright white and so naturally straight that he never needed braces, a fact I envied for two grueling years of junior high. Not only that, but he was also the only kid I'd ever known not to own a zit on his face. He made certain teenage aspects obsolete.

"Dad says I can drop Spanish," he said after a long pause.

I had seen Mr. Spencer only once since the divorce. It was the previous spring. He had grown a goatee and a bigger laugh.

Mrs. Spencer raised a warning finger.

"I don't care what your father says. My house and my rules."

I wish I could say Blake and his mom parted amicably, but they just seemed glad to be rid of each other as we reached the high school. Blake thanked her almost begrudgingly and the Acura drove off. I felt sorry for Blake, and knew the root of the problem. His mother was dating a guy for a year now who I thought was easy-going and funny, but Blake refused to like him. Mrs. Spencer began to spend notably less cordial time with Blake since she'd met Jim. Before, she'd taken Blake everywhere, even bugged him, trying to fill the hollow gap in her social life. Now she took notice of him only to settle a problem.

Blake's parents divorced seven years before. Since then, Blake refused
adults the necessary tolerance in coping with the year-to-year changes
we see in them and they in us. I guess he saw them as enemies and
marriage as evil.

I walked along the side of the parking lot toward the back entrance
of the school. I must have looked glum, for Blake asked me what my
deal was twice. I just hunched a shoulder to shift my book bag strap
and kept looking ahead. I'd been thinking about the park, and I didn't
know what to do with my confused feelings yet, so I decided merely to
shrug. I'd stay quiet until I had a decision on which to solidly stand.

Blake couldn't understand why I never vented my feelings. Known
to our friends for his overuse of the expression, "What the *heck*!" he
usually squeaked and beeped on just about anything he could think of,
though it could be funny as hell to hear him because he'd add his
sarcasm with this comically arrogant twist. Still, whoever stood where
was facing, that's who he complained to.

My homeroom was in the Wood Shop. I usually sat next to Chris
Noyes, who talked a blue streak. Today he was absent and it caused me
to notice the happenings in homeroom more closely. I wanted to shake
my head at Flexi Lexi, but held off. Her proper name was Lexi
Mercantanti, but she'd developed quite a slippery name for herself in
eighth and ninth grade. She'd since toned it down this year, and shifted
direction. Flexi Lexi was now a freaky weirdo who wore a cape to
school. Yes, a black cape like a witch. It was no seasonal coincidence,
either. Every day was Halloween to her. She'd been donning the
ominous apparel since the first day of school. Her lipstick of choice
was black and she had odd piercings—her nose, an eyebrow, her left
cheek. There were rumors of others elsewhere but I never pushed for
specifics. It was as if she was on a crusade of self-abuse to avenge her
prior reputation as a slut. One day Flexi wore a crown of thorns to
school, and the following day wore all her clothes backwards, even her
cape. Kids were generally too afraid to laugh at her. She kept to herself
and glared menacingly at you if you dared meet her eyes. Right now I
only glanced at her and turned away, sad. She could have been much
prettier in a more complacent state. I wondered what it might have
been that her parents lacked or overdid in rearing her. One thing was
for sure. She always made me very wary of the saws and sharp
machinery in the room.

Attendance was taken and I hurried out the door to history.

I had Mr. Flaherty for first period U.S. History. He was a tough man to admire. I liked most of my teachers, but found him cold and improper. Even when I received my class schedule that August, the first thing I heard about him was that he was famous for two things. One was shoving a desk at a freshman, years before. I couldn't get that image out of my mind whenever I looked at him. His size made it seem either improbable or more frightening. Mr. Flaherty's three hundred-pound physique carried a striking resemblance to that of Ralph Kramden's on *The Honeymooners*, though the comparison ended abruptly on his foul and distant disposition. A smile was like a holiday with him—pleasant but infrequent. In its place was the second fame— his moose-like yell. It tamed us all frozen to our seats in fear like tiny abused orphans.

Blake was in this class and took spree in the man's enormity. One rainy morning in September between the first and second buzzers, we arrived in room 323 chattering as we all did. Mr. Flaherty was in a rotten mood, evidenced by the curt removal of his thick, plastic-looking glasses and the nasty hollered comment directed at our talking. Blake was sitting next to me as usual, and under what he thought would be cover of sustained muttering and laughter, he tucked his face into his chest and blurted with frightening clarity, "Shut up, fat boy!"

All heads whipped silently between Blake and the teacher like spectators of a tennis match. Mr. Flaherty *had* remarked about our talking, so it wasn't any coincidence that he heard through the subsequent lull. Too bad Blake missed it by a second. Class started ten minutes late while Mr. Flaherty escorted Blake down to Mr. Peterson's office. I deduced by the brisk chipper manner in which Mr. Flaherty returned and immediately began teaching that Blake had met a cruel fate.

Blake was primarily book smart and street dumb, and he could be thoughtlessly cocky. Although one of the brightest kids in our grade, his brains sunk him in as much hot water as they rose his marks. He seemed *addicted* to trouble—crazy and wild in a coming-out-of-the-books sort of way—and instigated as much turmoil in the classroom as he did out of it. I guess he just felt smarter than whoever was teaching him.

This morning I met Blake again at our usual spot in the center right side of the room. He let his book bag drop with a heavy thud on his desktop. Next I was hearing about his exploits in homeroom and how sordid a reaction some had to his story about finding cat crap in his Reebok sneakers that morning. Our group of friends found Blake a receptive yet unwavering target for satirical abuse.

"I always feel like those people in Peppermint Patty commercials," he moaned against the settling-in gab. "Everyone looks at me like I'm nuts."

Maureen Egan walked in this morning donning an outfit considered vastly radical for her. Usually clad in large sweaters and long skirts, today she had on black jeans and a blue silk shirt. Maureen wasn't popular, a brainy nerd betrayed by her overly articulate vocabulary and crisp diction, but she was definitely pretty in a plain sense. Her small frame considered, she huddled down the aisle with her books cradled in her arms like a heavy baby.

Blake had just seated himself and was eyeing her. "Hey," he said. "You look pretty."

Maureen turned to him, smiling. "Thanks."

"Pretty ugly."

Blake's thin lips brought forth a conniving smile, parting just enough for his jaw to hang lazily as though waiting for someone to laugh along with him. His small eyebrows arched sharply in a crafty fashion as he lightly bit his lower lip, finally petering forth an even craftier sounding snicker. Maureen's shoulders dropped as she froze an exhausted, annoyed stare at Blake. She had more eye makeup on than usual.

"Blake," she said, "everyone has their 'ick' thing. *You* happen to be mine."

Maureen started transferring her books under her seat. Neglecting Blake further, she said a short hello to me and to Dustin "the dude" Noonan sitting two seats behind.

"How was your weekend, guys?" Maureen asked us.

Dustin replied first, nodding matter-of-factly. "I was beautifully hung over for half of it." I remembered Dustin at Melinda's party Saturday night, his face sunken deep into the cushions of the basement couch.

I called Dustin "the dude" because he used a rusty surfer-dude type of speech, which didn't quite fit his straight appearance. Dustin had stiff dark hair that he kept conveniently hidden under a baseball cap, except for a slick mat of bangs that stretched over his eyebrows. It inspired his irritating habit of wiping them out of his eyes. He was regular and normal and easy to get along with, and the only deviation from this was when he sent Val Reddington, his ex-girlfriend, eight balloons in the middle of class last year. A different guy's name was marked loudly across each balloon. The card read:

> *For all those great nights: Thanks babe*
> *—Your Boys*

"How 'bout you?" Dustin posted to Maureen. "Do anything crazy?" I detected a slight mockery in his tone, as though he'd asked the question for our sake. Maureen's idea of crazy was probably sneaking into an R-rated movie.

Maureen shrugged, and I suddenly found myself attracted to the girl's features—her tiny nose, the softness of her semi-blonde hair, the doe-like shape to her dark blue eyes, her smooth white chin.

"Friday night I went with my family to my aunt and uncle's," she began. "Saturday we went out to Colt's Neck and picked pumpkins. And then we made—"

"Yo," Blake cut in, "cherry pie." He sat lazily forward on an elbow. "I grow tired of this conversation."

Maureen fought back a smile and tried to look offended. She was in love with him and it was easily obvious, especially to Blake. It was part of Blake's charm, part of the friendly magnetic hold he had on girls. He took so much ragging abuse about his small frame and adolescent attitude that it was oddly inviting to receive any jeer back from him.

"Blake," she told him, "you're abnormal, and you're weird. You're very simply an abnormal weirdo."

Blake Spencer winked at her from behind. "Saturday night was raunchy, Maureen. Your type of gig. Next throw-down, you're definitely coming with."

Maureen turned forward coldly. "I don't drink, Blake."

Blake let an arm fall and looked at her mockingly as only he could. "What the *heck*. You've never gotten drunk?"

Maureen seemed flustered just to be getting this much attention from him. "No," she said defensively. "I have better things to do than get drunk."

"Oh my gosh. Anyone not drunk by now is a total diaperhead."

I blinked in a huff. I myself hadn't gotten drunk yet. Thanks, Blake, I thought glumly. A little water to help wash down that foot?

Little Blake's first drunk was the prior winter. Outside Jenn Dolan's house, he stumbled along in the snowy front yard with me to where we tried to write our names in the powder. I only managed A.M., but he'd had so much to drink, he successfully scripted Blake Scott Spencer. It was a hell of a thing to run out of steam, so to speak, and then look over at Blake, giggling as he went on and on and on, staggering in his steps for fear of losing his place until his name dwarfed my initials.

Two seats back, Dustin was begging to see Steve Capano's whoopee cushion. It was the kind of strange thing you'd see only in grade school. I wondered at the reason for its presence. Blake and Dustin, though, they just wondered how great it would sound in this drab room. Blake had shifted in his seat with a creepy smile washing over his prepubescent cheeks, and from it I knew there'd be trouble. Steve was anxiously checking Mr. Flaherty, who was sitting at his desk, pushing his big glasses further up his nose and listening to Jen Stirling. Without warning, Blake shot out his hand and snagged the rubber device as it dangled between Steve and Dustin. Blake immediately inserted the nozzle in his lips and blew air into the cavity. I could see the inked cartoon on the growing bubble—an animated man bent at the knees with a telltale caption: "Poo!" Blake tilted himself and set the pink balloon on his seat, glancing over at the front. Steve covered his head and Dustin Noonan's braces stuck out as he laughed in anticipation. In front of Mr. Flaherty's desk, Jen Stirling was nodding satisfactorily at the portly teacher. I had yet to notice even the thinnest smile coat the man's face since I'd entered the room. He leaned back as Jen retreated, shuffling a stack of papers and getting ready to start class.

"FFBBFFBBBFFFPP!"

Mr. Flaherty didn't rise, but his head did, directly at Blake. Blake was leaned over toward me and I guess heeded the sudden fear in my eyes. He neglected to sit up, his face squeezed in regret, reddened markedly. He made a futile pretense to fish through his book bag, but Mr. Flaherty wasn't going for it.

"Blake, sit up."

Blake slowly righted himself as Dustin snatched the deflated beef pad. Mr. Flaherty strained and pushed out of his creaky seat and walked to the chalkboard.

"Whatever is physically ailing you," he said in an easy-going voice, "would you please undertake measures to prevent it in the future?" He pinched a piece of chalk and wrote a name on the board. Guess whose?

"Mr. Spencer," he continued, his mellow voice echoing, "I'd like to wish you good morning by inviting you back here for detention at 2:45. Thank you."

Blake watched his desktop dumbly and crinkled his mouth.

It didn't take Blake long to thaw back to life, though. As soon as the lecture began on the Boston Tea Party, Dustin whispered up to him, "Is it me, or is he one day shy of exploding?"

Little clean-cut Andy Gibb whipped his head back and forth between Dustin and Mr. Flaherty. "I know! What the *heck*!" he replied just as softly. "Stay Puff wasn't that big *last* year. He must have gained another fifty pounds at *least*!"

"Blake, cut it out," Maureen murmured.

Blake sat forward, whispering to her in a strain, "I didn't think skin could stretch like that in one year!"

Mr. Flaherty glared tiredly over at the whispering. "Mr. Spencer, do you want to live to drink beer legally?"

"Yes."

"Then let's have some quiet."

I stared at the dirty tiled flooring, pondering how many other kids had sat in this seat before me. How many would be after me? There was that number thing again. I was soon pensively gathering my thoughts for tonight. I wanted my decision to be for the right reasons, more than just personal ones. Was I going to do this tonight for others? For myself? I had to be sure, know my reasoning for my final answer to Mr. Kellogg. I was snapped out of my boredom by Tim Corrigan's watch alarm accidentally bleeping off next to Blake. Heads turned in the vicinity.

"I can't be*lieve* this class disturbance!" Blake shot out with phony exasperation. "Mr. Flaherty just got us all quiet and this—this *nuisance* goes off!" He shook his head with slow dramatic disgust at Tim. "Horrible. *Horrible*! Absolutely de*spic*able!"

"Mr. Spencer!" shouted Mr. Flaherty. I saw he was getting ready to hand out copies of the map of the Thirteen Colonies. Now he just stood and held them, a glare tinged with fury.

Blake insolently ignored Flaherty and held Tim's wrist on high. "I found the culprit, sir!"

Mr. Flaherty's face was still void of any friendly expression. The door happened to be ajar at this point and another class was in the process of passing in hall. We all took envious notice, then Blake piped up cheerfully, "Hey, Mr. Flaherty! Let's play monkey see, monkey do!"

Mr. Flaherty threw the stack of copies on his desk in frustration. A scorching redness appeared on his face. It wasn't until he spoke these next words that I realized how angry he'd become. He often reverted to his Jersey City accent when his boiling point had been reached.

"What is it with y's," he said, "that y's always got somethin' to say?"

"I's don't know," Blake returned, keen on the slip-up. "I's guess I'll cut it out wit y's."

This time no one laughed. A huge expanse had been opened around Blake, who sat very alone. To show my distance to Blake and my timid loyalty to Mr. Flaherty, I glanced at my friend with wide eyes. I'm no part of this, my face said. Mr. Flaherty wasn't concerned with me at the moment. He now paced around his desk and squeaked the panels in front, elevating his voice to a deafening plateau—a booming megaphone heard five rooms down.

"IS MY UPBRINGING FUNNY TO YOU SPENCER?! WELL, *MAYBE* I SHOULD CALL YOUR PARENTS AND ASK THEM *WHERE* YOUR MANNERS ARE! MAYBE I'LL ASK THEM *WHY* YOU CAN'T BEHAVE IN THIS CLASS!!"

I caught sight of Jen Stirling cupping her ears. Mr. Flaherty usually spent more than enough time involved in these outbursts. Thinking about it now, I figure he was taking his size out on his pupils. Blake sat resolutely in his hardwood chair, red clouding his face.

Mr. Flaherty continued to step forward, and because I was sitting nearest in proximity to my best friend, it almost looked like the polar bear-shaped man was coming toward me. The teacher's eyes looked crazy and enlarged behind his dense glasses. His extended index finger was thrust so viciously at little Blake it could have gone right through his chest. I could see meteorites of spit burst from his mouth at every hollered consonant.

"IF WE CAN FIND YOUR FATHER," Mr. Flaherty shouted, "MAYBE *HE* CAN TELL US WHY YOU ACT LIKE THIS!!"

Blake unraveled his arms as Mr. Flaherty's finger drew closer with each jab. Under his bangs, Blake's eyes squinted, gleaming sharply. His thin lips were taut, his teeth clenched in defiance as Mr. Flaherty rested a pencil-clutching fist on Blake's desktop. Suddenly my fear gave way to anger. The man was trying to frighten Blake into submission, using the bitter sting of his father as a tool. Then Blake let go, and if I hadn't seen it, I would have heard it—a blunt harsh smacking sound. Mr. Flaherty began to yell something new and profound when his finger bumped Blake, who lashed out and swatted the big hand away.

Later I would find myself half out of my seat, but I didn't realize it then. Mr. Flaherty jammed the pencil in his teeth and clutched Spencer by the front of his shirt and yanked. Blake leaned back and I could see his whole entire future ebbing away as he chirped warily in singsong, "I've got somebody's job!"

Mr. Flaherty was finished yelling. He pulled little Blake up to a standing position. I can still remember the apprehension plain in Blake's agape jaw, which seemed to lengthen his face as he tried to balance himself while being dragged to the door. Mr. Flaherty stuck Blake against the wall as though taping him there. Agile for an acutely rotund man, he stalked back toward me and bent over Blake's vacant chair without even grunting. Scraping the kid's notebook off his desk, he carelessly clapped it shut and stuffed it into Blake's red book bag, which he picked up and literally threw twirling into the hall. Blake sank through the door and followed the course of his ill-fated sack while Mr. Flaherty pushed the office intercom. Spencer ambled around, dark in the hallway now, peering back in class with a timorous smile, hoping to include himself in our awe.

He wasn't alone for long. Mr. Flaherty neglected to wait for the office response. He simply huffed and waddled into the hallway and motioned for Blake to follow. Blake harnessed his book bag and was first to walk out of our sight.

We all sat pointlessly in the room after yet another of Blake Spencer's premature departures. It wasn't until the two had turned down the stairs when the loudspeaker barked.

"Room 323?"

No one answered. We were zombies, frightened speechless little zombies.

"Room 323? Hello? Room 323?" A few seconds later the woman who calls the between-period school-wide announcements snapped off. Quiet remained until Dustin "the dude" Noonan found enough bravado to break the stalemate. Lips pushed out by his braces, he shook his head in disbelief at Mr. Flaherty.

"Man, he is perturbed and dis*turb*ed!"

It was like leading the cows to pasture. Suddenly voices came alive in astonished wonderment. But it was Jen Stirling who asked loudly, "Why does Blake push his buttons?"

"Blake?" scoffed Maureen Egan. "Are you serious? He's why you shouldn't do drugs while pregnant."

Second period I had Algebra, with Mrs. Oliviera, a stern lady who hardly ever talked. All she ever did was write down notes on the blackboard. It made her job seem very trivial and so misrepresented the other teachers who put forth hard work and creativity in their field that I felt cheated for them.

Third period English was governed by one of my favorite teachers of all time—Mrs. Dowman, a thin, energetic, vinyl-haired woman who cracked us up day-in and day-out with her wit. She spoke briskly, adding her satirical comedy in the most appropriate places. Reason and wisdom were not lost on her however, and I would even say her expressive humor only served in evidence of the woman's intelligence. Needless to say, I set great store by her opinion.

"I don't listen much when someone speaks, even when I do," she'd said on the first day of school. "So when I speak, really pay attention, so one of us is listening. Someone has to keep track of all this nonsense, right?"

During gym class I wondered what doom had befallen Blake, since he was supposed to be on my soccer team. The class was big, divided into twelve six-person teams that played each other in a round robin format every Monday. My team was on first and wound up losing. We were missing Blake—he was the best passer in the bunch.

I sat and watched the second game, along with the rest of my team. Every grade was represented in gym. Thus, Dayle Tanner and John Kohleran were among some of the seniors in my gym class that year, and by their own design, were on the same soccer team. Right now they sat in the bleachers, having their loud way. Cupping their hands to their mouths, they mercilessly heckled kids on the floor, ragging meanly on bodies, hair, everything.

I had a filmy-vision recollection of them in Franklin School. During Tyler's fifth-grade and my third-grade year, they basically ruled the school. It's not like kids had parted for them to pass, but it did seem they had a lot of space to be recognized wherever they went. Squinty-eyed Dayle carried around a demeanor that anything could start a fight with him. John was actually all right, not directed toward trouble as much as his buddy. He at least had a dry sense of humor.

Out on the floor, Rich Hurley was calling a play to his teammates after a scored goal. He formed a triangle with his fingers and his teammates responded by shifting. Dayle and John, of course, found it extremely corny. "Oh yeah! Set up the triangle out there!" they yelled sarcastically. "Come on, guys! Set up that triangle!" They also tormented Hurley by chanting the "other" nickname for Richard. Names of other kids playing were being rhymed with dirty lingoes until Mr. Johnson made a strong suggestion that they stop. Watching these two added more significant apprehension to my decision.

Fifth period Science could've been much better with the right instructor. Mr. Dorevsky was okay, but he just—spoke—so—slowly! I hated being intensely interested in a subject in which the teacher's drawl caused me to fall into a daily doze. Blake was still absent from normal life, either on the lam from the administration or trapped by same. Earlier that month he had sounded very serious in suggesting to Mr. Dorevsky his idea for a science project—seeing how fast flatulence could occupy a small room.

During sixth period lunch, Dustin Noonan coaxed Chris Noyes and I into a game of Jell-O Squares Russian Roulette. The object of the game was to spoon a square of red Jell-O and flick it at the swinging faculty door ten feet away from where we happened to be sitting. If a teacher walked through at the precise moment, you most likely pegged them and lost. Four shots were taken before I was pushed into it. By this time a red sloppy mess was spread at the door's base. Chris voiced a concern that a lady in high heeled shoes would meet an untimely injury from slipping in the gook, yet no teacher had walked in or out for the duration of the game. I waited with my Jell-O wobbling on my plastic spoon while two tables full of kids anticipated a fateful splatter. Without regard for any proctors, I took the spoon back and aimed at the door. Flick! A quick streak of red smashed the door in a heavier mass than I'd envisioned. The action caused a deep thud against the wood, just below the plastic tab that read *FACULTY*. Drips and chunks splattered like fireworks.

Ted Cunningham gasped, "That was a *lot*, Ashley!"

At that instant, the door swung open and my friends whirled back to position. Actually they were curling in fright, their laughter blunt and incriminating. The man to appear was none other than Mr. Kellogg.

His head shot around the door, looking for whoever he supposed had knocked. He had no idea of what lay beneath him, mainly because he'd spotted me. Mr. Kellogg's dark furry eyebrows jumped.

"Ashley Munroe," he said, letting the rest of his body emerge into the cafeteria. He beckoned me with a finger. "Let's speak."

Mr. Kellogg started forward, then paused to check his feet and see what made them slide. His face slumped in irritation when he saw. He set his hands on his hips and stared sparks at my table.

"I don't have time to deal with you guys," he said loudly, and I could feel the stares and smiles from around the giant room. "Clean it up! Now!" He waved over the oriental lady who meandered around every lunch period. "Mrs. Ling, these boys are going to get towels." Mr. Kellogg snapped his long fingers with volume and one by one my friends lifted themselves from the table.

I made a move with them for the kitchen, but Mr. Kellogg led me away toward the back instead. The man was tall and lanky with a few gray strands in his slicked-back hair. His eyes were dark and concentrating, his face chiseled and hard. He was handsome, and from once meeting his wife, I could tell he'd been a bit of a stud as a young man.

Mr. Kellogg and I sat down on the same side of an empty table near the back windows. He seemed unprepared for an opening remark. His head tilted back and his eyes darted over the ceiling, his jaw suspended in thought.

"Ashley," he finally said, sounding regretful, "these are new waters for me." He crossed his legs as only adults do, and leaned back on an elbow. "I reread your article this morning and tried to see it as a student would, and—well, from that viewpoint, it—I'm a little spooked for you."

"I can't do it?" It would have been a great escape, saving me from making the decision on my own. But I was also touched with disappointment. A little. Mr. Kellogg shook his head quickly.

"Not at all. Just want to make sure you're comfortable. This—", he laughed and checked the floor. "There is danger. I won't lie to you." The man leisurely picked at something on his pant leg. "I want you to know I'm looking out for your best interests, and your—your family's as well. I think before anything else, two things have to happen."

I nodded eagerly, my pulse taking an alarming ascent, the reality becoming too apparent.

He licked his lips once and sat forward. "First thing. I want your parents to know about this. They have to be okay with everything. I'm responsible for you as the faculty advisor, you know. Second, we must—we have to involve the police." He saw my look and held my shoulder lightly. "We have to get them on our side, Ashley. Just a few quotes. You—", his head tilted to one side, "made a few remarks that could jeopardize your standing with them."

"That's part of the point."

"No, no, no. Ashley." He held up a long, bony finger. "Ashley, we have to know exactly where they stand. It will help your credibility, and mine. Believe me." Mr. Kellogg stared at me while I watched the window blankly, tapping my fingers together.

"Can I call you later tonight?" I asked.

"We have to have it by tonight."

I blinked repeatedly, nervously. "Let me just think about it and I'll let you know."

He shrugged. "We can push it back a week. Then you have to ask yourself, as I'm doing now—What if something happens within that time frame? How will we feel? Ashley, you've made me a part of this, and now—I'm the fool who can't let it go."

His laughter surprised me in a small comforting way. I finally told him I'd call him by sundown and got up.

After I threw my trash away I spotted Jerry Corcoran at the burnout table near the exit. Coors, spooning yogurt, waved his spoon shortly to me. His friends were beginning to disperse toward the garbage cans. Troubled, I sat down and watched him smile at me for what I felt would be the last time. I was confounded, searching for reason.

"Coors," I said softly—he was the only one left at the table now, "I want you to answer a weird question of mine."

He looked up from shoveling a large scoop of fruit slop in his mouth. Devoid of his usual black leather jacket, he was decked in jeans and a Metallica T-shirt of the same blackness.

"Yeah?"

I shrugged uneasily and tried to word it right. "I just—how about the Mindo scene?" He looked at me funny and I forced more purpose to my question. "I mean, how do you guys do all that so close to the police station?" Then I lied, "It's the only reason I don't hang there."

Coors smiled at his yogurt cup. "It's been goin' on for years, dude. Far back as like, Vietnam hippie days. Pigs are always goin' around town to find things to do. Think about it. What's the one place they won't check? Their back friggin' yard, dude! It's the safest place!"

I half-smiled. "Yeah."

Coors made a hollow sound with his spoon as he scraped the bottom of his yogurt cup, the kind where there's fruit on the bottom. His tongue jutted from his lips in a delectable fashion. I guessed it was pretty dang good. I decided I'd bring some tomorrow.

"Don't worry about it," urged Coors. "Just come out with us again. We're all a bunch of weirdoes, but that's okay. A little danger would do you wonders. You're kinda Peter Prep and all, but you'll warm up to it. Everyone does." He shrugged, lifted his eyes to me. "Your brother did."

After lunch I was pulling my book bag out of its cubbyhole when a strong hand gripped my shoulder tightly. I turned to see my brother backing away, biting his lower lip in a friendly smile.

"Dude." Tyler raised a hand and I offered a low five. He came crashing down, stinging my palm. He held it and said, "Meet me at my car today."

Tyler had stopped me in the hallway with Brennan O'Donnell and Scott Rinsky flanking him, all on their way in the cafeteria.

"You see what happened yesterday morning, Ash?" Brennan asked me boldly. His voice was always so confidently loud that I used to figure him for a hearing impairment. He indicated Tyler with a brisk nod of his chin. "Car almost ended up in your neighbor's frigging' den." He cursed good-naturedly then. It surprised me when Brennan cursed. I don't know. It just didn't fit him.

Tyler swatted lazily at Brennan's laughter. Brennan O'Donnell to Tyler was like Blake to me. Brennan, the good-natured young-at-heart joker with the short brown hair and wing-like ears; the loud senior class clown who treated me as a buddy in school, even though I was only a sophomore; the kid who had a shamefully bad habit of overusing the words, "Know what I'm sayin'?" Brennan O'Donnell, with his big dimples, huge smile, and loud laugh who got Tyler smoking Parliament Lights and drinking Bass Pale Ale.

Brennan smiled warmly at me. "Ash, your brother's turning into a raging nutball. Know what I'm sayin'?" He nudged Tyler and tilted his face at me. "He knows what I'm sayin'. Probably knows better than anyone." Suddenly he pealed his barking laugh. "Neh heh hah hah!"

Tyler and Brennan did everything together—played sports together, hung out in town together, dressed the same way, dated from the same clique of girls (Tyler's girlfriend, Jenn Dolan, was Brennan's closest female friend). They even got injured together. A few weeks before at a party on the Boulevard, Brennan cracked a toe on a chair leg and Tyler sprained his ankle from tripping like a jerk and stumbling down the back porch steps. Driving for my brother immediately became a nail-biting adventure. On that same night, Tyler avoided near disaster with a Scotch Plains (which the kids in Westfield called "Crotch Pains") patrol car. He was zooming a wicked trajectory down Lambert's Mill Road when the fuzz suddenly passed him in the other direction. My brother saw the brake lights in his rearview mirror and panicked, flooring it even further with his bad ankle as the cop made a hasty K-turn in a driveway. Knowing with all his heart he was about to be pulled over, he raced his Grand Am around the bend on Lambert's Mill and screeched off a side street, took another quick turn down a small road and parked in long dark driveway where he waited in anguished silence for over half an hour. He didn't see the cop again.

Tyler repeated for me to meet him in the parking lot after school, not exactly a regularity with us. He usually went his way and I went mine. I reminded him that he gets out later than I.

"I'm cutting my last class," he said easily. "Wait for me." At that, the three of them waved to me in a new, rather unfamiliar manner. I gathered from their demeanor that Tyler had since filled them in about my appearance at Mindo. Even though it felt good to have his acceptance of me heightened so suddenly, I couldn't help thinking as he walked away that the only reason my brother seemed to think more of me now was because he believed I was joining in on his park activities.

I walked on to study hall, catching up to Scott Rinsky's little sister, Kelly. From what I gathered Wednesday night, Scott had been frequenting Mindowaskin. Apparently he'd gotten so stoned one night he tried to ride a skateboard and ended up rolling into the brook. I asked Kelly Rinsky what her take was on the park scene. She had no idea what I was talking about.

After lunch every day I had only one class worth anything—French. The rest were study halls. As soon as I checked in with the study hall proctor, I got a pass to the library. I ended up studying nil. I immediately saw Donna Varano, my girlfriend from last spring, sitting with her new boyfriend, Timmy Waterhouse. She curled a finger several times for me to go over. They both seemed to inch away from each other as I did.

I held up a hand. "Hey, don't. Not on my account. Really. As you were."

Timmy and Donna looked at each other, sliding closer while I pulled out a seat opposite from them. Their hair was the same blond color and they had deep affection all over their faces. While we made small talk, they cuddled and kissed each other lightly. I just sat there and watched them, wondering why in the world their lovey-dovey show of affection didn't bother me, when just months ago this image would have devastated me. Now I just didn't care. It's amazing how time alters perception and perception alters time.

Donna and I went together from March thirteenth 'til May eighteenth. Exactly. We liked each other a very great deal, and acted in the first month much the same way she was doing right now with Tim. We idealistically thought we'd go through high school like that. But we soon found out how incompatible we really were and it was starting to strain at the binds of our adoration for each other. She became easily upset with me when I was just being me, and the feeling of disappointing her panicked me and piled on stress. Going out with her when she was ticked was like taking a cinder block on a date—same silence and a heavy feeling. She promised me at the beginning she'd grow on me, and now she was—like a fungus. It got so bad that I reached a point where I'd had enough and my emotions were dulled. What was once a fire was now a vaporized ember. I knew I had to break up with her sooner or later. It taught me how much more I'd rather spend my life trying to get *to* something rather than trying to get *out* of something. Eventually, Donna even tried using jealousy tactics on me, flirting with Blake. But jealously wouldn't even make me care at this point. By the time she took me to her church's spring youth formal, we were the worst couple in the world. I didn't think to get her a corsage—I didn't know it was going to be any big deal *dance* dance. I was astounded to discover she'd bought me a boutonniere a gift she put it on my chest with grudged force in front of her parents. At the fancy ballroom we only danced one half of a slow dance—practically over our seats. I made cracks about the food ("The meat's so raw I think the veins are still pulsing." "I could swear the rump roast just took a dump."), only to tragically find out later that she'd paid for both our meals. Then to cap it off I'd left her friend's post-dance party minutes after I stepped in the parentless house. Donna was stone-faced by then and seemed to be wishing my head to explode. Not knowing anyone there, I just thanked her, said good-bye to her in private, and left.

Today I smiled at Donna's happiness, and she smiled sweetly back at me. We'd parted ways rather comfortably that spring, and had a special, different kindness for each other now. I winked at her. She knew what I meant, and squeezed Timmy tighter, kissing his cheek.

As if to rescue me from what she thought was torture, Tara Vovens materialized in the seat next to me. Tara Vovens the Curb Owl, I called her. It wasn't to imply anything, trust me. I derived that term because this particular girl was always hanging out in town, in parks, near the train station, or at school after hours. But whatever it was she was doing at night, it occurred mostly outside. I couldn't be around Tara the Curb Owl without feeling some wave of sexual arousal. She had a sweet, delicate, soft chin that moved gently when she chewed gum, and a thin smile usually colored with ruby red lipstick. Her hair was teased a little higher than most girls', colored in streaks of blonde mixed in with natural brown. Her dark eyes were nothing short of glamorous when she smiled, twinkling in horizontal crescents. She was just a friend at this point, new for me since she was actually sort of a burner girl. But slight burnout or not, Tara had an incredibly soft inside. She was also forward, exercising that point a little too well to me months before. You'll find out how later.

Tara warmly put a soft thin arm around my neck and tilted her face to peer at me impulsively. I could smell her gum—grape. Her chewing was all I could hear until she blurted out in her sprightly voice, "Just read your story. Pretty spooky."

"Yeah," I said. "It really did happen."

Tara's cheeks were partially sunk in. It made her appear serious at times.

"Who was your anonymous friend?"

I shook my head coolly. "I shouldn't really say."

"I think I know who." Tara nudged me and winked. "I won't say."

Donna sat forward. "I heard about that. I never got a paper."

Tara slid a *Hi's Eye* from one of her notebooks and sailed it across the table. Donna and Timmy gazed at the third page.

Tara the Curb Owl removed her arm from me and sat back to fish in her purse for eye makeup. While she started to add eyeliner using her pocket mirror, she told us about the Halloween when she was eleven and dressed as a showgirl.

"I was on a porch the next street over from mine, on my way back home, like you were." She turned to look at me with effort, marking her eyelid with a finger. I giggled at the sight. "I will admit,"—she held up her other hand as though in apology—"I was a bit flashy for fifth grade. This car just like the one in your story appears in the road. I hardly even heard it drive up. I turn from the porch. I'm just, like, staring at it. And this totally freaky guy waves and shouts out to me, 'Yo! Come here, babe! Let me check you out!'" Tara paused to notice the attention in our faces. "As soon as the person's door opened in front of me, the guy tore off—" she looked at us, "not his pants, but tore off in his car."

We sat back, nodding, filling the air with, "Oh."

Tara elbowed me again. "So Ashley, your story kinda hits home."

"You were eleven?" I asked.

"Yeah."

"So this was what, last year?"

"Oh, beat it." Tara frowned at me and rapped my arm. I fell away and feigned serious injury. She tugged me back up and said seriously, "I was really freaked that night. Things like that make me afraid to ever have kids now."

"Now?" I joked. "I didn't know you were planning."

Tara started patting her face with some powdery pad. "Me? Kids?" She stopped. "Don't even dream about it."

"Shoot, then—what am I gonna fill my nights with?"

Tara's mouth tightened.   She raised a hand and tried to say something in return.   Instead she took her perfume bottle out of her purse and aimed at me.   "I'll squirt you."

"Oh—*my* gosh," I squeaked, mimicking her voice. "I'll like, squirt you."

"Okay," she professed, trying not to smile.   "I'm leaving before I get any more abuse."

I had met Tara Vovens through going out with Donna.   While Donna and I dated, Tara took on a best friend-like quality to me. Though Donna and I didn't last, Tara and I increased our bond.   Lately we'd developed a routine where she'd call and invite me to run over to her house near town.   By the time I'd get there, she'd still be on the phone, planning her night out as a Curb Owl, involving people with whom I really wouldn't click.   Most of our initial conversations revolved around the infamous Joe Chiavetti, her on-again/off-again boyfriend who spent two months in jail for breaking into his neighbor's house.   I remembered Joe Chiavetti from one quiet spring night out on Prospect Street two years before.   I was heading home on foot from a friend's house and Joe suddenly emerged under a streetlight from a crouched position in the bushes.   His features were dark and thick for a 17 year-old—his hair, his eyebrows, his stubble.   He was dangling a stick and asking me the best and most efficient way to get around the center of town.   I asked him why he couldn't just go right through it. His short reply: "Don't worry about it." From what I assumed, he was being restlessly pursued by others.

The night before school ended in June, Tara caught Joe in his house with a half-naked red-haired girl.   It was pretty much over after that, as far as she was concerned.   Joe didn't seem heartbroken about it, though. In fact, he kept right up with the other "lady of the evening", as Tara called her, during the summer.   I thought Joe was a fool.   The red-haired girl couldn't hold a candle to Tara's explosive figure and intensely attractive face.

For weeks after this, I listened to Tara talk about how Joe had the best seats in his car, how he had refurbished them himself, and now some "fire-headed tramp" would sit on them instead of her.   Tara kept wondering how that girl enjoyed the feel of those seats.   By the Fourth of July, Tara was in pretty bad shape.   The skinny little Curb Owl had turned into the shut-in boozer.   Almost every night we didn't hang out I was fielding countless post-midnight drunk dials.   Soon she'd start leaving her guard down in these states, telling me Joe didn't matter to her anymore and how much she wanted to be with me. She loved me. Donna finished scanning my article and was laughing at Tara and me continuing to goof on each other.

"I'm tellin' ya," she said to us. "You two should go out."

Donna winked at me and I looked across at her, abashed. Then something fondly stuck me. I remembered Donna calling me up the night her grandmother died, about two weeks after we'd broken up, and how I went over to her house and held her while she cried. I wondered if she was recalling that just then as well. Tara found out about that night not long after and started to really notice me as a person for the first time.

After school, Tyler was the one waiting for me first, smoking quietly in his silver Grand Am. As of late, he was always dangling a cigarette from his lips. I slung my book bag in the back, then folded my seat and fell in. Tyler drove off after a short hello. I watched the afternoon world in front of us; my nerves about tonight so worked up during the day that I was wrung out from the anxiety. Tyler drove slowly today, for leaf piles were growing in the streets, some yellow and orange maple, some red oak, but mostly soft, forky brown elm. I relaxed and listened to Tyler oddly explain why Brennan and Scott weren't here, as though I'd demanded a reason for their absence. Soon an alluring face blossomed into my mind. I remembered her sweet scent.

"Hey, Tyler?" I asked suddenly. "You and Jenn hang around a lot together. You always get along?"

"'Course." His head was drooped slightly, his forehead tightening as he raised his eyebrows to stare over at me with squinty eyes. "Why?"

"Well, naturally." I nodded away, watching kids on sidewalks pass us like they weren't moving. "You two are alike and all."

Tyler knew what I was getting at. He blinked slowly and seemed to say even slower than he blinked, "You're crazy if you don't hook up with that Tara chick."

"I don't know."

"Watch out for Chiavetti, though."

Tyler turned left off Broad Street and entered Mindowaskin Park. I felt annoyed. This was typical of his habitual self. I was actually shocked to see a few kids sitting on top of the bridge already, smoking cigarettes in patchy sunlit strobes.

"What are we doing here?" I asked rather curtly.

Tyler's head swung around lazily. His eyes fixed on me and I saw, in the rays of sunshine, the bloodshot lines. My brother seemed baffled as he reviewed the road.

"Why? We're not going over there. I just wanna see—"

"Tyler, are you—you're stoned right now, aren't you?"

Tyler grinned wryly as he passed the police station's front entrance. He kept the Grand Am rolling until he backed into the last spot of the parking lot. Here we had a clear view of the bridge. He cut the engine and left the windows down. It was a mild afternoon. We both stayed in the Grand Am, fifty or sixty feet from the nearest patrol car, and watched what we perceived to be another drug deal. Dayle Tanner was already there, standing close to a kid who had to have been no older than eighth grade. Tyler was silent, watching out his windshield with a hand over his eyes and sensing God-knows-what from me in his condition.

It took a few minutes before the small kid wheeled away on his skateboard. He made some laughing remark back to a kid in the bunch as he did so. "You suck!" the other kid yelled to him.

Tyler, meanwhile, rolled his head at me and mumbled, "Yeah, I'm kinda toked."

My face must have been a wash of incredulity. Tyler shook my knee with his hand and told me he'd been a lot worse before I showed up in the parking lot.

"Trust me," he said. "I wouldn't have driven you if I was really bad."

During the next few minutes, I watched those straight stiff bangs jumble as my older brother told me the truth about his car and the Wymer's lawn. "No one knows about this but Brennan and now you," he'd said. "Jenn doesn't even know, so don't say anything."

I promised him I wouldn't and then learned what I had already guessed. Tyler had gotten high on strong weed and ended up leaving his car in neutral that night. The slight incline on our street caused it to back up and settle there.

I took this pretty well, considering what I was feeling. I even laughed lightly. I took it so trustfully well that Tyler even told me how he sprained his ankle two weeks ago after hitting laced marijuana. John

Kohleran had sold him the "greatest weed I ever had. It was worth it." What it also did was make the near miss with the Scotch Plains patrol car that much more significant. If the "Crotch Pains" cop had caught him, he'd have been arrested instantly for D.U.I. That's why he'd scrambled to find a hiding spot. Tyler paused to smile at me. "Dude, it was close!"

I thought of us as young kids, playing with Transformers toy figures, running night games like "Ghost in the Graveyard" all over our neighborhood with the other kids, melting Hershey bars on sunny picnic tables at Memorial Pool, Tyler rejoicing at finding a sand dollar on the beach at Avon-by-the-Sea.

"I was high as a kite," he was saying in a laugh, "but those brake lights sobered me up quick!"

I was still thinking back when something popped into my mind.

"Hey, by the way," I said casually. "What does 'Bang Zoom' mean? The night I saw you here, that kid said 'Bang Zoom' to you."

Tyler was watching the kids at the footbridge. "Are you gonna buy?"

"Huh?"

"That's what it means. 'Are you buying?'"

My head lifted quickly. "Oh."

Watching Dayle Tanner and John Kohleran, all of them, all in the same vicinity as toddlers and young parents, it all became clear to me. A message screamed across my vision—Duh, kid. Drugs in Mindowaskin Park. A *beautiful* park, no doubt. A playground filled with lover's lanes and two blocks of nature, yards from the town precinct's front steps. Appalled, I sat forward, aware of my books in Tyler's back seat. I felt a chill run out from my stomach to the far reaches of my extremities, and before I could stop it, my head rotated shakily at my brother.

"Tyler." I took a breath. "Tyler, I don't—I really don't think you and Brennan and Scott shouldn't hang around here anymore after tonight."

Tyler frowned easily and waved a hand. "Don't—" I don't know if he was going to say "Don't worry" or "Don't nag," but I cut him off with nervous force.

"Tyler, I mean it. No more. As your brother, I'm telling you now. I'm working on an article for the *Hi's Eye* that's going to expose the drug ring going on here in Mindo."

Tyler blinked, thinking I was razzing him. He smiled in stunned fashion, like I'd just told him I'd lost my virginity. Cool so far, he leaned an ear toward me with a shaken smile.

I spoke with quick seriousness. "Mr. Kellogg and I are gonna rip this wide open in the paper on Wednesday. It was my idea—when I heard about that kid from Roselle Park who got stabbed here. That's why I was here Wednesday night. And then I saw you here Sunday, I knew for sure."

Tyler now exposed his best expressions of shock and anger. He sat speechless, his lips hanging stupidly open, his stony eyes searching my face. Cool became hot real quick. His cheeks flushed in random red blotches and he tried to think clearly, but too much was going through his head.

"Ashley—dude." Suddenly sounding different, he shook his head to the dashboard, scowling. For a minute he said nothing, and I waited rather patiently now. The air was out of the bubble at least. I stared at his eyes as they lifted once again to me. What he said he said with icy slowness.

"You seriously can*not* be that huge of an asshole."

I got out, folded my seat over to fetch my book bag, and started for Dudley Avenue.

4

My mother partially named Tyler and I after states, as her mother did likewise. Mom's maiden name was Virginia Browne. My brother's full name is Tyler Dakota Munroe. Mine is Ashley Nevada Munroe. Then there's Dad—Doug. Just Doug.

We had just started to gather in the dining room around five-thirty after Tyler and his girlfriend, Jenn Dolan, stepped in the front door with noses chilled red by the post-sunset air. Tyler was crazy for Jenn, who always made it a point that she didn't spell her name with just one *n*. Her straight brown hair was parted down the middle and draped around a pretty enough hazel-eyed face to pull it off. I was uneasy at first when I saw Jenn this evening. Who knows what Tyler had told her.

I waved shortly. "Hey Jenn with two n's."

Jenn laughed, her receptive appearance stopping my worry somewhat, though Tyler purposely avoided looking at me. He threw me a short knowing glance of interest before looking away. Jenn smiled pretty for me, her mouth the shape of a banana.

"Hey, I hear you're cookin' me dinner," she said.

My mother laughed her head off as she set six plates instead of the usual four on the dining room table. Her own mother's crucifix dangled on its chain over the neck of her sweater. She bopped into the hallway and greeted the two spiritedly, snapping her fingers to her chest once and making sure Jenn was staying. Mom's usually like that. Sometimes it's annoying and sometimes, as in this case, it's a nice icebreaker.

I often refer to my mother as holy-souled; a devout Catholic who has Tyler and me on our knees in church every Sunday and on every blessed holy day with our hands folded in the proper manner—our thumbs crossed in sanctified piousness. My father, however, is what I call a C&E Catholic, only attending Christmas and Easter Masses. He stays comfortably inactive while my mom involves herself in the youth program at St. Helen's, though he is indeed eager to gorge himself 'til he can hardly move at the church picnic every spring.

My mother had gone to the hair stylist that day; her blonde sides looked even and proper. She took Blake by the arm and jostled him, staring at his face with her hallmark gaze. With eyes the color of tropical waters, she sometimes looks at you so intensely as to appear confused.

"Blake?" she asked with concern. "Did you call your mother yet? Does she know you're staying for chow?"

Blake of course tried to avoid her with a short laugh to the wall. It wasn't easy. He ran his thumb down the side of the archway to the dining room and shrugged.

"I don't need to," he said.

Mom blinked, looked at him so worriedly and gently that Blake giggled. He didn't seem keen on revealing much and my mother shook her head to me. I knew what Blake was all about.

My walk home from Mindowaskin hadn't been a very long one. It was only seven blocks to my house from there, if you walked the right way. When I stepped in the front door, my head jerked in surprise. There sat Blake Spencer with my mom at the kitchen table, cracking her up with one of his scatterbrained tales. The dilemma at hand disappeared for one instant as I suddenly remembered his own catastrophe. It seemed weeks ago. Blake grinned dumbly at me, like the world had played a good joke on him.

"Hey!" I'd exclaimed laughingly. "How'd you make it out of school alive?!"

Behind my mother's head, Blake made a slashing motion across his neck with his finger. I clammed up. Later, Blake informed me that he had been issued a central detention and wound up cutting the rest of his classes after lunch. Bored and aimless, he'd been wandering around town before waiting here for a half-hour.

My mother got up, her hair shining in golden layers by the sun coming in the window.

"I just took a message from Mr. Kellogg," she said, handing me a note. "He left his number. Said it's important."

I took the note and felt a bit crowded when I saw his name. Mom went to the stove and tapped lumps on a plate covered by aluminum foil.

"We have an overload of pork chops," she told me. "Jenn Dolan's eating over." She rubbed Blake's hair and looked at me. "So I invited Blake, too, if that's okay with you, sport."

I checked Blake, who winked my way from his seat. He had this knack of slinking out of a situation by weaseling himself into another. From his smirk, I presumed he still hoped to avoid the inevitable ceremonious phone call to his mother.

Dinner had a rushed air tonight. My parents were attending a seven o'clock meeting to help plan the town Halloween parade, which they help to organize every year. Mom seemed to be dressed for it. A black and orange turtleneck sweater with a pumpkin pin met her dark blue jeans below the waist. Her standard hand towel adorning her right shoulder, she mumbled to herself what was missing from the table and then noticed me.

"Hey," she asked, "did you ever call Mr. Kellogg?"

Tyler, chin in hand, noticeably huffed. I glanced at him as he shook his head, eyes to the wall.

"Not yet," I told her softly, keeping watch on my brother.

The sun had gone down and I had remembered my promise to Mr. K, but my answer was still contingent on the eventual opinions around this dinner table.

Dad's brow twitched quickly. "Who's that?"

Mom leveled a plate in front of him. "Ashley's paper editor."

"What's he want?" My father asked, blinking at me through his rimless glasses.

I shrugged, feeling like I do before giving an oral report in front of a class. My eyes swept the table and I could feel a thumping in my ears. This whole thing was coming down to the wire!

My father's an Internet technical analyst. He is by no means a computer geek though, evidenced by his meaty arms, wide shoulders, and bulky chest. He's the picture of a Land's End father—a good-looking guy in fantastic shape with short, straight half-blond hair and a neatly-trimmed beard of the same color. One time he shaved it as an experimental look and my mother begged him to grow it in again.

Next to me at the table, Blake squirmed and offered to help when Mom brought out a plate of pork chops in one hand and a casserole dish full of au gratin potatoes in the other. She rebuked him pleasantly.

"Smells good, Mrs. Munroe," he told her politely. His head turned to watch my father lean back with a satisfied grin.

"Mr. Munroe," Blake asked, "you helped cook?"

Dad checked him with a warm smiling frown. "Be serious, kid. I can't bake. I defrost."

My father's intelligence is sewn on his appearance and seldom lost in his demeanor.

Jenn Dolan made a comment about my mother's pumpkin decoration on the front door, reminding herself about a tale she'd heard in school hours before.

"My health teacher said there's a legend in town about a ghost who haunts the Revolutionary Cemetery," she said, curling a few strands of hair over her ears. "That's baloney. I told her—"

"Lady Abigail," my father said, nodding. "I've heard it, too. I always thought it was garbage until I spoke to this one woman about it." He took a sip of wine as Mom stopped and listened in with us. My father has a gentle, smooth, deep voice like a hum, the resonant quality of a radio personality. He'd be hell on wheels for commercial voice-overs. "It was right after the Halloween parade last year," he continued. "I was passing through the Revolutionary Cemetery on my way home." He looked around the table and shrugged, playing with the collar of his plaid shirt. "I think it's interesting to read some of the town history on the old gravestones. Anyway, there was this woman doing the same thing I was, and I figured she had to have been coming from the parade. She was dressed in eighteenth century attire—bonnet, fancy blue and white dress—the whole shebang. I approached her and asked if she was in the parade. She told me yes. We got to talking and she knew how the town came to be named, how the north side of town was used as farmlands, told me about a hanging in town two hundred years ago— really informative stuff. Well, I made a joke about this so-called Legend of Lady Abigail and this woman's eyes kind of widened like this." Dad demonstrated with a jolt of his head. "Got a little freaky on me, told me, 'Oh, that's a fact. She's true to these parts.' I thought, Come on, lady. I'm an intelligent man. So I waved a hand at her, said, 'That's a myth.' The woman was persistent. She said, 'She does exist.' I asked her, 'How do you know?' The woman sort of walked behind me and whispered over my shoulder, 'I'm her.' I got these chills suddenly, and when I turned to look for her, no one was there."

When my father finished, the rest of us kept our heads still, but our eyes moved about the table, scanning each other. Blake was hunched forward with his lips apart, his eyes stiff to my dad's.

"When did this happen?" he asked.

"Last year on Halloween," my father replied. He picked at a drop of candle wax on the tablecloth and blinked placidly. "You know,

Blake, I also have a beautiful beach house along the Oklahoma shoreline if you're looking to buy that, too."

My mother burst out laughing, swiping his arm. "Doug, you jerk!" A crease formed between Blake's eyebrows as he took a moment to stare around at our laughter. Finally, "Oh, duh!" he said. "I get it." My mother made one last trip through the kitchen door before settling in across from Dad, finally ready to eat. Tyler still avoided looking at me and Jenn sensed something was not right with him. She inquired to the fact and he just shrugged absently.

During grace, in which we all folded our hands and bowed our heads under my mom's pious direction, a horrific though tragically funny misfortune occurred at the table—or just under it I should say. Mom was in the middle of leading us in a very soft and solemn blessing when Blake accidentally—how should I say it—"chimed from the south" before he could hold himself from it. It wasn't particularly huge, as was the whoopee cushion earlier that day; it was quick and sharp, like a modest upwards squeal from an old rocking chair. I opened my eyes and Tyler was smiling across at me from his lowered face, his shoulders bobbing. Jenn peeked over her hands to see if she'd heard right. My stomach muscles tightened like a rock and I was practically spitting on my folded hands. Next to me, Blake had cringed-curled himself into an embarrassed ball, his face a tense red mess of humor. "S'cuse me," he giggled softly. Grace went on through mirth pushing forth from lips in tight bursts and suddenly the table was alive in suppressed chortling. Jenn was wiping her eyes now. Mom paused in her prayer and snapped at us to stifle, only to fall into contagious tittering herself. Poor Blake was being avenged somehow, somewhere, by Mr. Flaherty, I just knew it.

To rescue the moment, my mother immediately unfolded her hands and got us all on the seasonal subject of Mischief Night. Kids have called it Devil's Night, Havoc Night, Wreck-up Night, or even Garbage Night, but we most commonly referred to it as Mischief Night, the ceremonial darkness that sets the stage for Halloween as the spirit first slips off its restraints. To me, however, it was always just another night at the end of October.

There was, however, something about Mischief Night that seemed restless, disorderly, and—pardon the obvious—scary. In fact, the very night before Blake and I were queerly assailed in third grade, my father's car was hit by a flying jack-o'-lantern. I know, because I was sitting right beside him. We were driving down Woodland Avenue in his white Honda Accord when a huge orange face appeared from out of nowhere and pelted the windshield. Had it been a full pumpkin, it may well have cracked the glass, but fortunately for our safety, it smashed into pieces and scattered behind us. The thunderous smacking sound was the worst part. I had started, freezing in my seat, not believing it. My dad cursed, swerving the Accord sharply before jamming the breaks. His face was flustered and patchy, his jaw tight. To this day I haven't—before or since—seen his eyes dart in stunned delirium like they were doing then. I found the whole thing funny, due to my dad's reaction. It was hard to keep from laughing on the way home.

With a swallow of wine, my mother aimed suspicious eyes at Blake.

"You aren't going out, right Blake?"

"Sure am," he professed proudly, his chagrin having passed quickly. He patted my shoulder. "And Ashley's comin' with."

"Don't even think about it, turkey," Mom stated warily. "My Ashley's not like that."

Blake slumped, his lips twisting sarcastically. He simply couldn't understand the mind frame. I'd come to understand his. I'd been with him when he was at his worst. Other than Halloween, summer was usually when Blake was most daring and adventurous. He had no studies, there was no intellectual challenge going on, so he found his out in mischief.

One of his highlights occurred between sixth and seventh grades while he was enjoying a hot shower at the club pool. Blake removed the cap of a trial-size bottle of Pert shampoo that someone had left behind and used it to partially relieve himself. We found out the bottle's owner the next afternoon when Mr. McCracken, a man in his mid-sixties, timely arrived in the showers next to Blake and me. He was a thin pale man with white hair and was frighteningly comfortable with his physique. Whereas we kids primarily used the showers to warm up after a cold swim, he routinely entered in the nude. After Mr. McCracken made small conversation with us while giving himself a horribly thorough washing, he reached up and retrieved the dreaded Pert bottle from its moorings in the eye-level pipes. With one motion he undid the cap, lifted and turned the small bottle upside down, and tapped it on his scalp. It may have been me, but it seemed that the man labored for lather. Blake and I spun around and shut off our showers before hobbling away, laughing drunkenly.

Blake liked to gather Crab apples from the Neilson's yard down the block from his house and hit everything in sight—trees, telephone poles, signs. I did, too, but it stopped there. Blake hit houses and cars by dark, inspiring great thunks in the night air. Under one afternoon sun, Mr. Neilson made the mistake of coarsely throwing Blake off his property. By the time that sun had been three hours set, there was a large hole in one of their upstairs storm windows. Blake lost thirty dollars for the effort.

Blake owned the dinnertime talk, keeping us entertained with other tales of his daring achievements and pranks, holding us in stitches the entire time. So much so, that at the feast's end, my father wiped his mouth with his napkin and stretched back, saying, "Well, Blake, you sure made this an interesting meal."

Tyler would only glance coldly at me now—sour dressing ruining a fresh salad.

I wanted Blake to stick around as support for my crusade in winning my parents over to my cause, but I knew it might be asking too much of him. A few minutes after Tyler drove off to take Jenn home, I got up and paced to the window. Mom and Dad were having seconds of coffee while Blake was just starting his first. I have strangely never developed a taste for it.

I pushed aside a lace curtain and watched the intermediate school field across the street. I could feel the fluttering of my breath as I walked back over to my parents and Blake. Their world was light and easy for one moment as all three involved themselves in another of Blake's tales. I hated to ruin it, but it was now or never. I cleared my throat when he finished. Mom took a double take when she noticed my unease.

"What's with you, sport?" she asked. Sudden quiet. Blake had a speculative look on his face.

"I, um—" I raised a hand in futility at the wall. "I think I'm going to do something that may be a bit of a bind."

Mom's shoulders sank. Enter her blue-eyed stare of intense scrutiny. She set her cup down.

I scratched the back of my head. "You know that call I got from Mr. Kellogg, um—before? You know, the message you gave me?" I dropped my arm. "Well, there's this—there's a big drug ring going on over at Mindowaskin Park. I mean, almost every night. It's been going on for *years*. And, well, tonight, I'm going over to Mr. Kellogg's house with a story that's going to expose it all."

My mother rested her chin on her knuckles. "That sounds dangerous. But, what—" Stumped by thought, she paused. "What's your deliberation? Why do you think it'll be a bind?"

"Because the people I'll expose are kids in my school."

My father stared at his coffee cup between his wrists. "Jeez, Ashley."

I heard Tyler's Grand Am pull back into the driveway. Blake moved his brown eyes back and forth between my parents and I with eyebrows raised. Nothing was said at the table for a while, even when my brother reappeared, leaned against the archway with wide cautious eyes, hands jammed deeply in his jeans pockets. He knew right away what issue had brought about the changed somber mood he hadn't left minutes before.

Mom finally spoke up. "Does your name have to be on it?"

"I can't hide behind it. I have to put my name. It's a matter of principle. Hey, you know, it may not be such a big deal. I just wanted you guys to know. Just in case."

As the unease of muteness built in the dining room, Blake started his rise from the table. "Well, that's my cue. Got homework."

"Yeah," I said sourly. "You have to go get it for Flaherty's class anyway." Blake's boldness seemed to vanish in the convicted smile he gave my parents.

At least it gave me a momentary excuse to leave the bomb where it lay. Blake thanked my parents, and as I led him to the door, I glanced back to see my mom and dad staring at each other.

I held the front door almost shut behind me. Outside in the dark, I relished the cool and lonely aura. Blake stayed in the light of the porch lamp and asked me a bit more about the story. After I briefed him, he had a weird look in his eyes.

"That's where, like, Joe Chiavetti and Dayle Tanner and all those guys hang out, right?"

I exhaled tiredly. "Yeah."

Blake looked off down the night street, thinking. On the bottom step he looked even younger than usual. He turned his head back up to me. "Ash, you think they'll do anything to you? Your mom's right. That'll be dangerous. I mean, Chiavetti—he was in jail."

I blinked at the front lawn. It was all I could do. I had nothing to tell him.

"Is he still with Tara?" Blake asked.

I shook my head. "She won't take him back."

"That's another thing. You better hope he doesn't find out she has the hots for you." Blake's eyes gleamed in the light. The nighttime made our words clear and loud. "I guess he's sorry he treated her badly, huh?"

I exhaled again. "Well, tit for tat."

"Oooh," Blake cooed. "I wouldn't mind being tat, whoever he is."

Suddenly he started speaking to me like nothing had occurred back inside. His mind was obviously deterred as he urged me to get with Tara Vovens, claiming she's this and that and he'd go with her no matter what the circumstances. He's a bit of a pervert.

"Ash, you have to hit that. She's awesome!"

I laughed shortly. There were just three problems—she was a grade older, we were different, and—well, I was not very experienced yet. I figured we were better served as friends. Maybe our differences were what we liked so much in each other. But I was gun shy after Donna. I knew that relationships weren't based on looks alone.

"Well," I told him, "we're just so damn different, you know?"

Blake slouched on the railing. "Ash, you don't have to marry her."

He didn't see the idea he put in my mind then. Tara Munroe. The idealistic sound waved an intoxicating, beckoning finger at me for a second.

Blake jumped a bit, smiled that crafty smile. "Look at her nerfs! I can't believe you saw them and blew it. Just get her back to the pool."

Blake remained the only one who knew about that. I had him sworn to our absolute secrecy bond Word as a Friend policy. It was a trust neither of us ever violated, since it meant we devalued the other as a friend if we disclosed such info to anyone else. Blake drudged over holding this true story in, and I appreciated it. But I'll tell you.

About three months before in July, Tara kept me fascinated with the idea of pool-hopping an aboveground swimming pool near her house. One hot and sticky night the pool's owners conveniently happened to be away, yet Tara waited until after midnight to call me for a swim. I sneaked out the back door and met her under a street lamp. Tara's parents, for that matter, went to bed early and never knew when she came or went.

Tara appeared in high-top sneakers and a huge shirt to her knees. She looked cute with her apparel and teased-up hair, like a doll I'd once seen. We walked a few houses down in the swampy night and she led me through a yard to a six-foot wooden fence, which we both scaled rather easily. We dropped into a very private back yard enclosed by the fence and a group of tall trees. In front of us sat a round pool fifteen feet across and four feet high. Only the humming of the small pool filter and a rumbling air conditioner next door breached the night's humid silence. Tara stood in the shadows next to me and put a finger to her lips. I slid out of my shoes and literally peeled my shirt up and squeezed out of it. As I tiptoed around to the ladder on the right, I caught a glimpse of Tara lifting her shirt off. I figured it was *some* bikini! Her breasts seemed well defined, silhouetted against a square of reflected light on the fence. I turned away shyly as her head popped freely out of the long shirt. To cool off, so to speak, I climbed the little ladder and slipped into the placid chilly liquid up to my waist. I waded to the other side of the small pool and was coming back when Tara dipped herself in and glided nearer to me. It took my asking her where the owners were to see she had no top on. She leaned forward silently to answer me, and in the darkness I was absolutely bedazzled to find no definitive string of clothing over her chest. I gasped, quickly smiling at the unexpected fortune.

"Aren't you wearing anything?"

Tara turned her shoulders and swished her arms in the water. "Yes."

I turned to see her. Nothing over her shoulders. Her breasts were barely visible to me, but there they were at arm's length. She giggled as I gave her the once-over.

"See?" she whispered, tugging a thin black string out of the water. "I'm wearing underwear."

An amazed laugh emitted from my throat. Blake would flip tomorrow! What a momentous event my life was about to record!

"Holy *crap!*"

"What? I don't have a bathing suit," she claimed shyly.

For the next minute I made small talk and tried to think of how to move on her. I just couldn't make myself do it. I was only fifteen and didn't want to spoil Tara's expectations with my pitifully young té. Plus, my biggest problem was that I was completely bothered ad to keep my knees slightly bent to shade the obvious from Tara's view. It was incredible—here she stood, in front of me like that, and I was worried that she would see how it was physically affecting me.

Tara finally took the initiative, splashing me lightly and moving away like I should give chase. I started feebly over. Apparently, the noise of the splash proved to be a saving and disappointing act at the same time.

Spotlight!

Tara whipped around to face the sudden intrusive brightness from the second floor of the house. She sank to her neck. I squinted with a defensive hand over my eyes and the only thing I saw on the surface now was her teased hair. Instinctively I hurled my legs over the edge nearest our clothing, nixing the stupid ladder, and landed stiff. The grass felt slimy on my feet. Tara scrambled over next, cursing the squishy moss. For a nanosecond, I lost myself in her gloriously pale skin. No one had appeared or yelled out to us yet, but I grabbed my sneakers and winged my shirt over into the next yard. With deep regret, I admit I fled in a rather ungentlemanly manner without waiting for Tara. I simply pulled at the top of the fence and hopped over in one adrenaline-rushed bound. I wondered what was taking her until she crawled over—fully dressed in her long shirt and sneakers. We walked home rather morosely, it never occurring to us that we had been the victims of a motion-sensor light.

After Blake started for home, I closed the door and ambled back to my family in the dining room. They weren't happy. My father rested his bearded chin in his palm, moving his eyes to me.

"Ashley, I'm worried," he said. "You could be going into this blinded by your zeal."

"Someone has to do something, Dad. A kid got knifed there over drugs."

Tyler was silent for the most part, still leaning in the archway wearing a hard dazed look. My dad just looked at me in stone silence, a jaw muscle under his beard flinching once.

I peered out the window for a hopeful break in the tension. A kid on a bike was passing under the streetlight by our house, his hair and shoulders glowing for two seconds.

Dad's tone was touched with ridicule. "What did the faculty editor—your uh—your school advisor—" He turned to Mom. "What's his name?"

Mom took her chin off her fist. "Mr. Kellogg."

Dad looked at me again. "What did Mr. Kellogg say?"

They weren't going to be okay with it. I looked at him blankly.

"What's his involvement with this?" He tried to keep his voice normal. "How much responsibility will he take as your advisor? I mean, is he going to make sure you have protection?"

"Condoms are another issue, Dad."

My father tipped his head and slouched. "Ashley, recognize the danger. You'll be attacking criminals here, and a smart mouth is the last thing you need."

"I'm just kidding, come on." I shifted and indicated them both. "Mr. Kellogg's the one who made me tell you. He wants to make sure you're okay with everything."

There was no response for a few seconds. I hated waiting. Every time the conversation stopped, the silence grew heavier.

Dad stroked his chin for a while. Finally he said, "I just don't think you know what you're—"

"Look," I interrupted, "I just feel like it's the right thing to do. Can you understand that? I just have my reasons, trust me." I checked Tyler and he glanced away. He was listening intently with his shoulder pressed to the wall but he certainly wasn't going to say anything.

I quickly briefed my parents on what nice little Mindowaskin Park was like at night, about Steven Durant from Roselle Park, about what I considered a lack of police involvement.

"Guys," I pleaded when I finished, "this is a chance to do something good. If I don't, it'll never get better and I'll walk around for the rest of my life knowing I totally chickened out when I could have made a difference."

I wondered if they sensed Tyler's guilt, his loyalty elsewhere. Dad's hand covered his beard. He blinked once as Tyler shifted in the archway.

"You know, it's really going to be okay," I said. "We're probably overreacting. It'll blow over in about a day I bet."

"You can't tell that," Dad said through his fingers. "You have no idea. How well do you know these kids you're dealing with?"

Out of the corner of my eye I glimpsed Tyler running a hand through his bangs, checking the floor, a storm raging behind his silence.

Mom finally straightened, flopping her hand to the table. "I think it's tremendous, Doug."

Dad still hadn't moved his fingers from his mouth, but his eyes shifted to Mom. I don't think either one of us had expected that. I had feared my mother the tougher egg to crack.

I rested my hands on my hips and tapped a chair leg with my foot. "Dad? I need to know you're okay. I'm giving the story to Mr. Kellogg tonight."

Dad sat up and brushed his fingertips around the edge of his empty coffee cup. "Well, it's kind of short notice. I'd like to speak to your editor before you go." He looked at Mom and said to her, "Other than that, I guess it's all right with me if it's all right with you." Our eyes met again. "Just know what you're dealing with and be careful."

The feeling of freedom was almost lonely all of a sudden. I nodded.

"It's the right thing to do."

I passed Tyler on my way upstairs to call Mr. Kellogg, who answered his phone on the second ring. He seemed irritated that I'd waited this long, but I explained to him that it took some time to coax my parents. He still seemed miffed. It wasn't until he reminded me that I still needed to include the Westfield Police in the article that I understood his anger. I was too anxious to feel burdened though. I ached to get this story off the ground.

"Ashley, you need to go over there right now and get some quotes to mesh into the story," he told me. His familiar adult voice sounded much more personal over the phone. "Don't worry. I'll call them before you show up and tell them you're coming. Just talk to them for about fifteen minutes or so. That's all it'll take." He stopped. "How's your homework?"

I thought for a second. "I have a math worksheet left to do, but I know the stuff pretty well."

"Good, then you can come straight here and input the edits yourself while we complete the layout work. I'll take a look at it once you have finished the story." He then directed me to where he lived on Harrison Avenue and told me to be there in 45 minutes.

"One last thing," I said. "My dad wants to talk to you."

There was no uncertainty in his response. "Put him on," he told me.

After my father and Mr. Kellogg spoke for a few minutes, talking about me as though I was somewhere far out of their hearing, I got up my courage and stuffed a pad and pen in my jacket. Dad finally hung up the phone and started getting ready to go to the Halloween parade meeting with Mom. I figured to get a ride with them, but then decided against asking them to drop their son off at the police station. Before I headed downstairs I heard the uncharacteristic sound of Tyler snapping the lock on his bedroom door.

I fetched my dirt bike from the garage and rolled along in the crisp cool air to the police station. I was surprised to be given a meeting with two officers—one of whom was the chief of police—and was even more surprised when informed that the cops knew all about the park. The kids there weren't fooling anyone. In fact, in their isolated location, they were making it easy for the cops to quietly hold them in check. The police chief eventually presented me past police blotter clips from *The Westfield Leader,* alluding to crackdowns on the footbridge activity over the years, and I asked to photocopy them. For much of the time I sat in a wooden chair with my pencil working furiously, lifting my head only to ask questions. The interview took a bit longer than Mr. Kellogg had predicted, about a half-hour. As soon as two uniformed men finished speaking to me I took everything over to Mr. K's house.

As usual with one of my pieces, Mr. Kellogg fashioned his red pen to delete a few weak sentences and change certain words he felt lacked journalistic sophistication. A couple of my phrases, he felt, sounded "young" and though he knew I was only a tenth-grader, he still wanted to add touches of maturity to a vital story. I had an idea to print one of the town blotter clips in the *Hi's Eye*, but Mr. Kellogg axed it. Incidentally, the only other times I read the police blotter were on curious occasions to see what Blake was up to. He would use the blotter, not only as confirmation of his activity, but to harass adults shamed in that section by calling them from a pay phone in town, anonymously haranguing them about their name being printed for a misdemeanor.

After my story was ironed out and we put the paper to bed, sending it to the printer, I borrowed the Kellogg's phone. I didn't want to go home yet. It had been a long day and too many emotions still raced through my brain. Thus, I called Tara. Her sweet, high, spunky voice so comforted me that I wished I could somehow will her through the cord. She told me to hold while she got off call-waiting with the other person. She always did that for me.

"Tara, meet me at the Rialto," I told her hastily when she clicked back.

"When?"

"Give me ten minutes."

"Give me twenty."

I whooped for the spirited reason she didn't know yet. "Fine."

I was charged as I bid the Kelloggs goodnight. It was just that feeling of accomplishment; I had written the story, and it would hit school Wednesday. It was real now. Outside the night was serene. Rather than race into town, I stopped and lay down on the Kellogg's front lawn. Forcing a deep breath, I relaxed on my back, legs crossed, hands folded under my head, and stared at the enormous sky. I picked at the grass and admired the shapes of the dark, puffy, 3-D-like clouds gathering over the stars. I was satisfied with my decision tonight, but savoring a calm before an imminent storm. The tranquil night and the smell of a chimney fire induced euphoric thoughts of adolescent Halloweens past. Maybe I was enjoying the anxiety rush of the oncoming chaos, or maybe I was just looking forward to seeing Tara.

Here goes nothing.

I reached the Rialto ten minutes before Tara and waited. Across the street in Haagen-Dazs a lady sat on a bench near the window, watching two kids eat ice cream. She looked bored; her elbow set tiredly on the backrest, her raised fist supporting her cheek.

Soon Tara appeared from Elm Street in a brown bomber jacket and whitewashed jeans, her lipstick bright in her face. She crossed the street and removed a hand from her coat pocket to wave shortly at me. I watched her with a smile, forgetting myself for a moment.

"Why do you always look at me like that?" she said with an abashed grin as she neared.

"Like what?"

"Like I amuse you."

"You just look like one of those club dance kinda girls."

Her perfume smelled like some sweet exotic fruit. I could tell she'd just put it on.

"What are you talking about?" she laughed.

"I dunno, but it's like, whenever I'm around you, guido beat music starts ringing in my head."

Tara rashly stuck a shivering hand through my arm and I started to lead us toward Mindowaskin. It didn't take long—just across the street and over the Presbyterian Church's lawn. While we walked, Tara swept her free arm over the rectangle of grass we were passing.

"Ashley," she said, "wouldn't it be great to just pitch a tent right here one night?"

I sniffled against the chill. "Sure. The cops would love that."

She jumped once and laughed. "Wouldn't they, though? That would be the funniest part, explaining to the police. Ashley, don't you ever feel like doing something outlandish like that? You know, not scary and freaky, but bold. Not caring what anybody else thinks if we do what we please." We reached the path around the big pond and she tugged my elbow. "You don't ever cut loose. One day we should sail out in an inflatable boat here in Mindo, in the middle of the day, right in front of people, and I'm gonna bring a camera so I can take a picture of your face when we get nailed by the fuzz."

Tara said something else after that, but I had now drifted into full notice of two things: the police station where I had just been an hour before, and the seven or so kids grouped under the lamp around the foot bridge.

"...sounded high as a kite."

I glanced at Tara the Curb Owl, wanting to smear that perfectly lined lipstick. "Huh?"

"I said when you called me you sounded high as a kite."

I walked along and smiled to myself.

"If I tell you why, will you promise not to change on me?"

Tara's eyes narrowed and an eyebrow raised. "I'll promise to change in front of you."

I bit my lower lip and giggled sheepishly. "Well, you're gonna find out anyway, but I want to you to promise not to hate me."

"Absosmurfly," Tara said. She watched me with funny confusion as we moved down the park sidewalk under the lamps. I thought of ways to tell her. Finally, her one interest came to mind.

"You better tell Chiavetti to steer clear of this place from now on."

Tara's comely face twisted at me in the lamplight. "How come?"

I didn't beat around the bush. After I told her about my article, she hastily turned us both around and started the other way, looking spooked. We went all the way through town, over the train tracks, and onto Summit Avenue where she lived. It wasn't anything new to be eventually sitting in her small room on her pink shaggy rug. We did that all the time.

She had some instrumental music humming on her CD player, like the stuff you hear in the background of a movie. Tara sat on her radiator and blew cigarette smoke out her second floor window into the darkness. From there you could see town and the train station a block away. Her walls were covered with posters of rock groups, and she had nailed to her wall a STOP sign Joe had stolen for her two years before. Her bed was soft and fluffy and only once had I ever seen it made. Tara wasn't the neatest person ever born.

She shook her head at me slowly, but with her most favorable smile I'd yet received. It wasn't so much that I was exposing a drug patch that bewildered her; it was the fact that I was actually taking a risk, doing something out of the mundane. The Curb Owl flicked her ashes in a mustard-colored tray she'd made in junior high.

"I can't believe you, of all people, are gonna expose the whole goddam *thing!*" She glanced at me and shrugged lazily. "S'cuse my French."

I scratched my chin. "You know, darlin'. I've taken three years of French now and I swear I've never come across *that* word."

She stared pensively out the window through her last blow of smoke and crushed the butt, swirling it around the little plaster bowl.

"I know most of those jerks. God, I hope Joe gets caught."

"You're not gonna warn him?"

She laughed shortly like I was a fool.

I lay back on my hands like I did earlier on the Kellogg's lawn. Tara stuffed a piece of gum in her mouth, hopped down, and sat Indian-style next to me on her pink rug.

"Clown still wants me back." She rested her elbows on her knees so her face was close to mine. The music on the CD was suspiciously romantic, but I didn't mind. I certainly wasn't used to it. It was rare and beautiful. "That's who I was on the phone with when you called," she said. I stared up at Tara's chin moving as she chewed her gum and nodded her head thoughtfully to the wall, her face upside-down to me. "My next boyfriend—I'm gonna be smart. I wanna be friends with him first."

I snickered shortly.

"BS," I said. "I've heard that tons of times before. That's too easy. Girls like a challenge, a guy who'll blow them off and keep them running. If you really like him, you won't hold back. Obviously. Or you'll get to know him too well as a friend. Then when he makes a move you'll beat him down with the lame excuse, 'I don't wanna ruin our friendship.'"

Tara didn't respond, simply because the music was climbing in a notably euphonious crescendo. She rose as the song did and increased the volume of pleasant violins to an alarming level. It blew me to my elbows and Tara invited me to a standing position with the touch of her soft hands and a seductive smile. She practically shouted to me over the strings, "You know what this is from?"

I stared back at her closely and mouthed, "No."

Tara glided her torso right into mine and I felt a hot flash of erotic embarrassment. The perfume intoxicated me, an intense flavor of levitating passion that warmed my blood. I watched her lips part slightly as she softly chewed her gum. I could smell the sweet grape. The tip of her nose floated inches from mine as we moved and her brown eyes grew bigger in our closeness. She draped her arms around my neck and I got a chilly rush from her skin's coolness. She moved her face in a way like she was going to kiss me, but then brushed by to my ear.

"It's the theme from *Field of Dreams*," she spoke loudly into my eardrum. "I love this stuff."

She began taking me into a slow dance. I listened to her hum next to my ear the exact melodies from the CD player, then a chew on that grape gum. This was definitely not the type of music I associated with Tara Vovens the Curb Owl. The violins were dreamy and dominant and I felt myself swaying around with Tara's body in my arms, felt her hands stroking my hair, the back of my neck. Her body bumped into mine and stayed there, I allowed one of my flattened palms to move over her back, and the feel of everything made faint, airy. She took her face from my shoulder and put it right in front of mine. I was totally out of my league. I practically gasped my next words.

"I have to get home after this song, darlin'."

I felt a warm grape breath.

After the song lulled but didn't end, Tara followed me downstairs, now with her saddest look I'd yet received. I suddenly regretted my stupid self, but couldn't bring forth any suggestion of going back up. Who knows? Maybe she'd have told me no in spite. I thought of her room upstairs and the blissful private ecstasy from which I'd just removed myself. I wanted to tell her I'd be thinking about this until I fell asleep, that it had removed any fear I'd had about my doom to follow.

"Hey," I said, just outside her back door. "Remember to look up at the moon at exactly eleven o'clock tonight." I pointed to the half moon beaming sharply over the next roof.

"Why?"

"Because then we'll know we're looking at it at the same time."

She changed her expression. Tara has a beautiful smile. I teased her teased hair a little more, ruffling it with my hand, and left. She stood at her door in stocking feet and waved every time I looked back until I rounded the corner to South Avenue. I later figured out why she told me that before—why she wanted a guy with whom she'd already built a friendship.

She was talking about me.

5

HI'S EYE   *Vol. 58, No. 8*   *Westfield High School*
October 28, 1992

Local Park Center of Drug Activity
by Ashley Munroe

*Editor's note: This issue contains an in-depth investigation of illicit drug use among young people in the Westfield area. The **HI'S EYE** has attempted to determine through this report the level of drug usage and some of the ramifications of this usage.*

Until now, few knew about the volatile drug culture in Mindowaskin Park and still fewer seemed to give a damn about it. But that should all change now.

For the violent act that may precede others to follow has just occurred. On Saturday night, October 10th, a Roselle Park youth who happened upon the park sometime around 11 p.m. was stabbed twice by a juvenile under the influence of drugs and alcohol. The problem has strong roots.

Three points help to define the borders of Mindowaskin Park—the police station, a large children's playground, the Presbyterian Church. Each site plays an important role in our community's well being. Yet in the middle of the park, just as much in plain view, rests Westfield's most frequented drug haven. Local youths infest a certain area of the park, assembling on and around what is commonly known as the footbridge—a cement and asphalt structure arching a few feet over the small stream that flows between the playground and Mindowaskin Pond. On any given night, teenagers gather around the footbridge to purchase drugs or simply use them. Fistfights are not uncommon, and activities there have turned increasingly violent.

It is unclear whether the curious problem has gone unnoticed or allowably ignored.

Lack of Strong Investigation

After being stabbed in the arm and neck, the Roselle Park boy was treated at Overlook Hospital where he remained for two nights. No viable or incriminating evidence has been assessed; hence, no charges have yet been filed. When reached at his house, the victim refused to speak for fear of disclosure.

The Westfield Police were asked why a thorough investigation was not active and it went immediately to the top. Chief of Police Louis R. Haverford stated that an inquiry was in fact made but that nothing has yet come of it.

"We have one detective on the case, but the investigation has been fruitless thus far," he said. "We still have the door open and are working concurrently with Roselle Park Police."

Asked why the footbridge has not been monitored more closely since the days following the stabbing, Haverford rebuffed the logic of perhaps placing an on-foot patrol at the site.

"We have been aware of the activities in the park for years," he stated, "and there have, in fact, over the course of time, been other more secluded spots around the park where under-aged drinking and drug-taking has occurred. If we disperse one area, kids are going to find another just as quickly, whether it's here or over at Brightwood Park. But in a situation such as this, there's only so much you can do to patrol a given area."

Getting Stoned

The two main drugs at Mindowaskin Park are marijuana and alcohol. The majority of youths visiting the park on a regula, nightly basis are commonly termed "burnouts" by both Westfield High School students and standards; juveniles who wear "tough" clothing (ripped jeans, leather-studded jackets) and listen to hard rock and/or heavy metal music. Hair is either shaved or beyond shoulder length. Recently however, kids from other "cliques" at Westfield have begun to drift in as well; kids from the "popular/groovie" crowd, lured by the promise of slight adventure and "great weed". Instead of clearing and dispersing, the problem continues to spread.

Systematically, kids familiar with the operation know how to keep inconspicuous. From information gathered during a covert visit to the park on Wednesday night of last week, it was learned that current "shifts" vary from night to night.

"We all hang out at the park and get stoned; there are nearly 200 of us that come from time to time, but no more than 15 at once," said one junior in our school. He stated that all sorts of people come to the park scene regularly; he estimated that about 100 WHS students, 50 junior high students, 20 assorted high school drop-outs, 15 older kids out of high school, and 10 kids in grade school go there. Some leave, only to be replaced by others, and the number is pretty consistent throughout the course of each night.

"On the average weekend," a WHS senior recently told me, "we burn out 'til about three in the morning. After that, we try to find homes to sleep in."

The kids who buy, sell, and take drugs use a "secret" language common to those familiar with the park scene. A term to inquire if someone wants to buy dope is, "Bang Zoom?" Additionally, other than "burning out," smoking weed is known as "filleting." A source known by the kids as the dealer of much of the marijuana smoked in Mindowaskin Park is referred to as "The Landlord."

Park a Problem

Detective Kenneth Geories of the Westfield Police Department stated that the Mindowaskin situation is a serious problem, and that in recent years it has been at its worst since the late 1960's and early 1970's. According to Detective Geories, the park at that point in time was filled with heavy users, with everything from LSD to heroine easily available. "Now the situation there is far less intense concerning the more potent drugs," he says.

According to Geories, the people who hang out at the park are "a group of misfits, who are the cesspool of Westfield." Detective Geories agreed that the number of people who hang out at the park amounts to a couple of hundred with only ten to fifteen people at any one time. This is a sharp decline from times like the early seventies when "groups of sixty to seventy kids would smoke, drink and take drugs through all hours of the night."

The reason for the decrease in the nightly average stems from the influence of the police force, years back.

"On a few occasions in those years," he said, "the precinct raided the group a few times, and since then, they've kept the numbers noticeably down. They're smart and lucky in that they've built a tradition of exclusively inherited information."

When asked why these youths are still allowed to stay at the park and violate the 10pm closing time, he responded by explaining that as long as they don't bother anyone but themselves the police basically leave them alone. However, Detective Geories did mention that after the stabbing incident he fears the number will increase this fall and that the Police Department will do everything in its power to prevent this.

"The point from here on in," he stated, "is foresight. Concentration should lie in awareness and deterrence."

A Night at the Scene

Most people involved with the park drug scene didn't seem willing to talk to me in school about exactly what happens, but I decided to go "under cover" to get an inside personal account of a typical night at the park. This is my story:

I ambled into the park looking as "grunge" as I could. My outfit consisted of large faded jeans with a hole in one knee, an un-tucked black Nirvana T-shirt, an old pair of basketball high-tops sneakers, and—since it was cool out—a jeans jacket borrowed from a friend. Ahead I could see something going on by the light of the lamp near the footbridge. As I approached the bridge I came upon about eight kids who were drinking alcohol out of a paper bag. A junior high school kid came up to me looking for a joint, but I had none to sell.

Another kid said, "I just copped a half ounce but I ain't sellin' any to you."

I then followed a couple kids into a dark corner of the parking lot to meet a few others in an open car. We squeezed together and suddenly I was crammed into the four-seater with six giggling, stoned kids; our ages must have ranged from 14 to 25. From the stench it was obvious the others had all been doing "many bowls", while Led Zeppelin's 'Houses of the Holy' blared on the radio.

After talking about whatever nonsense we could come up with for a while, one of the kids in the back seat broke out a half ounce of "Panama Red" and immediately started screaming shut up over and over again. He was nervous and needed quiet to roll his joints. He had trouble because it was so big, "the biggest stogie in Westfield," as he described it. His joint had about a 1/4-inch bulge in the middle. The kid was so high that his hands were too shaky to roll. So, someone else had to roll it for him.

While his helper was finishing the joint, a maroon sedan sped into the parking lot, screeching to a halt. I was scared. I thought it was the police making a bust, but the rest of the kids weren't, because they knew the police never made busts in Mindo. The car was filled with more people coming to the park, so we filed out to see who they were.

The driver of the sedan was a longhaired senior from our school who emerged quickly from the vehicle. Some sort of pipe in his hand, he left his door wide open and traced a stomping path toward a "preppie" kid at the footbridge. We all followed, some running over. Apparently, it was something anticipated. A heated standoff was now occurring over on the far side of the bridge from me. I walked over just in time to see the longhaired guy shove the preppie kid hard in the chest. There wasn't much else to see, only to hear. The two guys yelled and cursed at each other and it was so ridiculous and random that I still don't know what it was over. It ended when a couple kids stepped in just as the longhaired kid raised his pipe. A few tense minutes went by until they all settled down and ended up smoking a joint together. The night continued on as if nothing had happened.

I eventually hopped back into the first car on an invitation and we pulled out onto Mountain Avenue. The guy driving headed toward the north end of town to someone's home. He was speeding the whole way, going 20 to 30 miles an hour over the speed limit, ignoring stop signs and everything else. The driver was totally wasted. I hadn't noticed how bad he really was until I saw how he was driving. He hadn't the vaguest idea of what was going on as he ignored traffic and sped down Kimball Ave. No one else seemed to notice the speed or the danger; they simply stared straight ahead, stoned out of their minds.

I held on to the side handle and looked down, stunned. At my feet were items of drug paraphernalia (pipes, clips, rolling papers, etc.) along with pot spilled from an open bag of a "copped" ounce. Apprehension and sick fear began to sizzle through my body until I was practically shaking from worry. Had I gone too far? If the police stopped us, nary a person would be inclined to show me any clemency for my seemingly far-out excuse. Not to mention the sudden frightening potential of a fatal car accident. I was sitting center in a back seat with no belt available for that position, watching the windshield and praying to God not to let me see it too closely. One abrupt stop and I would have flown right through it. I swallowed and glanced all around the *car; no one else was concerned with anything but savoring his feeling. They were all used to this.*

The kid who was being driven home was literally booted out of the car where he fell face-forward on his lawn, and for all I know, might have stayed that way for hours. As for the rest of us, we sped away and somehow made it back to the park alive. How, I'm not sure, just lucky, I guess. I got out of the car and started home. I'd had enough and didn't want to press my luck.

This is the story that would change my life. All throughout school that Wednesday I was excited and nervous, trying to keep myself together until seventh period finally arrived. I grabbed a copy of the paper and saw my story all over page one with a green pictograph of a large marijuana leaf splashed underneath the words. A photo of the footbridge adorned page three, where the story ended.

The first casualty of the affair was Roy Lemaire, a junior who heard about the article from his chemistry teacher. Mrs. Hessler held up the new *Hi's Eye* and announced to her class as they got ready to leave for next period, "A tenth-grader wrote a fascinating story about drug dealing in Mindowaskin Park. It's outstanding. Be sure to grab one on your way out."

Tara was there in the classroom. She told me Roy just stood rigidly with a gaping jaw and fixed Mrs. Hessler with a wide-eyed look of disbelief. His tone was aghast and what should have been, "You're kidding!" was an accidentally drawled, "F— *me!*" His hands were at his mouth a second too late. Tara told me he was issued an instant central detention.

I was told this right after her class. Tara found me in the library at the start of eighth period just as Chris Noyes and Eric Solburg approached me with papers in their hands and amazed jovial expressions on their faces, like I'd just bought them season tickets to the Yankees.

"Munroe!" Chris laughed. "You're wacked!"

Eric sat next to me, his book bag slipping off his shoulders. "Ashley," he leaned in and said, "our whole class was just talkin' about it. Can't you get in trouble for this?"

"What does everyone think?" I wondered aloud to him.

"You really went out with them one night?" Chris asked me, ignoring my question. "Who got you to do that?"

They asked me two more questions at once and I shrank back in my seat, practically laughing at them. My small sense of famed victory changed when I saw Tara Vovens.

Striding down to the table where we usually met, she had blush over her cheeks and was giving me that intent stare of purpose.

"Come on," she said forcefully, taking up my book bag. "We gotta go."

"Why, what's goin' on?" It wasn't me who asked, it was Eric. "Who's after him?"

"Everybody."

I just stared at her. I sure didn't like the look on her face. I could tell she wouldn't take "No" for an answer, and figured she'd snap at me if I tried.

"You're in real trouble," she said breathlessly. "You have to split *now*. Come on."

I swore under my breath and listened to her tell me in her own quick terms how certain kids she knew wouldn't be receiving me favorably in school. Tara swiftly led me away from Eric and Chris. Her teased half-blonde hair flowed in the corridor ahead of me, the heels of her boots beating a steady knock on the hall floor. Even then, I took a sidetracked, approving notice of that sweet perfume.

"Where we going?"

"Away. Dayle knows he was all over the article. He and a bunch of his wannabes are totally after you."

"I have French," I called after her. We had reached the back steps and I was practically stumbling down from her tugging my shirt. She didn't reply. She didn't saying anything until we jogged out the Trinity Place exit and scooted up the hill to a sleek black Mercury Topaz across the road. Outside it was gray and overcast with a typical nippy October breeze.

"Tina let me have her keys," said Tara. She unlocked my door for me. "Get in."

I had never cut a class before in my life.

"Ashley," Tara laughed into the steering wheel, "I didn't think your story would be like *that*."

I held onto the dashboard as Tara pulled out.

"What if you get stopped, Tara? You don't even have a license yet."

Tara didn't reply. She was too exhilarated. The ruckus I'd so quickly caused back at school seemed to drown out the zany fact that she was driving alone. Her exuberance came dang close to annoying me. She just held a faint smile and kept her eyes on the road. I watched her, sudden heat building under my shirt and pants. I felt alone, helpless, and tight, wishing I was bigger.

"Well," I told her finally, "what did you think it would be like?"

She huffed out a quick laugh. "I don't know. I just thought you'd say there was some problem. You said a lot more."

"Well, duh."

"Hey, your article was cool. I read it in, like, a minute. It was just a little *too* good, if you get me." She ran a hand to her hair, then quickly signaled just as she turned left onto the town's circle. I checked out my window as a station wagon beeped and continued straight on.

"Speaking of trouble—jeez—one slip and you won't get your license 'til you get your social security."

"Oh, Ashley," Tara said worriedly. "I don't want you to get hurt."

We passed under the Broad Street train bridge and stopped at the light before the center of town. I couldn't tell if 16-year-old Tara looked smaller or more mature in Tina Rondinelli's driver seat. We both stiffened as a Westfield Police car crossed right in front of us. I watched the white vehicle with the blue specifics etched on its side as it trailed by and under the bridge from which we just came. Tara and I glanced once at each other and breathed heavily.

"Tara, where the heck we going?"

She shrugged, eyeing me from the side. "Warinaco Park." She pressed the gas and turned right on North Avenue. "I go there with Donna some nights. We can go skating and kill some time if you want. I got money. You wanna?"

I licked my lips and tried not to laugh. What a crazy idea. She was a kook, and I liked her more and more for it. I hadn't been to Warinaco Park skating rink in three years. I used to go every year 'til my mom thought I'd outgrown it.

Tara rolled down North Avenue, past Cranford, toward Elizabeth. Tina's Mercury smelled like fresh plastic, the interior so neat it shined. I fixed one of the heat panels toward me and noticed trees along the street becoming more and more sparse, leaves dwindling. It wouldn't be long now 'til they were all sticks against the sky defying the coldness of winter. A breeze sent dozens of red leaves out of a medium-sized apple tree to the surrounding grass below—an ever-growing circle of the same color. I always feel a bit somber at the passing of the leaves on to a new season.

I played with the radio, happy to bask in the tutelage of obscurity with a friend who I sensed for the first time truly cared about me. The twilight crescent moon outside the car window had swollen from two nights before. It followed us through trees and buildings. There was no escaping it.

"Hey, the other night," I said, reminded. "That was different music."

Tara smiled warmly, tucking a tuft of hair over her ear. "Nice though, huh?" she said. "I cultured you a bit. Why? What do you mostly listen to?"

I squinted back at her in suave fashion. "I listen to rap music." Tara glanced at me and I used a deep ghetto tone. "Hard-core, drug-dealin', house-robbin', wife-beatin' *rap* music, baby."

"Come on." She backhanded my knee. "Don't be a goof all your life."

I had other things creeping back into my mind.

"So Tanner said something? I'm surprised the guy knows I exist. He's always ignored me."

Tara laughed warningly. "Oh, he knows you exist! Trust me."

"What about Kohleran? Be a bummer if he wants to ace me. I always kinda liked him. Did he say anything?"

"Who, John? He wasn't in school today." Tara moved her face closer to the steering wheel and snickered slyly. "I wonder how Joe'll find out."

"This'll blow over." I leaned on a hand and picked at the side of the door. "You'll see."

"Ashley," pleaded Tara, "if it gets really bad, you know you can stay at my house for a little while. My parents like you." I couldn't believe what she was thinking. She acted like I'd be on the lam from now on. I smiled at the windshield.

"It won't be that bad."

"No, seriously. We have a spare room if you need it for a few nights."

I'd heard of girls instinctively mothering boys they liked. I figured this was her subconscious angle, so I held back from laughing at her like I wanted to. She was worried. I let it go.

Tara and I were on the ice in rented skates a few minutes later. It surprised me how many tough, older, burner-looking dudes hung out at the ice rink. Tara skated pretty well for a Curb Owl and could almost keep up with me. Out on the rink, coasting through the wind, I felt free and dominant. My cares and anxieties disappeared. Chase me if they wanted, they couldn't get me here! I could zoom all over that ice. I flew! There was no one who mattered right then but me and Tara, who was now somewhere amongst the throngs of small kids and adults flowing around the rink like suitcases on a giant baggage claim. I slowed down and waited against the side rail, feeling my heart beat. Locating her took a bit longer than I'd expected and for a few seconds I figured she'd gone off the ice. Then I saw her rounding the bend, her nose red against her whitened cheeks, her whirly hair thrown back, displaying her tiny forehead. She smiled at me through a hoard of speeding strangers and tried to get off. I laughed when her expression turned dramatically frantic as a guy whizzed by her. I took off after her and glided into her back, holding her shoulders. We soared over the ice plains together now. I wanted to tell her how her creative gusto and spontaneous playful nature was just what I needed. I hated myself for a tangled second because I knew she was confusing me. I didn't tell her anything. Perhaps it would have spoiled the moment. Rather, I just relaxed and moved to her side and we skated around and around and around.

It was dark when Tara dropped me in front of my house and sped away to Tina's. The moon was brighter in the sky. I walked up the porch steps with a good small ache in my thighs. My mother pushed open the door for me. I misread the look on her face to be pleasant.

"Where've you been?" she asked with concern blazing in her tropical eyes.

"Why?" I couldn't remember anything I might have missed.

"People have been calling. A lot of your friends—and some guy from *The Westfield Leader?*" She shook her head, her thin eyebrows twisting upwards. "He's been bothering me."

"Really?"

The kitchen phone rang and my mother sat on the top step with a hand to her mouth.

"You have to talk to them, Ashley."

I smiled excitedly and walked into the kitchen, setting my book bag on the counter. This certainly was getting a lot of attention. I picked up the phone on the third ring.

"Hello?"

Nary a voice, but I could tell there was no disconnection.

"Hello?"

"Stupid ass pansy," said a strange male voice. He hung up. I watched the phone for a few seconds after, stunned. This was real. This was suddenly all about my words, my idea.

My mother was at the kitchen door. "What'd they say?"

I only asked quietly if anybody else called. Four of my friends, notably early for this hour. I went to my room. I wondered what homework there was in French.

Later that night at dinner, we sat around the table, four confused and wary people. Dad said to me that he liked my style of writing and that I had a talent, but he was very skeptical about the reaction this was going to cause. He felt it was boldly versed against both my peers *and* the police. Dad even confessed regret at not having read it beforehand, and it made me feel like I'd lost his approval. I thought, What's everyone so surprised about? This wasn't intended to be your average trite "Just Say No" message. My parents finally asked Tyler what he thought.

"I think it was really stupid, to be honest," he replied, worming in his seat.

Dad had his elbows on the table and was playing with his beard slowly.

"You have to back him at school," he told him.

"Hey, I'm stayin' out of this," Tyler said with his hands in the air. He looked at Mom defensively. "What, Mom?! I had nothing to do with this. I found out just before you did."

Mom's lifted one hand off the table and pointed at my older sibling. "Tyler Dakota, you should back your brother."

"Fine. Figuratively. But I'm not gettin' beat up for this."

We were just about finished when the front doorbell rang. I was first up and heard a quick scurrying on the porch before I turned the outside light on. I unlocked and pulled open the big door to find the empty night in front of me.

For an instant I froze, fearing that someone was hunched up against the house. I pushed my face closer to the storm glass and peered sideways. No one was there on either side. I kept looking bravely forward and raised my hand over the window glare to see into the front yard. It amazed me that anyone could vanish that rapidly. I was so intrigued that my father's voice made me jump.

"Who is it?" he said behind me.

I shrugged blankly. "No one."

Dad was suddenly alarmed. He moved carefully in front of me, closing the door and calling out, "Ginny, turn on the yard light."

After the front lamppost blinked on, we went back to our routines and I called Blake and Chris back. I was in the middle of babbling mindful answers to Chris's questions when my mother's voice called from downstairs.

"Ashley! Tyler! Come here!"

The tone she used was similar to whenever one of us found trouble. I leapt off my bed and almost ran into Tyler at the top of the stairs. When we reached the kitchen, my father was leaning in the window, watching something in the back yard.

I strained to look along next to him. It was incredible. Two dark shapes, unmoving but not belonging to the shrubbery, stood right on our premises. The two figures then shifted in the direction of Clark Street, wandering the border of our yard and the Rosenbaum's. Mom mumbled something, and my father was already moving for the back door. He stepped out just as the back porch spotlight blazed the two from obscurity.

"What are you doing here?!" he shouted.

"...we'd cut through," was all I heard.

The telephone rang again. Mom picked it up—another hang up. I was sidetracked by it, but lost notice as I returned my vision to the back yard. The two guys seemed taken by my father's abrupt presence in the light. Now let me pause to remind you that my dad has biceps the size of my thighs and a wide hefty structure to his chest. He's maintained a loyally rapid pace over at the YMCA and could theoretically kick the crap out of Tyler and me at the same time.

"This is my property," my father snapped. "I don't want you cutting through."

"We're just lookin' for Tyler," one of them said quickly, and I recognized that vile voice. "Is he home?"

"You fellas go that way," I heard my dad command in his resonant tone. "You can talk to my son without ringing and running our house during dinner hours."

The other kid, a stout one, stumbled, "Well, I don't—I mean, we didn't—"

"Hey, either cooperate or I call the cops," my father said, extending a cautioning finger. "End of story." The voices in the night seemed hollow and short. My father looked back and forth at both of them.

The taller one snapped brazenly, "*Okay.* We hear you."

My father caught it. There was a pause as he stared at them. "I don't want any trouble, but I'm not stupid, fellas. I know what's going on." He pointed to Clark Street. "Move. That way."

It surprised the hell out of me when my brother left the door and jogged out into the yard toward the three. It surprised my parents.

"Chiavetti!" Tyler called over. I felt my feet slowly lead me out after him. The only noise out in the yard now was that of two crickets in the shrubbery.

Tyler Dakota took Dad by his stiff biceps. "Lemme talk to 'em, Dad. It's cool. I know 'em."

After a few seconds, my father placed his large hands in his jeans pockets and walked a pausing pace back to the door. He saw me and told me firmly in front of everyone. "Ashley, inside."

I noticed the hunched position of my dad's huge shoulders. I went quickly.

Back in the kitchen, I rolled the window open to the screen and listened. Tyler stood with his back to the light, flanked by the two. One was a slouchy kid who kept turning his head at me, and the other was Joe Chiavetti. There he was, even darker than I remembered. An odd thing—I'd seen Joe but once since I knew Tara, and that was only from a distance. Tonight I was the focus of his attention. Out casing my back yard, his big eyebrows sat heavily over his dark firm eyes as he half-squinted disconsolately at my brother. His black hair was short all around except for a thin blond tail extending down his neck. It called as much attention to itself as an open fly.

Tyler was getting visibly irritated. I caught a few exchanged words after he complained bitterly, "...why at my house? Dudes, that's not cool." Tyler was trying to use his school lingo, to show he was one of them. Chiavetti, though, was a validated 19-year-old criminal and a year had passed since he'd dropped out of school as a junior. He wasn't to be reasoned with. Tyler must have realized this, for he turned and stalked back to the house.

Suddenly, Joe turned his face right up to me and stung me with the horror of his dark eyes.

"You're *dead*, Munroe!" he yelled in his squeaky voice.

I stayed leaned breathlessly on the kitchen sink and saw my father's head reappear under the light. He shouted at them to get lost, his angered tone cutting the night. I shuddered from the definitive fierceness, wondering guiltily if the neighbors heard.

The two guys began taking tentative steps away toward the Clark Street side of our property. Joe took his eyes off me and was looking straight back at my dad. I felt a quick thrill, expecting something. Joe flipped his finger at me, failing at the instant to notice my father sink into a slight crouch.

"I'm comin' back to get your house and your whole f—in' family!"

Bad move.

My father covered the yard in three bounding strides and literally punch-slapped the weed-burner two feet in the air. Shock had frozen Chiavetti in the suddenness of the attack until my father's open palm appeared out of the lamplight and smashed into his face. Joe's entire body buckled off the grass, then went limp and lifeless. He thudded to the ground and stayed there.

Tyler hurried back over to them. A rush of gasped air flew from my mouth like I'd been squeezed. I followed my mother to the back door. She hopped all three steps like I'd never seen and ran onto the scene, yelling.

Out on the shadowy lawn, my dad's fists remained clenched, like his teeth. A vein was drawing a raised line in his neck. The red in his face glowed in the porch light and I could see the rigid course of his jawbone. He had both feet placed around Joe Chiavetti.

Tyler and my mother begged my dad to stop. Joe was calling to his stumpy friend, "Friggin' Scott, get him off!" His stunned friend, though, simply shrank away in retreat. My dad finally backed off, rejecting the impulse to kick Joe. His voice was rough and hoarse and *scary* as hell!

"Get outta here," he breathed. "Right now."

Joe Chiavetti didn't look so dangerous now as Scott Lucinski helped him up. Joe looked vulnerable and stupid but—unpredictable still. The two guys slipped quickly between our bushes and trotted to the sidewalk, heading left on Clark Street. We all followed my father as he went inside, rumbled through two rooms, and checked from the porch as the kids crossed Dudley and sank into the night.

The house was electric. Dad paced the den and living room floors, running a hand through his hair. His face remained flushed as he stalked and muttered. Throughout the whole ordeal, his rimless glasses had remained on his nose and intact. Mom spoke soothingly to him in the den.

I walked between them. It took a lot of nerve. "I'm sorry, Dad," I told him.

"Be sorry for that kid," he replied hotly. "Moron kid doesn't know his tail from his horns."

"He's not even a legal kid, Dad." I turned to my mom. "Really. He's nineteen. I know he is."

Dad looked into me. "That's right. Remember, he's the adult and you're the minor if he comes near you. But there's no way that punk's going to get to you. I'll beat him six ways from Sunday."

Tyler stood in the room with a less-than-friendly glare. It was too much. I sat on the couch and punched it.

"I can't believe this," I moaned. "This walks!"

Dad's understanding mode took a short hiatus just then.

"Did you inform the police before you did this?" he asked. "You know, they could come here tonight and get you."

I raised my head. "Huh?"

"They could arrest you as an accomplice."

"What in the world?"

"You knew and didn't tell."

"Doug, stop scaring him," my mother said, rubbing my shoulder.

I figured my dad's mind was cooked spaghetti. He set his hands on his hips. "Well, he didn't tell them first."

"Doug, just stop. You're not even making any sense." She looked tiredly at me. "They can't arrest you."

"Idiot!" Tyler stormed, slapping his leg. "I friggin' *told* you this would happen!"

The phone rang again and everybody groaned. Tyler rushed from the room for it.

"Yes, he is!" I heard him say crudely. "But he can't come to the stupid phone!" He hung up hard. "Your dopey friend Eric called," he railed.

I slumped, letting my arms fall to the cushions. "Don't take it out on him!"

Mom had stopped rubbing my shoulder. I could just hear her fingers over her mouth by her speech. "Doug, I'm worried. This is getting—maybe we need some help."

"Boys, out." My dad's tone did not leave room for questioning.

I sighed and got up. I needed to be alone anyway. We were all confused and startled and I left the den to head upstairs for my room.

I didn't get my desired solitude right away. Tyler followed me up the stairs. He opened my door wearing a face I'd only seen one other time—after his fifth-grade baseball team lost the championship game. I just wasn't in the mood for this. I huffed from my desk.

"Could you, um—close the door?"

Tyler stepped in and slammed the door behind him. I still looked at him tiredly.

"I meant with you outside of it."

Heedless of my wishes, Tyler moved about the room. "What the hell made you do this?" He shook his head with his mouth agape for a few seconds, like he couldn't find any words to express his thoughts. "I mean, you *had* to know this would friggin' happen."

"Oh, come on. It'll blow over."

"You're not a cop, Ashley!" he yelled. "It was none of your business! They're gonna kill you! They're gonna friggin' kill *me!*"

I scowled and waved a hand at him. "They will not. What reason do they have for *you?*"

"Duh, jackass! Put two and two together! *I'm* your brother! *You* wrote it! They'll think I told you about it! You exposed *everything* and some of them were my friends! They're in *my* classes! They're *everywhere*! This is about me, too, Ashley! Do you even give a crap?!"

"You know, you don't always have to curse," I told him quietly. "It's beneath you." I don't quite know why I said that. I was just flustered and angry and scared but—clear.

"Oh, go to hell," he said.

I sat in the eased position of my desk chair with my heart pounding, hot flashes steaming my body under my clothes, my vision blurred. Basically, a terrified beaten mess.

"You're gonna make me say it, aren't you?" I said finally.

Tyler's black bangs bounced as he held his arms out. "Say what?! Is there anything that—"

I jumped up. "Dammit, Tyler! I saw you going *right* down with them! Smoking dope and *driving*?! You fell down that hill high and ruined your ankle, you nearly lost your license, you were cutting out of work—everything!" I felt my face growing hot and dense with blood, embarrassed because I knew I was sounding like a dang parent. I motioned toward the Wymer's house. "And you wanna make noise about your car on their front yard?! How about the other day? Monday? I mean, stoned at *school* for crying out loud! You were getting so burned out it was in*cred*ible!"

"What makes you so holier than thou?!"

"Tyler, man, you're on a course to blow it."

Tyler had watched me the whole time with this one amazed droopy face. A shine coated his forehead and cheeks like he'd just survived a school wrestling match. His heavy breathing filled the room as anger and frustration fought to surface. Suddenly he turned for the door.

"I'm not goin' in to school tomorrow," he said.

"You're not?"

"Hell no." Tyler stared at me and started to say something when the phone interrupted us. He indicated the ringing. "That's why."

When my parents failed to call either Tyler or me to the phone, I figured it was another prank. I sat lonely on my bed as Tyler went to his room. Tyler and I had not been particularly close for a few years, but he was still my brother. Suddenly, I understood that we inhabited different worlds, and my connection with my big brother was fractured, if not broken.

The surprise of Mr. Chiavetti's phone call a half-hour later came as a fence-rider. True, I did not expect Joe to turn into a pacifist and leave things without retaliation, but I was astounded that he'd involve his father into his foolish mess. It became obvious that Joe had left out certain details, because I could hear the confusion in Mr. Chiavetti's unstable tone returning my father's remarks.

The entire event started after I decided to take command of the fallout, and answer each call. Silence greeted me the first time, so an adult voice caught me by surprise on the second call.

"Hello, is this the Munroe residence?"

Struck by wonder, I answered yes.

"My name is Louis Chiavetti," he said. "Is your father available to speak to me?"

For a few seconds I held the phone knowingly to my chest, wondering why in the world I would give this man the satisfaction of further complicating my dad's night. Figuring we should resolve things now, I told Mr. Chiavetti to hold and went to the den, whispering whom it was. My mother stayed on the receiver with me in the kitchen while my father took the den phone. I watched him sitting easily in the recliner chair, the lamp glowing on his half-blond hair and beard. Not surprisingly, the father on the other end lacked any real knowledge of what had taken place. He actually became understanding and cordial. It didn't take a rocket scientist to ascertain that, even though this man felt an urge to call for his ex-convict son's sake, he was shrouding an eventual apology. I listened to Joe's voice in the background, complaining that my father had busted expensive shades in his jeans pocket. God, I wished Tara could have heard him whine like that! She'd have flipped!

My dad began telling the composed man how his legal adult son had threatened our family, how he was caught trespassing on our property. He revealed Joe's obvious problem with me.

"Problem?!" I suddenly interrupted. "He wants to kill me!"

Dad told me angrily to get off. I did, leaving my mother in the kitchen and heading into the den to hear more. I wanted to have a voice, to be my own lawyer, but my father was clearly miffed, evidenced by the look on his face and his attempts to cover the phone, slashing his finger at me to quiet.

Almost on premonition, I wandered out to the living room. Lights attracted my attention to the window and I swept away a corner of lace curtain. Suddenly I witnessed a large red pickup truck with shiny silver trim pull into our driveway and back out again. Turning headlights shifted on the curtains, blazing them. Once back on Dudley, the driver spun the tires and peeled around the corner past Roosevelt School. I shut off the living room lights and stayed at the window. A minute later, I saw the same pickup pass again. The truck even made a *third* trip by the house from the other direction. As it did so, I sidestepped past the couch and flashed our porch lights off and on, signaling my awareness of their presence.

Whoever was driving noticed my signal and slowed considerably. I slid up against the wall and told Mom, who was suddenly watching, to stay put. Peering out again, I saw the red pickup with tinted windows rolling slowly now, boldly unafraid. It showed me how direct their intentions really were. I wanted to call the cops, but Dad was still on the phone and couldn't be bothered. Now even Mom seemed ticked off, telling me to stop.

"Ashley, it's not funny!" she nearly yelled. My jaw hung. She thought I was *playing*?

I moved to the window again when I heard an engine grow to a roar that eventually waned. The pickup truck raced down the street. Dad had just gotten off the phone, leaving it off the hook for the rest of the night. He passed me by and put his hand on the banister. I stared stupidly at him.

"Is everything cool, Dad?"

He wasn't going to say much to me, I could feel it. I stood behind him and watched his broad shoulders heave with a sigh. Disturbed by his silence, I asked again. This time he just blew out an even longer breath and started up the stairs. A little while later, Mom joined him.

I didn't know where that pickup was, or who else was might be prowling around our house now. It was way too scary to watch TV alone in the den tonight. I ended up going to my room sooner than usual.

I couldn't get much of my homework done. Thankfully it wasn't complicated or overly important anyway. I kept remembering the way Joe Chiavetti's body flew back in the porch light from my dad's palm. I was too worried about school tomorrow to think about anything else. The nighttime always brings out my worst fears, or at least brings them to a scarier, more focused dread. How was I going to face everybody tomorrow? What would happen from this? I couldn't hide until summer. I couldn't stay concealed in the protective safety of my own house for months. Boy, I wished it, though. Was everyone going to act like Tyler? Like Joe?! What would they call me? Was *anybody* going to understand? Would the only sympathetic people left in the world be adults? I chuckled to myself at that—I, perhaps the only teen in the world tonight who could form such an ironic thought.

I sighed like my father did and attempted my English assignment. The dictionary really bums me out sometimes. "Melancholia: n. the state of being melancholy." Gee, that helps.

6

"Doug, come downstairs, quick!"

My mother's troubled voice, oddly loud for the hour, woke me with a start the next morning. Jumping out of bed, I saw the back of her green bathrobe as she called into the master bedroom.

"Quick, there's something outside!"

She turned to me, her blonde hair tangled and frizzy, her brow furled over sky-blue eyes sharpened in alarm. "Something big is hanging from the tree outside!"

My father flipped off his covers, his eyes tight from sleep. He clutched his glasses and came to the hall. Mom was acting like she'd seen Lady Abigail.

"Doug," she said, "I want you to see this." She started downstairs, clutching her robe. "Scared me to death!"

Dad and I stood in confusion. Suddenly I remembered him trudging up the stairs the night before. I made sure I was down on the landing before him.

Mom led us to the front door, where it was already open to the storm door. It was just about dawn and one half of the sky was coming to an early light. The street lamp was still glowing. All three of us crowded in the doorway and peered out the window. Something bulky and foreign was silhouetted against the horizon in front of us.

"What is that?" my mother whispered. "Is that a person?"

Something possessing the shape of a human body was dangling from our maple tree.

Behind his glasses, Dad's eyes squinted. His head cocked to one side, his mouth hanging open in his beard. "What *is* that?" he echoed.

I strained to see. The body turned slightly in a breeze and I swallowed back. The person had blond hair and was dressed in light blue jeans, a flannel shirt, and what looked like a navy windbreaker. White sneakers hung untied on the feet, the laces blowing softly. I could see the thick twine rope wrenched around the neck, descending from the branch I'd always climbed. The "prankster" had bound the arms of the victim behind the back and covered the eyes with a handkerchief. Much of the face was dark, streaked black, as though smeared with dried blood. My stomach tightened like a cramp and I felt a wave of dizzy nausea. A large carving knife protruded from the chest, pinning a note. Mom unfolded her arms and turned away with a hand over her mouth, making a sound through her fingers like she'd just come up from water. Something made me push on the door. Dad held me back with a strong arm.

"Don't," he said in an oddly sick tone. "Stay put. Ginny, call the police."

Someone emerged beside me, and I thought it was still my mom until I heard a breath above my ear. I turned to see whites in my brother's rounded eyes I'd never seen before. Transfixed, Tyler gasped a low stinging curse, his breath visible on the glass.

"Tyler!" Mom shouted. It was the foulest thing she'd ever heard either of us utter.

Dad backed away from the door. "What are we doing standing— Let's get the police!"

My father himself had to call the cops, and it was grotesque and almost surreal to hear him describing what was on our property. After he got off, he told us to stay away from the windows, that the police would arrive in a minute. Minute nothing, a Westfield patrol car came to a speeding halt across the street in less than thirty seconds, followed by two others. The first rays of sun were just climbing over the walls of the junior high school.

The police only stayed for ten minutes, which was good in that the scarcity of their time, and the early hour, didn't allow for a build-up of driver stop-and-gawks or a gathering of curious neighbors. I was stupidly relieved that no one we knew saw what really happened. The officer in charge vowed to notify the rescue squad and call the local hospitals in hopes of finding out how someone on the outside had come into possession of a life-sized Annie resuscitation doll, the actual "victim" hanging from our maple. No one laughed at the joke. As a matter of fact, my mother went into a half-panic when she saw the note stabbed by the carving knife into the doll's plastic chest.

"MUNROE!"

I was alert from that moment on. After the police left with the painstakingly made-up dummy, the four of us again sat in the living room in disbelief. I tried to relax, but sitting amongst my family's gloomy faces, it was impossible not to contemplate the foolhardiness of stubborn will. The whole problem sat over me like a wet quilt. I thought about Joe Chiavetti stumbling off our lawn last night—down, but certainly not out. Something was just bound to happen today.

Tyler held steadfast in his refusal to go to school. I decided to follow my own ethical but partially suicidal honor code and made the stand to go. It was school property, I figured. What was the most anybody could do there in plain sight? I, however, did not reaffirm the decision easily. It took me fifteen minutes of stress after my shower, and I was actually leaning toward not going. But the decision to suck it up may have actually saved me.

After I was dressed, I sat at the kitchen table, having trouble eating even the greatest and junkiest of cereals—Kaboom. For a moment I felt like there was a giant bubble around me and the rest of the world was walking by it. Events had seemed to detach me from reality. That may sound melodramatic, but that's what it felt like. I could not rationally connect tenth grade and my story with drive-bys, death threats, and a dummy hanging in a tree with a knife in the chest.

Mom came in while I was eating, acting different, not mean, but far away. She took an audible sip of her coffee, her mouth twisting. In her free hand, she picked up a small piece of paper and set it down in front of me.

"Here," she said, almost sickly amused. "This was on the back door."

I stopped spooning Kaboom and looked down at a hand-sized note. Above a poorly sketched skull and crossbones, this written in red ink:
We watch while you sleep

Guilt has always driven me more than any other emotion. I seem to possess this annoyingly overbearing conscience, one reason why I'm writing about my experiences. Guilt brought me to school that morning. Guilt in small part made me write the article. But I can honestly say that this particular Halloween week seems more fate than chance to me now. How do you feel guilty over something that seems destined to happen? I'm wondering lately about destined fate. It sure is a funny thing. You live your life and think that all roads lead to something you can take. But nothing could prepare me for what I was about to learn in the halls at school that morning.

Again I was in the back seat of the Spencer's Acura, watching the world float by without heed to anything but what stirrings lay ahead at

WHS. My presence, to some, would seem as welcome as a rank bum on a crowded elevator. It's amazing how well I can still feel those deep breaths as I finally got out of the car and walked with Blake down the steps toward the back of school. I knew bad things hid inside those walls, but I had to confront this. It would be the hardest morning of school in my life. I must admit, I felt relieved when a group of my friends met me at the door. I mean, just like that, I was surrounded in a protective circle. I couldn't understand a word that was flying by me until someone told me that John Kohleran was in the hospital.

I stopped. My first thought was, So *this* is why he wasn't in school yesterday. I wondered if he'd had a bad trip, which in a bizarre sense would have served in small purpose to vindicate me. A painful thought—I pictured how his blond bangs would always hang stiffly just above his eyes. For the moment, my excited friends were giving me too many confusing angles about it, too many wrong turns and inconsistencies. So as not to do the same to you, I'll just tell you what eventually came to be fact.

On Tuesday night, Westfield Police, facing my imminent public details, decided they should raid the Mindowaskin Park footbridge. Three kids were arrested—one of whom was John, drunk off Vodka. He stuck around a little too long and gave the police officers trouble. Why people do that is simply senseless. Didn't Kohleran ever watch the show *Cops*? Those staggering, backwoods, shirtless, pot-bellied, toothless junkies who were manhandled like rodeo cattle for their conduct? Apparently that night, John pushed one of the officers and ended up receiving a police escort to the hospital. What was devised to be a method in doubling John over, in order to control his resisting manner, was a blow from an officer's billy-club that struck high of its intended mark, fracturing two of the kid's ribs. I was now being told that John was laid up in Overlook Hospital, and an apparent lawsuit would likely be pending.

I walked along and stared at the floor moving slowly in front of me. The cops had stormed the night before my article even came out. The kids on the bridge had no chance, another result I'd feared. Only one interpretation existed, and I shook my head morosely, realizing that everyone would see it for the truth it was. I had told the cops before I told the kids.

Blake had a funny serious look. I say funny because serious has never been one of his traits. The kids continued to follow, and I felt safe in their sociable attitudes. It was as though I was avoiding the press as I walked along the halls and up the steps to my locker. Some dark-haired girl hurried by coughing "Snitch!". Other kids stood and watched our noisy clan pass.

"Look what someone did!" I heard Blake suddenly say. He had stopped in front of me, and I had a bad feeling about the vicinity. I pushed through kids, approached my locker, and suddenly felt blood leaving my face.

Sometime between yesterday afternoon and now, someone had administered my locker a series of brutal dents. Whoever had done it had rendered it useless. A series of makeshift marijuana joints were taped along the busted door. Blake tried to break the tension by snatching one and sniffing it, comically disappointed that it was only a rolled napkin. Various phrases associated with the idea of my mortality were etched in colorful, cheerful ways along ill-fated locker 354. Clarity arrived for me that morning in permanent magic marker: *DIE YOU NARC FAGGOT* and *R.I.P. NARC*. The fact that I had no idea who was behind any of these threats was really starting to bother me. Usually, when you have a problem with someone, it's specific and targeted. When a small percentage of an entire school wants your head, it's tough to direct any anger. You just have to keep your senses alert and accept it.

I turned around to everyone. For the first time yet, I both admired and envied my brother for his decision. Right then, Tyler was back home, most likely comfortable in his bed, watching TV. I really started wishing I had followed his example when I saw Dayle Tanner.

He was making a faster pace than anyone else in the hallway, trailed by a few others, looking over heads to find me; that shag of his swayed behind his neck. I was so wary of him over the years that he almost appeared infamous to me now. I had chosen to challenge him in this way and now he had poison for me. I felt a sudden surge in my chest when my eyes met his glare.

Dayle, wearing a hooded blue sweatshirt and white jeans, moved right up to me. In his eyes he held an unavoidable contempt, like he couldn't believe what he was seeing. They were light brown. I never noticed that before. He squinted and his braced teeth appeared.

"How do you like your hospital food?" Dayle said down to my face. "Hot or cold?"

A group of burnouts surrounded me. One thrust a middle finger right in my face.

"Good to seeya," the kid said. "Sorry we missed each other yesterday."

Dayle's breath was horribly warm on my face.

"Hope you got a lotta friends," he spat loudly. "You're gonna need 'em."

I don't know what the hell he ate, or when he last ate it, but he was definitely suffering from a chronically hideous case of zacolees—his breath smelled *zacolee* like his armpit. The burner squinted past my head and gestured easily, like he pitied me. "Nice locker, narc."

A silent gathering was growing around us. A few of my friends watched with rigid faces, like they knew there was nothing they could do. I remember Blake's eyes glaring wildly over one of the burnout's shoulders. I had a fleeting vision of Joey Apel's expression in the face of Benton Crossey. In a situation like this, a kid has two options. A, he can save himself by bowing down and losing his dignity, or B, he can risk his life by showing cocky and saving face to those watching. No one likes to be singled out, and in this case, I felt more alone and helpless than in any time of my life, before *or* since.

Dayle's face lost that inquisitive glare. He didn't want to know why I did it. He just wanted me to know I'd be dealing with him. He never took his light brown eyes off mine. He wasn't going to let me ignore him. I'll never forget his next words.

"Know what happened to my friend, asshole? You know John Kohleran, right?"

There was no getting away from his question. Blood had returned to my face and I felt its hot sting. My eyesight swam in a daze from the pressure. I looked around sharply, felt my book bag brush against my smashed locker. In years to follow, I would go back to this moment, relive it with me as a black belt, decking this kid in front of everyone.

"You know I didn't mean for that to happen," I finally muttered.

"Who made you a narc?" he snapped quickly, spreading his arms and frowning meanly. "Huh, Munroe, you little fag? That was the stupidest thing I ever—I mean, what are you even doing here?" He shook his head. "You're brave to come back, but I'm still gonna have to kick your ass so far in you'll be tastin' shit for days."

I thought of my two options and chose option B. Taking my face back, I grimaced at him, waving a hand in front of my nose. Maybe it wasn't the best thing to say.

"You have got some *bad* breath!"

A strong palm smacked against my left eye. I was startled by my own instincts, which made me shove him back before leaning in a slight crouch. I heard yelling around me and someone else bumped me from the side, someone big, with short hair and sunglasses. I was surprised to look up and see Brennan O'Donnell jump between Tanner and me. Usually both hands were jammed in his jeans pockets. Now they were raised, his book bag slipping off one arm and falling to the floor.

"Dayle," he cried, "come on!"

"Screw off, O'Donnell," Tanner seethed. "Don't act like such a fairy!"

"Come on," Brennan urged, leaning against Dayle to hold him off. "Look at the size difference, dude."

If it wasn't for this bald teacher with a bushy mustache approaching, I don't think I would have made it through the day. I blinked through my good eye at the man as he barreled forward.

"Hey! HEY!" he shouted. "Cut it out!"

The kids made room for the teacher. The tangle started to relax itself and Dayle backpedaled, glancing at the teacher, then back at me.

"Faggot gets his daddy and everyone else to fight for him!" He and four other tough wiry kids strutted down the hall between passing kids. "Fight your own battles, Munroe!"

I felt a hand on my arm. The teacher's eyes were dark and probing. He asked me in his coffee breath if I was okay. I nodded yes and told him not to worry about it. He wasn't about to take my advice. He left me with intentions to inform the office of what happened.

Brennan, meanwhile, twirled in place with his hands out. "Nothing else to see," he said. Everyone knew him, liked him, listened to him. It wasn't long before kids started clearing away to homeroom. Brennan sensed the extent of my haggard condition. I couldn't help it. I felt like I had asthma. I wanted to turn right around and run for home or at least for the soft pink carpet of Tara's room.

"You all right?" Brennan's voice was too loud next to me. He grabbed my shoulder strongly with a smile. "Your brother told me to look out for you."

I swallowed, nodded, darting my eyes right and left, re-exposing myself to normal things in the hall. My left eye stung badly and I could feel the tears on my palm. School was going to go on. I had to face it. I had sent John Kohleran to the hospital.

"...should be doing this," Brennan was saying. "He ever coming back to school?"

I had trouble seeing for a second. I wished for the cool comfort of a wet towel. I took my hand from my eye so as not to draw too much attention to it as kids passed. I resorted to looking away and blinking. I wondered who had been there for the exchange, wondered what they were thinking of me now, what stories would be circulated. Finally I started to relax, relieved that the horror was gone for the moment. Brennan was staring down at me through those big bug-like sunglasses.

"Ash," he said with that huge, inviting, toothy smile, "why'd you do that in the paper?"

I started along with him. It felt good to be next to his size and know he still accepted me with some reasonable favor.

"It's been done before," I said easier than I felt. "On much bigger scales than this. It shouldn't be that big a deal."

Brennan nodded thoughtfully. From the side I could see his eyes.

"That's why it *is* a big deal," he said. "Because this is such a small town thing where everybody knows ya. Know what I'm sayin'?" He spoke in his usual, somewhat overbearing tone. I dug him, but twenty feet away you could hear every word out of his mouth. I needed softer, confiding, LiteFM-like talk now. "Dude, if you had the protection of the press," he explained boldly, "it might be different. But this is so confined, and that's why it's kinda nuts to do what you did."

I stopped at the hall stairs, out of earshot from most. "You think I was wrong, too?"

Brennan paused. His shades reflected the window behind me. He leaned on his pocketed hands to cushion his frankness.

"Well, I don't think you had a clue what you were getting into. I mean, *I* never would've done it. I actually think it's a hell-raiser of a thing you did, but I never would have used *my* friggin' name. Know what I'm sayin'?" His eyebrows rose above his shades and he took my shoulder easily. "No, Ash. Honestly, dude? My respect for you has totally gone like—" he pulled a hand from his pocket and flew it over his head, laughing through his lips. "Know what I'm sayin'? I think it was brave as hell. But you couldn't have sold *me* on the idea."

"Everybody in your grade thinks I'm a bastard, huh?"

I wanted him to shake his head quickly no, tell me they're with me. Instead he bent to one side and his mouth twisted halfway.

"Well, people just think you're bein' judgmental." He waited, staring plainly through those large shades, and once again came that, "Know what I'm sayin'?"

I blinked, studied the dim wall behind him like the blocky patterns had answers.

"Look what was going on," I said quietly, my eye starting to feel better. "I mean, a kid was knifed for Pete's sake. Some dope's out there supplying the whole school—"

"Oh, I'm not sayin' you're wrong, dude," said Brennan. "I hear ya, totally."

"All this going on in a park for little kids—"

I stopped, knowing I sounded desperate, like I could have told him reason after reason all day and it still wouldn't have changed anything. But I absolutely could never tell him how much Tyler, and even he, had affected my decision.

Blake and Maureen were at it again in Flaherty's history class that morning. It began when Spencer came in just before the second bell, overdoing a frown at her.

"*You're* here?" he whined, dropping his book bag.

"Stand easy," Maureen ogled back, fanning her face. "You're just *choking* me with your charm."

Blake considered me as he sat in his creaky chair. "Your eye's a little red. You all right?"

I nodded like it was nothing.

"Everyone in homeroom was squeakin' and beepin' about what happened."

"Leave him alone, ding dong," Maureen told him sourly. She tapped my knee and inquired politely, "How about— What are you going to be for Halloween?"

I huffed shortly. "Invisible."

"Hmm, that could be tough."

Before Mr. Flaherty started class, Jen Stirling came striding down my row. As confidentially as she could, she kneeled at my side and began telling me about the scene last night in front of *her* house, which bordered Mindowaskin Park playground. She told me that she and her family watched out the windows for half the night as cops walked around Mindo with flashlights and dogs. Jen said she could see German Shepherds sniffing around—probably females, because her neighbor's male dog was wailing and baying the whole time, wanting *serious* action. She said the barking kept her up 'til three. She wasn't mad, though.

Class was twenty minutes old when it all started happening. At exactly 8:50, the room's intercom clicked on rudely. Right away I had a very weird feeling.

"Room 323?"

"Yes?" Mr. Flaherty responded, walking underneath the speaker stupidly, as though to get a better view of the voice.

The lady sounded hollow through the resonance. "Is Ashley Munroe in your room?"

About a dozen kids sang out, "Yeah!"

"Please send him to the main office right away."

"Gee," Dustin said, tapping his finger on his temple sarcastically. "I wonder—what could that be about?"

On my lonely parade down to the office, I saw only two people. The first was a hall monitor; the second was that big kid, Benton Crossey, his identity exposed from afar by his Westfield baseball cap turned backward on his scalp. We were walking opposite directions along opposite walls when he saw me and began approaching at an angle, hands flopping lazily at his side, his mouth a brazen curl. I figured this wasn't the best circumstance to meet, me being alone and all. I wondered momentarily what the people in the front office would think when I didn't show up. But Baseball Benton put his hand out.

"Bro, you are the *stuff*."

"Huh?"

"I am so glad you did that." His arms hunched forward from his shoulder muscles and his fist went up in greeting, coming down lightly on my palm. Just from the weight I could feel his strength. I was so taken I leaned into a huge smile.

"Really? I thought you were cool on them."

"Bro, gimme a break." Benton smirked colorfully. "I hate all them jerk-offs. Buncha phonies. I only wish I did it." He walked on, shaking his head. All I could see in him was Joey Apel crumbling to the sidewalk. "When I heard Kohleran got aced by the cops," he called back, "I wanted to cheer."

I turned again to the office and froze, pausing before moving to the door. There, a bevy of adults stood waiting for me. Mr. Kellogg greeted me with a grin of subtle regret. I felt my brow twitch when I saw my mother standing with Uncle Joe, next to Principal Peterson. My uncle took his hand from his pants pocket and a trace of lint floated down to the floor. A handshake.

"Hey!" he cheered rather happily. "Some piece!" Uncle Joe was just like my mother, high strung and spirited. I'd never known him to be anything but. I have yet to attend a funeral with him, but it would be a heck of a thing to witness. It figured his interests would bring him here. Aside from his personal stake, he's a local real estate agent and Town Councilman. He has blond hair like my mom's, though not half as bright, and a Jay Leno-like under-bite.

My mother looked at me and I could tell she was agitated.

"The police want to talk to you," she said.

Uncle Joe just watched the road ahead, his face calm in the rearview mirror. I sat forward from the back seat, regarding the fine texture of his gray jacket.

"Did they say why they wanted to talk with me?"

My mother stayed quiet. Uncle Joe looked up and squinted at me in the mirror. He rolled his hand in the air in explanation.

"Your principal called your mother, told her two things. He said you had trouble already, and also, the police want some questions answered. She couldn't get your father, so she called me immediately."

I clung to the headrest on my mom's seat and sat forward. "Why only me?" I asked bitterly. "Jeez, why now and not sooner?"

Uncle Joe remained placid and explained to me that since I'd involved myself on such a level, I'd opened a can of worms. It wasn't sitting well with the police that some kid had shown them up. For appearance's sake, they wanted to make it clear that they really cared.

When Uncle Joe turned into the precinct at Mindowaskin, we all subconsciously looked ahead to the footbridge, but two islands of yellow and brown leaves blocked our view. The three of us got out and walked around the big bush in front of the precinct door.

As we rounded the bend, a ghostly-skinned guy with gray hair stepped off his perch on the wall. Poor man looked like he hadn't seen the sun in five years.

"Ashley?" He stuck a pale cold hand out to me. I shook it, said yes.

"Oh, great," he said. "At last. Um—Ashley, my name is Sal Pocatelli and I write for *The Westfield Leader*. I, um—I know it's kind of crazy now," —he started to follow us through the front door— "but I'd appreciate the chance to talk with you about your story."

My shrug was as colorless as his skin. "Okay."

"Great." He smiled, showing his upper gums. "I appreciate it. When can I ask you just a couple quick questions?"

"He really shouldn't give anything anymore," my mother cut in. Her head cocked and she looked at him as though studying him for a makeover. "Don't you think he's in enough trouble?"

Like a compliant prisoner I followed my mom and Uncle Joe up to a steep Formica counter with a protective window. A black lady whom I recognized as one of the town meter maids, pushed a button and greeted us.

I leaned forward, gave my name and offered why I was here. The lady told me to hold on and picked up a phone. Nothing happened after that for ten minutes. My mom, her blonde hair bright under the hall light, grew increasingly edgy, holding herself tightly—arms folded, heaving up and down from breathing. The black lady finally made the mistake of speaking to her.

"Someone will be here to talk to you soon," she said.

"All you're trying to do is bully my son," my mother snapped, "because he had the nerve to do something about this mess you couldn't do yourselves." She shook her head and glared past the counter. "All this was going on right outside your front window, for heaven's sake!"

A large black man popped out from the main hallway door wearing an expensive suit and a cautious look. His face was square and wondering. He introduced himself as Detective Spera, head of the Juvenile Bureau. The man gestured my way.

"I'd really like to talk to Ashley in person here." He smiled tightly. "I'm being told certain kids aren't too happy with him right now."

What happened next I can only relay secondhand. My mother and her brother asked to speak to Mr. Spera privately. I sat on the wooden bench in the lobby, wondering if this detective was on my side. When the three of them came back, I was told I could return to school.

Apparently, nothing would happen without my father present. I was glad for my Uncle Joe. He knew the rules. But I was offered to come back on a day when both of my parents would be able to make it. Hence, a tentative date was set for Saturday at noon. My mother said we'd think about it and let them know. Standing there having all my responses spoken for me, I began to wonder about the reason for my presence. When we finally turned to go, I was mildly disappointed. Now that ignorance was behind me, I wanted more drama. I wanted to stay and observe life out of school. No one, however, particularly cared about my desires.

I felt sour on the way back to WHS, dreading the wolves I'd have to fend off for the rest of the day. My mother still had her arms folded tightly, complaining of the ironic disorganization in the precinct, "...probably the reason they needed you to clear the park," she said. I just sat in the back and watched my mother and uncle's heads, dreaming of the day when I'd no longer have to watch the world from back seats. I wanted my license suddenly, sick of looking at people's hair. I squirmed restlessly and sighed. It all seemed preposterous. All I did was spill a nasty truth.

"What do I do now?" I said out of the blue. "I can't make anything go back to normal. And I don't want to run away. There's no going back to normal in school. Everything's changed now."

"Well, it certainly is a major turning point in your life," my mother told me in a surprisingly more relaxed manner now. "But you're unique, Ash. You're special. The courage that inspired you to write this article will carry you through this as well."

"That's right, Ashley," said Uncle Joe. "No one else in your school is going through such a stand. You and only you have chosen this honor."

My eyes felt hot and I crossed my arms in my mother's fashion.

"You just have to deal with what's in front of you now," Mom continued. "You have to look at today and say, This is my life now and I have to adjust. I have to decide how to make this change good for me."

It was silent for a few seconds as they sensed my gloom. I heaved another sigh and mumbled to the window, "This is the act I'll always be judged on."

"Ashley, you're a good kid," Uncle Joe reassured. I could feel him watching me in the rearview mirror. "You're not spoiled, or rude, or punkish, like some teenagers I've known. You're mature. You're definitely a thinking, mature kid. I guess it takes that kind of kid, that kind of mentality, to do what you did. As for being judged, six months or six years from now, the only people who will remember and judge you on this will do so because they view it as heroic."

A heavy sigh blew from my mother's lungs. She looked out her side window and said, "But I'm still going into church after this to pray for you, Ashley."

My holy-souled mother, I thought. I remembered her surprising approval at the dinner table Monday night and wondered how much she wished she could go back and recant her "tremendous" statement.

"Kids at school think I'm judgmental," I told her out of a sudden following silence. I figured she could offer me some pious encouragement, something to keep my spirits up, so I sat forward. "Hey, Mom? What do you think God thinks about that?"

"I don't know," she finally said with an air of pension. "Only thing that comes to my mind about judging is Matthew 7:1."

I squinted at her questioningly. "Matthew 7:1?"

"I could be wrong. Look it up for yourself. See what it tells you."

Back at Westfield High, I was somewhat perplexed when my mother and my uncle made me stand in the hall outside the main office while they went in and spoke with Principal Peterson. Slouching and staring at the trophy cases, I could feel the tension grip my body like an ache. I was reading about the '86 soccer team's state championship when a few faces appeared next to mine in the window's reflection. I turned around. My mother and Uncle Joe had reappeared with Mr. Peterson.

"Ashley," Mr. Peterson stated, stroking his tie with his knuckles, "your mother is worried. I told her you had some trouble today. We're going to let you stay in here for a while until this settles down."

Mr. Peterson led me by the shoulders into the office. I was taken through two rooms and into an adjoining hallway where I dropped my book bag on a desk between a window and a main hall door. I was told that this would be my classroom for the day and that someone would get my lunch for me. I couldn't understand how the school could not come up with some other arrangement. At the very least, they should have allowed me to attend the important classes and nix study halls. Besides, it wasn't even school I was worried about—it was *after* school. My mother sort of commanded me to do this, and I just rode with it. She kissed me goodbye with her glorious blessing. Watching the door close after she and my uncle moved through it, I felt their support lifting away. Like a little child, I wanted them to stay.

At first, I enjoyed the serenity and the time with which I had to contemplate everything. Fifteen minutes was all I seemed to need, though. After that it grew more boring than a four-hour Mass. Teachers kept coming in and out of the hall door, snapping my thoughts. I wanted to go home, wanted to *something*. A sense of unfairness grew as I thought of my friends out and about the school without me, laughing and joking easily and socializing while I sat alone in quiet, damned by my own words, with no one around but adults and shelves full of the same books. I already knew all my lessons and had read all the day's material, so I sat with my chin in my hands and stared out the window at a cloud cover just moving in. Every so often a small hole of blue sky would appear, but the sun couldn't find sync with it and the day remained gray and fall-like. I killed some time by making several intricate paper airplanes.

I was allowed to ask for a friend to get my lunch for me. Of course I chose Blake. He ate with me and confirmed the buzz that the burnouts had marked me. He seemed to dig the whole affair, basking in his secret role so close to the center. It was one of the first conversations we had had in five years that didn't involve girls or my lack of knowledge on the subject. Well, that is until I asked him to tell Tara Vovens where I was. He laughed and scooted back out to the wild.

Blake came through like a champ. Within ten minutes, the prettiest face I'd seen all day stopped by the hallway door and peered in the window confusingly. Smiling when she saw me, Tara opened the door and slithered around it, eyeing me prudently. I wanted to squeeze her. She stood over me, brushing my hair slowly and making a face otherwise reserved for kittens and puppies.

"What have they done to my friend?" she drawled.

The copy machine lady appeared and stared at Tara through her reading glasses, like a blaring alarm waking me from a pleasant dream.

"You have a pass?" she asked. I felt guilty. Tara laughed.

"Of course not."

Copy machine lady raised her brow. "Get to class."

Tara started away, the lady blocking her out of the office like I was quarantined. I rose quickly and followed.

"I'm coming over after," I told her firmly, looking right into her eyes. "Be home."

Tara nodded as the door was shut.

As soon as that, the door opened again. It was my favorite teacher, Mrs. Dowman. It occurred to me as she leaned into the table and wrote my homework assignment that we'd never really spoken to each other much. I was sad for that, and I guess that's why she did it so briskly. She acted as though none of this really fazed her, like it happened every day and she had other places to be. She made one good-natured quip about my predicament and finished writing. I sat eased back and watched her at the door.

"Mrs. D," I said, causing her to pause, "you think what I did was foolish?"

For a second, I thought I'd stumped her. Then, just before she backed through the door, she darted her dark eyes from one wall to the other and shrugged.

"Well, if you didn't want the trouble, it lacks wisdom."

I received my last piece of homework nearly two periods in advance, and the delivery girl surprised me—Maureen Egan. Five minutes after blunt Mrs. Dowman left, Maureen arrived wearing the soft pink sweater and slacks I'd recently admired in history class. Along with a smile, she carried two night's worth of French homework and class lessons. In my bleak isolation, I had already finished most of my night's drudgery. Clearing the deck was part of my preparation strategy in dealing with whatever was to surely occur later tonight.

"I won't bore you with the rumors and threats," Maureen told me. "Although they are setting up a gallows in the courtyard." She winked. "Just kiddin'. Actually, no one's said anything for an entire period. It's amazing. Oh, by the way, there's a quiz on Monday, just so you know."

"This is only a temporary thing," I told her hopefully. "I'll be back to daily life tomorrow."

She paused at the door, then turned around on wobbly lazy legs. I figured she wanted to ask me something unordinary, but was totally unprepared for the subject. She touched the desk top, her finger twisting.

"Hey, I want to know."

I blinked at her. "Yeah?"

"Does Blake like me?" She tilted her face. "Or is he—I don't know."

I shrugged a smile up at her, slightly envious of my best friend. "I don't know. Why?"

Maureen pursed her lips bashfully. "Just—wondering." She twirled back to the door, waved, then walked out.

Principal Peterson stopped at my side not long after and gave me incredible news. The school was releasing me early, right then. He made sure I had all my homework assignments and simply excused me for the rest of the day. Tyler would be waiting with a big "I told you so."

I was let out the front door around 1:30. On the way home, I passed Holy Trinity Church, reminded of my holy mother's words to me— "Matthew 7:1."

The door to a house adjoining the church was being opened and a man came bumbling out with a big box. I glanced at the door and saw a young bald priest standing watch behind it. His collar was undone and hanging off his neck. Though it was overcast, he squinted out at me in question. I felt really goofy, and decided to just walk on.

I went home to show my mom I lived through the day, and had to plead with her to let me go back out to the Memorial Library so I could research John Steinbeck for my English term paper. The idea was to be there and get my information while school jailed my predators. I wound up staying a little longer than I should have and figured it was too light to walk back toward my own neighborhood. I had to have somewhere to hide out 'til dark and had told Tara to meet me at her house anyway. It was nearing 4:30 when I left the library and jogged over to the Curb Owl's residence, later than expected, and knocked on her kitchen window. Inside the Vovens's kitchen, Tara was jabbering on her cordless and munching her usual peanut-buttered bagel. She waved the bagel at me and gestured for me to come in. I comforted myself with some candy corn while she laughed and goofed on the phone with some girl named Patty. As soon as she hung up, Tara put on a leather jacket and pulled on my sleeve.

"Come on," she said. "Let's go hang in The Magic Forest. It's safer."

I followed her back down the porch steps. "Safer?"

"I don't want to be here in case Joe decides to pop over," she said.

That's all I needed to hear. We cut through her neighbor's property to the next street and scampered onto the Boulevard. On the way, Tara told me how she heard from Joe that I was in trouble with a lot of kids. It certainly wasn't anything new, and I was growing tired of people reminding me. We finally reached her "Magic Forest"—a simple stretch of woods leading to the lumberyards south of town. Hidden in the obscurity of tall trees and overgrown shrubbery, it was darker here. Tara sat on a log and took out a pack of cigarettes.

"I'm so psyched about your dad," she said after her first drag. "He really decked Joe, huh?"

I stood with my hands in my pockets and kicked the log. "Yup."

There was a single puff of soft laughter. "Your dad's big."

I smiled uneasily at her, thinking about my mess at school. I wondered if Tara knew about Dayle Tanner and me. My eyes watered from a small breeze carrying allergens of dead leaves.

"You wanna try a drag?" Tara asked, holding out her smoldering cigarette.

I shook my head and twitched, watching her staring at me funny.

"You ever once in your life smoked?"

"I hate cigarettes."

"Ever a joint?" She bent her head to the side and smiled. "Never once?"

I shook my head like I was irked she'd even asked. Tara the Curb Owl took another puff and blew smoke. In the faint light of the woods, the orange ember glowed like a tiny illuminated plastic pumpkin when she dragged. Those were the only times she didn't look appealing to me. I don't know. There's just something about smoke emanating from a human orifice that doesn't do much for me.

She still had this sly grin, peculiarly bordering on lust. "I gotta get you to smoke one night. Get you stoned just so you can get a feel for what you reported on." She scraped leaves out of her way and tapped cigarette ashes onto smooth dirt. "Ashley?"

Her tone was odd and I mimicked her. "What?"

"If I asked you to smoke with me at this moment, would you?"

"For Pete's sake." I peered around the woods coyly.

She giggled at my face. "I'm serious. Would you or not?"

"Oh, sure." I regret that Tara didn't catch the sarcasm that time. Moreover, I felt myself sink inside when she picked her purse off the dark log and unzipped it. She stopped once to hide her hands inside and looked up at me.

"Remember you asked me at Mindo that night not to change if you told me something?"

"Yeah."

Tara lifted her wallet to her waist and opened to the bills. She had recently gotten her nails done, bright red. She pulled something out that looked an awful lot like those things that were taped above my locker that morning. My vision was a bit funny, maybe because of the pause in my breathing. I had to be sure, so I stepped forward and put my hand out. She recoiled on the log.

"Not if you're gonna do something with it."

"Just lemme smell it," I said. She held it under my nose and I whiffed. It was definitely the real thing. I'd hoped for a second that she was joking. It was nothing *too* surprising, since I had known her to do pot before. I just felt sapping betrayal.

I could not hide the disappointment in my face. I backed away, blinking like I'd just seen a dead animal or something. In my mind, this was ruining any chance of Tara and me having a larger meaning. Most of all, I was depressed, realizing the distance between us.

When I looked at Tara again, I was ten feet away with my hands on my hips. I watched her fail at a smile and bounce the stick in and out of her wallet.

"Hey," she called, "I'm just schooling you on what you wrote about. I won't do it again if—"

"Why are you doing this?" I looked at a dirt hill near a small swamp.

"Ashley, I won't do it anymore if you don't want me to." I had never heard her plead with me before. It was like I was being introduced to a new version of Tara Vovens.

"Tara—" I flopped a hand out of my pocket.

"Okayokay." Tara's mouth twitched. "Watch." She crushed the joint in her fingers until it was spread on the small forest's floor in dozens of shards. "See?"

I was so flabbergasted by the bold-souled move and girlish look on her face that I started laughing. Tara jumped up and playfully hit me.

"Eat dirt, you clod," she said. "That took a lot of strength."

I backed away and fixed my eyes on a little swamp next to a dirt bike trail, finding a successful way out of the happenstance. When I noticed a rope hanging into the still water from a tree limb just above, I started walking over.

"Let's go check out that pond!" I called.

Tara took up her purse and followed me noisily over the leaves. She talked with a newness in her words to me now, about how she admired my character, confessing a wish that she had it. I was a little maze-minded and thrown off my feelings for a spell. I decided to shake it off by offering a simple dare. I'd swing over that small swamp.

Tara was taken. "What?"

"Yeah. You said I don't do enough spur-of-the-moment outlandish anything, right?" I mocked, "Be crazy, man."

She held my side. "That was before I knew about your article."

We both stared at the swamp. The water did look black and gross, but the width from one end to another was only about twelve feet at most. It was obviously deeper in the summer, given away by the steep layered walls of mud around the perimeter.

"You don't know how deep it is," she laughed. "And besides, that vine won't hold."

"It's not a vine, it's a rope. Look." I pointed. Although it was discolored, you could see where the rope was tied around the limb. "*Some*body swung on that once." I circled my arms around in lively fashion. "I'm into doing crazy stuff, Tara. Just like you said. So let's go, darlin'."

Tara folded her arms tightly. "I'm not goin' *any*where! You swim with the rats. Not me."

"Ah, ya hypocrite. Watch."

I picked up a stick and stretched for the rope dangling in the water. I think the muck's first movement in months was the ripples that upset the stagnancy when I scooped the rope into my grasp. The wet part of the cord was slimy and cold, but I tugged and found enough slack to give myself a few feet of dry grip. Here it was. Like my article, I was going to take a risk. Like my story, I was leaping over uncharted, unknown territory. Setting myself with good tautness to the rope, I tested the strength of the limb, swiveled my head to Tara and used a ghetto tone.

"In yo' *face*, disgrace!"

I flexed my legs and leapt from the bank, clinging mightily to the rope. The wind rushed through my hair and I felt myself submit to gravity. Something hit my back and I realized it was the water. Splash!

The surface stopped my momentum immediately and I found my body sunken in wet coolness. Very suddenly, I was in trouble. The part of the rope to which I had been holding fast was maybe only a *foot* out of the water! It wasn't the strength of the rope I had misjudged. It was my weight on the stupid branch!

In up to my chin, the filthy water was seeping heavily into my clothes and I was slimed to the neck. Humiliated and shocked, I gripped further and further up the rope, looking about the shore and cursing my brains out. I had this crazy notion of climbing all the way up to the limb. The stupidity of my cold wet blunder so consumed me that it took a few seconds to notice Tara. She was literally rolling on the leafy ground in scream-laughter, gripping her stomach like her intestines had burst. I don't know what she was laughing at more—me in the water with my panicked face or my alarmingly foul yells.

"Hey, it ain't funny!" I finally quivered. "I need help!"

Tara stumbled up, sucking air and pushing it back out cruelly. Seeing me claw my way up the rope in futility with slop draped over my body, she fell back down in a ball of mirth.

Once above the water with only my legs in, I could gauge my options. I breathed hard and swore at Tara. I really couldn't blame her. Hell, I would have laughed just as hard if not harder. It was just the idiotic feeling of looking so incredibly half-assed in front of her. Not to mention, how in the hell was I going to get back to dry land? The limb was too complicated a shape for a shivering idiot like me to scale. No way was I going back down into that thick black water! So I held onto the rope like a squirrel clutching a thread, dripping cold liquid and already dreading the way Tara would be telling this to everyone. Jeez, my gallant metaphor comparing this risk with my article ended with me in the same place both times—stuck deep in the muck.

Tara was standing again (doubled over, I should say) when I peered back around at her. She tried yelling for me to swim back, but her eyes met mine and she caved back into bellowed spit-laughter. Finally I saw the humor in it all and couldn't hold back. I started laughing, too.

"I'm gonna kill you when I figure out how to get the hell outta here!" I yelled, throwing in a few more profanities at myself.

My laughing and joking took away some of her thunder. Tara calmed enough to tell me news I didn't want to hear.

"You have to wade back to me, Ashley. I'll help you."

She reached out her hand, only some *ten* ghastly feet away!

She was right. There was no other way than down and in.
Reacquainting myself with the stinging cold water, I dropped in and felt
my sneakers sink into the muck at the bottom, stirring it up to my chin.
Tara got down to one knee and kept her hand stretched to me. It didn't
take long before she blew a strong laugh at my cringing face. I moved
through the chest-high water with my arms above it and clawed my way
up the muddy embankment. Tara tried to help, but I warned her off,
telling her not to touch me in such a gross state. When I stood up, I had
a new appreciation for ground. But my transient relaxation was quickly
replaced by shivering cold. The sun had just set and dusk was coloring
the area. I started to move like a robot out of the woods. A totally weird
thought swam into my mind as I ran. It just seemed that whenever Tara
and I were around water, *some* zany story was bound to come out of it.

What irony, I kept thinking as I slicked back to her house. She
wants to do dope and I won't have any part of it, yet she's dry and I'm
a muck-covered river rat. Nobody was out on the road, but it wouldn't
have concerned me if there had been a parade. My only desire was for
warmth and comfort. Tara, worrying that I'd catch cold, kept me
running by staying ahead and waving me on like a coach. I had this
funny desire that, if I could, I'd rewind the whole event to where I'd
commented about the swamp, push stop there, and start re-recording.

Thank God Mr. and Mrs. Vovens weren't home yet! Inside the
house, Tara opted for me to take cold refuge in the bathroom next to the
kitchen.

"Now I get to watch you take off all your clothes," she giggled,
turning on the bathroom light.

I crinkled my mouth and pushed the bathroom door closed on her,
ashamed of the mess I was making on the white and blue tile floor.

"We have to put your clothes in the washing machine at least," Tara
called from the other side. "And take a towel from the closet there. I
don't want you to get sick."

I started with my jacket. It peeled off me like a tarred banana skin.
Tara heard me grunting and started laughing again from the other side.
I reluctantly lifted my soggy shirt and felt the chill of dirty swamp
water slide down my side like icicles.

"I'll bet you," I gibed loudly, throwing my heavy shirt on my
jacket, "that at one time this scene *must* have been filmed as a hot set-
up in a porno flick."

"Ashley," I heard Tara sing out, "you're gonna have to open the door for me, sweetie."

Fearing the inevitable, I tried to stall. I said into the door, "How long do you think this'll take?"

"Depends on your experience." She waited a couple seconds. "Ha."

"In that case, don't even bother opening the door. Really, how long will my clothes take?"

"Hour maybe," I heard her say against the wood. "Don't worry. My rents shouldn't be home by then. I'll give you some sweats anyway. Now come on. Lemme have 'em."

I slid the gold handle down and the door opened. Embarrassed, goose-pimpled and shivering, I held an arm across my chest from the arching of Tara's eyebrows as her face appeared from around the door, eyes wide and wondering. Luckily I had a line waiting.

"I envy how warm and dry you are."

Tara pushed the door wider and swung her shoulders. "I could warm you up." She then looked down at my crotch. "I need those."

I checked my sticky jeans. "Can't we do it in two washes while I wait? I'll wait, you know."

The Curb Owl set herself sternly and impatience filled her tone. "Let's get this done with. Look at you, you're freezing." She slumped tiredly. "Just close the door and throw your jeans out. I won't look, you wimp."

I did as she told me, only I left the only article of clothing on I could trust—my boxer shorts. It eventually did matter. After I squirted and scraped my pants off, I tugged my boxers firmly back to position and opened the little linen closet. Nothing. The only things for cover were Tarzan-like face cloths. I took about three of them and patted myself dry, starting to feel warm at last. Standing there like that, an extremely empty feeling curled in my gut, like my stomach was squeezing against itself. Here I was, nearly stark naked in a hot girl's bathroom, no one else in the house. The possibilities suddenly seemed massive. As if that wasn't enough, when the bathroom door opened again to reveal Tara's face shining in the light, a weird extension of my body began taking a horrible form just south of the border. Tara didn't help matters. Sensing sure victory when I dropped my two-ton jeans around the door, she started flirting with me to come out.

"Tara, please," I cried, hiding my body behind the door. "It's embarrassing enough."

"Come to think of it," Tara observed plainly, crossing her arms, "you practically are em*bare-ass*ed. I guess that's where they got the term."

The Curb Owl unfolded her arms and took my jeans, winging them down the cellar stairs where they hit the floor with an obscene flop. She then danced back toward me, smiling seductively, peeling away the shoulder of her shirt, exposing a creamy white softness of skin. Her right eyebrow twitched, and I could see a distinct twinge of lust behind the playfulness of her eyes.

"You think you're gettin' anything to change into?" She moved her face near mine and laughed. "Think again."

I stood behind the door, grinning at her. You know what the worst thing about this was? I felt way too slimy and mucky to really allow myself to into the moment. I was about to suggest she even the odds when Tara lifted her hands. I had a feeling of what was about to happen, but whatever her intention was, it was cut short by a soft banging down the hallway. The noises took the character of what seemed to be the front door opening. A cheerful holler broke into the house.

Tara's face was suddenly vivid with shock. I saw her eyes fly open just as she pulled the bathroom door shut. I heard her call weakly from the kitchen, "Hello?"

I locked the door, tested it, and waited, my thumping heart the only sound in that bathroom.

Deep mumbles resounded two rooms away from me.

I stayed still and listened at the sink, holding every muscle in my body gripped in a mad convulsion. My abdomen burned from the strain.

The voices were instantly louder, sharper.

"What are you all doing?" Tara sounded shaky, guilt-ridden.

I heard a number of guys walking around the house, their laughter bold with volume. It was hard to tell how many there were from all the banging footsteps.

"Bustin' in on you for chow."

You know, it's amazing how well I could tell that voice by now, though I hardly knew the guy. The squeaky toughness always distinguished that barking petulant tone.

"I'm sorry to tell you," I heard Joe Chiavetti say, "but your little friend's a dead duck."

He didn't know how right he was.

Holding the edge of that sink, I watched my full reaction in the mirror, stricken by how I looked. Practically nothing on and some of my archenemies right on the other side of the wall. Great. A horrid notion caught me stunned. First I thought they had tracked me here, but then I realized the absence of anger in Joe's voice meant they were ignorant of my presence. Send them away, Tara! Joe had even threatened me in front of my father last night. God forbid I get caught like this! If Tara could get them out of the house, I might survive with my flesh intact.

Someone neared the bathroom door, so close I could hear the wood creak under the weight. Too big to be Tara. The line of light under the door must have attracted attention. I eyed the lock on the handle. It seemed so frail!

Panic seared through me like a pulled muscle when Tara's voice, just as close as moments before, repeated, "What are you doing?"

God, *please*, Tara! Don't act suspicious!

"Someone in there?" a guy asked softly. I could just hear the humored wonder in his voice. It wasn't Joe; it was someone else. Perhaps Scott, the stocky dude from the night before.

I looked momentarily for anything, a knife, a hammer, *anything* to keep these guys at bay from me in my wet, shrunken boxers! There was nothing. No towels, no weapons. Only a sink, a toilet, my Godforsaken three-quarter naked body, and a window. It was obvious my only choice. I scooted to the small window. Whoever had stopped near the door called out with frightening clarity, "Joey C! Come here!" I grabbed up a toilet brush and held it like a sword, then took a frowning double take at my feeble and impossibly ridiculous tool of defense. Setting it gingerly back, I moved my hands to the window. As I held my breath and slowly undid the lock, I noticed one good thing out of this sudden predicament. Adrenaline had risen my body temperature dramatically. Pulsating hot flashes dimmed my hearing as much as they sharpened my intent for the outdoors. I made a small noise in my throat sliding up the first pane. The storm window, though, was complicated and I lost my breath when I thought it wouldn't open. After I figured out the two buttons on the sides, my dizziness cleared and I slid the window slowly up, setting it to its highest limit, amazed to find my tongue protruding comically from my mouth. I backed off to survey the opening. Now how was I supposed to do this crazy thing?

Across that bathroom, another voice came from behind the locked door. Eight feet away, Joe Chiavetti roughly asked who was in here.

Tara's answer was stinging with annoyance. "It's my mom, you sick twisted pervert! Get away from there! Jeez!"

In a rush of fear, I leaned my head out into the cool air and could just hear Joe spit back, "Bull. Your mom's car isn't even home. Who's in there?"

Half out the window now, I inched along, careful of the thin cold edges. Outside, the evening was much darker, porch lights sharp and bright. The atmosphere was silent, free, inviting. I checked down. The ground below me was a six-foot drop into some sort of flat juniper bush. I mulled for a second the possibility of landing on my head. It was either a complicated fall or face a potential pain and mortification. Suddenly from behind I heard a short laugh, and something that almost made me drop straight down—a single hard knock, a punch against the door. It seemed to vibrate through my body. I balanced myself on the house siding and peered back frantically. No one had busted through like I had supposed; the white door still shielded me. Joe was getting loud and gruff, cursing at Tara. She was still trying her best to stall them.

The door handle jiggled once.

Literally panic-stricken, I moved my body further into the night, swirling my legs as though treading water—until my hands slipped. Trying wildly to balance myself I heard another knock hit the door and I banged my knee. The next second, I was falling ridiculously through the air, landing hands and face first into the flat scratchy juniper bush and rolling forward to cushion the blow. Branches snapped and I turned on my stomach. Out onto the grass I crept like a kitty cat, hoping Joe and his friends weren't on to my escape and heading around to trap me in the back yard. I wasn't leaving anything to chance. Like a frantic kitty cat now in flight, I sprinted across the Vovens' back yard and kept going, feeling myself detached from the drama. My momentum sailed me through two more yards until I found myself trapped by a fence lined by bushes. My feet rested on a soft patch of grass and I waited and listened, my heavy shock panting the only sound. A stiff breeze swam over my skin, smacking me with an appalling realization.

I was, beyond belief, basically streaking. My hot skin contested the evening air. I made a pitifully intuitive attempt to cover myself, hunkering under cover of a shadow, surveying the nearest windows. Clear. I checked all around me carefully now, wondering if I was better off waiting out the time when everyone would leave Tara's house. She, by the way, would be beside herself when she discovered I'd fled. I should wait, I thought. Then a breeze blew over my goose pimples and I didn't feel like waiting around. There were no sounds but cars passing over on South Avenue. I watched the Vovens's house a couple hundred yards away now, feeling victory in my escape. But it was enormously apparent to me that my problems were just beginning. I now had to navigate a hidden trek home clad only in thin, dampened, pathetically outgrown boxer shorts.

About a thousand thoughts ran through my mind in the first pensive moment. Where to go? Dang it! It was dark out now and I had to be home for dinner soon! Jeez, how in the world would I ever spin this to Mom and Dad? Think on it later. I had to get home! I stood timidly, held to my hiding spot, trying to think of a plan, but a dog's sudden bark from the back porch of the next yard startled me right out of myself. It was a good indication that someone might show at that back door and look around warily. I hustled away, for it wasn't every night you peered out your window to see a boy in his underwear running around your property.

My first adventure was slipping through the driveway I was in and scurrying out into the wide open across Summit Avenue without being seen. It was a stone driveway, so I tiptoed swiftly along the scratchy grass behind an old station wagon. My step hurried when a man's mumbled voice resonated above me in a kitchen window. With each move I felt nippy air swim over every extremity of my body. I reached a thick tree and hid behind it, keeping a sharp 360-degree watch. A truck turned off South Avenue, delaying my charge. I maneuvered uniformly around the tree trunk, keeping the headlights from me as the truck vroomed past, watching with relief as it continued down Summit.

I drew a huge breath and lunged for a darkened house across the road. The chilly pavement made me feel just how bare I was. Careful not to stub a toe or jam my tender feet, I hopped the curb and sailed onto the leaf-strewn lawn. The grass in the front yard was long and the gray house up close seemed almost vacant. I soared around by the side and the darkness and solitude I then encountered in the back yard offered comfort. There was only one problem. The fence.

Right away I found out climbing fences and snapping over little twigs were going to make bare feet almost intolerable. Creeping over this unkempt yard full of dry leaves, every crackling footstep could be heard. To further my plight, in the really dark spots I couldn't tell where a stick was until I stepped on it, adding to the noise with a muffled yelp. I moved along the fence, squinting from spotlight strobes through panels of wood, and at last I found what I was hoping for. The fence met up with an older one at the edge of the property and I was able to wedge my near stitch-less self between the weak opening by pushing on it.

Entering the next property, I was stunned to find it wider and much brighter than the previous. Instead of wasting time squirming to avoid the light, I scampered straight through, passing under a strong spotlight, and arrived upon the openness of Westfield Avenue. Pitter-patting briskly across the street, I came to rest in a hill choked with bushes and shrubbery. Up on the raised front lawn, I saw the most blessed thing my eyes could behold—a scarecrow.

The makeshift dummy stood drooping against a lamppost, decked in sagging jeans and a red flannel shirt. I was crouched on all fours, my panting lungs the only movement as I watched it. I groped my way up through dirt and leaves and stepped carefully through an array of early elastic maple trees. My heart banging, I literally held my breath and ran.

When I reached the scarecrow, I grabbed it and tugged violently, only to realize with alarm that it was attached to the post by a complicated twisting of thin wires. The lamppost jerked, throwing light around the yard in haphazard flashes. With a fierce rush of adrenaline, I held the post and jerked hard, ripping the decoration free and hauling it away with me. I was so consumed with zipping off with the steal that I made a costly turn around the corner of the yard. Before I saw it or knew what happened, something seemed to pull me to a messy spill. I had slipped in the loose dirt from a new garden, my cheek hitting the soil and the first hard bump spraying dirt all over me. The scarecrow left my clutches and split apart next to me. I sat up and a groan sprang from my lips before I could stop it. Cold mud was all over my left side—legs, back, smeared over my neck and chin. My tiny boxers were a skid-marked mess.

With a careful watch of the side windows, I swore bitterly and gathered what was left of the mangled scarecrow, dragging it on my knees with me to a thicket of dark bushes. The head, which had been created of hay wrapped in burlap, was strewn over the dirt. I emptied the hay out of the shirt and jeans and slipped on the scratchy clothes. As I dressed, I grew increasingly worried about time and missing dinner, since I was usually responsible about calling. Considering present distressing circumstances, my parents were probably worried I'd been kidnapped. I finally stood up in the darkness and surveyed myself—a sorry fool in a wrinkled old shirt and huge crusty jeans, itching and barefoot.

From there I jogged home lightly on the soles of my feet, skirting around the center of town, the whole time holding up the enormously fat jeans with one hand. At times I paused and ducked, zigzagging through the darkest parts of properties, avoiding detection from cars, streetlights and porch lamps.

I had mixed reactions when I finally zeroed my house from behind the Mackay's line of bushes across the street from Roosevelt School. I had come into sight of a group of burnouts surrounding the bike racks. One was silhouetted against the library wall, lifting a cigarette to his lips.

Home. It didn't matter if my story sounded too fantastic or not. I'd deal with that later. I was sick of hiding scared. Strangely though, even at that moment I knew I'd had an adventure, a tale worthy of widening eyes in the future. Now I was freezing and my feet killed. I wanted warmth! I wanted a bath! I wanted to know what in the world happened to Tara Vovens. Finally I gritted my teeth, hopped out onto the Mackay's front yard, and dashed madly across the asphalt. It hurt my poor feet to slow down on the pebbles lining our property. Ready to face twenty-one questions inside, I crept around to the back and eyed the kitchen window. Suddenly, something moved from the darkness.

"What the hell?!"

I was so shaken by the brisk shout that I waved my arms and rocked completely in terror. Kicking the air with my right leg through the giant jeans, I crouched defensively. My face, I knew, looked utterly ridiculous when I stared up. As quickly as I heard it, I realized only one person could belong to that voice.

"Ashley!" the voice cried again. "What happened?!"

I was so relieved I fell to the grass and groaned. I sat there for a few seconds while Tyler flicked his cigarette butt to the bushes and tried to help me up. Irony of ironies, I had actually stumbled onto *him* sneaking a smoke from Mom and Dad. His face was a wash of alarm. "Ashley!" he kept saying. "What happened?! You all right?"

Still on the grass, I kept waving him off, telling him hoarsely to shut up lest anyone should hear. His concern showed faithfully through his eyes, warm and pleasantly compassionate. Even the goofy shape his mouth was taking and the swinging of his dark bangs relaxed me. I must have looked a sight to him—covered in rags and mud.

Triumphantly but tiredly, I briefed him on the story and he absolutely laughed himself lightheaded. Even though I was still outside in the night, sitting in my yard next to the kitchen made me feel warmer. I kept begging Tyler to hush, but it did seem as though he was over his anger with me. He finally helped me off the grass.

"I just saw kids over there," I informed him, pointing to Roosevelt.

"Could be anybody," he said easily, like it was nothing. "This time of year."

Suddenly his breathy laugh—"Tara called."

Still puffing, I enlisted him to get me pants and a shirt. Tyler ran inside. In a moment he returned with sweats and a pair of his sneakers, as well as a warm damp cloth for my face and neck. As soon as I was properly assembled, I hid the scarecrow outfit as a keepsake and walked inside.

Holding a glass of wine, my mother came into the kitchen from the den as I stepped through the back door. She stopped to glance at Tyler's sweats on me.

"Where've you been?"

I could smell meat loaf. Red potatoes were cooking in a pot on the stove. I hadn't missed dinner! Immediately, my mind concocted at least three different tales. I gave them all up quickly, though.

"Just out," I said, hurrying past.

"Wait," she called. "What are you doing in—"

"Seeya!"

I was anxious to call Tara, but instead, headed straight upstairs for the bath. My older brother was amazingly filling the tub for me when I got there.

Wonder of wonders, two miracles occurred that night. One, I never caught a cold, and two, the Munroe family ate dinner in peace. No one called, no doorbells rang, no one scared up any hi-jinx around the property. None of that happened. Not until nine o'clock. The threats seemed to prefer the later hours. For a while after my journey home, I was convinced that the drama with my story was fading quietly like I'd predicted and now the good would come from it.

Burnout anger though, took its time tonight to hit the corner of Dudley and Clark, but when it did, it hit in full force like a hurricane.

Lying on my bed, I could feel the stress from the past two days catching up to me. I was sliding off into sleep when the ringing telephone shook me off my doze. I hopped off the bed and picked up the phone in my parents' room.

"Hello?" I said.

The silence on the other end chilled me sharply awake. I decided to chide this one on. After all, I wouldn't put this past Blake. I tried to sound casual, to keep the confused shake out of my tone. "Name and desire, please."

Still nothing. We had no caller ID, but from the background noise of cars, it seemed to be from a pay phone. Miffed, I looked at the clock.

"Isn't it a little too late and a little too early to be prank calling people?"

A loud cracking hurt my ear. The person banged the phone against something and hung up.

I was helped out when the second prank came a few minutes later. Down in the kitchen, my dad waved me off, grabbing the phone.

"Munroe's residence," he voiced comically. "State your request." He paused for a few seconds until a disgusted frown creased his face. "You guys are pathetic." The receiver clacked on the wall.

Right away the phone rang again. My father's lips tightened in a scowl through his beard.

"You get this one."

"Munroe's Morgue," I answered. "You kill 'em, we chill 'em."

"You better not go to school tomorrow, asshole," a guy's voice told me. At that, the line went dead.

Burdened by anonymous anger once again directed at me, I left the kitchen and went back up to my room. Mom had said, "Matthew 7:1." I opened my Bible to the Book of Matthew, chapter seven, verse one: *"Do not judge and you will not be judged."* This passage was far from the support I had expected. I kept the book rested in my lap and stared at the wall. Judgmental. Do not judge. I was so caught up in it that I neglected the phone.

"Ashley!" my father called up the stairs. "Telephone."

I went down and returned to the kitchen wearing a befuddled expression. Dad just cupped the phone and told me softly, "It's some lady."

"Oh." I took the phone. Her name was Mrs. Leslie, and she was calling me on behalf of "myself and many, many parents" who were impressed by what I did. Everyone, she told me, found my article bold and long overdue. She said that the story had been the talk of the ladies at the supermarket that morning. I felt tiny bursts of air like laughter coming from my throat. It was incredible to hear. I needed it like water to a wilted plant. Suddenly the pranks were worth it. The worry was worth it. Even the bizarre events of this very evening were all worth it. Mrs. Leslie told me that she and her friends were sending deeply felt Thank You notes to both the school and me.

The call waiting beep crashed into her talking. Mrs. Leslie kept chattering through it. I asked her to hold.

"Pardon?" She seemed perplexed.

"I have another call coming through, ma'am. Could you hold on for just one sec'?"

"Oh, I'm sorry. Sure."

I pressed over. "Hello?" The anonymous silence was getting annoying. "Oh, come on," I huffed. "This better be good."

"It should have been *you* in the hospital," an oddly mature voice then said.

I spoke back. "Oh, you think so?"

"Yeah," the voice told me. "Next time it's gonna be you—"

I snapped back to Mrs. Leslie. The poor woman probably thought I didn't care much about this call of hers, so I told her how much I appreciated her gesture, and the support it offered. Then I explained that my family and I were in the middle of being harassed and this woman drawled, "Oh, that's too bad." She did sound extremely concerned, but I reassured her it was all right. Still, the calls were starting to really spook me, and due to my absent lack of involvement, the conversation didn't last much longer. When I hung up, I remembered what I had been doing when the call came.

I went to the den and sat across from my father. The TV glare glinted off his glasses. He raised his chin and smiled warmly. "Pretty nice of her, huh?"

"Dad, did I do the right thing?"

My father scratched his beard under his chin and looked at the TV. He laughed in a light tired manner. "Well, I wouldn't want this again, that's for sure." He took a heavy breath and said on his exhale, "Time will tell, I guess."

I groaned as I got up and went to the dark living room, peeping out the windows. I was watching headlight after headlight float down Dudley for about two minutes before that red, silvery-trimmed pickup passed slowly by the house. My head fell against the glass as it rounded Clark Street and passed by Roosevelt School.

"Ashley!" Tyler called, breaking my stupor. "Tara."

I drew my face from the curtain. Tyler was draping the phone in his hand and watching me with a funny grin. Astonishingly, I hadn't even noticed the phone ringing.

I bounded over and grabbed the receiver. Tyler had the presence of mind to leave while Tara and I commiserated about the misshapen evening. She was apologetic and worried silly, but above all, amazed that I'd made it home. It so happens that Joe Chiavetti and three of his friends eventually went around the back and saw the open window. Hearing this shook me. I really *had* to do all that!

"You okay?" I asked.

"Fine," she said. "They just split after that. I have your book bag. Want me to bring it over?"

"No way," I returned adamantly. "Don't come anywhere near this area. They've already started hassling us."

"God, really?"

"Yeah. And the last thing you need is for Joe to see you."

"Oh, Ashley," she moaned. "I'm so sorry. You must have frozen!" Her tone changed. "You looked so funny though!"

"Not a word!" I demanded. "Got it? Not to Donna or Varsity or *anybody*!"

Tara laughingly complied. With concerns to my abandoned possessions, I told her I already had my homework done and not to worry. Just see me with everything in school tomorrow. She apologized again and we got off. That was the last moment of peace for a while.

The fifth prank call was the worst. After picking up what I expected to be foul anyway, I chirped something light to hopefully throw them.

"Munroe's Bakery!" I called out. "Which crumb do you want?"

"Are you Ashley?"

"Yes."

"Little pansy ass mother."

"Oh, it's you! Thank God. I've been waiting to hear from you."

A coarse voice, like teeth were gritted. "You know, tomorrow night is Mischief Night."

I just couldn't place the low, raspy tone. It definitely wasn't Dayle or Chiavetti, or even John Kohleran. My mother walked up from the laundry room and knew right away what was going on. She set her basket on the counter.

"You better be careful, Ashley Munroe," the guy said to me. "You know what kind of crazy stuff goes on tomorrow night."

"Didn't you call before?" I said easily. I didn't want to mock or crack back like I really wanted. There was enough danger.

"Who de hell you think you are?!" the guy demanded. "Huh? Who de hell you think you are? God or somethin'?" I deduced from his tone that he was much older, though not very educated. That worried me. I didn't know of anyone but kids who'd been going to the park. He went on, "You just havin' trouble with your fagulitity, it's all right. I already know you a homofagual." He laughed. "Don't even bother hidin', prissy boy."

He stunned me. Absolutely held me to nothing. I'd never experienced true, rigid, icy fear on the phone before. But it was happening now. The letter from those kind women wouldn't help me against this. For the first legitimate time in my life, I feared for my safety.

"You gonna get into it with me or not, bitch?" The man waited, then measured his words slowly. "I'm gonna have to promise you somethin'. We will see each other. Uh-huh. And you're not gonna like it. I'm gonna be watchin' tonight and every night until we alone. Don't even bother hidin'."

I swallowed. "Don't you think you're taking this just a bit too far?"

My mother had the phone out of my hands before I knew it.

"What kind of a jerk are you?!" she nearly shouted into the receiver. I watched as she paused, her sky blue eyes aiming sharply into her fiery words. "I said, if you can stop for a second, What sort of loser threatens a 16-year-old kid? Do you think you're cool or—Oh, that's very intelligent. Your parents raise you with that kind of mouth? Oh, I bet. Excuse me? Oh, I'm sure we are, mister." She slammed the phone down and looked at me. "That's it. I'm calling the cops." She leaned sideways to spot my father. "Doug, I'm calling the police!"

Dad set the leg of his recliner back under and pushed himself free. He just about made it to the living room when the wall seemed to explode.

It sounded like a huge bowl had fallen off my mother's china shelf. Something had crashed through the living room's bay window. Dad ducked for it. Even though I'd seen him lay out Joe Chiavetti the night before, his speed still amazed me. He rolled out of the room and popped back up as two heavy swears escaped his lips. He had just risen when a second crack and a loud tingle of glass waved the curtains over the dining room table as if in a strong breeze. Shards of glass bits and a solid object skipped across the tablecloth. My mother backed against the cellar door and gasped the first curse I'd ever heard from her. In the same second, a large piece exploded one of the upper den windows facing Clark Street, clanking loudly to the floor. My father streamed to the front door, his face a swarm of red. He ripped it open and sprang onto the porch. Guilt pumped through my body like hot liquid. Tyler came racing downstairs, swinging himself around on the banister. Mom ripped the phone off the wall and started dialing. Whoever she called picked up quickly.

"You have to send someone to my house immediately!" my mother hollered in a frantic rush. Her free hand was holding her forehead and her face looked like she'd been on a jog. "We're on Dudley and Clark and we're under attack."

While she talked to the police, a strange eerie wailing began to echo from the corner of the den. My stomach went in and out from panting as Tyler and I glanced at each other, then back to the den. I started creeping toward a sound, the sound of a hollow amplified voice shouting in patches between heavy crackling hisses. Dad stormed back in the house, slamming the front door. He hollered something to my mother and stopped as he heard the strange echoing in the den. Whatever it was, it sat behind the coffee table. At first I thought something had hit our stereo and a speaker had fallen. But stereos don't curse. I leaned over the coffee table, then backed away.

To recognize it was not to believe it. A walkie-talkie was buzzing with bleeps as though the radio itself was alive. The crackles suddenly became words and I listened to what I can only describe as some kid running. "We got you, you bastards!" he shouted twice. There was an audible sound of feet crunching on leaves. Some burnout was still in this vicinity, running away in a random direction, verbally taunting us. Whoever it was started threatening me and even Tyler in a breathless savage voice.

"Don't go near it, Ash," my father said, pulling me back with a powerful arm.

"What's wrong?" Jeez, for all I knew something was about to blow up.

Dad shook his head, telling Tyler and me, "Don't touch anything 'til the police get here."

The three of us stood still at the den door, staring at the walkie-talkie, quite spooked as this strange kid now attempted a breathless rendition of the chilling *Halloween* movie theme. The kid's breath crackled unevenly over the radio, forced, like he was climbing over something. "You're *history!*" he finally raged.

I looked left. Tyler's dumbfounded face was next to me, listening as the sound reverberated through the house. In his hand was one of the rocks that had broken the living room window. I looked over my brother's shoulder and there was the first police car already stopping out front. I hoped their arrival would halt the lunacy for a while, and for the first time in days, I felt safe.

A strong sharp knock clacked on the front door window, then the doorbell chimed. Thankfully that window was still intact. Flashlight beams blazed intrusively through the glass, lighting up Mom's face as she pulled open the door. She greeted two men with relief and put a hand to her chest.

"Thank God," she breathed.

The first policeman who entered looked hulking in his thick black jacket. I felt like singing the "*Bad Boys*" song when I saw him. He had close-cropped light hair, a tight round face, and appeared very businesslike. The walkie-talkie on the den floor had just gone quiet, as though the person on the other end was aware of what was happening. Now it was the cop's radio that echoed against the walls. He walked around with a discerning stare, discovering on his own the broken windows.

Tyler and I looked outside where two other shiny white police cars with that horizontal blue town lettering were now parking in back of the first. For the second time today, the law was at our house, but the police created a very different image at night. The rotating red roof lights and headlights illuminating our part of the street had a sense of urgency and rescue. They were here for *us*, focusing their full attention to our situation. Every day we see patrol cars on TV, but never really feel the personal energy and titillation of the real thing.

I had done this. Single-handedly, I had caused all this to happen to my poor family.

Dad was stiff and straight with crossed arms, talking to two men, pausing while an officer's radio sent a shriek of banging noise into the hallway. I plugged my ears from it. How could they stand that all day long? The cop reached to his waist and turned down the blaring volume.

"I had trouble with a couple kids sneaking around the house *last night*," I heard Dad saying tiredly.

I cut in, adding that a red pickup truck had been passing over and over again. The first cop nodded at me absently. Mom led everyone into the den and sounded shell-shocked as she explained the disturbance on the den floor. She pointed to the cracked hole in the window above.

"These kids are *amazing!*" she cried. "They were yelling and cursing and—oh my *God*—saying all *sorts* of stuff on that thing, threatening my children with *murder!* I'm sorry, I'm just a little shocked. I didn't know stuff like this went on. It's not even Mischief Night yet. I mean, this is like ten of the worst Mischief Nights put together."

One cop shined a flashlight beam on the hole in the glass. The other bent over the broken shards on the rug, dangling a handkerchief, which he used to gently handle the radio. He lifted the piece slowly, inspecting it in his fingers with the earnest concentration of an auto mechanic reading a dipstick. Finally he waved a plastic lunch baggy out of his back pocket, snapping air into it, and dropped the radio inside. Despite my dad's cool outward appearance, we were all stunned. The cops' serene and casual demeanor helped out a lot. It reminded us that they'd known far more excitement.

I didn't think I could do anything else but get in everybody's way, so I went over to the front door to join Tyler. We looked at the radiant scene outside. Incredibly, in a matter of seconds, our neighborhood had the look of something rivaling a stakeout. Other police cars were driving aimlessly up and down Clark and Dudley. One moved onto Roosevelt School's premises, throwing a spotlight at the base of the library and cafeteria buildings, then out over the fields. Tyler and I stared at each other in amazement as we overheard the first officer telling my parents that they had stationed on-foot patrolmen at specific pay phones around the center of town in an attempt to trap the callers. For a second, everything seemed surreal. Right out in our front yard, a group of uniformed men stood silhouetted against the bright headlights of their cars. A subsequent and expected gathering of on-looking neighbors began to assemble. Mrs. Getty from across the street leaned forward to ask a question that went unanswered. At first I felt really awkward about how they were all perceiving this. Then my feelings changed and I felt kind of brave and proud if you can get into all that.

A minute after the police arrived, the phone rang. It was perilously amusing how everything fell silent. A second ring. I watched everyone and finally shrugged as I went for the kitchen. The big officer immediately stepped forward.

"Hold it," he said. He took his radio from his waist and put it to his mouth. "Four oh, trap this call." He signaled to me. I answered plainly this time.

"Hello?"

An adult said excitedly, "Is—Hey, Ashley?"

"Yeah?"

"Ashley, it's Mr. Kellogg. Are you having trouble?"

I waved off the two uniformed men. "It's Mr. Kellogg," I informed. Everyone still listened anyway. I returned my face to the receiver.

"Well sir, right now I'm surrounded by a few policeman."

His voice was troubled. "Ashley, what's happened over there? I've gotten some threatening calls. Is everyone all right?"

"Yup." I then gave him the short and hasty form of the evening's events.

"At least it seems to have settled down," he assessed. "Listen, I'm going to come over to your house to talk with everybody about this face-to-face. If there's anything the police need me to do, let me know now."

I asked the cops. They shrugged brazenly. No.

My faculty advisor impressed me with how quickly he arrived. The bell clanged, one of the policemen strutted to the door, and there was Mr. Kellogg. His chiseled face was longer and his dark eyebrows tilted upward. The officer escorted him into the living room where he shook hands with my parents and offered them a tough apology. No longer did he appear different out of school. I was used to seeing a lot of him now. He unzipped his softball coach's jacket and sat on the footrest in front of Tyler and me. The news he carried was startling to me and heavenly to Tyler.

"I've just spoken to Mr. Peterson," he said to everyone in the room, "and he's excusing both Ashley and Tyler from school for a week, maybe two."

Tiny voices sounded from the waist radios attached to the four policemen standing around. The only other sound came from my mom. She said, as though finding a gray hair, "Oh."

Mr. Kellogg looked about the room almost timidly and spread his arms. "Everyone feels this is eventually going to blow over. These kids will cool off with time." He fixed a few streaks of stray hair hanging over his forehead and glanced at Tyler and me. "We need to get you guys out of there for a while. For now. It's the best we can do."

Tyler happily accepted, then made everyone chuckle as he thanked me. As for me, I just couldn't see how avoiding people would resolve anything.

"I'm still going," I professed lightly.

No one said anything. Tyler finally blew a sarcastic puff through his lips.

"Screw that," he said aloud. "I'm on vacation as of now."

Mr. Kellogg blinked, tried to sound easy. "Ashley, being in the school just gives them an excuse to cause trouble." I knew the stares wouldn't be approving ones, so I kept my eyes to the carpet. Mr. Kellogg moved himself to the edge of the footrest. "Ashley, kid. I'm offering you the path of least resistance."

I looked at him. "Are you going tomorrow?"

Mr. Kellogg glanced up at my mom and a police officer. "That doesn't matter. I'll be okay."

"Well, Tyler should stay away. I mean, he didn't do squat. But it's my mess and I won't just run from it. If it's going to fizzle out, it'll fizzle out with me in the middle of it."

Mom shook her head sickly and backed away. Dad followed her into the kitchen, and I could just make out a soft momentary exchange. The first policeman, whose name was Detective Falcone, went to push open the swinging door, asking them to come back in the living room. Once they did so, he suggested something that blew me away—we should leave the area for a few days.

"Find somewhere to stay," the man said in an explanatory instructive tone. He looked at Mr. Kellogg. "You mentioned that you and your wife are staying at your daughter's for a few nights?" Mr. Kellogg nodded and the detective turned to my father. "Sir, my strongest advice is to keep away from here at night for a little while. Ashley here should just get his things and stay away from here as much as he can, day *or* night. We can offer him some protection, if you prefer."

"Especially this weekend," advised another.

Falcone checked around the room. "That's right, this weekend. Unfortunately, this is a whopper of a time for this to be going on. Mischief Night and Halloween will only multiply the problems. These kids will find any excuse. Every kid will be out this weekend and it makes it harder for us to target anyone. We'll post an all-night guard out front for the next three nights. That way, nothing more should happen to your home." He held a flattened palm to my parents. "You guys have homeowners insurance, I hope, for these broken windows?"

That was last piece of advice Detective Falcone offered, and after that, we were clear to follow his directive. My mother called her brother and that was it. Mom and Dad decided that they would move for a couple nights to Uncle Joe's house on the north side of town. Someone would fix the windows tomorrow during the day, and I was to have no contact with these premises until kingdom come.

It was time to bail. Tyler was first to leave, packing a rucksack and heading over to sleep at Jenn Dolan's house. In any other normal peacetime circumstance, Mom would have vetoed that in an instant.

Mom wanted me to come along to Uncle Joe's, but I didn't really feel like it. Instead, I convinced her to call the Spencer's. Blake's mother okayed the idea, and I knew Blake's lunacy would ease my tension.

Mr. Kellogg left soon after, and we thanked him for coming over. My mother seemed the most impressed of anyone by the courtesy. I threw some clothes and shower stuff together, thanked the police officers shyly, and a squad car took me over to Blake's. My parents got some things together and locked the house, leaving it to the cops. A police car would guard our house all night, sitting lightless but for a small red dot glowing on the dashboard.

Blake met me at the front door and pressed his thumb into mine, our usual greeting. Still charged, I sat in the living room for a while, telling my story to Blake, his mother and his little brother, the raw nature of it coloring Mrs. Spencer's face in awe. Much to Blake's dismay, I told them how I'd declined a police escort to school. All of the attention that this was getting fascinated him.

"You'll be in the news for this, I'll bet," said Blake.

I shrugged. "Never thought about that. Maybe. But that's not what it's about."

Mrs. Spencer shook her head and rose. I guess I had sighed one too many times because she put a hand on my shoulder. "You look exhausted." She waved shortly to Blake and Trip. "These little rug rats want to camp out with you in the basement. They've laid out some sleeping bags. Okay with you?"

I looked up tiredly. "Any idea of unconsciousness is fine by me."

We went down the few stairs to the basement. I always liked the Spencer's basement—heavily carpeted and snug in arrangement. After a few seconds of watching little Blake and his littler brother Trip play Nintendo, I set my possessions on the couch and literally fell on a green sleeping bag. Not a good idea. It wasn't as padded as I thought and my head banged through the soft pillow to the carpet. I was too bushed to do much about it, though. I just turned on my back and nearly fell asleep.

Blake's little brother, Trip, who sounds and acts like a sarcastic little Blake, was sitting Indian-style on his blue sleeping bag. I felt my brow twitch when I opened my eyes and saw him. Littler version of little Blake was just staring at me. I rested an elbow across my eyes and laughed weakly at his blank expression. Coal-haired like his mother, he was a thirteen-year-old eighth grader who walked through each day with a wise smirk, thinking most everything was corny. Tonight his face was full of question. He wanted to know more, and I wanted to roll over and conk out, but I had come into full notice of Blake carefully hiding one of his stinky Reebok sneakers—with which he never wore socks—right under Trip's pillow. My lips crinkled in a spreading grin.

Wonderful little Trip scratched his nose and finally fell sideways. From his position, his nose couldn't have been more than six inches from the hot and steamy opening of Blake's rancid sneaker. Even I plugged up. It was pretty bad.

"*Iiww*!!" Trip suddenly gasped, pushing to rise. "This is *gross*! Guys, my sleeping bag's *nasty*!"

Behind him, Blake rubbed his hands together and bobbed back and forth silently, his top teeth glistening from his suppression. Trip looked around at him bafflingly, saw the expression, and tore Blake's sleeping bag from the floor next to him. With one motion he tossed his at Blake and laid the replacement down in front of his pillow. The sneaker hadn't moved. As soon as Trip's head was down, it was back up again, as if in a spasm.

"*Oohh*!" he moaned in a fit. "This one's even *worse*!" He looked at me. "Ashley, lemme smell yours." He brought a corner to his tiny nose and sniffed, then backed his head away, perplexed. "Ashley's isn't bad. Forget that, I'm sleeping on the damn rug." Totally unaware of what lay below him, Trip crashed back again and an amazing expression of complete illness formed on his face. He squinted at the ceiling. "What the heck *is* that?" He sat up and frowned. "It's my *pillow*!"

Blake doubled forward, his clamorous laughter now filling the room. Trip lifted the pillow, took one spectacular realizing look at the mangled Reebok, and hurled it like a boomerang into the dark laundry room. When the two brothers ended up tangling, I sprang to my feet and separated them.

"For criminy's *sake*," I laughed. "*Sleep*!" I held them apart and chuckled to the wall. "This is unbe*liev*able."

A few seconds later, Blake made sure Trip and I were in our sleeping bags before he shut the light. Suddenly the basement was thick blackness. Blake's footsteps pounded next to me and he dropped to the floor. When he was flat and tucked inside, he said into the pitch darkness, "Hey!"—I heard him sit up in his sleeping bag—"Anything happen with Tara? Dude, were you slidin' tongue?"

"Oh, jeez." I cringed the instant he reminded me. Magically, I had forgotten about my cold adventure home.

"What happened? You get any nerf?"

"Blake?" I begged tiredly. "Just for now? Please. Whatever you do—don't ask."

"Who's Tara?" Trip, of course, wondered.

"Only a hot chick who wants him to treat her dirty," Blake replied. His pause was reflective. "Perfect nerfs."

When I begged for them to go to sleep, Blake agreed, only if he could tell me one more thing. Apparently, he'd spent his evening casing Mr. Flaherty's house in Cranford. My eyes opened to darkness as I listened to how he'd smoothed a specially-made bumper sticker on the back fender of the plump man's car. He wouldn't tell me what it said yet, but he did say that Flaherty had a pumpkin whose humongous proportions mirrored its owner.

"I have to smash that bubba!" he exclaimed eagerly. "That pumpkin's thirty inches across!"

"Yeah, right," sneered Trip. "How do you know?"

"Well, I took my peter out and measured," Blake returned plainly. "Then I knew for sure."

"Whew," I jibed. "Guess you had to take out about thirty of your peters."

"Ash," little Andy Gibb said, "you're cruisin' Mischief Night with me. I insist."

He went on, gabbing about all the fun we'd have. Blake simply couldn't wait for tomorrow night. He obviously had a substantially opposite reaction from me about Halloween Night in third grade. He seemed to want to avenge it by hailing October 30th and 31st as his craziest two nights of the year. But I didn't want to lie awake analyzing all that garbage. It was late on a school night.

7

"Happy Mischief Day!"

I could hear that characteristic snickering; could picture his top teeth pressing his lower lip. Always that sneaky hilarious laugh I'd know as only Blake's. I looked through the grogginess, forgetting where I was until I saw his sleep-pressed face smiling slit-eyed at me. I blinked rapidly. "Blake—huh?"

He pushed me softly and his tone changed. "Wake up. Your mom's on the phone."

Out of the calm quiet I felt Mrs. Spencer murmur quietly from the top of the stairs, "I really feel bad getting him up."

Awakened by quick recall, I automatically scampered out of the sleeping bag, wondering if something else had happened to my family. I hid my face from the upstairs light as I hobbled over to the stairs. Thanking her as politely as I could, I took the phone from Mrs. Spencer.

My mother's familiar voice sounded wide-awake. "What in the world are you doing up?"

I rubbed my eyes. "Funny, Mom."

"Wanted to see if you were still alive," she jested. "Wait, your father wants to say something."

My father got on with his gentle bass voice. "Everything go okay?"

"Sure," I grunted. "Oh, um—how's Uncle Joe's sloppy place?"

His laugh was almost a whisper, nearly undetectable over the phone. "They managed to dust off a place for us."

My mom reclaimed the phone, telling me directly, "Ash, you go to school, you go incognito, got it?"

"Huh?"

"You're going as something so no one recognizes you today. How about Bill Clinton?"

"Whatever." I haggled with my mom for a bit, but finally agreed to do it if Blake dressed up as well. It seemed corny to me. She said she would drop off the masks shortly, then asked to speak with Mrs. Spencer again.

As soon as I got off with my mother, I looked over and saw Trip ask Blake something in a whisper. Blake fell on his sleeping bag with his nose plugged.

"Aw, *man!*" he choked. "You have *death* breath!"

"No I don't!" cried Trip, smacking Blake with a pillow. "*Your* breath walks!"

I rolled my eyes and went for my things. They were still arguing about who's breath was worse when I headed for the basement shower.

My father had chosen to call in late at work and oversee the repairs to our windows. He and my mother swung around the Spencer's house within the hour and walked in holding a brown grocery bag full of masks. The ridiculously huge rubber face of Bill Clinton looked idiotically up at me from the bag, and the minute I saw it I felt pushed and embarrassed. Still, anonymity had some appeal. Maybe I'd blend discreetly at school. Dad had brought along my dark suit, which was saved for family functions, as well as his red "power" tie. They were serious about this. As soon as I slipped on my jacket, Mom pressed the big mask my uncle would wear tomorrow night at the Y's Halloween party over my head. The price tag read: "I didn't inhale!" Everyone stood there laughing at me. I hated the smell. I stumbled to the hall mirror and backed away in awe. I looked frighteningly goofy. I always go to the mirror expecting me. Here I found a very good miniature replica of then-presidential candidate Clinton. Everything fit but that enormous face with its long, sloped, almost phallic nose.

My mom had brought three masks for Blake. His choice was this huge, creepy, bald criminal face with gawking bulging eyes. The head was the shape of a fireplug, with no discernible neck. Blake really got into it, taking his most beat-up clothing from the attic and stretching it all on. Today, Bill Clinton would walk into school next to a giant-headed, drunk-looking bum.

Having my father drive me to school was weird enough. Having both my parents take Blake and I looking the way we did didn't even feel like a school day. It was actually starting to feel fun. An old pang of the Halloween aura warmed me for an anxious instant.

Instead of going directly to school, my dad turned down Birch Avenue to swing by the Dolan's and check on Tyler. Spencer and I ripped our masks off simultaneously when we looked ahead. A cop car sat in front of the Dolan's driveway. Tyler stood by his Grand Am with his hands at his hips. A policewoman was studying the insides of the Pontiac. I felt dizzy all of a sudden. I feared his face if something happened to—he loved that car. My father pulled over and we discovered the reason for the fuss. Tyler pointed to a blockbuster, a D-battery-sized explosive plug with one-quarter the strength of dynamite. Sometime during the night, someone had taped this potent and unholy firecracker—still intact—to my brother's windshield with a note.

I Coulda!

The morning weather was bright and mild for October 30th, referred to by Blake as "good potential mischief weather." It expanded his possibilities for the night's impending town torment, which he kept disillusioning himself I'd join in on. His tradition had already begun last night and I was about to witness his first prank. My parents dropped us off and Blake, in his tattered shreds, took me on a deliberate wild goose chase through the parking lot. Walking in costumes wasn't so bad when I got used to the smiling unsure stares. It was the discomfort of the mask that irritated me. Every time I spoke my mouth scratched lightly against the tough lining. Breathing caused an unpleasant humidity and I could feel my eyelashes when I blinked. Through it all, for safe keeping, I kept my mask on and my voice down. Not as many kids as I hoped were dressed in costumes. I was thankful for Blake's hideous participation, believe me. The parking lot didn't feel safe and I started to wonder what we were looking for when the humongous bald head in front of me swiveled. Under the mask came a hollow laugh as Blake pointed. Most assuredly, Mr. Flaherty had missed the homemade bumper sticker on his green Oldsmobile that morning. I gave a casual glance to the back fender. There it was, fiendishly funny. You know how people have those bumper stickers that say, *I'd rather be playing golf* and all? Well, even though I was prepared for anything, it still surprised me how authentic and bold it looked:

I'D RATHER BE SCREWING YOUR WIFE

Laughing hard under our masks, Blake and I turned and headed into the school. Once inside, it was hard to focus in dark hallways. Kids laughed at Blake and me and it seemed we were getting away with our hidden identities.

John Kohleran was still big school news, made clear to me by the mention of his last name by two kids in passing. I suddenly found myself wanting to visit the hospital, have a one-on-one chat with John and tell him where I was coming from. It wouldn't work. He'd never see it my way.

I passed my locker out of curiosity and faintly saw through my mask that the door had since been removed, most likely by a janitor. The cavity and shelves were bare. I was glad no one could see my annoyed face at yet another new decoration. The now legendary *Hi's Eye* issue was posted above where fake joints had been the morning before. There was circle over Detective Geories's words: "...a group of misfits who are the cesspool of Westfield." Someone had drawn across the page in red magic marker: *C U 2NITE.*

I left Blake at his homeroom door and decided to go find Tara. It was a funny thing to see more kids dressed up in costumes on the junior floor than on the sophomore floor. I had to hand it to my mother. She really knew her stuff. Here I was walking an unobstructed path in an expensive silky suit among kids I knew wanted to squash me, but instead, grinned unknowingly at me. A few made good-natured disparaging remarks about Bill Clinton, and others wondered aloud, "Who is that?" When I caught sight of Tara at the door to the stairwell, I rushed down the hall. I must have looked ridiculous running, for she paused to stare warily at me. My mask twisted slightly and I gripped it back to position. Tara wasn't in costume, but she did have on small pumpkin earrings. She hadn't taken seriously to my suggestion of dressing as an owl.

I led her down the stairs, away from people.

"Got my stuff?"

Her eyes blinked in enchanted surprise. "It's *you!*" Sudden regret squeezed her brow attractively. She pinched the long rubbery Bill Clinton nose as we walked down. "I'm *so* sorry about yesterday."

Along with a huge orange sweater, she was wearing small hiking boots tucked into black leggings that displayed every curve of her knees and calves. I felt dumb around her lately, always noticing stuff like that...her legs, her dark hair teased and streaked with blonde, the neck opening in her shirt, the shape of her—elsewhere.

My voice was muffled inside the mask. "You didn't tell anyone?"

Tara held up a hand in oath. "Nope. Not a soul." She stopped me privately on the middle platform and ran a hand over my pressed suit. "I love this. Who's idea? Yours?"

I shook my head freely inside the mask. "Negatory. My mom's."

Tara the Curb Owl smiled coolly, tried to peer in the slits at me. "Smart woman. No one will know a thing. I guess you have the good fortune of timing."

I shrugged in the smooth clothing. Tara, with her fruity perfume scent, suddenly came forward with a soft hug, the aromatic Curb Owl embracing Slick Willie.

"I heard things," she said to the side of my mask. "What happened last night?"

The door above opened and a group of noisy kids made corrupt plans for tonight on their way down. One guy passed right by me and leaned to point at my mask. "Dude, he'll never get elected," he jaunted. I backed away from Tara, forgetting she couldn't see my expression.

"Tell you later," I mumbled.

Tara jerked a thumb. "I put your clothes and books and stuff in my locker. We can—"

"Keep it, for now. I'll see you later."

The bell rang and sent us in different directions. I headed down to the first floor empty-handed, smelling nothing now but musty rubber. I wondered if anybody would try to wing my mask off curiously. I could just see it. Me fighting off Dayle Tanner and everyone in my suit.

Halloween had arrived at Westfield High School, and off-the-wall get-ups filled the first floor hallway. Gary Walton, a humorous black kid in my grade wore a KKK robe with "DUNCE" marked several times around the hood. Dustin "the dude" Noonan figured in as a half-and-half guy. I was shocked to see his head half-shaved, one side colored red. He wore one sneaker and one loafer, a T-shirt and a dress shirt sewn together down the middle, and jeans on one leg with trousers on the other. I swallowed in shock and anger when I saw Jerry Corcoran and a couple burner guys pass right by me. They were wearing nooses around their necks and *ASHLEY MUNROE* on their T-shirts. He had abandoned me after all. That stunk. I always liked him. But the most shocking costume of the day was about to exhibit itself. When I stepped inside the woods room, I saw Flexi Lexi Mercantanti sitting peacefully in homeroom, dressed completely normal.

I cut my homeroom so as to keep shut about my identity. Out wandering in the hall, I heard the Friday morning announcements blaring over the loudspeaker. At the conclusion, Principal Peterson bid everyone a pleasant weekend and a safe Halloween. But he didn't earn his leadership from naïveté. He knew the score when it came to kids, evidenced by his strict warning that cops would be on bikes tonight, patrolling neighborhoods.

Maureen Egan swiveled in her seat hotly. "Oh, Blake, kiss my ass." "Shave it first."

Another routine morning for Maureen and Blake.

Blake had been sticking his helmet-like face in her soft white one, giving her the works.

"Hello?" he'd said in a deep goofy voice, a pretend phone to the ear of his mask. "Is uh—is Maureen home, ma'am?"—A pause—"No? Oh. Well uh—could you tell her that, like, Rick called? And that I, like, need my underwear back?"

Hence the cause for her above comment.

Since some of us were donning costumes in Flaherty's history class, we extended the mystery by sitting in different seats. Kids looked around with gaping smiles, chuckling at makeup and costumes. Even Mr. Flaherty accepted the humor of the day. Amazingly, one corner of his mouth was curled in a half-smile.

Blake, in his tattered shards and monstrous eerie head, was next to Maureen Egan over at the front left side of the room. I had a suspicion Maureen would feel odd in my presence, considering her remarks yesterday. She was dressed as Snow White, and when asked why the inspiration, replied that she might as well go along with her stereotype for a day. I was growing more and more impressed with this girl. She eyed me curiously and got up in her big dress. I turned my body to see out of my eye slits as Maureen stepped softly over and quietly sat in the seat next to mine. She sure looked funny, oddly sexy. Red was caked on her cheeks and she blinked her long fake eyelashes twice as she leaned toward me.

"My friend said she saw police cars in front of your house last night," she whispered with concern. "Is everything all right?"

Before I could answer, I saw that huge bald head sneak up and bend forward behind Maureen. Suddenly she jolted and frowned. "Ow, jerk!" She glared back at Blake's successful if inept bid to get her attention. Annoyed, Maureen turned my way again and scratched her back where he'd snapped her bra. The poor girl liked him since grade school, but was usually forced not to show it by fending him off.

"Maureen, you look hot," Spencer cooed, sitting behind her, "in your own completely dorky kinda way."

Now Maureen gave him his due. Her made-up face turned sour.

"Blake, is there a normal nerve in your body?"

The big bald head leaned forward on his small elbows and muffled, "Duh, is there, like, a normal nerve in your body? X equals the sum of the square root of five-eighths. Hi, I'm Maureen. I love school, and I'll grease your keister if you're a teacher." From inside the mask, a giggle. "Really though, Maureen. You look like a *babe* this morning! I'll be your eighth dwarf—Horny."

Maureen shook her head and huffed. "Oh, God, more like Stubby."

"Whatever you say," the mask murmured in that hollow tone. "But honey, tonight—we're gonna get some *lovin'* on!"

Maureen tilted her head to the side. "Actually, Blake, I'd love to, but I have some blank tapes I haven't watched yet."

"Duh!" he said, sounding a lot like Trip. "That was old before it was told." It was incredibly funny to hear this kind of talk coming from that God-awful mask. "Come on, cherry pie. I wanna see Snow White get down and *dirty!*"

Dustin Noonan giggled beside him, and I twisted to look at the kid bewilderedly. I just could not believe he'd done that to his hair. Eventually he'd close-crop his entire scalp, but today he just looked queer. In his half-shaved head and all his absurdity, he told Blake, "Dude, you've got a way with people that makes them get away from you."

Blake turned his head, losing himself in the mask. "Dustin, you know what? I'm gonna marry Maureen 'cause I can tell she's the type who won't get fat on me when we're older."

Luckily for Egan she had that rouge on her cheeks or she'd have been plum red anyway. She still faced me coyly, resting her head on her fist.

"I swear," came Blake's resonant voice from the mask, "if I was ever married and my wife got fat, I'd divorce her. Your honor? She's too fat." He banged his desk with an imaginary gavel. "Motion granted on grounds of obesity."

Maureen ignored him and tried to look into the eyeholes at me.

"They won't bother your house from now on with the police there, right? I mean, even with the announcement before? Did you hear that? Bike patrols? That's so funny." She snapped her fingers in sarcastic regret. "I guess I'll just have to be more careful tonight."

"You're a bit like me," I told her, jerking a thumb at Blake. "I don't get this character. He wants me to go out with him tonight."

"You are," Blake's voice said. He pinched Maureen's red cheek. "Egan's gonna be out eggin' houses, I bet. She's probably a closet psycho."

Maureen shook her head bashfully. "*What*ever."

The big gawky bum mask aimed her way. "Have you ever done a mischievous deed in your whole life?"

She put a hand to the puffy garment at her chest. "Me?" She considered it for a second. "I don't know. Well, one time in the Rialto I threw a Raisinette at someone talking."

"Whoa!" cried Blake. "Batten down the hatches!"

Maureen squinted at him. "Shame. Just a few beatings shy of a good kid."

Mr. Flaherty shook his head to his attendance book and asked for costumed kids to raise their hand when called. When completed, he lifted his large frame from the poor chair and strode wordlessly over to my desk, placing on it a note. It was a message from Sal Pocatelli, the guy from *The Westfield Leader*, explaining a "sudden, slight drug dealing paranoia" over the town and how my story was affecting Westfield. "Please touch base with me!" it concluded.

Waddling back to the front, Mr. Flaherty held his hands up to settle everyone for another lesson concerning early Boston. Although I had to borrow a few sheets of paper and a pen, it was the first full class I made it through since fifth period Wednesday.

Later, right after history, I saw Blake and Maureen kissing at her locker. His mask was in his right hand and her small waist was in the other. He pressed against her as kids walked by and whistled at them. I guess the tension just built up 'til they were "slidin' tongue" as Blake put it.

After a second and third period of nerves dulled by boredom, I decided to cut gym, again leaving nothing to chance. I had seen Dayle Tanner and two of his friends push through the gymnasium door, clueless of my very proximity. I knew I couldn't keep my mask on in gym, and the direly real fear of being hung by the boys' room pipes via supreme wedgie stung me with apprehension. I decided to skip it altogether in favor of the asylum of the library.

This is where I was when the bomb threat occurred.

I was floating near the microfiche just after eleven o'clock when Principal Peterson's voice cut into the period.

"May I have your attention please?" his voice commanded.

Everyone in the library straightened faithfully.

"In a moment we will hold a fire drill," he said. "I would like to ask both students and faculty to take your belongings with you for the duration. Thank you." He snapped off.

Immediately the fire alarm started whirring annoyingly. In my mask I followed kids and librarians in single file order through the turnstiles.

Outside, WHS was clearing, everyone with books, purses, bags, jackets. I didn't really think much of it at all, except I figured the interior walls, ceilings and dim light inside the building offered better protection. Usually with a fire drill, only kids and school personnel are lined up outside in an orderly mob. Today, however, the atmosphere was stimulated by the presence of two town patrol cars and an enormous yellow snorkel fire engine, all three spinning their roof lights, as though something was really happening inside. My first thought was that an experiment had gone remiss in a science lab. I found my friend Mike Cicero, informing him privately who was under my mask, and we stood out in the mild air on the front sidewalk among countless students wondering verbally about the matter. The guessing went on for close to twenty minutes or so before anyone even hinted of a bomb threat.

Inside that mask I thought about it. Bomb threat. It sounded overdone, newsworthy, like something bigger than the school itself. There had actually been one ten years before, I later learned. It turned out to be bogus, but the police found the caller, and he was charged, convicted, and sent to juvenile detention for six months. I don't know how they caught him, but he was only a sophomore and the school never allowed him to return. As I stood next to Mike, a horribly anxious feeling grew inside me like hot butter under my skin and my mind began to swirl. Probably just rumor. Don't get panicky. Then a couple of juniors suddenly passed by with news that confirmed growing suspicion.

"Bomb in the school," a soccer player announced with an excited grin.

"Shut up," a kid in my grade said. "Really?"

The soccer player kept going, an emphatic confidence in his expression making me believe him.

Two more police cars appeared from Rahway Road and turned onto Dorian.

"Told you so," he called back, pointing to the vehicles. "School's gonna be called. Just wait."

"How do you know?"

"I just know."

A few cheers rang out. The juniors continued down the line, making the same proclamation. Hundreds of teenagers hummed up in commotion. Everyone's first thought was to applaud it as a Mischief Night prank, but I doubted the theory. I have awkward premonitions and I had the definite feeling that this in some way involved the drug exposé.

It's amazing how a quickly a small confidential piece of information or baseless speculation can travel when kids are involved. Apparently, from what I was overhearing, someone claimed to have planted a bomb to avenge John Kohleran. Rumor placed the bomb along the school wing where the *Hi's Eye* office was located. I heard something else being circulated. Dayle Tanner and all the noose-necked kids wearing my name on their shirts were mentioned as being held for suspicion at that very moment. From witnessing Dayle's prior entrance into the gym at the start of the period, however, I was sure he didn't do it himself. But then again, that doesn't mean he had no hand in it.

All in all, the worst thing about this was, I knew in my heart this was a perpetuated bluff. I knew from Resuscitation Annie and from the note on my brother's Grand Am windshield. I wanted to find Mr. Peterson or whoever received the call. I wanted to tell someone high up, but figured I better keep my mouth shut. It was suddenly dark and lonely in that rubber mask.

We were kept waiting outside for almost an hour before school was finally called just after noon. Faculty members and hall monitors walked up and down the lines, shouting that we could head home. Everybody celebrated their "Get out of Jail Free" cards, knocking by me on their way to oblivion. I sighed and turned for home. It was quite a week of school.

I had just rounded the corner to Trinity Place and was passing the temporary classrooms affectionately termed the Porta-Johns when I noticed Domino Hackett. Usually a reserved kid, he came walking strongly toward me from the side, wearing a sort of weird maroon shirt. He had dark greasy-looking hair and a face with puffy features—his brow strong, his nose flat and slightly turned up. Over his thick lips he wore a feeble mustache that only served to display his pubescence. His war with nature was on a current losing streak, exhibited by his tragic acne. Kids secretly called him Domino's Pizzaface. He had somehow found out that it was I under the mask, and his intent was made very clear from the onset.

"Ashley?" he asked strangely, staring his small marble eyes right in at me. "You know John Kohleran?"

I focused through the slits on certain scars peppering his face from recent zits he'd scratched. It made me a bit sorry for him. I didn't know what he wanted me to say, and I was through with hearing about it. Domino was stationary, trying to see in at my face as kids moved away, crowds thinning.

"He's my brother's best friend, dude."

I'd never heard this kid use the word "dude" before. I suddenly noticed his angry manner. It was finally going to happen, compliments of a most unlikely source. He looked down that wide pug nose at me.

"My brother's best friends with him," he repeated, squinting sourly at me. "You know that?"

Lee Hackett was simply a larger and more advanced prototype of Domino. A senior, Lee's acne had passed and he was better looking and more popular than his younger brother. He also wore tougher clothes—army boots, ripped jeans, radical image T-shirts, spiked black leather jacket, colorful feather earrings, occasional dark lipstick. In short, he was out there.

I felt hot in the chest and neck. How was I to know this kid's brother was best friends with Kohleran? It wasn't my job to keep tabs. Okay, so he was. The only thing I could think to say through that mask was, "I thought Tanner was his best friend."

Domino amazed me when he stepped toward me.

"He's *not*, snitch."

For the first time that day I felt like taking my mask off around kids. This might get ugly and I didn't want it to hamper me. Who cared if anybody saw me? There were outdoor proctors waltzing around and Tanner and other burnies were held up anyway. I was somewhat safe. A thought formed behind my eyes. Could Domino be among those harassing my family? I was sick of the whole blown-up business. This zitbag breathing on my mask was it.

"Good God," I spat in a tired mocking fashion. "So now you wanna *fight* about it, Hackett?"

I'd never called him anything but Domino before. Out of the slits I saw his chin lift. A force caved my chest in and I backpedaled. The son of a bitch had shoved me. It angered me how much he wanted this. The betrayal left me crazy.

It must have been freaky and comical to see a big-headed Bill Clinton strike an expressionless defensive pose. I stepped back to wing the mask off and there he was in full light. Domino didn't seem fazed. I let Bill drop to the ground—a sign of the challenge accepted—and in the sudden brightness I studied the zits on Domino's chin more closely now, picking a string of them as my target.

Not lavishing any time on fear, I shuffled back up to him and swung two-fisted, catching him under his arm and on his other shoulder. I thought he'd laugh tauntingly, the way he was, but his face was wary. He was seeing something in me now. I ran onto him and we literally wound up hitting the ground, grappling, me in my suit. I guess it was my wrestling skills or the anxiety level brought up from the whole affair because I was soon dominating a kid who was by no means buffed—even a bit lanky—but at least four to six inches taller than me. I hardly noticed the kids forming quickly around us. I remember knowing in the back of my mind not to pay attention to them or it would hinder me. The mere sound of them, though, made me brutally aware that we had turned this into a real fight. I hadn't been in a school fight since third grade. Domino seemed to let the reality of attention bother him. By now he knew he'd bitten off more than he could chew. He allowed his body to become subdued, relaxed almost, as though he'd just changed his mind, and I used it as an advantage. Aggressively, I got him into a headlock and slid him down where I squeezed tightly and leaned toward the earth, blinking at an imprint of a sneaker cleat in the ground. Domino was almost giving up now, and I had no idea how or when this would end. Quickly my ears took in the noise—hollers, happy barbaric shouts, apathetic whoops; a condensed claustrophobic mass of annoying celebration ringing with bloody thirsts for more. All sounded above and around my head. The chanting of a particular name over and over finally caught my attention. Impossibly beautiful to realize, almost everyone was cheering for me.

I held Domino's head and rocked myself into a leaned position. I was in command, but I wasn't going to rest on my laurels. If Hackett wiggled out of the headlock in a sudden frenzy, I was in a new trouble. Quickly I found myself ashamed, wondering who was watching us. I was about to find out. A new large weight fell into me, raging a stab of blazed fire through my skin. Was I being bombarded? Set up? I felt the massive body next to me and knew it too strong for my control. But the body was favoring its weight and energy on Domino. The head in my curled arm shifted awkwardly and I dreaded serious injury. I didn't want Domino hurt. I just wanted my space. I checked next to me and relaxed when I discovered Benton Crossey's face glistening tightly, his teeth clenched in purpose.

"I got him, A'," he said strongly. "Let go."

His white baseball jacket brushed me as he spun himself onto Domino's back and pressed his frame, his enormous chest pushing Domino's face to the grass. I rolled off and stood up, airing out and looking with disdain at the ruination of my costume, *my stained suit!* I was loose and unafraid and swore bitterly at my findings to those around. I didn't care about them or what they thought. I would have mouthed off to all of them for staring, if Mike Cicero hadn't started brushing me off and congratulating me.

Back on the ground near the portable classroom wall, the action wasn't over. Baseball Benton had twisted himself, still flat against Domino's back, yet their bodies faced opposite ends. Domino wasn't about to move on his own right. Benton took a second to stare up at my clothes and my irritated expression. He turned mean, just like Sunday evening at the park, mumbling into Domino's lower back, "Look at his friggin' *suit*, Pizzaskin!" He tried to shake the kid, but Domino was too wrenched on his stomach. You could hear his breathing, then he cursed at Crossey. Athletic Benton stared down. "First he kicked your ass, now he gets to watch me screw up *your* clothes."

As if there wasn't enough to see, Baseball Benton reached up and slid his fingers to the elastic band of white exposed under the opening of Domino's jeans. He found enough for a fistful and suddenly Domino squirmed, his expletives chewing loudly into the grass. With a fatefully good grip, Benton pulled an enormous tug and Domino Hackett's briefs came into view—thinned out, labored against the strain, frail white contrasting the blue denim. Benton grunted and the briefs stretched into a loud rip. The elastic band finally separated from the white fabric.

Hackett was downtrodden, and as I think on it now, I regret the memory of that face. After Benton pushed off, Domino stood and fixed his pants once without concern for his torn underwear. He began stalking back up to the street, red patches and a streak of mud coloring his face. His maroon shirt was wrinkled, speckled with leaf bits. I watched a friend join him, watched Domino wave the kid off angrily. He had stopped fighting me before Benton jumped in. I had felt it, known it, could feel the break soften his body. I could've probably let go and pushed off easily. I accepted and furthered a fight with him that was below me, and because of it Domino was made to suffer in humiliation. I still think about that sometimes.

About half the group of kids who'd watched the fight followed me down Trinity Place and through to town. The rubber mask was at my side and the wind felt refreshing against my face. Bill Clinton's countenance had served its purpose. Benton Crossey was one of the stragglers in the group. He had never hung out with us and seemed to be in attempts to make up for the unfamiliarity. The expression on his face was one of conceit as he talked about a game-winning home run. By the time we reached Cosimo's Pizzeria, everybody had taken to partial worship of Benton's heroics. After Cosimo's, Blake and I split up from the group and marched home. Along the way I gave him an elbow.

"What was that with Maureen Egan before?"

Blake half-smiled as he stared ahead. The wind blew at his hair, exposing the whiteness of his upper forehead.

"I still don't know," he said. "Usually I go with bimbo girls. This is the first girl I've ever liked who actually has a brain. That scares me."

We reached his street, Colonial Avenue, and started passing the weird old Huelett house. Tall, thin, almost gothic, painted dusky gray like the old lady's shade of hair; like the way she and her husband lived their lives—dark, dismal, reclusive. Their yard portrayed them as people far from societal norms. On either side were seven-foot wooden fences, more like walls, both lined with tall fir trees. A row of chest-high thorn bushes bordered the front and back yards. The property was literally enclosed from the world, enclosed from light—a strange hermit's paradise. Huge trees, which they never pruned, dominated the yard. One night Blake and I cut through their yard and found broken branches on the fir trees *taped* back together.

The Hueletts had a jagged history of giving Blake and his little brother Trip trouble. During Blake's sixth and seventh grade years, the grumpy couple made quite a fuss over the "clanging" made by the two boys playing basketball in their driveway. So much so that Mrs. Spencer, flustered beyond her senses, had the basketball rim taken down, much to her sons' dismay. Once, on a Saturday morning, after Trip had fallen off his bike, the Hueletts drove right by him in their gray Lincoln, turning slowly in their driveway as he lay injured and gasping through his tears.

I speak of this yard and of this peculiar couple because Mr. Huelett himself was now rolling down the sidewalk behind us on his old bicycle. I wondered comically to myself if it had been inspected lately. The old man's gray presence quickly interrupted all rhythm of talk, and it seemed really puzzling to me why he didn't just wheel into the road to pass. Still he trailed us for a series of seconds, scouring us both with an unfriendly eye, his bicycle so close to our heels that I could have tucked a book in his front basket. The ash-haired man's bony legs pushed gaudy yellow cocktail trousers to the limit as he pedaled slowly in his vanilla Izod windbreaker. I did admire his balance, but not that wretched ugly stare—pale blue eyes that burned under his angled brow.

Automatically, Blake and I parted to either side of the sidewalk, politely inviting Mr. Huelett to pass. But the man stopped, too, opening his lips in angered alarm.

"Why are ya stoppin'?!"

For a brief instant, Blake's eyes swirled from mine to Mr. Huelett's. Before he could ask a taken thing, Mr. Huelett flew a hand backward to the air, as though swatting a fly. "Why don't ya just get on your way!" His voice was an unprompted and immediate bark. "Don't gimme any trouble! I'll arouse the police!"

Blake's head slumped forward and his jaw fell as he frowned. "What the heck," he then mused softly, as though checking with himself for something missed. "What did *I* do?"

"Ya crossed in front of ma *property!*" the old man yelled hoarsely. "For the love of Mike, I don't wanna *see* ya here n'more!" In a rashness that frightened me, the man let his bike crash to the sidewalk and stepped his lanky figure out of the way. He converged upon Blake like a madman and pointed a bony finger in his face. "Y'always pass in front of ma yard and spoil ma *view*, dammit!" He thrust his arm to Blake's property and his yellow teeth showed. "Don't make me tell y'again!"

Blake twirled around stiffly, like a statue, a rotating figure with a smile of bewilderment and a twisted look in his eyes. I just stood there, not noticing how tightly I'd been holding my body until after I, too, started moving away. Mr. Huelett still stood over his downed bicycle with his hands at his hips, glaring sternly at us as if he would come running if we dared stop.

As soon as I was through gasping to Blake in a hushed whisper, I managed a short chuckle when I saw his front doorstep. That morning, next to their three pumpkins, Blake had placed a big tomato in honor of Mischief Night. The only house in America I was aware of that venerated such a tradition. Once inside, Blake and I set our masks on the kitchen counter and I changed out of my stained suit. I tried to picture my parents' reaction. It was their idea anyway. I settled into myself, for now it was Friday, the beginning of the cherished weekend. I was back in street clothes and wanted to relax, to assess in my mind that strange and wacky confrontation.

Blake and I spent most of the free afternoon lounged out in front of cartoons, munching on Oreo's dipped in milk. Trip came home around 3:30 and Blake sang out, "Ha, ha! We got out of school early." Trip's face was an amusing twist of disappointment when he heard why. It wasn't until late sunset when Mrs. Spencer's heels clogged through the door and onto the kitchen floor above us, keys jingling. Blake sat up and listened, eyes darting left and right. Suddenly he pushed out of his deep-cushion recliner, leaving it rocking back and forth, and hopped up the stairs. Soon I heard him having a conversation with his mom about Mr. Huelett, an issue that had the irritating adhesive quality of not going away anytime soon. Trip turned the TV volume down and we crept to the top of the thickly carpeted orange stairs.

Mrs. Spencer wasn't saying much. It was all Blake, complaining about the maniacal treatment he'd just suffered from a man who lived in a decrepit old house that was probably haunted for Pete's sake.

"Mom, listen to this," he said in a flustered tone. "He goes, 'For the love of Mike!' You believe that? The love—of Mike. What the *heck*!" Trip and I covered our mouths from spray-laughter, half-choking as Blake went into a wildly sensational impression. "Ya spoil ma view! Uuhhh! For the love Mike, ya spoil ma *view*, dammit!"

A long deep breath was audible, then Mrs. Spencer said plainly, "I'll give him a call." Her bored tone was ruining the drama of it all. In a minute I heard the woman fumble around for something and pick up the phone. As she did so, Blake's stocking feet thumped our way. Trip and I quickly backed off the stairs like the carpet was electrified and barreled to the recliner chairs. When Blake came down and saw us both rocking with red cheeks, he made a dumb face at me. "Why'd you eavesdrop?" he asked me. "You should've just come up. I needed you there."

"He *is* in school," we heard Mrs. Spencer saying. Blake picked up the remote and zapped the TV black, his eyes watching the wall, ears alert. Mrs. Spencer's weight squeaked on the wood above us. "They were let out early today, George. No, he's not blackening the neighborhood. Oh, yes, you do like him. George, no, he's not evil."

Blake's face was a mass of stunned anger. I could see his rapid breathing from across the room. He stood like that until his mother hung up. Stomping back up the stairs, he returned to the kitchen. What Mrs. Spencer then demanded of him amazed me.

"Here. Take these over to him and apologize."

"Flowers?!" Blake cried. There was a pause. "What the heck for?!"

"Just go over and apologize."

Trip and I looked at each other in puzzlement. There was the sound of chopping in the kitchen, like Mrs. Spencer was cutting celery. I could feel how infuriated Blake was made by the action, which had the uncanny quality of a brush-off. His laughter was high-pitched in disbelief. "What?! No way. Forget it. Get dorky Jim to do it."

"Leave Jim out of this," Mrs. Spencer replied in a soft warning tone.

"No," Blake challenged hotly. "What if your precious Jim was chewed up and spit out by that geek? Would you send him back over with friggin' *flowers*?"

Something crashed into the sink, perhaps the cutting knife.

"What the *hell* has he ever done to you?!"

Blake's cotton-covered feet reappeared at the top of the stairs suddenly. For a second they creaked there. My breathing was small, rushed, lightly controlled, as though I didn't want anyone to hear it. Finally the socks bumbled down and Blake came into view with flushes of red on his cheeks. Passing me, he faded into the darkness of the wash room. When he returned, a stuffed black book bag had magically materialized on his shoulders and he was changed into black jeans and a gray sweatshirt. Little Tripper stayed deep in his recliner as Blake instructed me to put on my dark jacket. We were going. This was his night. This was when he would take his vengeance out on the world. Tonight his father was in every house, on every block. Tonight, Blake would strive to fill his voids. He would play out his hidden guilt about Jim and his mom on the streets of Westfield. Every property would represent adulthood, misunderstanding, the unheard anger of the last six years.

After turning to Trip with a finger to his lips, Blake hurried me up and out through the basement window, knowing his mother would chastise him for going out dressed like he was, and above all, for that Godforsaken mischief pack clinging to his back. Once I had squeezed through into the side yard, I pulled him up after me and we tiptoed to Colonial Avenue. The outside world had grown dark. Blake's angry appearance turned excited when we approached the Huelett house. All the lights were ablaze on the first floor. At this Blake smiled.

"Hmm. That house needs a new coat of paint," he observed. "Perhaps something in Egg Yolk Yellow?"

Blake knew where I wanted to visit before he attempted to lead me on anything. We trotted several blocks over to my Uncle Joe's and Aunt Diane's to check in with my parents. Blake placed his merciless pack outside their front yard in a bush. When we got there, I was mildly disappointed to find that my parents had already gone over someone's house to help plan last-minute things for tomorrow's Halloween parade. They left a note for me asking to tell Uncle Joe where I'd be at all times. Aunt Diane told me that a police car was still faithfully stationed at our house, as it would be for the next two nights.

I slapped my leg suddenly.

"Damn," I said. "Uncle Joe, I forgot your mask."

"That's all right," he said, sipping motor oil-colored Scotch.

"Well, I'll definitely get it to you before tomorrow night."

A soft serene nod, as he'd always give at the beginning of a Scotch. He asked how the costume scheme worked. I shrugged and looked at Blake, hoping he wouldn't mention my suit.

"Did Dad get the windows fixed today?" I asked, veering slightly off the question.

Aunt Diane sat next to my uncle on the couch and nodded. She sipped her drink and forced it down quickly so she could make words. "Ah—yes. He did. And I believe he's covered."

My aunt and uncle couldn't make Blake and I stay long, but we did have a go at some Chicken and Stars soup. They watched us sip it vigorously and spoke to us through our slurping. Aunt Diane voiced her hope that Uncle Joe's real estate values wouldn't go down since my article would cause the town serious reputability damage. I stopped sipping and looked up.

Aunt Diane laughed shortly and waved her glass at me. She got up to refill and said in a huff, "I'm teasing. This is going to be fine in a matter of time. You just hang in there, kid."

Uncle Joe savored that Scotch, staring at Blake and me with a fine squinting eye. His voice was slow, incriminating. "What are you two dressed for tonight?"

Blake's little Andy Gibb face rose slightly from his bowl. We looked at each other. That told all.

After we finished our Chicken and Stars, Blake politely thanked my aunt and uncle and was out the door into the night. I shook my head as he directed himself toward his hidden sack of goodies.

With a guilty smile, I started out the front. "Help."

"Ashley," Aunt Diane said suddenly to me.

Something about her tone made me stop dead at the open door. I turned and watched her stare the most seriously worried expression she'd ever aimed at me.

"Be careful," she warned. "It's Mischief Night."

8

Mischief Night

I couldn't help but wonder how different tonight would have been had I not chosen to sleep at the Spencer's house. I remembered the year before, when Mischief Night fell on a school night, and how I opened my front door to Blake's frown at me holding a pencil in my hand. He absolutely couldn't understand why I had no gusto to head out with him. Well, under this clear night he would finally trap me by my own curiosity into testing my mettle.

We began our march toward Wilson School. A coolness that hadn't been present before my uncle's house now coated the air. The wind kicked lightly, flapping a Halloween flag over a porch light—a witch flying against the moon. The whole town seemed to be on guard. A top window of one house on Oak Avenue was crowded with small shifting shapes peering out at us. A powerful flashlight blinked on from its second story window and blazed us, peeling us from the cover of night. Another small light hit us from the porch of an old suburban ranch on Linden Avenue. Blake and I laughed shortly at the sudden intrusive beams causing us to squint and blink. Uninvited though I felt, there was still this crazy stir about, as though we were celebrated, expected, owners of a higher more tempting fate. Porches had life sneaking around them tonight. Kids crouched in their bushes, giving themselves away by crackling leaves and sharp whispers. It was almost freaky how alive yet hushed this atmosphere was. Something to the right, close to the street—a first floor window blind was slowly drawing shut in front of a small head. I grabbed Blake's elbow and tugged.

"You see that?!"

We teetered on aimlessly around Wilson School. Other moving shapes were coming quietly into view ahead. Of all the zany sights I'd eventually see tonight, perhaps the most peculiar one was this man, hands jammed in his coat pockets, walking in the middle of the street with his two boys, smiling contentedly as they sprayed shaving cream on cars. It was as though he was their delinquent chaperone.

Blake's impatience pressed him toward action. He swung his pack off his shoulders and set it on the street in front of a shiny black Jeep

Grand Cherokee. I checked the area, then myself. No one could look more suspicious. I wasn't used to wearing darkness all over, and the fact that I was in the middle of the dang road kind of defeated the purpose anyway. Blake unzipped his pack and revealed rolls of toilet paper, soap, shaving cream, a pack of chalk, a carton of eggs, two lighters, and a jackknife. Blake pulled out a can of Barbasol and handed it to me. Palming the bar of soap, he was just about to go to work on the Grand Cherokee.

"Don't touch that car!"

We slammed our heads to the sound. A man was sitting leaned forward on his dark porch, eyeing Blake and me.

Suddenly the door to the Cherokee opened right in front of us.

Blake backed off with a sharp yell. There wasn't even time to run. A second guy got out, agile-looking, thirties-ish, a slight resemblance to Robin Williams, only with black hair that curled over his ears. He slammed the door and stepped forward.

"All right," he said tiredly, like the catch wasn't even fun for him. "What's goin' on?"

Blake was quick to speak. He held up the soap and smiled in a boyishly engaging manner.

"Well sir, we were just about to go get your hose and wash your car for you."

The guy on the porch walked over and stood at the fence, crossing his arms on a post.

"We spotted you two down the road," he said.

Blake and I shifted and checked each other. Something was blocking my throat. Black-haired Robin Williams spread his arms out and smiled.

"Hey, it's all right," he said. "I did the same damn thing in high school." He backed off a step and laughed to the other guy, "Let's let 'em go. They're just hormonally confused."

He then pointed to the can of Barbasol. "Take my word for it," he said. "This stuff goes better on your face than on a chassis. Go on. Get outta here."

After thanking the guy, we made haste down Kimball Avenue, a couple of lucky punks. Once we turned up North Chestnut, Blake veered right onto a lawn. Up to the porch and past the spotlight thrown against the house, he cast a huge distorted shadow that shrank as he neared the door. He leaned forward, put his hand against the doorbell, and pressed.

Backing away in speedy motion, Blake winged his arms and jumped off the step, his shadow dancing across the face of the house. He ran in a sharp cut to the next yard, the contents of his backpack jiggling noisily. I pulled my arms and legs quickly and matched Blake's pace, my sneakers playing a pattering beat. Blake was already ringing another doorbell. Behind me was the sound of the first door pulling open. I hauled onward without looking back, slightly ahead of Blake now, and crossed to Raymond Street. At last we slowed our steps to a walk and the night became quiet. It wasn't until Blake spoke that I saw he was brandishing a nicely rippled, small, flat pumpkin.

"Where'd you get that?" I panted.

He shrugged. "Got it with a five-finger discount at the second house."

"You what?"

"Took it."

It's not hard to figure what happened next. Blake checked around, lifted the small pumpkin in one hand, and crashed it to the asphalt. It crumbled apart with a thunk and spread around our feet. He looked at me like a maniac.

"God, that's addicting!"

Without another word, Blake ran over to the nearest doorstep and cursed when he found he'd mistaken an orange mum for a sizable pumpkin. I didn't know where to go next. I just followed along the street, an idiot lookout, watching him comb the next porch like a stalking tiger. To my dismay, he found a family of three pumpkins; two small, one large. Guess which one went. Little Spencer hoisted the huge momma to his stomach with scaled adrenaline and walked a few hunched paces toward yours truly. I looked to the windows of the house and backed away. When Blake saw he'd get no help from me, he staggered to the edge of the curb and let go. The giant fruit spilled onto Raymond and split in half, both pieces rolling around freely of each other. Seeds scattered, sprinkling out on the road. We left the ill-fated pumpkin halves rocking back and forth and took off.

Blake kept me anchored to his mayhem. Every time I wanted to bolt, he would swerve to one side and dash in an angle up someone's property. He ceased casing windows and porches and smashed any pumpkins he saw, except for those basking in the safety of well-lit yards. After a while, I deduced from his panting shouts that he was on a quest for a hundred pumpkins. I looked back at our path of destruction. A sea of broken pumpkin pieces, lying under streetlights like rotting corpses on a battlefield, now peppered Raymond Street, Parkview, and Harrison Avenues.

A faint idea came to me when I saw Blake running back from one house palming two small pumpkins with carefully painted jovial faces. Every October, at her friend's boutique shop in town, my mom likes to help by indulging herself in painting pumpkins for sale. I thought about that just as Blake hurled the two artfully designed pumpkins to a heightened death, littering the road fifty feet in front of us.

"Hey," I said angrily. "I'll bet my mom painted those pumpkins."

Blake walked easily now, taking a break from his rampage. Cans of Barbasol clinked once in his pack. He kicked a gooey smashed pumpkin wedge along the road and shrugged.

"Ash, you gotta help out."

I didn't want to help smash. I missed Tyler. I felt like detouring a few blocks to Jenn-with-two-n's Dolan's to see if he was around.

"See, Blake," I told him. "I look at pumpkins as decoration, something to admire and be creative with. You look at them as things to decorate the sidewalks."

We had reached Highland Avenue and started rounding back down toward Birch and Colonial when Blake amazingly coerced me into riding his coattails up to a huge mansion of a house. The yard was long, dimly lit, and the door, far from the road, was shaded in almost zero visibility. Up we went, tiptoeing over crunchy leaves. The sound of it made me cringe, remembering the near-naked night before. I didn't see any pumpkins and figured I was in the clear for now. A few steps more and the vision became apparent. There indeed *was* a cluster of something to the right side of the door. I tell you, this kid could sniff these things. To Blake it was Christmas morning, presents under the tree. I heard his taken gasp and my face grew hot. Just as we reached the shadowy steps in utter silence, a sudden sharp clank broke the serenity.

The dark door swung open!

The pressure sounding against the storm door and the banging of the metal doorknobs blazed us to a panicked jump. Blake barged into me and sent us both running toward the street just as a flash of porch light opened brightness around us. For a second I couldn't tell if it was

Blake or someone else whose pace had overtaken mine. Then I heard an incredible sound—Blake's laughter. I slammed around the last bush of that huge yard and jumped to the street with his creepy giggling followed me. Finding somewhere to aim myself, I booked toward Colonial. When Blake finally got me to stop at the corner of his street, I leaned on a telephone pole and nearly collapsed trying to catch my breath. All I could see or hear now was that door pulling open.

With brain-clotted stubbornness, Blake wanted me to give it another try, insisting that what happened back at the mansion was a fluke thing and that I had to christen the night with at least one smash so I could know for sure it wasn't for me. Everyone seemed to think that since I'd written that article, I needed to feel the madness of life. The goof hounded me for two house lengths before stopping me cold near a row of pine trees lining a drive.

A white house in pleasant sky blue trim sat over a modest and carefully groomed front yard. Blake held an arm against my chest like a roadblock and kept careful observance of the house. A porch lamp shone off pumpkin tops. It was a modestly impressive display— cornstalks on either side of the door, orange ribbons from a Halloween wreathe waving softly in a breeze. A bale of hay served as a prop for a family of gourds while four glistening pumpkins sat around the base.

"Been eyein' those beauties for weeks," whispered Blake, "saving them for tonight." He nudged me. "They're all yours, bud."

I crept from the line of pines and out onto the foreign driveway. It seemed vaguely intrusive to me just to be standing there on that property. These neighbors of Blake's never did anything to me. They bought and arranged those pumpkins in a cultured manner, and who was I to disturb them in an uncultured spasm? I said back to Blake, "They never did anything to me."

"Go!" he nearly shouted.

Across the street, a dog's bark seemed a warning. Just get this over with. The first step felt like lifting a sneaker out of thick pudding. I could hardly believe it when my feet started taking me closer to the door. The display grew larger. Everything became sharp, especially those smooth pumpkins, whose stationary pose made them appear as naïve victims who should be running away. A strange tingle wormed into my abdomen. The crunch of leaves grew more distinct under my feet as I neared. I watched the door, even the crack of the mailbox. Leaning into the pumpkins sitting placidly beside the hay bale, I reached out my hands and took a medium-sized one into my palms, pulling it up gingerly. It felt solid and cold to the touch. Done.

I turned, holding my breath, and walked back onto the lawn. A jolt froze me when I looked ahead. Blake had started running early for some reason, his body streaking in a moving light. Suddenly my hearing returned. Everything went back to normal. I don't know if it was the headlights I noticed first or the humming of the engine, but behind the screen of pines, a car slowed. A silver Cadillac appeared and pulled into the driveway, snaring me in its headlights.

I nearly hyperventilated. Pitching the pumpkin, I dashed out of the light to the next yard. My cheeks bouncing from the frightened pace, I ran for Blake's figure sprinting ahead of me and could almost hear myself think: Blake, is it worth all this? We tore around the bend and Blake stopped me a little before his premises, holding my sleeve so I wouldn't keep going.

"Man!" He panted with a hand on his knee. "You have the worst luck!"

We hung out there for a few minutes, surveying the area, keeping a watchful gaze toward that last house. The road was surprisingly quiet and desolate again. Standing on the sidewalk in front of Blake's home, trying to keep out of sight, it was almost as though he didn't live there. He zeroed in on his neighbor's porch across the street, shaking his head once.

"Those dorks carved their pumpkin like, three nights ago. Now it's so rotten they can't even light it tomorrow night."

"A lot of people can't light theirs now."

Blake smirked dumbly and started his creep.

"I'm gonna splatter that rumpled pumpkin all over the front door."

Annoyed with him by now, I suddenly had an idea. Without any provocation, I zoomed ahead. Blake nearly squealed with elation at my waxing participation and tried beating me to the door. Poor kid. Had no idea. All I kept thinking about was that mess he'd left me in back at the last house. We bounced into each other closing in on the step. It was indeed a sorrowfully rotted jack-o'-lantern, like a half-filled kickball, its face sunken shut with dark blotches caking the skin. Blake giggled and tried butting me out of the way. I positioned my feet with a steady grunt and jabbed my hand down into the sloppy center. The carcass was softer than I expected. Blake leaned under me and tried to get at the remainder of what was once a proud pod on a sunlit vine.

With his uncontrollable laughter just under my head, I scooped deeper at the cool insides and came up with a huge squishy handful. Suddenly I slammed it all across Blake's face. I could feel the tiny cartilage in his nose, the smoothness of his teeth, the ridge of his jaw as I swiped a sloppy mess. He flew back like a firecracker had exploded in his nostril. When I saw the gook dripping down his cheek, I reeled away, gripping my belly and laughing in course jubilation.

Blake's backpack jagged as he dove at me, attempting to share his face-smear. I lunged away at the last second, and Blake bumbled by, falling to the lawn, looking more ridiculous than ever. With his backpack at his elbows, he peered up from his sprawl. I thought he'd go home and leave me for the night when I saw his face. He looked hurt, dejected, suddenly fouled.

"G-*ross!*" he exclaimed. He sounded inquisitively stunned. "Ash, why'd you do that?"

I tried to hold back laughing as Blake got up and stomped across the lawn to the street. I made sure to keep a good distance from him now. He could've just gone home and washed his sticky slimy face, but he jogged past his house toward Mountain Avenue. I saw why.

Someone had been here recently. A few someones. The signs were all over, like animals marking their territory. Starting at the old Huelett house on the corner, they had draped toilet paper strands over several houses down Mountain Avenue. Blake wrapped a fistful and swabbed his face with it. I snickered when he slobber-spit the last bits of pumpkin grime from his lips.

There was a mild peace about the scene. Around us and ahead of us, the trails of white tissue, created for such a nasty purpose, had a strange, eerie, romantic quality. Under the corner street lamp, their hanging glow added scale to the tree limbs. I stood admiring the creatively tangled work, like streamers at a dance. It was just a weird and interesting sequence of thoughts I was having. Hanging toilet paper was a funny thing to me. It just drooped in suspension from tree limbs, tall and still in ghostly strips, some reaching the ground. I wondered who did it and how long ago. Were they nearby?

Blake found his own form of delight in the mess. Unhitching his black sack, he swung it around and zipped open to fetch a lighter, which he scratched until a tiny flame ignited into appearance. Handling a line of toilet paper, he held it to the dancing tongue of light. Suddenly a bright fire was climbing up to the branch, swallowing the T.P. strand as it went. I must have stood on that quiet street for five minutes like a kid at a magic show, gazing at flames soaring into the bottom half of the big maple while Blake lit any strip within grasping distance. I got a little scared, though, when he set ablaze both ends of a piece draped over a live wire.

"Enough of that," Blake finally said into the darkness. "Time for Huelett's."

As far back as I've been hanging around Blake's neighborhood, I've always known these Huelett people to leave one side of their garage curiously open, a direct incongruity to their private bearing in life. Little clean-cut Andy Gibb began tiptoeing down the old man's driveway. Moonlight scattered in patches through the trees like white slates on the pavement. I stood guard, as much a support as I would allow myself to be, as Blake inched his small frame beside the Huelett's old gray Lincoln and disappeared into blackness. Suddenly a dim light uncovered him from the murkiness of the garage, his small face gazing upon the contents of the refrigerator like a toddler spying the window of a toy store. That was about the extent of the innocence. A soft clanking sounded as Spencer slid an object into his hands from the top of the fridge. The door gently shut, suction the only sound.

I backed away, stepping over leaves with barking volume, as Blake emerged into the dim light of the street. He held something out to me, something dark and shiny. Begrudgingly, I accepted this cold smooth bottle. The liquid gulped around as I read the label: Beringer.

"A little White Zinfandel with your best pal?" he said gaily.

Right then I could view the anger for these people, for his mother's irrational flakiness, for Jim, for the betrayal by his father—all of it dissipating with every step now. Blake snared the bottle and reversed his backpack to his front, stuffing the "fine year" between a stash of toilet paper rolls.

"For later," he said, zipping back up. "There's a party up at Candy's house. This'll be a hit."

After Blake spanked the Huelett house with four eggs, we doubled down Mountain Avenue on our seemingly endless foray and headed up Alden Avenue, parallel to Colonial and Birch. On the way, Blake kept his lighter in his hand and grew increasingly destructive with it. A ghost decoration, made of a white sheet and impaled on a lamppost, was in flames by the time we were fifty yards away. He burned another one hanging from a tree, as well as a cardboard pumpkin decoration on a storm door.

"See, Ash," Blake said as flame glow danced on his back, "I'm making you experience things you never have before, things you'd never see if it wasn't for me. This is a better lesson than you'll ever get in school, bub."

I stared sourly at him. We had spun a web of destruction half an area code wide and were now hiding from any cars sighted. My mind kept exposing itself to this one truth: If I'd never written that article and sent my family on a town-wide flee, I wouldn't be out on this circus of a night.

"Great," I said. "A lesson in life from Kid Puberty himself."

Leah Hamilton lived ironically on Sinclair Place, the fateful street on which Blake and I had our now-infamous encounter seven years before. Leah was Blake's ex-girlfriend and the breakup had been anything but sweet. Their subsequent trades and taunts had no soft cutesy quality like Blake's exchanges with Maureen Egan. These rank-outs were heartfelt, stabbing, evil. Leah was a dark-haired turquoise-eyed beauty who never seemed ignorant of that. She was also the only girl I ever knew who could pass disgusted snobbish insults like a schoolboy bully. You knew her opinion of you very easily. Most certainly the biggest bitch in the entire school. Blake would deal with her tonight the best way he knew how. He would hail her abode with a storm of hen embryos.

Just across Lawrence Avenue, and there it was.

Blake detoured us through to the back yard of the Hamilton's house. Tall bushes surrounded the yard in a square perimeter. As we cleared the line of thin trunks, people became visible inside. Leah herself stood in the den with two other girls we knew, clear to us through the large patio doors. A TV was on but no one was watching. Clad in jackets, it looked as though they were just about to head out for the night. Blake acted quickly, placing three eggs in my hand.

"You gotta do this, Ash," he pleaded, his eyebrows twisting up like a dog's. "For me."

He fixed his pack and we stood facing the huge windows. On his count of three, we stepped from the bushes and whipped six eggs toward the light. I was on my second egg when I saw golden yellow spray like a can of paint over the glass door. Running through the next yard, I could still hear the sharp thuds against the glass.

After cutting through a few properties, we found ourselves in back of our old school, Franklin Elementary. Blake was breathlessly congratulating himself, saying he should type an anonymous note to Leah, asking how she'd like her eggs next time. Sunny?

I held Blake back as I spotted something to our left. Three burnouts were in the process of rounding the bottom corner of Elm Street. We waited and watched them in full light as they passed under the street lamp and suddenly the message emblazoned in my head: *C U 2NITE*. The threats started coming back. I thought of the walkie-talkie through our window. Could these be from Dayle's bunch?

After the three guys cornered up Elm, Blake and I circled around the school the other way. It was a critically good move that granted us the fortune of spotting a parked police car. Blake quickly released himself from the binds of his mischief pack and set it under the slide. The bottle of wine clanked on one of the supporting legs. Right off I could see he wanted to have fun. Over the field and around the chain link fence we walked, approaching the dark cop car, a painful reminder of last night. We leaned into the window with a friendly greeting, disappointed to find the car empty. I cupped my hands over the glass glare and Blake followed my example. A laptop computer jutted out from where a car radio would be.

"Who are you?"

We spun around and looked. This guy just appeared. Just like that he was standing there, staring at us in a manner that told me who he was and why he was there. A flashlight beamed in my face and I put a subconscious hand up, blocking the brightness. Again, Blake did the same.

He was a cop all right. Through the blinding light I could see his navy blue uniform. Even from what I'd been through with cops in my house last night, this man's presence threw me.

"Who are you?" he asked again strongly. From the tone, I could tell we'd made a bad move. He was prejudging us, and I was irritated by the fact that whatever he suspected, he didn't know the half of it. He back-and-forthed his flashlight between Blake and me. Neither of us said a word.

"What are you guys doin' out here? Huh?" After all the silence of the night, he seemed very loud. "What are you doin' hangin' around the school?"

"We're just walking," Blake said in a small feeble voice.

"You kids have identification?" the cop asked. No time to answer. Right away: "Where do you live?"

Blake lost that small feeble tone. "Why?"

"Hey, I'll ask the questions!" the man snapped.

Blake's courage surprised me. He gestured around the area. "I'm not allowed to just walk around with my friend?"

"You gettin' smart with me?!" the man yelled.

I tried to recognize him through the glare—tall, slicked-back dark hair, thick mustache. He wasn't anyone who'd been at my house. It seemed we were in some trouble.

"I'll ask the questions," he repeated. "You keep speakin' back to me and I'll take you to jail."

That seemed awfully hasty. A weird scenario indeed had formed. Ironically, I was on the other side now, not as the protected, but as the antagonist. This was too much, and I wanted out of there. I simply started walking away. Incredibly, the cop let me.

"Wait," cried Blake. Bull-headed, he wanted the challenge. That damn pent-up anger of his. I wasn't going to let it ruin *my* destiny. He could go to jail without me. I'd had it. I walked down to the gate and swung around back over the field, feeling the freedom of allowance. In a moment my mind cleared and my conscience returned. I decided to stop at the line of trees behind the batter's cage and listen. I honestly thought that any minute Blake would be escorted into the patrol car. Maybe the Hamiltons had phoned in about the eggs. Jeez, if that policeman only knew.

"...not allowed to walk around without you harassing us?" Blake was saying, only snippets of his voice audible to me.

"I'm not harassing you." The policeman was still talking loudly, coarsely.

"Yes you are! It's not a school night. I have rights to be here. It's not even town curfew yet."

"Town curfew is seven tonight."

"Well, I mean—I never knew about that. Nobody told me."

"Listen to me!" the cop half-bellowed, standing close to Blake. He raised a finger in Spencer's face. "Listen. Hey! Be quiet for a second.

I know what tonight is. I also know your face and your clothing. If there's any trouble and I spot either of you again, you're going to jail. Got it?"

The bickering simmered, and in a minute Blake's figure was jogging over the field. I stepped out of the shadows and he shuffled when he saw me.

"Ash! Cool. You didn't leave."

I folded my arms. "He seemed to like you."

Blake Spencer glanced back, his eyebrows curling up in caution. Out of sight of the cop, he dragged his dirty deed case and we made through the woods.

"I'm so glad you didn't leave," he told me again.

I said nothing. I'm your best pal, Blake. I'm not your father. I'm not going anywhere.

We met Dustin Noonan and his tragic-looking hair out on Lenape Trail. I knew we were passing his house, but didn't think he'd be home then. I figured him for the municipal parking lot, skateboarding with the other bodaciously narly dudes. A voice called our names from a dimly lit porch. We looked over and saw a fume of smoke spewing under a hanging plant. A shape appeared from it.

"Dudes!" he called. "What are you doing?"

There was no mistaking the do. He sided up to me and hung out a hand. I just couldn't get past that hair; still half-shaved for Halloween with the long side completely red. I took his hand and told him about the cop. Dustin "the dude" replied, "Cool. Let's go bomb him."

It was somewhat disorienting to see his house—a modern design with spotlights hanging down from the middle, giving the appearance of one of those rich houses on Beverly Hills 90210. The lawn had recently been cleaned of leaves, and a trail of lights oversaw a fancy pebble path to the porch. Everything looked so affluent, proper, normal, everything except Dustin.

Dustin abandoned his private smoke hole in favor of including himself in the drama of which Blake was boasting. It didn't take long to find some.

"Dudes," Dustin said in his hoarse narly voice, "my 'rents went out to my sister's college tonight. Her car's in the garage. I could take it out and drive us around."

"Illegally?" I said. "Dustin, you can't even drive."

"I drive," he said defiantly.

"Yeah, what?" I replied. "A Tonka?"

A few minutes later, Dustin was proving, for all his "radness" that he was a fairly stable driver. I wondered how he got his knack. Most likely from his sister in this very Volkswagen Rabbit, in which I was sitting, again, in the back friggin' seat watching backs of heads. Blake led Dustin through a purposeful tour of Cranford. At the edge of a park he sat forward with his hands on the dashboard.

"That's it," he said softly. "Dustin, kill the lights and wait for me."

Mr. Flaherty lived in a plain white house on top of a hill. A brown cross-pattern rail decorated the surrounding porch. Tonight the windows were dark, as though no one was home. The back of Flaherty's green Oldsmobile, however, sat parked along the street in front of us with that horrible bumper sticker describing what he'd rather be doing to other men's betrothed.

Dustin left the car running and shut off the lights while Blake hopped out with a baseball bat he'd taken from the Noonan's garage. This time I enjoyed a comfortable distance in that back seat. The shaved side of Dustin's head faced me as he watched out the passenger-side window.

A small shape glided up the hill in a crouch to the darkened front porch and raised the baseball bat over its head and very quickly I remembered the night before—"*That pumpkin's thirty inches across!*" I stuck my face out the window for a better look. There was the sudden thunk of the bat, then nothing, followed by the small clatter of the bat dropping. Dustin and I regarded each other, then looked out again for a few seconds. Blake was running back down, his steps inconsistent, awkward. He stopped at the car and squeezed his hands between his knees.

"It didn't break!" he groaned over the engine. "It's a rock! I just killed my hands!"

"Where's my bat?" Dustin demanded.

"Back there." He jerked his head toward the door.

"It's got my *name* on it, dork!" cried the half-and-half kid. "Dude, go *get* it!"

Blake frowned in agony and trudged back up the hill for the bat, shaking his hands.

Ten minutes later we were back at the same spot, having been informed by Blake that he had aroused the big history teacher's attention inside the house. Melanie Noonan's VW Rabbit was parked on the street around the corner, and we had just scaled the dirt hill on Mr. Flaherty's property with Mrs. Noonan's eggs in our hands. A line of soft light crept over Blake's face as he peered over the mound, scratching his nose.

"I've checked that house's cholesterol level," he whispered, "and it's apparent to me that we'll have to add some egg yoke to its diet."

I felt like a commando in an army movie, spying through a patch of weeds. On my pinkie finger was a plastic spider ring I'd just found on the street. It was one of those cheap little things given out as Halloween party favors. Watching it, I flexed my finger and the spider lived for an instant.

Blink!

The porch light turned on. All whispering stopped. Blake, Dustin and I crouched deeper into the hill, waiting to see what was happening. Kinks and bangs sounded as the front door opened, and there stood Mr. Flaherty. Large and round, he came out on the porch and stared at us as though the hill and bushes weren't even there.

"Whoever you are," he suddenly shouted in his famous tone, "get the hell out of here before I call the police! Go wreck your own neighborhood!"

It was defeating how well he was on to us. I lifted my face just a tad and saw the eerie image of Mr. Flaherty's eyes flitting back and forth in alarm, checking over the hill line. I held a gulp as he stretched his glare twice to the left and caught my slight movement. He was staring right at me. Our silence must have freaked him. He seemed apprehensive in his frozen stance. The biggest problem for us though, was that we were shackled to a hill. If we ran, he'd be able to identify us in the light, a discovery that just might hinder our chances of getting a good grade in his class. Blake giggled breathlessly and his whisper lifted the silence.

"I'm gonna count to three."

I kept my eyes on Mr. Flaherty. "Blake, no way. If—"

"One"—I looked at him as he counted—"two, *three*!"

Blake straightened with fiery eyes and cocked his arm. In a matter of two seconds, eggs were being sailed toward the doorway. Dustin managed two hasty throws that flubbed and hit the upper part of the house. The barrage shocked Mr. Flaherty into silence. I don't know if Blake scored a direct hit, but it had to be close. I jumped down the hill to the road and smashed my two eggs to the ground. More fright running. Behind me, Blake and Dustin were laughing as we hauled for the corner, each of us hiding our faces within tugs of our collars. I reached the car first and looked back. The two scatterbrains were stumbling around the corner, heaving with breathless mirth.

"You guys are slower than a *freight* train!" I yelled hoarsely. They both hastened their steps.

"You see his face?" Blake snickered as he finally grabbed a handle. "That's the look I've been waiting all *year* to see!"

Once we were safely coasting back into Westfield in the Rabbit, an idea began to peel in my mind: What an interesting story for the *Hi's Eye*—to interview kids on Mischief Night. The quotes alone would make for a great juvenile human-interest piece. Only my zeal was interrupted by a truth which had thus far escaped me. Very viciously, I realized myself a total hypocrite. I was stuck in the middle of conflict yet to be resolved. My article had disrupted my family, my house, part of my town, and a select group of kids—all swirled together in a collective controversy. I had just written a scathing finger-pointing article about the actions of others, yet here I was.

Sparks outside Blake's window clapped my reverie off like a wet face-slap. Spencer had lit one of a series of skyrockets that Dustin had brought along and was holding the live shooter out the window like a flaming torch. Dustin checked him cautiously—the road, Blake, the road, Blake. I ran my face to the window and watched as the rocket fell from Blake's hand and bounced around on the road behind us. Suddenly it ignited, sparking in a blazing zigzag until an array of dazzling light bloomed over the street. Dustin continued on, dashing the Rabbit through early leaf piles, scattering them. God forbid kids should be playing in any.

We snaked our way onto a small curvy street called Wallberg Avenue, where a number of kids from our school were hanging out, as if waiting for a bus. Geoff Lightheiser was the first kid to approach the car after Dustin stopped. He leaned in and began jawing with Blake about heading over to Candy Kane's party just a few blocks away. I could tell some of these kids were a bit uncertain of it though, since they weren't too friendly with the cheerleading, bubble-gum, preppie crew that would certainly be chancing upon Kane Manor tonight.

Candy's friends were mine and I knew some of them as ones inclined to treat these kids with snobbish cynicism.

The focus of the attention here centered around an act occurring behind the street in the pre-developed woods. Geoff made the drastic mistake of telling Blake that, deep in the trees, Paul Miller was busy feeling up Leah Hamilton. All I could think of was her patio door.

I could have smudged another handful of rotten pumpkin slop across Blake's face and he wouldn't have diverted his attention from Geoff Lightheiser. He stared up through his side part into Geoff's eyes with an animal look. I guess Geoff didn't sense anything because he went on in a dirty mode like he envied Paul. I could only imagine what was going through Blake's head. He only asked one thing.

"Where are they?" He sounded interested, although not much more than Geoff, not like it mattered.

Geoff pointed into the small, dark, wooded area. Somewhere in that abyss big Paul Miller was having his intrusive abusive way with the only girl Blake ever loved. Little Spencer wasn't about to let this go easily. He grabbed another rocket and told Geoff to get out of the way. The lighter was thumbed.

"Dustin," Blake commanded in a trance-like firm tone, "you will do me the gracious honor of peeling when I tell you." Dustin nodded uneasily. Around Blake, when he was like that, it didn't matter who you were—you just did what he said. I can't explain it.

Blake lit the huge skyrocket and stretched his arm out, holding the very tip of the long stick in his fingers and pointing it toward the clump of trees. He took one last glance, made sure of his aim, and squeezed his eyes shut. SWOOSH! The rocket left his fingers in a loud blaze of sparks and slammed into the woods. For one incredible second the trees and thick shrubbery were alive in light as the ensuing fireworks exploded all over the area. Blake held Dustin's arm in a halt. There was no noise. I watched; my eyebrows raised in awe. It was a spectacular gesture, a stroke of fine marksmanship.

Leaves rustled and a pattern of breaking branches broke onto the neighborhood as a huge body moved through the thicket of growth toward the car. Paul Miller's shape came rumbling through the smoke.

Blake hollered, "Go go *go!*"

Miller very nearly closed in on the Rabbit, and Dustin seemed to sense it, screeching around the corner with just enough speed to avoid the charging lineman. I kept flinging my head back and forth to get a good look. All I could see out the back window were the jerking knees and that bullish oncoming torso of Paul hauling after us like he'd grab hold of the bumper if he could. Finally his steps shortened as we rounded the turn to Oak Avenue. Blake was shouting out his window at the top of his lungs.

"Leah, you're a loser! You! A loser!"

Candy Kane's house sat on a rise at the steepest part of Topping Hill Road. Tonight, lights and laughter spilled from the windows. Candy had at least three parties so far this year, so many that they grew boring after a while, all the same flavor each time. This get-together would prove different.

Mrs. Kane, a single serene-faced lady, usually sat at the kitchen table dragging cigarettes one after another. She was oddly tolerant of allowing Candy and her hulking older brother John to have their friends to the house on weekends. I got to know Mrs. Kane about as well as anyone hanging out there that fall. She'd just inhale, blow, and tap, the whole time listening to me ramble about school.

Tonight the woman was absent, away for the weekend with Candy's aunt, and the house had a crowded untamed atmosphere. Whereas booze and butts were usually conducted in hidden little places like the back yard and the dank wash room when she was present, both substances floated freely about the first floor.

Candy, dressed as Raggedy Ann, glided toward us through a throng of my friends squeezed together as if bunched on an elevator. Now let me explain. Although it sounds like a porn star name, Candy's genuine label happens to be Cathy, but she's been called otherwise since diaperhood. A bright-eyed attractive cheerleader whose dirty-blond hair bounces on her shoulders in thick curls, Candy has a high-strung friendly nature and is rarely seen without this broad smile, like she'd just won a prize on a game show. Tonight, in red curls and blush, she gave us each a hug and demanded good-naturedly to know the whereabouts of our costumes.

Thinking quickly, I slipped off the spider ring and spread my arms. "Hey! It's me!"

I soon got separated from the other two and began to mingle. Those who had only stared at me in school yesterday were buzzed enough to ask me candidly about the drug story, and John Kohleran, and who was after me. Chris Noyes told me that John was rumored to be getting out of the hospital tomorrow. Two different kids thanked me for influencing the premature ending of school. Someone also congratulated me for my showing against Hackett. Chris's eyes sparkled at me in laughter upon the subject's rise.

"That kid Benton really ripped Domino's underwear?"

I looked to the carpet. "Kinda."

"That's hilarious," Chris chuckled. "Hey, are you going out tomorrow night?"

"Trick-or-treating?" I dropped inside, remembering my duty. "Don't know. I have this thing with the cops tomorrow. No idea how long it's supposed to last. Why? Are you?"

He swept his hand. "Hell yeah. We all are. Why don't you come with?"

The thought of the cop shop tomorrow at noon burdened me. How would I face them after tonight? What did they want to ask me? I didn't think at the time that there was any way they could punish me for my intended silence. Still, I couldn't go back on that stand just to save my hide.

Kohleran's partial girlfriend, Varsity Carnoustie, was just coming up from the basement as I was squeezing down. There was no mistaking the lining under her eyes, the tangled strands of her frosted hair.

"Oh my God!" she exclaimed, putting a hand to my chest. "You're here!"

We really didn't even know each other that well at all. It puzzled me why she was so thrilled to see me until she took my hand and said, "Don't go anywhere. I'm gonna page Tara."

Varsity Carnoustie, proper name Jennifer, had acquired her nickname in eighth grade after dating three guys on the varsity soccer team. Strangely, she accepted her pseudonym with an odd pride. She was not what you'd call a regular with either Candy or big John Kane's clique. Like Tyler, Candy Kane had been stretching her vision lately, denying her image and including a wider spectrum of friends, the foremost of whom was Miss Carnoustie. I never really liked Varsity much, probably because I never really knew her. What a stupid thing. Why do kids view each other badly just from lack of acquaintance? It's amazing how familiarity can change everything. But with Varsity, she always seemed to glance at me like she was above me in sincerity, like she thought I was some snotty prep with no depth. Now, since her best friend happened to be Tara, maybe she realized I wasn't so bad after all. Being led upstairs by her, I still didn't know what to make of this. Her name was famous to me for things I was completely scared to even try. I know it's horrible, but I couldn't look at her without picturing her in certain positions doing some of the things for which she was both heralded and abused. What made it worse was that she had a beautiful figure that only now seemed broken of its luster and violated of its appeal.

Varsity sat me across from her in the retreat of the second floor hallway while she paged Tara. Her jeans were whitewashed, more ivory than blue now from wear and tear. All the while I sat and watched her, confounded. I couldn't understand why she would be here while John was laid up in the hospital. I wondered if she ever even went to see him at all.

The ensuing phone call was quick. Tara the Curb Owl was at a junior burnout party over on Lawrence Avenue and would be here as soon as she could coax a ride from Tina Rondinelli.

Out on the raised lawn, Varsity waited with me, my price being I had to sit and fan her smoke from my face. A few younger kids passed by in the road below, indiscreetly making their mischief rounds in black wool hats.

"Look at those dorks," Varsity said, waving a cigarette at them. "They'll never get laid."

Tina's sleek black Mercury Topaz drove up and stopped in front of the Kane's driveway. The door opened and a soft inside light shined on the thick waves of Tara's hair. I felt a helpless tremor at the sight. She stood out with a black leather jacket draped over her arm, then closed the door and smiled up at us. My lips parted lazily and a warmth tingled my cheeks.

"I'll be shot out of a cannon," I gasped.

Even though it was fall, Tara was wearing white jeans and tight soft-fabric shirt with a wide neck. She usually dressed fairly conservative for an aspiring burnout, but this was a new look for her. I almost hated how unsteady it made me feel.

"Heard you had a bit of a tangle this afternoon," she called as Tina drove off. "Had your way?"

I don't remember exactly how I responded to that, because as I started to, a terrible sound screamed into the lovesick aura. Heads in the yard whipped left. A maroon Volvo stormed around the bend and

skidded to where Tina's Mercury had just been. A side door burst open
before the wheels stopped.

Tara hunched forward in alarm, throwing her hands at me.

"Ash*ley*!" she screamed, scaring the hell out of me. "Run! Now!"
I started across the lawn. The front door came zooming toward me
and I grabbed the handle, nearly yanking it off as I flung open the storm
door and whirled my body around it. The face I saw rumbling up the
front steps after me was a larger version of the one from that afternoon.
Lee Hackett had just reached the first step when I slammed the main
door in his face, frantically relieved to find a hand-turned lock on the
inside. I pressed my body to the wood and twisted the latch 'til it
clicked and held. The storm door ripped open on the other side and Lee
strained at the main door handle, the lock banging in its socket. I
backed into the front hall, half-expecting the door to break. All the kids
in the hallway and living room were looking at me. I waved a hand to
my right and my yell was strong.

"LOCK THE BACK DOORS *NOW*!!"

I was cornered, looking all about the windows, the rooms, not
trusting anyone or anything. A dozen calls of "What's wrong?" clouded
my hearing. Candy came forward with concerned expression on her
usually boisterous face. I hated letting them all know what was
happening.

"Quick—" I grabbed her in front of everyone. "—is there a
window in your attic?"

I had a rushed notion of climbing out on their flat roof and spying
a good place to jump if predators infested the house. The atmosphere
was frenzied. Candy's brow wrinkled under her wig.

"We don't have an attic."

Some began to sense what was going on. Chris Noyes and a couple
guys jammed themselves down in the basement and plugged the doors
in case Lee or anybody else should try to come in from there. The
porch door was slid shut and bolted with a pole for good measure.
Candy and a few others led me to her upstairs room overlooking the
front yard.

Well, I thought, here is where it would happen, in front of my
friends. I wouldn't have any family or police around me this time. A
cop was back at my house, but there would be no car stationed in front
of the Kane's. Yet for all I knew, those who'd been prank calling and
spying in the house and breaking our windows were now forming a

circle of entrapment around a party of kids two grades younger. How long would they wait? Certainly not all night. What of Tara? It was clear to me that they'd used her naïveté, knowing she might lead them from her prior party to me. I had to hand it to them. For burned-out druggies, they were methodically smart.

In Candy's dark room I sat on her bed, thinking about Lee Hackett as he'd raced up for the door before I'd closed it, his expression purposeful, stone-faced, dark icy eyes fixed, not on me, but on the screen door handle. It occurred to me now that if Tara hadn't screamed for me to run, that crazed kid would've caught me. The reality of tasting violent pain put me in a stupor. I'd never been beaten up before, and it wasn't only the idea of pain that scared me, it was blind fear of the unknown. John Kohleran's ribs were fractured because of my impulsiveness. I had just been in a fight with Domino Hackett, who ended up stalking home with ripped underwear. Now Lee was outside. I remembered Sunday evening when Benton Crossey beat up Joey Apel for messing with his little brother. I blinked at the wall. Now I was Joey Apel.

From outside, a series of voices began to ring up to the windows.

"Munroe! Yo, Munroe! Just come out a second! We wanna say hi!"

Two porch lights enabled us a clear view of those standing out on the lawn without them having the same fortune on us. I rose, took the slightest glance, and sat back down. It looked like a small lynch mob. Dayle Tanner, of all people, stood in the driveway, Lee on the lawn, and a few other tough-looking senior burners moved to join the two. The numbers figured to be about six or seven. They were leaning their heads back, swiveling their faces side-to-side, searching the windows with their eyes. None of them had been able to squirm their way inside the house. There was no sign of Tara.

I could end this particular act right here, I thought. We could call the police and I could delay this for another day, and this conflict would just keep raging further and further on.

A powerful knock at the bedroom door.

"Where's A'?"

Slight stirrings followed in the dark room. Any other time I would've dug being in a lightless bedroom with chicks. Small talk around the room confirmed a number of kids were in here, but Candy, in her wig and deep blush, put a soft finger to her lips. I felt ashamed that they should have to go through all this because of me. Just like my poor family.

The knocking was strong, pounding.

"A', it's Benton. Open up, bro."

For two seconds nobody moved. I looked at Candy questioningly.

"He was in the basement," she whispered.

I rose for the door and opened to the light. Ironically, there was the frightening hulk of athletic Benton Crossey in a guinea T, wearing that baseball cap backwards. His ominous presence was a pleasant welcoming as he stumped into the room. Although I wasn't a good eye for detecting a drunk, I could tell he was a bit warm and sloppy by the glossiness of his brown eyes.

"Close the door," Candy ordered.

"Forget them retards," Benton professed loudly. He grimaced. "They seen me fight." Candy wasn't too impressed at the moment as he bobbed, bragging, "You think any uh them lowlifes'll bother with wit' A' Munroe while I'm here?" He put a hand up to me. "Bro, I gotcha."

I tapped his palm resignedly. Benton seemed like one of those kids who carried that unfulfilled toughness around. Like he was trying to show he could be rugged so as to get back at his stunted grammar school years when kids treated him as a goof.

"How long are they gonna stay out there?" Dulcie Robbins asked from out in the hall.

"They'll go away," I heard Chris Noyes answer. "Just give 'em time."

Confusion filled the hallway as kids made suggestions. One was that everyone group to the basement. Another was for all guys to run out and gang up on what would be a powerfully outnumbered group of seniors, but for some reason, no one but Benton was up for that. Sean Fitzpatrick figured to "call the police on those degenerates." I looked at Candy, whose painted face broke like she didn't know what to do.

Outside on the front lawn, the calls persisted.

"Come on! We just wanna say hi to Munroe! Let's see him!!"

Kids peeked in the room at me and I could feel the concern. More yells from out on the lawn directed painful infringement on my freedom. I was getting really embarrassed by the attention.

Benton bumbled to the window and cracked it to the screen.

"Hey!" he yelled in a squat. "Go home, lowlifes!"

What we heard next sounded like someone smashing a wide hammer on the wall. Right beside and underneath that window, a series of hard whacks shattered against the aluminum siding. It was as though small bombs had been placed under the paneling and were exploding outward in a ring of fragments. In two fantastical seconds, the Kane's house was being pelted with beer bottles.

I heard a series of hollers downstairs and couldn't hold myself still any longer. I jumped past Benton and barreled into the hall. Below me, kids were cutting a swath to the front door, intent on some form of defense. I hopped to the landing, only to back up toward the kitchen when I saw the front door pull back, revealing Lee, Dayle and another kid coming up the steps. I took off down the basement. Someone grabbed my shoulder on the way down. I glanced strongly. Blake.

"Wait up, Ash!" he shouted over the noise.

I pushed forward past kids in the dim light of the basement steps. Benton and Blake were yelling something behind me, directing me. The patio door opened to the night and I ran outside.

One question was answered when I streamed past Tara on the patio. Her arms twitched in shock, as though she thought Dayle might be right behind me. I didn't bother to say anything. I just kept running from a group of wiry burnouts who wanted to do God-knows-what to me. Into a pitch-black patch of Rhododendrons I bashed, pattering noisily over ivy leaves, throwing branches out of my way. I slid in the dirt under a low tree limb, scratching my face on a twig, and got momentarily stuck. Twisting my heat-panicked torso free, I rose and scrambled wildly over a chain-link fence and made for the street. Behind me was the sound of running.

I was almost proud of the way I scaled obstacles and cut through neighborhoods to find refuge, but was wasted from the fierce sprinting. I reached the line of houses on a street called Wychwood Road. Zeroing in on a two-story white Colonial, I took one breathless glance behind me and hauled up the driveway. I stopped at the dark corner of the house and put a hand to my chest in exhaustion. Peeking around, I saw one side of a two-car garage open to the back driveway. I took a huge breath and jumped around the corner, disappearing into the garage.

Darkness, serene quietude, safe now. Around me was a black Audi, a wheelbarrow, some sports equipment, and a ten-speed bike into which I banged my knee. I made like a feather to the edge of the side wall and slumped against it, panting, assessing for a moment what had just happened, and what options I had. Outside the garage was a view of a golf course extending far from the back yard. I tried to listen for voices or footsteps. If Dayle or Lee showed up, the vast obscurity of the fields ahead offered me a chance.

After a little while, I caught my breath. Still shaken, I finally leaned my head just outside the garage and peeped my eyes carefully up at the kitchen door. In a funny way, it was the last thing I expected.

Inside that brightly-lit kitchen, some strange guy at the sink turned his face right at me.

My head crouched back into my shoulders like a turtle and I slunk deeper into the garage. A swallowing in my stomach, I tiptoed all the way to the upturned wheelbarrow against the back wall. Like a glow still visible after closing my eyes, I could still see that face spotting me. I took a huddled curl behind the wheelbarrow. Just as I expected, more as I feared, the kitchen's storm door opened with a short whine.

Someone stood at the doorstep. In a second, the light door clicked very softly closed, indicating a sign of caution. The guy was outside now, moving on the other side of the one closed door with what I can only describe as alert footsteps. I faced the floor and kept the same breath of air for half a minute. Every muscle was tight.

Whoever it was now stood rigid in front of the open garage, and for a second, I couldn't tell who was the more quiet of us. I *knew* I'd been seen! A sound arose just a few feet away, the shifting of a sneaker. For all I knew, he could see some piece of me. I felt the clenching of my teeth and let out a very slow breath of air, my lungs shrinking comfortably. Should I rise? Give myself up?

The click of a switch and it just got worse. Brightness shocked me as if I'd just been doused with freezing water. Air now pushed through my throat in tiny pants. Hunched tightly into a stiff ball, I started to cramp up. A clinking sound—the kitchen door opened again.

"What's goin' on?" a man asked into the night.

Not more than fifteen feet from me, a reply echoed into the garage.

"Swear I could have seen something," a younger voice replied.

Jeez, what would I tell the cops, or even *The Westfield Leader*? Nah, the investigative reporter bit wouldn't work.

"You better shut that tonight," the older voice said at the kitchen door.

"Who'd steal anything from *here*? I imagined it, Dad. A breeze shadow maybe."

"Well," I heard the father say, "there's bikes and golf clubs in there and—and anyway, nothing should be left open on this night."

"Want me to bring the clubs inside the house?"

There was a pause, like something was really wrong. Had the guy discovered me?

"No, that's all right," the father finally said. "But you know what you can do? Here. Put the car in the driveway so nobody joyrides through onto the golf course like last year."

"Oh, yeah. That's right. Where're the keys?"

"Here. Catch." A jingling of metal flew through the air and stopped where the first guy stood.

"Make sure," said the father, "you shut the garage when you're finished."

Consequently, I was screwed.

Why is it, I thought bitterly in that crouch, that whenever I'm with Tara, I always somehow end up trapped? The guy, who really *had* seen me, entered further into the garage, pulled open a door on the Audi, and plopped himself in the driver's seat, so nearby I could hear the shock absorbers slightly creak. The hollow thunk of the door clamping shut bounced across the walls. The engine started up right next to my face against the wheelbarrow and all known to me became lost in the sound of the blaring patterned humming. I actually cursed inaudibly frustration. Headlights blazed all around my hiding spot. Cramps and all, I steadied myself to keep out of the light. The engine rumbled louder, the tires rolled over the garage floor, and the headlights trailed away, the glow dimming as the vehicle turned in backward motion. The stranger pulled forward and the headlights disappeared, replaced by the garage light. Outside the wall next to me, the Audi's engine silenced in the thin stretch of driveway.

Damn! I thought. I could make a clean dash for it if the father wasn't at the kitchen door!

I heard steps dragging as the guy strode back up the driveway, turned the corner, and crossed in front of the garage. His pace paused for a second as two clicks sounded. The light shut off and the automatic garage door started lowering. I felt the disbelief on my face as I listened to the mechanics and watched the wall. The big door met the floor, coating me in blackness. At last I stretched out, easing my muscles, and settled in for a long, dark wait. I would have to sit here for hours before I could feel confident that the owners had gone to bed. Suspicions already alarmed, these people would be on the watch. For a few seconds I half-panicked, wondering how long I'd be trapped in here. Jeez, I had to talk to the police tomorrow! Plus, it was the start of the weekend for dirt's sake!

I finally stood out from behind the wheelbarrow and walked around, stretching my legs again. The large door spring along the ceiling was still vibrating. My eyes adjusted to the dark. Moonlight streamed in the windows above me like a spotlight from Heaven. While waiting in empty anguished quietude, I looked out to the front yard and was happily surprised to see the black shapes of Blake, Benton and Tara standing in a hesitant manner out on Wychwood Road. So those running steps behind me had been *theirs*. Huh. I was in here for nothing then. I could only imagine what they perceived of my fate. No doubt they saw and heard the Audi, but for all they knew, I'd either been caught or had run somewhere out on the golf course.

From the sound of their worried chatter, I discovered a cracked hole in the bottom corner of a window pane. I put my face close to it and was about to say something when the front porch light suddenly blinked on. I backed off quickly. The front door opened to my right and the voice that had just been at the kitchen stoop now had a face whose bespectacled profile was silhouetted against the lamplight. The man stepped out.

"Cops are coming!" he called. "You better get on home now!"

I returned to the windowsill and watched the issue with saucer plate eyes.

"Oh, BS!" I heard Benton insolently cry back.

The man's college-aged son appeared next to his father.

"BS nothing!" he hollered. "They are! We're calling them right now!" He turned and disappeared back into the front door.

I looked again to the street and watched in deserted gloom as my three defenders vanished. I slouched in the moonlight and cursed the night. Now the police were being called!

Satisfied for now, the man shut the door and the front step was empty. I quickly relaxed. There was little hazard as long as I kept my movements soft and waited in the cool quiet. That was it, though. Other than being totally trapped, I was fine. I wanted to find a way out quickly, to rejoin my friends. With a slithery tender touch I undid the locks on both windows and tried to push, emitting a slight grunt on the second one. No escape. An old paint job had sealed them shut. I slouched morosely against the back wall and crossed my arms, blinking at the moonlit floor and noticing the feel of my lonely heartbeat. Finally I lifted my eyes across that unfamiliar dark garage.

By the faint light from the windows, I straightened off the wall and took my time stepping carefully over to the center post, where I ran my fingers to find with rapturous relief the electronic door buttons. After a minute, I figured which one went where and planned my escape. It was all on good timing, of which I had no way of knowing for sure. I had a fleeting thought of opening the garage to a couple men leaping on me from the kitchen door. Twice I had a hand on the button but couldn't punch it. It was such a fifty-fifty gamble. This was it. I covered the right button with my hand. My heartbeat was strong, healthy, punching. I blinked and took a deep breath, feeling the air through my lips. With a big inhalation I squinted my eyes and pressed.

The cacophony made by the garage door brought startled quivers to my skin. I dropped on all fours to the cement. The outside world looked beautiful and grand but the stupid door wasn't going fast enough. Bumping my head on the bottom edge, I scrambled under the enlarging space and pushed myself to an immediate run. Too scared to even glance at the kitchen door, I slid around the corner, snaked beside the Audi, and sprinted into the next yard, vaulting a group of azaleas with one mighty jump. Soon my sprint toned down to a jog and I aimed to where the others had fled. Never before had the nighttime looked so inviting and bright to me.

Needing a place to stay tonight, I went searching on instinct. I wanted to find Tara. I also wanted to jog along the street, a winding road called Woodland Avenue, but the idea of keeping a low profile appealed to me, particularly when a police car passed under the streetlight a hundred yards ahead on Kimball Avenue. The headlights moved closer around the bend, like two bright specters, sliding the stretched shadow of a thin pine tree along the yard in which I now hid. I wondered if the police were responding to a call from that prior house. No doubt most of my other activities had jammed the phone lines at the precinct tonight. This one would be suspicious. What was it that cop told Blake? A seven o'clock town curfew tonight?

I waited 'til the cop car passed, then headed for Kimball, hoping I hadn't taken a drastically wrong turn from the others. They had to be somewhere looking for me. On that idea, I wondered what that guy and his father had done when their loud garage door raised mysteriously from the inside.

I was about to find out.

I had just reached Topping Hill Turn when I spotted something at the bottom of the hill. Floating under the street lamp were two police bike patrols made famous by Principal Peterson that morning. True to form, their "flight path" seemed to indicate that they, too, were headed for the happenings over on Wychwood. Suddenly I was stumped. A dash to the right would only bring me back to the vicinity of Candy's house. I made a quick cut left through to Canterbury Lane, beginning to like the tactility of traversing unknown territory while remaining as elusive as the darkness itself. I watched between two houses as the bike patrols passed, complete with nightlights and helmets. All they needed were masks and black capes. I hopped over a back yard fence and came out into the open of Canterbury, instantly recognizing this tiny street as somewhere my mom took me to when I was little. I walked along, feeling tranquil. The lane was barely big enough for two passing cars. Living room windows in one home were no more than ten feet from the street. All in all, this place had the quaint appearance of a gift shop Snow Village.

I felt a smack against my shoulder and knew right away I'd been hit with something bad. Freaked, my hand went to the spot and came away wet and oozed with seeds. Tomato.

"Mischief Nighter! Get him! Get the intruder!"

A group of kids that numbered upwards of twelve cheered from the next yard. Dismayed by their blunt rotten deed, I wanted to roll ass, but unfortunately, the numbers didn't dictate a pretty outcome. So much for obscurity. I ran up the nearest driveway and found myself closed off by a garage and a tall wooden fence. I made a momentary stand, dipping under the car in front of me.

"No cuttin' *through!*" a high-voiced boy yelled wise-assly over to me.

"Yeah!" they all shouted. "Don't cut through!"

A chorus of roars arose, like two little league football lines colliding when the ball is snapped. Suddenly that wooden fence didn't look so high. I heaved up from the approaching rug-rats, leaping to the top of the fence and bending my body over. With deep regret, I admit that I was in this state when their barrage of ammunition found their targets. Tomatoes smashed against my thighs and butt as I swung a leg over. Before I fell to the other side, water from a hose doused me, sloshing my pants and socks. I gained my balance and clenched my fists in anger as water droplets continued to rain over the fence. A kid's face hung over to snoop at me. What else could I do? I flagged a pathetic middle finger at him and jogged away from the triumphant shouts.

Tired of the night as a whole, I decided to head for the Spencer's.

The journey back to Colonial Avenue was fine until I saw the Volvo. I'd kept to the shadows as the walk lulled down Kimball and past Wilson School again. It was second nature now to hide whenever any car headlights appeared like two freaky eyes. For the second time tonight I turned up North Chestnut, hurrying by familiar pumpkin pieces in the road.

Thank God Volvos have a distinct sound. My heart started pumping against my chest when I heard the motor. A dark chassis with yellowish headlights appeared at Kimball and made a right in my direction, almost as though they were tailing me. I couldn't tell from the distance if it was maroon or not, but I sprinted diagonally across to a driveway on Oak Avenue. Peering over a pickup truck, I watched, horrorstruck. Like a death camp patrol, that exact same maroon Volvo passed at an irregular speed as the passengers, no doubt, scanned the neighborhood. Even though the Volvo continued on, I cut through the yard. Little did I know I was about to meet my next and most chilling encounter.

It amazes me to this day that I didn't sniff out the little bugger prior. As cute as he might have been, one step more and he would have reduced me to an instant social reject for a week. I had made a successful endeavor through the first leg in a train of back yards when I nearly ran right into the path of a skunk, conveniently camouflaged near a long stretch of pachysandra. When I saw the striped bushy tail I hollered shortly like I'd touched a hot pan. Suddenly the tail extended to the sky in an eerie hush. I fluttered my hands to shield me and took off to the left as though blown that way by a cannon. Fearing the little son of a bitch would chase me, I vaulted over an old white picket fence into the dimness of the next yard.

Terrified of the skunk behind me, I neglected to see the outline of a particularly dark pool. My feet ran on nothingness before I came tumbling down to a nasty splash. The water came crashing into my face as I fell flat on the mesh covering. At first I felt a stab of panic, like I knew I'd just fallen into a deep hole and seriously jeopardized my neck. It was a stroke of luck that I hit the pool where I did. My landing spot was the wide part of the deep end and I slid along the mesh covering to a spread-eagled spray at the other edge. I grabbed immediately at the cement and pulled myself up to a yielding standing position, feeling the wetness soak into my hair and clothes. That did it. I stood on that damn deck and shook my arms free of cold water.

"What the hell is going on around here tonight?!!"

No one answered. I slobbered on, my tomato-stained pants succumbing to the chill of the water. My sneakers squished from the moistness as I glanced back for the skunk.

I climbed what I hoped to be my last fence and dropped into what I wanted to be the last back yard. I had no choice. Only private fenced-in property surrounded me. I glared up at the windows defiantly. Let them catch me, I thought. If anything they'll pity my God-awful appearance. Hell, at least I'll be safer and warmer in a dang jail cell. I was prepared to go. What I *wasn't* prepared for, however, was the sound of a chain dragging slack off the wooden porch.

I knew what I was in for right away. A meat-eating schnauzer was rapidly closing in on my space. The sound of those little patters on the leaves almost gave me a heart attack. For a second my body seemed to leave my head as I hauled mad-ass for the other side of fence. Before I knew it, the little maniacal hot-dog had me clinging to a tree limb. I swung my feet clear of its loud barking jaws and wished feverishly for Dustin's bat. I managed to kick my legs up around the branch, hanging like a ridiculous koala bear as the vicious schnauzer screamed and wailed directly beneath me, trying to alert half the stinking neighborhood that I was trespassing on its precious territory. Blowing wild pants, I looked up and found an escape. It took me a minute or so, but I grunted and groaned and clawed my way in a fierce crawl to another branch hanging over the next yard. At last I jumped down, putting the fence between me and the incessant howling. Feeling the rush of escape, I jogged a few steps and glanced back to the fence, almost jumping from what I saw. A human head was silhouetted against the previous yard's spotlight, looking straight at me.

I should have known when I heard the sirens over on Mountain Avenue. Wherever there were sirens, Blake Spencer was surely nearby. I had just crossed that busy street and slipped into the unknown of a tiny dirt road. When I came out on Standish Avenue, I felt my body wrench tightly. There was a small leaf fire in progress to my right, downwind of me. The worst looked to be over. Small flames laid flat for twenty feet against the pavement. A dark figure in motion, very faint against the orange glow and billowing smoke, was kicking at it to keep it from spreading. It was an older man who turned and froze when he saw me.

"No you don't, son!" he called, waving his arm to me. "Where are you off to? Come right back here!"

It was then that the siren sounded. The shrill blast of an air horn told me it was a fire truck. And for that second I was Joe Chiavetti. I was now the carbon copy of that guy two years before out on Prospect Street, dangling the proverbial stick, being restlessly pursued by others.

Despite the drag of my wet clothes, I started pumping my fists and legs like they were too fast for my body and zoomed away from the man. I decided to have fun with this one.

"You didn't see me!" I shouted.

I ran down Standish, away from the fire truck's intended path, and angled a sharp right to Birch Avenue. I had just started to round the bend when I was halted by more action.

A running Mercedes-Benz sat paused two houses down from the Dolan's. Tyler's Grand Am, however, was nowhere in sight. A door slam was audible to me in the clarity of the night air. Then I heard the rumble of the fire engine blocks over as it turned a corner. Talk about a rock and a hard place! I positioned myself behind a large needle bush and watched the Mercedes.

"I saw them run up these stairs," a man yelled, gesturing from the sidewalk.

"No, over there," a woman replied faintly from the car. "I think they went around the back."

"Little peckerheads," I heard him seethe.

"They're gone, Henry," the woman called out. "Let's just go."

The man, dressed like he'd just come from fine dining, trotted back down the steps, and with a last glance around the area, shook his head to his windshield.

"We'll get it off later," the woman said. "Just use wiper fluid for now."

The angry man sank into the driver seat and the engine hummed. After a slow searching pace, the Mercedes stopped at Standish, taillights reddening the area. Noticing the fire truck ahead of him now, the man turned his car to the scene.

Out in the open again, I trailed further up Birch, past Jenn Dolan's. Down the street, a dog with a large deep bark echoed a lonely call over the neighborhood. I jogged on, listening for cars, and very suddenly, I saw Tara.

She was standing out in the middle of the street like a gunfighter ready to draw, her white jeans glowing under the streetlight. I could see she was watching a particular gray house with black trim, like she was waiting for it to move. The sloshing of my wet sneakers heralded my arrival, and the Curb Owl saw me and gasped in a smile. Tara ran over and hugged me tightly. She whispered "Hi!" then backed away to give me the once-over, questions in her eyes. I greeted her and she put a finger to my lips.

Something was happening here. Two shapes were sneaking up to the front door of the house, where a streetlight threw a dancing tree shadow. Suddenly, from the shadow of that front doorstep:

BANG! CRACK!

One loud bonk, followed by another, with the telltale sound of scattering seeds. Two midnight shapes started sprinting savagely through the next few yards. Exhaustively, I trudged along in tow. Ahead at the corner of Colonial, Benton Crossey slowed to a walk and swung his big arms at his side. His baseball cap snapped on his belt buckle, he high-fived Blake casually. It appeared they had made quick friends. Tara giggled, tugging at a rip in my shirt.

"We tanked Blake's wine," she said. "I'm a little buzzed."

"A'!" Benton ceased his movement when he looked back. "What happened?!"

They all took sudden notice of my appearance as I passed under a street lamp.

"Well I'll be hog-tied to a fat chick!" cried Blake. "What happened to *you*?"

I looked around insultingly at their laughing. They were too drunk, too wired with adrenaline, to really care. Blake started showing me where two eggs had accidentally gotten crushed in his pockets. I skipped the tomato stains and seeds on my butt. I didn't need any more stories at school. Tara tried to apologize for what happened at the Kane's but her speech was a little sloppy. All three were tipsy and I looked at them with disdain. It occurred to me, as I listened to their ranting details of riffraff that none of them could help me now. Dayle, Lee, Joe and others were somewhere out on those streets hunting me. I was terrifically paranoid now and wanted home, *my* home! For crying out loud! I had to go to the police station tomorrow!

"Hey, Ashley," Tara said. "Cheer up! Watch this."

In her black leather jacket and fragile shirt, the little Curb Owl shook a can of Barbasol and literally white-walled a small red Mitsubishi, laughing like she did when I fell into the mucky swamp. The whole can was used up until the car was draped in white foam. There was something vaguely outlandish about a girl doing this type of stuff. Tara took an egg from Blake and threw it in that girlie way on the windshield. Her laughter was uncontrolled, like she couldn't believe what she was actually doing.

I started away, checking for any signs of cars and wondering what that old man was telling the firemen. The three followed me down the street. Baseball Benton now had a clod of "dip" under his lower lip, spitting tobacco saliva in sloppy amber gobs. He checked me from the side with a weird trace of caution, fixing his dip wad with his tongue, causing a funny hump in his lip.

"Ooo, Benton," Tara laughed playfully, "show off that bulge!"

Benton's shoulders hunched in a laugh.

"I been around," he said, "and I can tell you that dippin' is without a doubt the most anti-social habit there is. Kids are always gettin' grossed-out by it. I get it all the time." He tried grabbing my shoulder as he stumbled along. Funny how I wasn't scared of him anymore. "A'" he chortled loudly, "'member Mindowaskin Park? Them bum's all standin' around puttin' pot in their lungs and then sneerin' down their schnozzes at me for doin' *chew*?! It was a*ma*zing!"

Tara was noisily shaking orange Tic-Tacs out of the famous little container.

"I'll have one," Benton said, unsolicited. As a rule, no one really eats *one* Tic-Tac. Taking the little pack, he flipped open the lid and gulped several straight from the container with traces of dip on his lip. I wanted to giggle from the wash of revulsion that came to Tara's face.

"Ash," Blake was calling out sloppily behind me. "Ash! Wait. Watch this!" I heard him set his pack down, then grunt. Suddenly—

"Ow! *Shoot!*"

A metallic object clanked on the pavement. I turned around. Blake was squatting tightly on his knees, his head tilted down at his joined hands like he was praying hard.

"What'd you do, bro?" Benton asked into the sudden suspense. He leaned into him and spit sideways. "Aw, bro. You gotta get that wrapped."

Benton backed off and I saw a trail of blood seeping down Blake's fingers. A bent jackknife sat between his knees and the front tire of a Ford Taurus. Unbelievable. In his drunken vigor, he'd lanced his index finger trying to ice the tire. Blake got up, biting his lower lip and grimacing. He took his hand away and looked at the cut appendage, covering it quickly and sucking air through his teeth. Suddenly I was sorry for him. I took up his depleted backpack and then his jackknife, trying not to look for blood on it in front of him.

"Blake, run home," I said. "You might need stitches."

He took my advice quickly. His body twisting like a washing machine head, he ran a stunted pace around the bend, clutching his finger to his chest. Benton, Tara and I walked on sullenly. We had to be getting home, each of us.

We arrived at Blake's house a few minutes after he did and stood watching the windows, wondering if we should just beat it. I didn't want to go in at first. I knew Mrs. Spencer too well. But I needed a place to sleep! Jim's truck was in the driveway, so maybe she'd be too preoccupied to rail. The image of stitches and a bandage on Blake's finger prompted me to the front door where I rang the bell. Inside light spilled onto us and small Trip stood with a knowing smirk.

"Come on," he said in his mocking little tone. "I'll show you to the intensive care unit."

Tara and Benton followed me in. I looked into the den where Mrs. Spencer and Jim were sipping wine and conversing lightly, both checking us with suspecting eyes.

"He's upstairs," Mrs. Spencer called in an oddly slow tone. "Ashley, I want to speak to you later."

"Yes ma'am," I said.

The four of us made haste up the stairs to Blake's room. When Trip pushed open the door, I felt an astounded twitch in my face. Blake was on his double-bed watching TV with his finger bandaged and an ice pack on his head. An *ice pack*, for gosh sakes! A perfect illustration of his mom's melodramatic care. I guessed she and Jim had experienced a good night. Blake's face was still, his eyes directed at the TV. With all he'd done tonight, *he* was playing the poor wounded soul? Jeez. Staring at him looking like a hospitalized private on M.A.S.H., I couldn't hold it any longer. Sudden howling laughter pushed from my lungs and I fell face-forward on Blake's bed in hysterics. When I lifted my head, everyone in the room was laughing except Blake. He fixed the ice pack on his forehead and spoke softly.

"I can't have anyone sleep over tonight."

My stomach stopped convulsing in elation. The room quieted, my breathing the only sound.

"What?"

Blake brought his ice pack from his forehead.

"My mom's not letting me have anyone sleep over," he repeated. "I'm in trouble for the cut. I had to make up a reason for the knife, and I think it was worse than the truth. But the hardest thing was explaining to her why I had crushed eggs in my pockets."

I just stared at him in confounded anger.

"Sorry, Ash." Blake looked dully at me, then pushed that ice pack over his eyes. "I'm grounded tomorrow night, too." His lips twisted stupidly. "Grounded for Halloween!"

I stood off the bed. "What the hell am I supposed to do *now*, nerd?!"

Benton's family was something to behold! All were Bentons. Thirteen-year-old Bentons, fat Bentons, old Bentons, female Bentons. Everyone looked like Benton.

The Crossey household, plain by the artistic sign over the back door, was virtually one street over from Tara's and right on the edge of town. The house was tall, like the Vovens's, but a lot less kept up. The interior smelled like something—something that wasn't quite living anymore.

Benton and I had done the chivalrous thing and walked Tara home. I'd had mixed emotions when I hustled away from her back door. Her alluring intense-featured face had looked worried. Glancing back I saw her turn a sad pensive expression to the door as she opened it slowly.

Benton's mother was sitting on the couch when we came marching onto the bare wood floors of the small quarters. Little brother Corey sat in the adjacent armchair. An old man in a hooded sweatshirt looked crimped in and comfortable on the couch next to Mrs. Crossey.

Baseball Benton's mom had short black hair plastered to her head and was dangling a lit cigarette from her lips, the way Tyler was doing lately. I wondered how people never choked or coughed from the smoke trailing up into their nostrils. Right in front of me, the woman sat in a bathrobe and kept sawing at the soles of her feet with what looked like a giant nail file. Benton appeared huge in the room as he backed away and flew a hand at her.

"Ma, why are you doin' that now? I got a guest. Come on."

"I'm gettin' the calluses off, ya big pain," the lady said in a smoke-husky tone. "Big deal. Your friend can handle it." There was a toughness in her, like an aging burnout. In my mind I was cursing Blake for this.

"Hi, I'm Benton's mom." She twisted her free hand over. I took it reluctantly. Baseball Benton shook his head remorsefully at me.

"Does this every night," he groaned, rolling his eyes and waving an arm, "and there's like, a big pile of sawdust on the floor. She leaves her feet everywhere." He turned to her. "Ma, I could swear it's makin' you shorter and shorter every day."

A fat bumbling ball of yellow fur was coming sluggishly down the stairs. My lips quirked once as it scraped its nails loudly on the flooring and dashed toward me. I tried to look pleased and politely interested until the furry dog rammed its wet snout right into my crotch. I must have pushed and fought this blubbering mutt for half a minute, its nails tapping on the wood like Morse code. It couldn't decide which side it wanted to explore more.

"Uh, Benton?" I finally managed. "You uh, wanna call your—"

"SISSY!!" he yelled, freaking me to shivers. "GET AWAY FROM HIM!! *BAD* GIRL!!"

They were the sharpest consonants I'd ever heard him use.

Mrs. Crossey left her perch on the couch and hustled over with eyes ablaze and her file raised.

"GET OVER HERE YOU STUPID ANIMAL!!" she literally screamed.

Gritting her teeth, the woman reached out and grabbed the dog's collar, yanking fiercely. The dog audibly lashed its tongue. Benton's mom dragged the cowering blob back upstairs where I heard a door slam.

As shocked and grossed-out as I was thus far, I was hungry as I watched beefed-up Benton dump a container of chilled curly pasta into a frying pan and coat it with thick red sauce. The sizzles made my mouth water. Benton stirred with his face close to the pan, smelling the aroma. After a testing with his wooden spoon, he waved me over with his mouth full and gestured to a drawer. I opened it and grabbed two forks. Soon I was having a late dinner in not so different a manner than their dog. Benton and I stood and lifted forkful after forkful of some pretty amazing stuff right from the pan as it cooked. I kind of envied how he could come up with a meal like that so quickly.

The TV was on to *The Tonight Show*, where a fat man was performing a ghastly and brutally obscene trick with his jelly gut. The old man on the couch, though, sat staring at me. I waved. He still stared.

Benton rose and leaned to the refrigerator. Still chewing, he grabbed two beers and parked them on top of the stove. I laughed through cheeks puffed full of pasta and shook my head.

"Don't want one?" he mumbled. Baseball shrugged and cracked one for himself. Corey (Benton Lite) watched from the couch while his older brother swigged beer.

"Yo, Bense," he called. "I'll have it."

Benton tilted his head back. "You won't, lowlife." As he said that, I suddenly saw him punching Joey Apel's lights out in Corey's name. I don't know why I did. The vision just simply appeared.

Mrs. Crossey came back down and lounged again on the big sofa, scratching the side of her head harshly. In front of her, Benton casually brought the beer to his mouth and tapped me. Already buzzed from Candy's party and part of the Huelett's bottle of White Zin, he snagged the other beer can and led me out the back door to a pair of steps.

Out in the coolness, Benton sat on the top step as I stood and listened to him talk about Candy's party and fake kids at school. Then he got stuck on the ending to my fight with Domino.

"Ripped the shit out of his underwear, bro," he kept saying.

He stopped jawing enough to down both beers in less than four slugs. After he chugged his last, he dropped his head, swallowing and staring at me with fixed eyes as though waiting for approval. It was late now, past eleven on an unforgettably long night, and the air was still and crisp. I huddled my arms to my chest and could feel the crustiness of the smashed tomatoes.

The storm door opened above us, and Benton's bathrobe-clad mother stuck her head out. "You best not be drinkin' beers out on those steps," she said. "Someone's gonna see you and report it. You wanna get me in trouble?"

Benton tilted his head back up to her and squinted. "Ma, who pays most of the bills around here?"

"Benton—"

"Ma, just go back inside. No one's seein' anything."

Mrs. Crossey made a grunt and shut the door. Benton then leaned to reach inside his pocket and slid out of it a small round container, peeling it open to reveal what looked like jet-black dirt. He pinched a wad and pulled out his lower lip, stuffing moist tobacco in front of his gums, then mashed his mouth, squeezing the dip in place. He bent forward and a dark drivel fell from his mouth, splattering with an appreciable thud on the rocks.

"This stuff greases me up *so* good after a few beers," he said, rolling his head.

I kept my hands in my pockets and gazed over at the train station, thinking about Tara.

"Your dad pretty cool?" Baseball Benton asked out of the blue.

"Huh?"

He spit again. "You and your dad get along?"

I shrugged. "Mostly. Why?"

"Just wondering." He swayed his head at me. "*My* dad died when I was eleven."

"He did?"

"Five years ago," he mumbled over the swell in his lip. I figured he needed someone to talk to, so I watched him closely. Benton's eyelids hung a bit low now. "I held my dad like this,"—he cradled his arms—"just like this in his hospital bed until I could feel his last breath of air." He nodded, his eyes thinned out in slits, giving a mature appearance. "I've lived, bro."

At this I knew right away why he was the way he was. He was the man of the house, the ruler of his own authority, taking care of his mom, his little brother, now me. The inalienable Protector for the cause of right. Maybe that's why he was such a great athlete.

I sighed, weighed down in the drama of reality.

"Bro, what's wrong?" Benton inquired.

"Just this whole week," I returned tiredly, flopping an arm at my side.

Benton suddenly took his head back and kind of glared at me. "What are you so worried about, bro? You got everything! Look at me." He brought a hand up and gestured to the door. "Look at this house."

I hated the biting sound of his tone, and of his truth, both of which my life had given me no prior preparation in dealing with. Instead of backing away, though, I sat next to his colossal frame in a slump, watching the step. I still felt his face turned my way.

"You got *every*thing," he repeated through his bulging lip, hammering away his incredulity. "Bro, I held my dad when he *died*." There was a marked break in his voice and I looked up, amazed to see a gleam of tears beginning to build on his lower eyelids. "You know what that's like?! You even imagine holding your dyin' father in your arms like that?!"

I thought of my father; proud, strong, smart, so neatly attired, his light beard always groomed perfectly. My head shook slightly, "No." Benton blinked and looked ahead, so I added softly for good measure, "I can't."

He suddenly appeared to me as a small boy, the need to be heard making him helpless in his fight to save face. Here was this soundly and thickly built athlete succumbing to tears right in front of me, and we hardly knew each other that long. Without notice, I did something I could never have fathomed that one Sunday evening in the park. I put an arm around his big shoulders and patted. For a few seconds we sat like that and stared out at this strange neighborhood of night, two lost kids in the crazy opposite confusion of our teenaged lives.

After a few minutes, Benton jabbed fingers under his lip and raked until his nauseating clump of dip plopped out. Out on the step it looked like a little turd.

I was set up in the sloppy conditions of the Crossey's living room with a dirty pillow and an old stiff nylon comforter. I relaxed and asked Benton to tell me a little bit more about his dad before he headed upstairs. After he finished and left, I thought about him in that hospital room at eleven, about a pain of which I couldn't even begin to imagine. In that respect, I refused to mind my situation.

That is, until I found a porno flick and a half-eaten wrinkled hot dog just underneath me. It wasn't my intent to look, but when I reached up for the lamplight switch, the cushion folded in a manner that exposed something between the crack. When I peeled away more of the weak cushion, I froze, a gap-jawed horrified expression plastering my face. I got up in the quiet of the downstairs and went to the kitchen. I guess I could have slept over *Sheepless In Montana,* but not that aged hot dog and its crusty bun, for which I rolled three paper towels to handle. I squeezed it off the bottom of the couch as though handling a dead squirrel and dumped it into the smelly kitchen trash.

Returning to the viral sofa, I lay carefully down again and cringed with the awful realization that I was going to sleep right over where Benton's mom had been sawing at her feet. Checking warily for callus dust on the floor, I pulled the musty comforter fearfully over my head.

If that wasn't enough, hard nails came clacking down the stairs. I flapped the covers off my head. That old, gross, vomit-colored dog bounded onto the hard floor. I tried not to move. If I don't move, I thought, maybe she won't see me. Too late. The dog circled by and stared me right in the face, pointblank. For a second it was a stare-off—me and paunchy Sissy. Her tongue lapped at her nose. Suddenly she tried to get on the couch with me and I sprang into action, kicking my legs. The dog backed off, lapping her nose again and staring her two brown eyes at me. A hand went to my brow as a sigh closed my eyes. God, *why* did I have to write that article? Suddenly the brown/gold mop walked by and farted at me in passing, like she was trying to mark her territory. It wasn't audible or anything; it just absolutely stunk. I covered my nose with the blanket until Sissy clogged her fat gaseous belly back up the stairs.

I let my nose free when I thought it safe enough and stretched to shut off the light. Suddenly something was crawling on me. A huge insect of some sort was inching its way up my calf. I froze to feel if it wasn't my imagination. At first I thought it was part of the scratchy comforter, but then this small itch began to have a soft pattern and when I realized what it was I flipped, throwing off the comforter and slapping furiously. Whatever it was had mysteriously disappeared. I took everything off the sofa until I was sure the bug had gotten the message.

Reassembling everything, I plunged down into the softness, and by the grace of God, finally fell into a narcoleptic-like deep sleep.

9

"Disgusting slobs!"

I awoke in the morning to Mrs. Crossey saying this over and over again while banging pots in the kitchen sink. I didn't know what time it was, but I was awake in a shot. I almost wanted to do something like get up and help the lady, but chose wisely to stay safe under the blanket. In a moment, the woman came out of the kitchen and stood in the living room. I heard the scratch of a lighter, then a cigarette being puffed, this early in the morning. My body was a stiff block of tissue as I kept my face toward the backrest of the couch. I could swear she was standing there watching me. She finally walked past the couch and headed upstairs. I sneaked out before she came back down.

I went out to a gloriously clear and sunny morning, making my way across town. Despite an initial nip in the air, I could tell it would be very comfortably mild all day, and more importantly, a beautiful night. Though my muscles ached from so much running around hours before in the darkness, my deep sleep had refreshed my mind. Memories of Mischief Night invigorated me like a humming wire. I could take anything now.

Confident that I was one of the first kids in town up at this hour, I decided to chance walking by my house. I hadn't even seen it since Thursday night and felt a touch of homesickness. I passed by yards littered with toilet paper and an occasional smashed pumpkin in the road. My friends and I certainly hadn't been the only group out and involved last night. For that matter, what would half of Westfield think this morning? Pumpkins amiss, cars soaked in shaving cream, eggs splattered on windows, other various acts of minor mayhem marring the streets; it all seemed to add a decoration of clean fun, and my usual guilty conscience remained silent.

I passed Roosevelt School and saw my house for what felt like the first time in weeks. It appeared normal, but barren—a hollow shell of past warfare. The absence of my family removed any sense of life from the house. When I cruised up to the door, I saw the broken windows had been replaced with gleaming new ones.

Something in front of the door caught my eye. Advancing closer, I spied, of all things, a vase sitting on the top step. In it was placed a headless rose stem. The flower had simply been cut off. I almost laughed at the overexerted creativity. I had to admire their tenacity, however goofy it was all starting to seem to me. I did wonder how they'd slipped this behind an all-night guard.

The smell of sun burning dew off the grass lifted humidity to my nose as I jogged down Dudley Avenue, crossed Mountain, and cut over to Topping Hill Road to see the Kane's house. I had a notion of apologizing to Candy and her mammoth brother John, and especially to Mrs. Kane, though I feared it was too early to ring the doorbell. When I got there I just stood on their dewy lawn sprinkled with early sunlight. My body stiffened, transfixed by the view. The morning light shed an awful reality on two sharp holes cut into the aluminum siding, just under the window where I had been stashed. This *had* happened. This indeed *was* my life. My mere presence had created damage to someone else's property, and I had fled; escaped like a coward. What had my friends thought? Did they understand? Or were they shaking condemning fingers against me for desertion?

"I'm really sorry, Mrs. Kane," I wanted to say. "I'll figure a way to get your siding fixed. I'll find a way." I wished for the guts to go up to that door then, but I left without a word.

I headed back to town, figuring that the annual Halloween parade would be in its preparation stages and I could find my mom and dad somewhere in the midst of the side fair. There would definitely be some good grub around them, the promise of bagels and doughnuts.

People were lugging pumpkins in every direction when I got to the center of town. I checked my reflection in a store window, happy to discover that I didn't have a horrid bed-head. Strolling by flashy Halloween sidewalk displays, I enjoyed being among people again. Aside from choosy pumpkin buyers, almost everyone here was helping to set up. The smell of burnt coffee corroded my nostrils, robbing them of the pleasant memorial smell of a humid fall dawn.

I found my father near the hay-strewn pumpkin lot. He was wearing a New York Jets cap, leaning over a folding table and handing change to a lady with a cane and a head of huge red hair. Next to him, two kids were invading the haunted house hut that he and two others had put together. *Monster Mash* filled the air from a radio situated on the roof of the spooky little mansion. I giggled from the corny melody. *"I was working in the lab, late one night..."* I walked closer to the laminated sign hanging off the edge of the table. A skeleton pointed a finger: "Hey you!" it read. "Please do not pick up pumpkins by stem— or else! If you break it, you bought it!" Quite frankly, I found myself looking at pumpkins very differently this morning.

My father greeted me with a grin when he turned and saw me. "Happy Halloween, kiddo. You're in one piece. That's good." He shuffled briskly around the table and offered a shake. "How was your night? Stay outta trouble? Trouble stay outta you?"

I shook his hand and felt the scratchiness of his fingers, chapped from hay and pumpkin stems. Then I jerked a thumb at the bagel joint. "Dad, can I get something to eat?"

He nodded with a wry grin and wiped his forehead with the cleanest finger he could find. I paused and asked how it was going.

"Well, you seem to be the big news around here," he told me. "I've had a dozen people ask about you." He smelled like hay. At Christmas he volunteered to run the tree lot and came home smelling like Christmas trees. I went to help him last December and quickly learned how heavy Christmas trees were. Every night I'd come home from that lot, dog-tired, pull my clothes off for a bath, and smell nothing but pine.

"No, I meant, how's it going with the fair?"

My dad smiled again and shrugged. "Just started now." I don't know if it was the rush of the Halloween festive spirit or the buzz about my story and newfound status that excited him, but my father was unquestionably drunk with endorphins. My parents dedicate weeks of help each year to help coordinate the parade and fair. They always seemed to rediscover their creative youth in planning the event.

My father walked me through the little hay maze, which ended back in the pumpkin lot. Even as I followed him in this magical kiddie playland, I snickered, remembering how he clobbered Joe Chiavetti. I squinted through early sun glare as he sifted through small pumpkins, rolling a few rotted ones off hay bales. A twisting grimace came to his face as he lifted a large pumpkin covered with fuzzy spots. Juice and seeds suddenly poured out of a hole on the bottom and slopped between my dad's boots. He held the wrinkled disfigured squash like a severed head and watched until the dead pumpkin vomited all its entrails to the hay flooring. My dad checked me from the side and was about to smile when the stench hit him hard. His eyes squeezed shut as though pain burned them.

"Awhh!" he gasped. "Something *horrible* crawled into this guy and did a *dance!*"

He started carefully around the back booth, balancing the smelly muddle with outstretched arms. I peered around the corner and watched him push-dump it onto a pile with a squish. Behind the booth my father stood amongst flies swarming over a small mound of orange rot.

"Dad," I said, hanging on the edge, "believe this, you've never looked so impressive to me."

"Hey," a familiar voice called out behind me. I turned around to see my mom in a black sweatshirt with a smiling pumpkin designed in sequin on the front. "A friend of mine suggested you can always move to another state and change your name."

Above her, the radio in the fun house now played *Thriller*. It was becoming apparent to me that, like Christmas, Halloween was developing its own musical themes. Mom stepped over a box of miniature pumpkins and kissed my cheek. She backed away and her tropical ocean eyes squinted at me as though detecting something sinister.

"What did you and Blake do last night?"

"We went out."

Her shoulders dropped and her eyes pleaded with mine. "Ash—"

Dad stepped forward onto the hay.

"Ginny, he's all right," he said easily. "He can't be closed from all walks of life."

Mom walked a few steps away, then came back with a sigh.

"I can't keep you from doing the things you're going to do," she said, "obviously. But—" She paused. "Do I really have to tell you?"

I nodded, picking at the crusty tomato spots on my jeans. "I'll be careful."

Mom backed away, keeping that watchful skeptical stare. To my surprise she made mention of mischief in Blake's neighborhood.

"I'm beginning to hear tell of various acts," she said. "Leaf fires, smashed pumpkins, eggs." She crossed her arms and very nearly broke a smile. "Did you see anything peculiar last night?"

"Yeah," I said. "Now that you mention it. Last night on TV this guy came out and did an incredible routine where he rolled this jelly bean up and down his stomach."

As if to save me, a lady approached the table with three pumpkins. Mom zipped over to handle the sale. "Confession's at ten over at Holy Trinity, you know," she called over. My father's laugh was quick. Mom handed the lady change and turned to me seriously. "You're going."

I scanned the hay at my feet. "All right, whatever." In this fine and holy instance, it was useless to argue. "I'll go if I can bum money off you for food."

A minute later, Mom finally brought up the subject. "There's been some more fallout from your article," she said, ruffling the side of her blonde hair with her fingers. "You know the police still want to speak to you."

I nodded.

She glanced at my father. "If you're going, we're going with you."

I figured my father was choosing to avoid the water until the sediment had been swirled. He took a light hold of my arm and sat me down on a hay bale warmed by the morning sun.

"If you're going to do this," he told me, squatting next to me. "Just remember. You're only sixteen. They can't make you do anything. You're a kid. You have rights." He set his eyes to the bagel joint across the sidewalk. "This has been enough trouble, and as your father,"—he stared at me and raised a finger—"I'm not even going to ask. I'm telling you. Don't give names."

"I'm not." I looked at him, waiting for the surprise. He just kept that same straight face and concentrated on my eyes.

"We went along with this at first, but—"

"Dad, I'm not going to do anything anymore. Trust me. It's over."

He blinked resignedly. "Well, good. But even if this thing ever got out of control to a point where it went to court, you can just plead the First. Which means you're protected by free speech."

I laughed at him now. "Jeez, Dad. This'll never get *that* far. Look, I'm just going to walk in—I don't know what they want."

I remember how he studied me through his glasses, his face now devoid of that fun-loving cheer so evident minutes before. "You never know, son."

After a banana, orange juice, and a blueberry bagel, I waltzed under the train bridge and over to Holy Trinity Church. I read the sign in front and figured I was a bit early for ten o'clock confession. I never realized how slow a morning was, how long a day could be just from being outdoors since sunrise. I pulled on the handle to the big door, happy to discover it open. Inside, I tapped the holy water and sat in a pew far from anyone else. One lady kneeled forward in a shawl, clutching rosary beads in her folded hands, pressing them to her forehead and squeezing her eyes like she was constipated. When an elderly man in a wool coat burped loudly, no one took notice but me.

The confessional offered two doors to enter when the time came for me to give my recent God-awful testimony. A placard on one door read: *Face-to-Face*, while the other read *Screen*. I paused for a second between both points of entry. The whole idea of confession seemed silly if I hid myself. The point was, I reasoned, to *face* my sins.

I felt a small laugh push from my lips as I entered the tiny closet-spaced room. There sat the young bald priest, whom I'd seen on Thursday. He waved his hand politely, and in this room, his smile seemed soft and unusually silent. Brown carpet hung on every wall to absorb sound. On a small coffee table was a plastic card with what looked like a short play in black and red letters. I realized I had to start, yet for some sudden reason, had no recollection how to do so.

"Hello."

"Hello," he returned affably.

His eyes were bold green, a vivid shine not unlike those of my mother. The countenance I beheld was unsettling and friendly at the same time, like I couldn't tell if he was mocking or about to smile. I shifted, glanced at the table, then back at him. His hand lifted.

"Is there uh—anything you'd like to tell me?"

"Huh?"

"Well, this is confession. You've walked into the fire, young man. I'm afraid I get to hear your dirty deeds. If you'd like to brief me on them now, I'm willing to listen. You've made the brave jump so far."

I sat forward and twisted for comfort, clearing my throat. "Um, well actually, I'm here more out of my mother's urging."

He tried to keep his grin down. "That's okay."

We read the first few lines on the card and got right down to it.

"Well," I started, "last night was what you might call a kid's holiday, and I took certain liberties with people's pumpkins and sides of their houses—why I'm here of course."

"Of course."

I chuckled at his expression, then changed mine. "Actually Father, I really do need to know something." I stopped to glimpse at how the soft yellow overhead light shined on his bald scalp, then blinked to the table again. "Matthew 7:1 says that we shouldn't judge others." I caught his nod and went on. "How do you make things better without judging others? See, I recently reported to the public a drug ring in town involving kids at school. And the whole—"

"That was you?" His notice shocked me, took me off myself for a moment. I watched the carpet around my feet and nodded. Finally I raised my head and studied him.

"Father, did I do it the right way? I mean, was I wrong to judge other kids?"

The young priest's face was serious enough for my liking. "I'm glad you came to me," he said. "No, you weren't wrong. It's a pleasure to meet you, by the way." He offered a shake and I gave it. Then he folded his hands over his knees. "I don't really think the passage in Matthew relates to this idea, at least so much as how you're perceiving it." He took a hand from his knee and twirled it in an explanatory fashion. "That bases judgment more along the lines of shaming others before God. In other words, we cannot say who's going to receive God's salvation and who's not, especially when we all fall short of His grace. Your article, conversely, did not pass on the worthiness of someone's character. I suspect that a concern for the safety of others motivated you in writing the article."

"Hmm." I thought of Tyler.

"Indeed your actions are consistent with the efforts of the Church, which views drugs and under-aged drinking as divisive acts that prevent an individual from growing physically, intellectually, and spiritually. I've often told my youth group that, as for our schools, I consider those activities viral in that they're beginning to spread through the grades. Of course, peer pressure, for lack of a better term. Given the high currency such actions enjoy, the church, in part, emphasizes information, including the effects and consequences tied to drinking and drug use. Your story has not only caused a crack-down on one sales point, but, more importantly, it has focused for teens, in a voice they understand and respect, the inherent dangers of drugs. Dozens or even hundreds of kids in the future will benefit from your single act. That's how you should view it." He tapped the table. "That's how I view it."

I stared at his knuckles on that table and fought with a smile. The young priest leaned back.

"As for your actions last night," he said whimsically, "I'm sure you'll grow out of it. But the fact that you're here is a good sign, a good indication that you don't wish to—repeat that type of activity." He winked, not knowing I was still draped in the night's dreadful clothing. "So your penance is to say three *Our Fathers.*" He leaned forward and made sure I noticed his grin. "And be good tonight."

I blinked and bowed my head as he blessed me. Once more he thanked me for coming. I felt a need to ask him to pray for my family, but instead, I just left and headed to the front of church. I think he sensed it anyway. I decided I'd ask God myself.

Ghostbusters was blaring from the speakers on my return to the town fair, another song rapidly becoming a Halloween carol. The parade was in full vigor, each age group marching along the East Broad Street blocks of town, coloring the area in a sea of individual design. Numerous princesses, a big Hershey bar, a walking lamp, pumpkins, cows, robots, miniature celebrities, kitchen appliances, and football players whose bodies could hardly support their giant helmets paraded past the stores. A boy in fourth grade, dressed as a witch, won Most Humorous for his age group. A blonde girl, squirming about with great difficulty in a serpent costume, was awarded with some medal for her efforts just to move. The festivities lasted about an hour, with the fair to continue on through to mid-afternoon.

Blake Spencer got up at what he refers to as the "crack of noon" and found me at the haunted house hut. He came riding up behind me on his silvery dirt bike and slid his back wheel into me. His thumb was bandaged and the sight of his conniving smile shook me slightly out of my blissfully sanctified state of pristine glory. In his other hand dangled my uncle's Bill Clinton mask.

"I'm the only one who knows how to keep up with you lately," he said, handing over the rubber face. I remembered ripping it off during the fight with Domino Hackett. I took the mask with thanks and handed it to my father.

"Rough night, Blake?" my father observed, indicating the thumb.

Blake recoiled in his little smile, searching my face for a helpful answer. Maybe he thought I told. I almost lied to my father for him, but refrained on the grounds of where I'd just been.

Clean-cut Andy Gibb set his bike on its kickstand and said softly, "Sorry about last night. I was kinda noodled." He stared off toward a Halloween wreath display. His mind was working on something deep. I found out quickly when he rolled his eyes and huffed.

"Jim slept over last night," he said. "Dork. Truck was out front the whole night. No shame."

I folded my arms and looked at him. "So where's your ice pack?"

"Shut up."

I laughed lightly. "Talk to your mom about going out tonight?"

His lips curled wryly and he nodded.

I felt more laughter in my chest. "No use?"

"Like selling snow tires in the Bahamas."

Tyler appeared minutes later. I told him about John Kane's house and how I'd seen the outside this morning. I could tell Tyler's attitude toward me had changed. He was no longer that elusive angry brother with that distant betrayed hurt. I could feel his growing pride in my endeavor. Standing next to both him and Blake, observing all the animation of grinning jack-o'-lanterns, skeletons, ghosts, and witches in windows, I felt warm and relaxed in the sun, enjoying the calming company. Oddly, for the first time in years, I felt part of this holiday again. All the ghost stories I used to listen to, all the spooky songs I used to sing in grade school, the costume parties that the PTA mothers would throw. Everything here enveloped me in that hay-scented, crescent-moonlit, cornstalk country feeling of Halloween.

Tyler was standing on a mailbox and holding onto a telephone pole to watch everything when he told me out of the blue, "Ashley, it would be a good idea if you didn't go out again tonight."

I put a hand to my eyes and squinted up at him. He wasn't even looking at me. The noise around us was drowning enough for this kind of talk.

"Be careful," he still said. "I heard a rumor. I was at Brennan's gig last night and some kids were talking about what happened to John Kane's house." He looked down at me. "They heard Dayle and some other guys are threatening to hunt you again on the streets all night."

I watched a cowboy bending down to give out handfuls of candy corn to a group of kids. My thoughts sank deeply into the vision of Dayle and Lee looking up at the windows last night. Blake was tilting his head to watch Tyler.

"Don't worry," he vowed waggishly in the sunlight. "I'm sneakin' out tonight. *I'll* watch him." He fixed a tough homeboy slouch. "Any d'ose honkeys show up, I'ma just deliver an east-side ho-slap!" He raised a flat palm. "Startin' all the way up in Maine and coming right across to Cali*for*nia, baby!"

A laugh sounded from on high. "Exactly what I'm afraid of." Tyler jumped down and looked me in the eye, the most mature stare I'd seen from him in weeks. "Dude, I'll be at Jenn's tonight. She's havin' a few people over her house. Just hang with us tonight. No one there's mad at you or anything. You'll know most of 'em. They're cool people."

I grinned at the sidewalk. "Could be. If Blake can get out, maybe we'll head over after a bit."

"Jeez," Blake mumbled, elbowing me lightly, "you're more tolerant than I thought."

"Oh, Blake meboy mebucko," I spoke with an Irish brogue. "I'm afraid you misperceive me, thar."

He smiled, but didn't understand. The thing was, I now held a funny addictive urge to be out in the neighborhood tonight. Oddly, it almost felt like a call to return to innocence. Something about the night, I felt, would remove all the interference from my life and permit me to move on. Tied to the Night itself as well was a memory of when I was six. Blake and I had once trick-or-treated Colonial Avenue in August because we couldn't wait for Halloween. We simply donned capes and masks and walked out in broad daylight. Ladies laughed but gave us ice cream sandwiches and Fla-vor Ices.

Just before my family and I walked over to the precinct at noon, my father handed me a letter with my name written in script. At first I thought it was just another threat. Dad said someone had delivered it in secret while I was at church. Uneasy about talking to the police, I was happy to find a way to deter my thoughts. I turned, ripped open the envelope, and felt a softness growing in my chest as I read.

Ashley,

Couldn't sleep so I thought I'd ramble. You seemed kind of mad when you and Benton left my house. I'm sorry. I guess you were right. I forget myself when I drink. I don't want you to be mad at me, though. We should have tried harder to find you, I know, but we really had no clue where you were. And I swear on my life, I had no idea those guys were following me. I know it's been a cruddy week for you and that certainly didn't help. I don't blame you if you're mad. But you sure do make me laugh lately! I'm just so confused. I've sent so many signals to you but I guess you either don't get them, or do, and just don't want anything with me. Yeah, this is corny, but I don't know any other way to say it. This has been weird for me because you're definitely different from any guy I've hung out with before, that's for sure! But I have more fun with you than anyone. I love the stands you take, and the risks you take (even though you always wind up in trouble). I still laugh when I think of you in the swamp, but I haven't told anyone. Someday you have to let me spill the beans to somebody.

Love,

Tara (the Curb Owl)

Blake came with my family and I to the precinct out of his curious hatred for authority. He seemed to revel in the drama of it all, keeping our ears occupied with anecdotes as we rounded Mindowaskin Pond. My father and mother were like two moving temples of turmoil, yet telling *me* not to worry. Oddly, I was relaxed, almost euphoric. I had the good protective fortune of age, had the blessing of the church, and had just finished heart-beating words from Tara.

Mr. Kellogg was sitting on a wooden bench inside when my dad pulled open the police station doors for me. I took command, strutting toward him.

"They called you in, too?" I said, shaking his hand.

Mr. Kellogg shook his head and his dark eyes seemed uneasy.

"Actually, no," he replied, gesturing behind me. "I've been in touch with your dad." He offered a nervous smile to my parents and extended his hand. "And how are you doing? Had enough craziness?"

They shook hands. My father then grinned once to the floor and slid both of his hands in his back pockets, rocking on his heels.

"Well," he said rather pleasantly, "it's been a ride. I wouldn't wish it on my worst enemy, that's for sure."

The two of them laughed loudly in the hall. I looked around at all of us. Blake and my family appeared new and different to me, out of place; none of us belonged to the atmosphere.

The same black man from Thursday appeared from a door in the corridor wearing another fantastic dark suit and tie.

"Ashley Munroe," he chirped.

I stepped forward and the man put out his hand. Another big handshake, another big smile, but there was something more behind these gestures.

"Detective Spera again. I appreciate your coming. How've you been?" He chuckled warmly. "Rough couple of nights, huh?"

Mr. Spera had a carefully trimmed mustache and seemed businesslike in his brisk approach. The crack of a smile formed across his cheeks as he greeted my parents in repeat fashion. When he leaned in to shake everyone's hand I could smell his after-shave, like peppermint and fruit.

"I tell you what," he said. "Since there's a lot of us, why don't we just move into this room since it's bigger?" He indicated a door to his right, sweeping his hand rashly. "We have a nice new carpet in here." He stopped and tapped his forehead with a set of fingers, crinkling his mouth in a show of unease. Suddenly I liked him. He smirked at me. "I don't know why I said that. Just come on in."

When I stepped into the hollow room and saw wooden seats around a long glossy table, and beheld the town seal on the wall, the ambiance took on a sudden serious air. Even Blake had shut up.

I noticed a funny skeptical alert in my mother's face.

"Is he in trouble?" she asked the man. "We—because we have our own attorney in town."

Mr. Spera put one hand on the table and raised the other. "Don't worry, ma'am," he reassured, shaking his head. "I know it looks to you like some big deal, but it's all right. We're not here to put your son in any harm or anything."

He pulled out the chair at the head of the table, his dark jacket taut from his bulky muscles. Even though he was okay to me, I wished for laughter's sake that seams would rip audibly at the armpits when he bent over to sit down.

Six of us took seats while Detective Spera introduced himself again in his boldly loud tone, told us what he dealt with in his job, and repeated that he had no intention of taking any action against me. He actually lauded the article, and gave us more detailed historical information about the local drug scene. I sat still and listened, remembering my Dad warning me on the walk over to let the police do all the talking. Mr. Spera tapped his fingertips together and sat at ease. His tone was like that of a confident salesman, who knew for all he was worth that his product was the best and his word was law.

"Now, as I said," he told us in his heavy bark, "I will not force Ashley to say anything he does not want to say. But Ashley may have information that I lack, and his actions on this knowledge have opened up a heated situation, one that has had a rippling effect on different aspects of the town. We've gotten calls from newspapers, a cable news channel, and,"—he indicated my mother—"and I understand your brother is Joe Browne?" My mother's nod struck me as peculiar, like she was dazed and wary at the same time. "Well, I'm pretty friendly with Councilman Joe. And we spoke yesterday"—he smiled boyishly at us through a lowered face—"about rumors of town realtors who have concerns that publicity like this could affect both real estate values and sales. While I don't exactly agree with that, I'm just hoping that Ashley might be comfortable giving me a bit more information about the activities in the park so I can start putting this to rest. Anything he says will be strictly confidential."

He checked his clipboard in front of him and straightened. Then he sat back, his eyes raking the ceiling. One hand flopped lazily to accentuate each point. "On the other hand, I know that a number of kids have already threatened you and damaged your house. Implicit in all of this, I'm sure, is that Ashley will suffer worse consequences if anything happens to some of these kids. So we're stuck on a tight rope here, all of us."

"Not necessarily," I said from my raised palm, already forgetting my dad's advice. Silence grew weighty by the second. Mr. Spera's eyes were white in his face, glancing over those around the table and then back at me. At least he was looking to me. I was expecting him to keep ignoring me, talking to and looking only at my parents. I thought quickly of the young priest. I sat forward on my elbows. "The park's cleared. The problem, I thought, was—"

"Ashley, you know better than that. Clearing the park has not resolved the problem," he said, patting the table. "Which is why you've been asked in here today. I admire your character, and believe you wrote that story to end, not move, the drug sales. So now I'm going to slip my hand into the oven and ask you if you might have any names of frequent visitors to the park. It's my understanding that a number of older kids were mixed in with kids as young as grade school?"

"You know," Mr. Kellogg suddenly spoke up, "he *is* protected. He doesn't have to give any further specifics to anyone."

Detective Spera spread his arms and smiled. "I know that, but he can if he feels he wants to. My job is to find out how much he may want to disclose."

Mr. Kellogg now sat forward. "See, I knew it. I knew you'd try to do this to him."

"Sir—"

Mr. Kellogg held a hand up. "Look, I'm his advisor, and I feel most directly responsible. What's happened to this family is—I feel terrible. And as his journalism teacher I *have* to remind you of his First Amendment rights."

Detective Spera nodded. "I'm well aware of that. But what I'm trying to get at is, we need someone to identify this guy they call The Landlord. Now, I don't wish to offend anybody or get anybody worried, but our department has cooperated exceedingly so far. We've been open and helpful with our comments, as his article manifests, we operated a raid the night before the story ran,"—he looked at my parents now—"we've protected your premises, we were on immediate call when you were being harassed and what have you." He looked back to Mr. Kellogg. "Now, yes, as far as his First Amendment rights, he had the right to free speech, but he also had the right to remain silent. Now *my* job here is to obtain as much information as I can to find out who is this main supplier. As far as I'm concerned, that's the single most important thing. The other kids, the footbridge itself—that's nothing. The supplier is our main objective."

For a second I watched Blake and Tyler. Both of them were sitting like hunched zombies, their heads held stiff and the whites of their eyes brighter than usual. We were all learning new lessons today. My parents were also silent as Mr. Kellogg circled a hand in the air in response.

"I realize that," he asserted, his furry eyebrows arched. "Supplying *is* the great crime, but why put this on a kid's shoulders?"

Spera's eyes widened as he shook his head. "I'm not trying to attack Ashley at all. We're really jumping off the wrong foot, here. All I'm just saying is that, if he and his parents feel it's important, if it's relevant enough to his cause, he may give me anything else he knows, strictly in our confidence. But there *is* a major supplier still out and about there somewhere, and if we can find someone willing to identify him, this whole story will have a much more severe positive impact." Spera sat back and pointed his fingers to his chest. "Now, to help clarify things, I'm going to part with a dirty secret. I myself know"— he paused, his eyes floating to each one of us, his face held in bright suspension—"that there's a male in his thirties living near the high school who's abetting kids in school. We just haven't been able to catch him in the act, but I have my reasons for believing. Kids want booze? He goes out and buys it for them. Now, between you and me and a rock, I think he may just be our man here. I'm very close, you see, so I'm going to try every angle."

Mr. Kellogg was still leaned far ahead in his seat, as though he was about to jump at any time. He held his palms up impatiently. "Look, what I want to know is, what is the worst that can happen here?" He gestured to me.

"What *can* happen?" Detective Spera offered in his booming tone. His eyes went to mine now. "Well, he can be subpoenaed to the grand jury for indictment. That's what can happen. If he is, the judge will ask him on the stand if he knows the source, or if he knows kids involved. He can refuse to give testimony, but then the judge can find him in contempt of court." He cleared his throat and put his stare back on Mr. Kellogg. "Then, as *you* say, even if knows *every*thing, he still has his First Amendment rights. He would tell this to the judge, and the judge would say, Yes I know you have your First Amendment rights, but I can hold you until you testify. See, the way the judge would see it, Ashley here is blocking the issue. He is—how would you say it—he is obstructing the administration of justice. Now I myself can't force him to say anything—he's still a minor—but how likely is this scenario I've mentioned? Not very likely at all."

There was a second of silence as we all pondered the facts. My mom took the first chance to speak.

"What did you say would happen if he goes to trial?" she asked with her head cocked pryingly. "I know you said it already, but I just want it made clear."

Spera's big hands were folded on his tie in a relaxed manner. His eyes searched the back wall as he speculated. "If the judge doesn't care for his conduct—his refusal to give testimony—he can throw him in juvenile hall and he'd be fined maybe"—he threw his hands up and rolled his face pensively at the ceiling—"I don't know, five hundred dollars. Again, this is worst case scenario."

"Just because he dispersed a drug ring?" she fired, her eyes blazing angrily from their sockets. "That's the thanks he gets?"

"Ma'am," the detective chuckled, leaning forward to ease her with his complacent stare, "don't worry. Really. This probably won't even get that far. It's not going to get any further than this." He smiled and pointed a finger at me. "May I just ask a few questions and that's all? I will make sure he's okay."

My parents looked at each other and finally nodded through troubled frowns. Dad winked at me reassuringly, and very suddenly, I thought of Benton.

Officer Spera bounced the eraser end of his pencil on the table, holding part of his upper lip in his teeth. "Ashley?" he then asked me. "Maybe you know who's behind the harassment to your family? You can give me something that might help us help you?"

The room was thick with quiet, like the Huelett's garage. I thought about that frighteningly realistic dummy hanging in bloodstained fashion from our tree, about the radio through the window, about Candy Kane's house the night before, about my father's spectacular altercation with Joe Chiavetti. I was responsible to my parents. I owed them for everything they had endured. Certainly, a world of difference existed between smoking some pot and driving a family from their home. Still, we had borne more inconvenience than anything else, and I simply did not want to become an informer. I just couldn't do it.

"Sorry. I can't help you," I told him at last. "I've only been to the bridge twice, so I could only guess. I mean, with your view from your office, you probably have more information than me anyway."

The man scratched the dark skin over his temple. I hated to make him angry.

"In your article," he went on, "you state that there's a *known* source of the drugs and under-aged drinking that had been going on. You said he's referred to as The Landlord." He jabbed the pencil toward his chest and his eyes were wide into mine. "This is what I want to know foremost, why we're here, the cream of the cookie. There was a kid caught the night before your article was published who—"

"John Kohleran?"

Mr. Spera nodded once big. "News travels fast in high school. Yes, John Kohleran. Well, since this Kohleran kid was arrested Tuesday night and also happens to be eighteen years old, the county prosecutor, whoever that might be, can subpoena him and bring him to court. It all depends on who wants to give me this guy's name first. With that said—how about you? You want to tell me who The Landlord is?"

"No idea."

A crease appeared in Mr. Spera's forehead.

"Well you wrote a source *known* among the kids," he said with a touch of incrimination in his voice. "Now if you wrote *suspected*, that's a different story. But you wrote *known*."

"Slight erring of words," Mr. Kellogg bumped in to confess. "That's more my fault than his."

Detective Spera nodded but still spoke to me. "Known to whom? You state that you visited the park area one night. If you swear by grace that you don't know this guy"—he checked his pad—"who The Landlord is, fine. But some of these kids you saw over there are probably the bigshots in the park scene and might name and identify this dealer. And you, Ashley, could further your cause."

"'Course I could," I agreed. "But no way. I mean, no thanks." I took a deep breath and watched the glare on the glossy wooden table. "I've had enough. I may be a journalist, but I'm through with being a target."

The big detective rested his cheek in his hand and I could smell that cologne again. My mother's wooden chair creaked. I turned my head and her blue-eyed face was over my elbow.

"As much as he'd like to," she said, "we've had just too much trouble. If things continue to happen and this doesn't get a chance to simmer down, my son won't even be able to go to school anymore. I'm sorry. We're just in enough hot water as it is. Too much unrest, and I want peace."

Mr. Spera smiled warmly, a bittersweet grin for our benefit.

"That's all right," he laughed lightly, the tension leaving the room like an implosion. "I have to try, you understand. We all have a job to do."

Mr. Kellogg rose, signifying our exit and the completion of the affair, and suddenly there was the small relief of chatter in the room. I looked at my parents and pushed out of my chair, Blake and Tyler following suit. In a minute, we were all on our feet and heading to the door. Before anything further, I turned back and shrugged to the detective as he stood tall from his seat.

"Sorry I couldn't be more helpful," I offered.

Detective Spera closed the flaps of his jacket and shook his head easily. From his size I imagined him playing professional football, a lineman. He was that big. He offered a huge hand. I shook it and he began to lead me out.

"I understand completely. Just don't ever lose your pizzazz."

I turned once more and nearly bumped into his big frame. I wanted to joke with him about his cologne but chose a sentiment.

"Look, I, um—I wanted you to know that I'm sorry if I insulted you guys with my story."

Mr. Spera held the door. He didn't say it was okay. He said, "I appreciate that. I would have liked a voice, though."

I jerked my head to the hall and blinked coolly. "Mr. Kellogg's right there. Still time to get something in if you want."

Once outside, I started walking around the pond. My parents were still back at the precinct house talking with Mr. Kellogg, and I wanted a little solitude. Blake was first to me. He had to skip steps every so often to keep up. He tried to ask me things, but for the moment I could only huff and try not to curse like a truck driver. Five hundred dollar fine? Juvey hall? And I never touched a drug. If I ratted everyone I was a *hero*?

Tyler ran up to me near the dam at the front of Mindo Pond and stopped me with his renewed troubled face.

"Wait for Mom and Dad," he said.

Pretty soon the five of us were making our way sullenly back to the fair.

"Mr. Kellogg wants you to see him on Monday," my mother told me, "but you're cooling it for a while."

After that it was Blake who hounded much of the talking. I was glad for him. The silence that had followed my mother's remark sucked, and I was of no mind to do much about it. He kept up a good tirade about the justice system, if I should face it.

"He's not going to court," my mother cut in. Dad quickly concurred.

I glanced at Tyler twice on the way. The idea that he hadn't spoken a word since the fair troubled me. He was back to his apprehensive and cautious self, studying the sidewalk panels with deep concentration, like he couldn't hear us. The reason why would eventually amaze me.

10

Halloween Night

Knowing how the circumstances under the time span of this particular darkness were to eventually turn out, it's hard to say if I had to do it over again, would I go through with it. Everything seemed to happen for a reason. My mother says I was on a collision course, and could not avoid my fate. My father just said I had the luck of the damned. I'm not sure about either, but I know how dangerous a stubborn will can be. After all, I decided to go out and about that night, against the wishes of my family, against common logic, really. But for pigheaded determination, however, nothing would have turned out like it did. This was the night that would change everything. This was the night that Tanner, Chiavetti, and everyone else would finally catch up to me.

Events began to unfold just after I took a shower around five o'clock that afternoon. I sat in my uncle's living room, no longer trusting the instability of the Spencer household, and took turns with my mother giving candy to pint-sized dusk-hour trick-or-treaters. The temperature was still mild and tiny costumes were rolled at the sleeves. Most kids at this hour were toddlers under parental escort. I'd hold the door open with my butt and present a bowl of SweeTarts to kids who could hardly speak, while Mommy and Daddy watched carefully, almost scrutinizing me from the sidewalk as though I was going to steal their infant. It was easy to assume, from the carefully labored detail on some of these elaborate miniature costumes, that Halloween is a holiday that truly stays with us. Adults use children as an excuse. But I know the truth.

Sucking on a SweeTart, I called Blake. No surprise to me, he had managed to get his mother to overturn his sentence tonight. She had waffled, as usual, and allowed him to go trick-or-treating—conditionally. He would have to take his goofy cousins with him. I figured the two grade-schoolers might serve to calm him down a bit, so it wasn't a total loss. After church today, I was staunchly against any mischief. Bad risks had returned too many hints lately.

The evening had a special thrill to it, driven, in large part, by the hint of romance. I had called Tara earlier in the day and invited her out quickly before she could make any mention of her note. I wanted to avoid any path to squirmy talk. I wasn't ready. I just wanted to have fun and think later. She got the point.

My parents and my aunt and uncle were getting ready to ship off to the YMCA's Halloween Party. My father was an Arab. Crowned with a turban, his beard scraped black with a piece of charcoal, he set a very striking resemblance. My mother squeezed into an expensive Catwoman suit and actually managed to make it work. Of course, my Uncle Joe was Bill Clinton, and Aunt Diane was dressed as a witch, complete with pointy hat and puke-green toned face. Their enthusiasm seemed to fill the house.

Originally that afternoon, I hadn't a clue what I was going to be until I hung my jacket on my uncle's basement door and stopped. I suddenly noticed my great-great-great-grandfather, thickly bearded, posed in his dark uniform with a musket, looking down at me from a picture atop the wall before the stairs. Family legend had him as part of a valiant Minnesota regiment that fought at Gettysburg. Pride melted through me like syrup in my skin.

Two hours later I had scrounged together a pretty good replica of my ancestor's Union soldier apparel. Light blue trousers, a rather large dark cap that made me look twelve, cruddy old black sneakers, a canteen harness, and a makeshift coat—blue blazer with the collar up and gold buttons pinned vertically—just like my great-great-great-grandfather before me. My Mom added the final perfect touch when she suggested a fist-full of dry dirt on my face for a true effect. The idea of licensed sloppiness appealed to me like pizza and a movie, and I hustled out to the back yard. Minutes later, I had managed to change my complexion with charcoal flakes and parched earth. When I got back in the house, everyone was upstairs making last minute dabs. Good. I could know what I looked like before anyone else. I moved into the hallway and stood in front of the same mirror as yesterday. Incredible. In a matter of twenty minutes I had magically gone back in time. The change appeared quite real to me, and I couldn't wait for Tara to see. I gave myself a full-uniform salute and heard my mother coming down the stairs. I turned to face her. She held the rail with one hand.

"Oh, that is just too much. Let me get a camera." Standing there in this shiny Catwoman suit and ridiculous black mask, she was telling me *I* was too much. "Doug," she called, "you have to come down and take a look at this."

I opened the basement door again and stared at my forebearer, studying the way he looked. I remembered a program on the Civil War and how certain generals on both sides wore flashy full dress uniforms, sported long beards and handlebar mustaches, and kept plumes in their hats while riding proudly on their mounts. Wars before camouflage suddenly seemed like elaborate bloody Halloween costume contests. Why did they want to stand out like peacocks? Why did they require so much flair just to kill? Why does everyone admire such historical slaughters? Standing there in replicated fashion of men who had died horrible deaths made the Civil War come clearly alive to me. Tens of thousands of men had sacrificed their lives to preserve the Union and end the tyranny of slavery. They had fought and died to preserve a good and terminate an evil that had no direct impact on their daily lives. Here I now stood, testing the idea's irony.

Another group of trick-or-treaters rang the doorbell—four kids about Trip Spencer's age. Ironically, one kid appeared to be a Gulf War army private with black under his eyes. They barely glanced at my dark face before using their hands to scoop up SweeTarts. Thanking me, they trotted back down the sidewalk. The private started a bustling pace.

"We need to run, guys!" he cheered fervently. "We're not gonna get *anywhere* walkin'!"

I checked down both ends of the street and saw little creatures traveling through the dimness of the sweet dusk. Several groups of kids appeared from doorsteps and around corners, invading the neighborhood. I gauged how long it would take them to reach my uncle's and fell into a peace, a beautiful hue coating my dirty cheeks. The sun had just set and the horizon was a stretch of pink, a few clouds outlined by a dazzling orange border. It all meshed upwards into a daytime-like blue sky, where clouds still floated cottony white. A tepid breeze bounced down North Chestnut Street and swam around me. I remained leaning in the doorway, dreaming of the proper way I could describe this.

Back inside, a last minute Scotch was in my Uncle Bill Clinton's hands. The radio was set on 101.5, a Jersey station, and the discussion involved real-life ghost stories. Callers phoned in with personal accounts of having witnessed apparitions, of hearing unearthly sounds in houses, or merely mentioned anything of the supernatural happening to them or a friend. During a news report, the DJ cautioned drivers to be careful of trick-or-treaters out on the roads.

I could feel it all around. The energy was building. Listening to the radio, watching other kids pass outside, knowing I'd join them soon—it kept burning back to me. The childhood feeling I used to have about Halloween. Inside me, all those years, had been that left-out emptiness, comparable to being the only kid without fireworks when dusk falls on the Fourth of July.

I hiked over to Blake's house, armed with a pillowcase. Street lamps lit my path and I questioned whether I was made-up enough to avoid detection. Three crickets whistled random lonely twitters about the area. A large illuminated plastic pumpkin's bright gleam threw faint orange over a front door. Sheeted ghosts hung from the low branches of a maple in the same yard. Another home's porch was adorned with cotton spider webs, a hanging mummy, and two candlelit jack-o'-lanterns that flanked the entrance.

Jim's truck was in the Spencer's driveway when I got there. Someone had transformed all three of their pumpkins into angry jacks. Standing above them, I could see bright candlelight flickering through the lid slits in the tops, could smell the insides burning. I rang the doorbell and found myself face-to-face with a huge, jointed, glow-in-the-dark skeleton taped to the storm door. What a holiday, I thought, where its appropriate for people to happily arrange in public display a life-sized totally decomposed human being. And the thing smiles.

The black door opened with suction and there stood Jim, six years younger than Mrs. Spencer and looking all of it. He acted it a bit, too, but it was a friendly approachable quality I liked. He pushed on the storm door and the skeleton swayed out and away from me. Jim's glance contained a smile.

"Hey soldier," he chirped. I walked in and spotted a trick-or-treat bowl in the hall. An aroma of spices and cooked meat hit me and made my stomach growl.

"Mm-*mmm!*" I said. "Something smells good."

Jim leaned into me and held a hand to his mouth. "Must be coming from way down the street."

"Hey," I laughed softly, "her cooking's not bad."

"Sure, if you're a dog and don't know the difference." Jim led me down the hall, patting my back in laughter. I liked this guy. I was too young too really understand any of Blake's hostility towards him.

In the kitchen, Blake and Trip sat around the table eating hamburgers while Mrs. Spencer washed pans at the sink. She smiled delightfully when she saw me. Blake raised his arms.

"Awesome!" he cheered. "Ashley finally rises from the dust!"

"Dirt is more like it," stated Mrs. Spencer. "What is that on your face?"

I saluted. Before I could answer, Blake piped up. "I wanna do that, too."

Mrs. Spencer indicated a plate on the table. "Have you eaten dinner?"

I flopped a hand to my hip. "Chicken and Stars at my uncle's again."

"Well, I made an extra burger if you're hungry."

I smiled, thanked her, moved to the table. Next to me, Blake and Trip were considering my face. I laughed at the attention until I saw Blake's half-eaten meat sitting slogged between his bun. Blake likes his burgers rare in the middle. Gross slop. I had one like that once, and it was like I couldn't tell where the meat ended and my tongue began.

Blake was going as a pirate, using that as a pretext for dirtying his face. He still had that bandage over the base of his thumb. Trip was begging to join us instead of wandering with his friends. When Blake refused, Trip vowed angrily that he was going to reek havoc anyway and perform his own mischief with his friends. Oh, the rewards of a twisted fraternal influence.

"You guys better behave tonight," Mrs. Spencer told us with a stab of seriousness as Jim leaned against the counter with an amused smile. "These are my sister's kids you're taking with you. I don't want you trick-or-treating down past Friendly's tonight. We don't know those people."

Blake glumly ripped a bite of his burger in a way that showed he wasn't thrilled with the idea.

"Don't jump in any leaf piles, either," she warned.

"Dog pee?" Trip asked.

Mrs. Spencer ran the faucet and went back to scrubbing.

"That, and people sometimes put cinder blocks in leaves to deter kids from driving their cars through them. Your father left his axle behind him in high school one night from doing that."

After I had wolfed down my hamburger (cooked through, thank the Lord), Blake and I retreated to the isolation of his room. A Neighborhood Watch sign he'd stolen during the summer decorated the wall above his stereo. There was terrific irony in it.

I sat on Blake's bed and watched him put together a pirate as best he could.

"Dude," he asked, "what are you gonna do if you have to go to court?"

I rose with a burdened sigh and watched his fish tank. I wanted to close the subject, to think on it later. "I don't know what they want from me." I blew a breath. "I served my purpose, Blake. Mindowaskin's cleared. But I can't give names. And anyway, I don't even know this—this Landlord guy." I leveled a hand. That's all I would give him.

Despite strapping a patch over one of his eyes and rolling up his pant legs, Blake still didn't look much like a pirate. Maybe, I thought, some good dirt on that smooth mug of his would help. We went back down to the den, where Trip and now three of his friends who'd since appeared—all four dressed as monks—sat with Jim and watched *Halloween*. The front doorbell rang and Mrs. Spencer went to give out candy. It turned out to be Blake's cousins, two boys who entered, then shied at the mass in the den. Cheap plastic outfits, the ones from a box, enshrouded each of them. One kid portrayed Hulk Hogan and the other was dressed as some Star Trek geek. Mrs. Spencer touched their shoulders and her voice rose over the TV, regarding her boyfriend.

"Jim, this is Paul and Ryan." She bent over and smiled at them, then looked at Blake. "And Blake and Ashley have agreed to take them on their rounds tonight."

A stifled giggle ran through Trip's nose. Blake mumbled something with a frown and stalked off to the kitchen. Mrs. Spencer blinked irritably, running a flustered hand through her hair, and directed little Ryan and Paul to the big couch. The geeky kids, thin plastic masks in their hands, became instantly transfixed by the movie. Mrs. Spencer followed Blake, and out in the kitchen, bickering could be heard. Blake's voice was suddenly loud and sharp, audible to all in the den.

"I don't wanna trick-or-treat with nerds!"

Trip coughed over a laugh. Blake's goofy cousins sat with folded hands, eyes to the screen, pretending they hadn't heard. Suffice it to say, Blake got himself grounded again.

"Ashley can trick-or-treat with someone else tonight," I sullenly heard Mrs. Spencer chew.

"Mom, what the *heck*!" Blake cried. "It's Halloween and you're icin' me with nerds!"

"You're grounded, buster. Period!"

It's incredible how embarrassed you are for someone when they get yelled at in public. I prayed Blake wouldn't slip up again, perhaps use Jim against her now. But as far as his mother was concerned, the matter was settled. When Blake reappeared in the den light, now missing the eye patch, his face looked tired, beaten, like he was about to cry. Trip's suppressed laughter taunted him and I could just see it—Blake tearing off his dingy sneaker and whipping it at Trip in front of all of us.

Blake led me to the front door, his hushed tone suggesting a plan. He told me to come back and meet him at his basement window at exactly eight o'clock. Jeez, it was already quarter after six and I wanted to hit houses for stash. Plus, his mother scared me. I really didn't feel safe rebelling against her ruling. Blake's escape changed everything. Now I had to get Tara and come all the way back here. As much a part of this as I didn't want to be, the plan for sneaking out was laid and I left sourly.

I made haste in jogging to Tara's house. On the way I passed kids in all sorts of costumes carrying pumpkin candy carriers already weighed down with loot, and I grew increasingly more annoyed with Blake and what his pent-up anger had brought us. The sun had long since set, and I had yet to trick-or-treat one house. When I came around to Summit Avenue, I noticed the Vovens's garage was empty. I tiptoed quietly up the back steps and looked through the screen door. Tara was punching beeps on the microwave, dressed sexy, looking made-up and sweet. My lungs filled with air as I cupped my hands to my mouth—

"BLAH!"

The Curb Owl let out a short scream as her shoulders bobbed violently, her hands waving in vibration. A spoon clanked on the floor. I backed away and held my stomach in laughter. Suddenly the door slammed.

My laughing slowed. I returned to the door window and made a puppy dog face. Poor Tara was leaned against the wall with one hand to her heaving chest, rigid fear widening her eyes. I felt alarmed pity for her.

"It's *me*, Tara!" I took off my infantry cap and smiled excitedly.

The breath of air she let out displayed her relief and humiliation at once. On jelly legs she came forward and opened the door. A loud sharp curse left her lips.

"Sorry," I giggled. "Where're your 'rents?"

"Out." Tara was panting. "Nice—get-up." Her made-up eyes were resentful—a touch of mistrust. She swallowed. "That was just—wrong." She leaned on the counter and put a hand to her heart. "I didn't—know who you were in the dark." Tara swallowed and slapped the counter. "Ashley, you scared the *blood* out of me! Promise to never do anything like that again."

"I can't," I teased. "Your reaction was too priceless."

Tara turned, smiled nervously. "I'm gonna get you back for that." I thought of her letter, wondering if she'd be different now. I saw an opportunity to hug her with playful consolation, but chose to let it be when she went to the microwave and pressed start.

"I love your face," she said away from me. "But you look five years old in that cap."

I wanted to say the same about her face, wanted to tell her what I was thinking about every soft inch of her, and her get-up certainly aided such thoughts. She wore fishnet stockings that tinted her legs, a black leather miniskirt, a red sequin shirt, and a bright-white fur coat that went to her waist. Twin patches of blush defined her cheekbones more deeply. I almost didn't recognize her eyes—heavily arrayed in blue eye shadow. Her hair was pinned up on one side like a duster. In the light, I could see sparkles on her face. She turned and noticed my concentrating stare. I leaned forward and squinted.

"Are you a hooker?"

Tara hunched. "No, you goof. I'm a showgirl."

I fixed my cap and rested against the fridge. "Is that the light term for it?"

"Ashley," she said gently, "this was what I was dressed as when I was—"

"Eleven, I know."

She looked down at herself, then shrugged her head up.

"I figured since you were tackling old ghosts, so would I."

Just the sight of her made me forget myself for a second. Suddenly I wanted to just go somewhere alone with her instead of trick-or-treat. My urge compelled me and I felt stony as I moved toward her and took her into my arms. Even with my soiled face she let me rest my head against hers. Her arms crossed behind my neck softly, like they fit right into place. Suddenly the kitchen was quiet, only the microwave hummed, as I stood squeezed against Tara. We had hugged before, but not like this. Definitely not like this. I smelled Tara's fruit-tangy perfume and moved my hand on her back. She felt the cue and did the same to the shoulder of my jacket.

"How'd it go today?" I heard her say delicately to my ear. The proximity was new and unusual and, I realized, announcing a change. I had crossed a certain line now. We weren't an item as of this moment, but there was *something*. It was all my call, and I still wanted to be sure. Tara's soothing hand squeezed my neck. I felt the vibrations in her small torso as she murmured, "You a fugitive yet?"

"Almost." My voice sounded funny to me. Holding her so close had done something to it. I tried to relax. I breathed deeply, embarrassed by how intimately Tara was aware of it, and stared at the plate spinning slowly in the microwave.

"You want to know the worst part about being me?" I finally said. "I can't escape this at all. Usually when you're tired of someone you can ditch them. With me, I'm just stuck. Just once. Just one time, I'd like to step outside myself and run away for a while."

We backed slowly out of each other's arms and I dropped my stained face. Tara kissed the tip of her finger and pressed it to my cheek. A smart play. Charcoal would've stuck right to that bright red lipstick.

"It's Halloween," she said. "Tonight you can."

Eventually we returned to our normal selves, and maybe it was all the activity of running around the past few nights, because I was soon having a third dinner while sitting in her den watching *Halloween*. Tara phoned a few friends while I ate a dish of macaroni and cheese, and Jamie Lee Curtis tried to tell little Tommy Doyle there's no such thing as the boogie man.

When Tara was done, I told her we had to be at slippery Blake's at eight. At that point, she seemed torn about something. She kept watching out the window. Finally the Curb Owl asked me to take out the garbage so she could throw together some last minute things. After tying the plastic sack and lifting it out of the container, I took it past the treacherous bathroom, dismally reminded of The Ordeal. Yet it wasn't until I was bobbing down the steps when I felt an arresting dread. Joe Chiavetti. I pulled my Union soldier cap tighter over my eyes as I walked out into the night and approached the garbage cans on the side of the house. I pulled up on one of the lids.

From behind it, a figure sprang out at me, screaming.

At the very first I thought it was an animal I'd disturbed—the scream began at such an inhuman tone. Then I feared one of my predators. I leapt back with a spasm and tripped over the gutter, cursing on my landing. This could be bad. Very quickly, my night had turned on me.

Someone was under an ape mask, laughing a girl's laugh. The ape face was torn off and Varsity Carnoustie was in hysterics.

"Are you all right?" she gasped, her cackling ticking me off.

Tara stood behind me now, helping me up while celebrating her victory.

"I told you I'd get you back!" she cheered.

I straightened, fixed my cap, and brushed my uniform without a word, figuring emoting would only serve them better. But I was alone in their laughter. Tara tried to hold my sleeve.

"Hey," she said brightly, shaking me. "It's Halloween Night. I had to."

Blake was already standing on the side of his yard when we reached his house. He appeared from the shadows, his jumpy and agitated figure revealed by the glow of the streetlight. He didn't want to stick around his house, so he greeted us, checked Varsity with a glance, and started walking past. "Come on," he whispered. "I just snuck out the basement window. I gotta get far away from here, quick."

He wasn't dressed as his pathetic version of a pirate anymore. He looked much the same way he did the previous night, only with an enlarged gut. I saw why when he tugged his dark sweatshirt out of his black jeans. A black wool hat and a green pillowcase fell to his feet. He searched through the wool hat for something.

"Trip and his friends got stuck with the doofus twins," he said.

He found what he was looking for—a stored piece of charcoal. After fixing the hat over his hair he cracked the charcoal in half and began rubbing it all over his face. When Tara told him he was overdoing it, he smiled. After a minute, he looked like a Zulu tribe king. He chucked the coal and regarded Varsity with unusually white discerning eyes now, staring at the thin pointy lines on her brow. He thought Varsity was hot, but was virtually dead in any respect for the girl, as his first words to her demonstrated.

"Do you pick your eyebrows?"

She frowned at him. "Are you a jerk?"

Tara quickly asked, "So—what are you supposed to be?"

"A crook. What else?"

I forfeited a laugh. "Ask the Hueletts."

We crossed the street and headed for Wilson School. One of the first houses we trick-or-treated was on Raymond Street, a housewith a porch whose giant pumpkin had fallen prey to Blake's little hands the night before. Once a boastfully great sphere, the pumpkin was now a flat orange mess in the road. I found it ironic and cruel the way Blake took a six-inch Three Musketeers from the lady's hands and turned away.

The younger groups of kids had started to disappear at dusk. As night fell deeper, parents became more and more scarce until only teenagers, once again, roamed the streets. Jack-o'-lanterns gleamed more sharply as darkness surrounded their eerie stationary faces. Walking along dark shadowy sidewalks, crossing under streetlights, I could sense something different. It seemed a lot more alive out in suburban Westfield than the night before. The streets weren't as foreboding or empty. They were friendly. Trick-or-treaters would pass each other with common purpose, crossing uncommon nighttime paths, yelling and laughing, feet hitting the asphalt at a run and crunching leaves on lawns.

I took a moment to soak in more of the night, then went with the other three up to the next house. A jack's face blazed out into the night, orange light dancing sharply from its mouth and eyes. Someone had carved its face to look like it was scared of something on the ground. Blake probably couldn't believe he'd missed it last night. The door opened and we all seemed a little bit younger.

"Trick-or-treat!" the others yelled. I glanced at Tara in the door light, her blush-covered cheeks glossed with the elation of a small child's. She took a step up, careful of the burning fruit at her feet, and leaned in to select from a wide bowl. In her fancy make-up, she smiled.

"Thanks. Happy Halloween." It was funny to behold her so prissy and polite.

I was next. A woman about Mrs. Spencer's age stood in a bright green sweater and held the door with her body, a heap of goods at her waist. I reached out and grabbed a Mars bar. It seemed vaguely intrusive to me, but a growing stash was helping me to become acclimated to the idea.

We crossed North Chestnut to hit the homes around Wilson School, focusing on houses with elaborate decorations or a simple welcoming light, zigzagging the area, ringing doorbells and taking candy like frank little beggars on both sides of the street before reaching Kimball Avenue. Depending on where we faced, I could see the half moon reflecting on storm doors. I'd ring the doorbell and watch the moon on the glass. Suddenly the door would open and the moon would seem to fly across the sky.

Shouts echoed in the neighborhood, ricocheting off quiet houses. The landscape was alive, a huge town party catering to the young. It was uncommon for a house around the school to be bare of a creative display. Across-the-street neighbors on one street had strung up two ghosts made of long white sheets, using wire and electric pulleys to bring the phantoms to life. In ski-lift-like fashion, the sheets glided high above the street, crossing each other, their bodies blowing spectrally in the wind, floating momentarily bright under a street lamp.

Since Blake hadn't spent much time here last night, many jack-o'-lanterns were abundant. Spotting the glow from the flickering candle beams before you reached the house caused a slight tingle. There was union with those people in that house. The greatest thing about these big fruits was the varied designs flashing the faces to life. You never knew what face you were going to see next. Every house was a new discovery. I wondered how many people collaborated on the pumpkin until it could be placed on the doorstep with pride as an expression of their creativity.

In one extreme case, someone seemed to want to send a subtle message. Lined up along the sidewalk, eight jack-o'-lanterns threw candlelit words that twinkled on the grass in front of them. In what had to be a painstaking process, a direct hint was carved into each one: *SCRAM! GET LOST! TURN AROUND, BEGGAR! BEAT IT! ABOUT FACE! GO AWAY! WRONG HOUSE! TAKE A HIKE!* The four of us approached in wondrous laughter. Blocking our way to the front door was another pumpkin, a gigantic one with words painted: *SMASH ME AND YOU DIE!* Signs hung in haphazard haste filled the two windows bracketing the door. Inked in magic marker, one read *BEWARE OF CHILD MOLESTER,* while the other—shaped like a yellow car window sign—warned *FONDLER ON BOARD.* A cardboard cutout of a hand giving the middle finger was taped right to the door, and a sign below it indicated, *IF YOU'VE REACHED THIS POINT, I'VE CALLED THE COPS.*

We kind of left this magnificently deranged house alone.

My pillowcase was starting to get some good weight by the time we had circled Wilson. Huge leaf piles lined the curbs as we moved into the side streets—crisp brown oak leaves—some fluffy piles as tall as our heads. I thought about Mrs. Spencer's prior advice when Tara and Varsity fell back into a feathery heap and got into a vigorous leaf war.

Blake thought of something else. Watching the two, he fixed his wool hat and turned his coal-blackened face to me. "I should jump in while the going's good and try to start somethin' with Varsity," he said low.

I watched Tara and Varsity spit leaf dust from their lips and brush their coats as they sat in the leaves like preschoolers. They pushed up and walked out, kicking the light foliage, walking it into the streets.

Further down the street, Tara grabbed a handful of leaves and doused two younger kids passing by, shouting gleefully, "Happy Halloweenie!" I rushed to their defense and pushed Tara back into the pile, falling comfortably with her. I took her wrists and held them to the leaves, pinning her, and she let me. Thrown against the auburn petals, her painted face looked defined, placidly waiting. I felt a squirming in my gut and was just about to kiss her when a stockpile of leaves bashed into my face, crunching loudly against my ear. Tara screamed something that grew muffled under Varsity's scooping. I reached under and picked the Curb Owl up out of the leaves, balancing her like a puppet on the road. Her pinned-up hair was a tangle of leaf bits and I pretended to pull them all out, leaving the big ones dangling for fun.

Above us, the orange leaves of a giant maple were blazed like a fluorescent fireball by the streetlight shining in the middle of it. Tara suddenly twirled around in the light like she was listening to that song we'd danced to in her room, her sack revolving in the air like a propeller. Finally she stopped dead, wobbling. "Spin ten times really

really fast, and then stop," she gasped. "That's what it's like to be really bombed." I felt the smile spread across my face. Ever the Curb Owl. She wasn't going to change.

We resumed our course, though not on the bare streets, but trudging through the big leaf piles. Tara held my hand faithfully, tugging my arm as she laughed and hopped. I was aware only of the soft warm feel of her palm and fingers. The dead scent of fall surrounded us as we spilled pile-to-pile, clogging entire roads. Blake jumped out of the leaf humps and ran onto a lawn, grabbing a tacky pumpkin leaf bag from the base of a tree. He literally tore it open, gutting it, and whipped it viciously from side to side, dumping its leaves on the cleared lawn.

The strangeness of Halloween decorations continued. Blake led us purposely to a Victorian house on Winyah Avenue. He rang the doorbell and winked at me for a reason about to be revealed. I faced the door patiently and saw a frighteningly realistic cutout of a severed hand taped to the window.

"Jeez." I shuddered. "Why don't they just cut to the chase and hang pictures from medical books?"

The door pulled back and there stood a youngish-looking, pale-faced girl in PJ's and socks, with traces of dark make-up circling her eyes. She looked drained from the night, or maybe sad because her Halloween was drawing to a close. When she came into the porch light my mouth gaped in a smile.

"Maureen Egan!" I declared. "You live here?"

Maureen's face came to life with a big drawling "Hi!" She hung in the door, clutching in her arms a wooden bowl filled with bite-sized candy bars. "I love all your outfits." She checked Tara and Varsity, pointing at Blake and me. "You think their faces look better as dirt clods?"

I eyed Tara. She was smiling, checking me from the side and nodding quickly, over and over. Maureen was plainly attractive, but compared to Tara she was as regular as anybody to me. At that moment, I knew I was completely entranced with the Curb Owl. Thank God for the charcoal to cover my red face. Talking slowed and the air grew crisp with silence.

Blake spoke up. "You're in already?"

Maureen nodded, aimed her head wearily inside.

"My parents are just about to go out," she said regretfully, "and I'm burdened with baby-sitting my little brother. My friends and I had to take him out earlier."

I elbowed little Andy Gibb beside me. "Sounds like destiny to me, Blake." He grinned smugly.

I pointed to the door. "And whose is that?"

Maureen balanced the bowl and leaned to eye the decaying hand. Her eyes rolled. "Oh, that's my brother's charming touch. Don't you love it?"

She leveled the big bowl in front of me. "Choose, cadet."

I selected from the collection of bite-sized Snickers, Milky Ways, and Three Musketeers bars, so tiny I could write a sad ballad on them. Blake squeezed rudely in front of me and hung an arm over the bowl. Maureen smiled bashfully at him and held up a finger in fake caution. "Only one, now."

"One?!" Blake wailed, quickly back to his old self. "These pinkies wouldn't fill my best cavity!" Suddenly Blake sneak-attacked the bowl, pushing it down and dumping almost half of its contents into his green pillowcase. Maureen backed away and light-fisted Blake on his head. I found it virtually impossible to resist joining in his muffled guilty laughter.

Varsity was glaring. "You have to excuse him," she said to Maureen. "His diaper's leaking."

Blake disregarded her and moved into Maureen, who took her head back from his dirty face. Directly in front of us, Blake ripped off his wool hat and stepped in the door. Sliding his bandaged hand around Maureen's shoulders, he pulled her into a French kiss, char-faced and all, resuming with a lengthy passion the preceding day's act. Through the silence, the rest of us glanced at each other and back at them until we heard the abruptness of a strong voice.

"Hey! What the hell is—!"

He was too shocked to finish. A tall man with a full head of premature gray hair and wearing a suit of a matching hue was bearing down the hall toward Blake and Maureen. His brow was furled in a noticeably wrathful angle, his bulging eyes contorting his expression. Maureen shrank away, mortified.

Whipping his head several times back, Blake insanely danced away as though his feet were on fire and barreled between the three of us out on the step. Instinctively, we gasped and jumped off the step after him, our candy sacks banging against our thighs. As though evading a herd of elephants, we flocked to the left, jumping over a leaf pile and making loud patters on the street with our shoes. This pace continued until we just about reached Wilson School again. Tara grasped my hand and looked back. Other than trick-or-treaters, the streets were devoid of any quick movement. Blake rested his hands on his knees.

"Well, Blake," I breathed, resting an arm on his horizontal back, "if there's anything to come of you and her, you just stunk up quite a roadblock for yourself."

Blake straightened, took a deep breath, and walked on, watching the pavement in thought.

"Oh, God," he moaned. "Maureen's turning into *such* a babe! I wanna spank her nerfs *so* bad!"

"Blake!" Tara laughed.

He only went further with it. In the tradition of The Beatles' *I Wanna Hold Your Hand*, he mimicked in tune, "I wanna spank those ner-r-r-r-rfs. I wanna spank those nerfs."

Varsity Carnoustie shook her head and spat, "What are you, like, twelve?"

"Thirteen next month!" Blake kiddingly defied.

I wish I could say it ended there between those two, but soon after, Varsity let loose, in more ways than one. Regardless of our hearing, she went into detail with Tara about her lewd affair with Chuck Henshall upon walking over to his house late last night after Candy's party, clad only in sneakers and a robe.

"What about John?" Blake asked incriminatingly before she was finished. "John Kohleran? You know? Your boyfriend?"

Varsity reached into her sack and retrieved a piece of gum. She waited until it was in her mouth before she shrugged with a hard chew. "What about him?"

Air puffed through Blake's mouth as he swung a lazy hand at her. "You are, unbelievably, without a doubt, the biggest hussy I've ever known in my *life*!"

"Shut up!"

"In my *entire* life. You're unique. No, I mean, really. You're at the top of a very distinct list." I heard his voice aimed my way. "I don't know about you, Ash," he called sarcastically, "but this slut's got me poppin' *serious* skin!"

Varsity walked closer to him. "Why don't I just give your mom a call and ask her to get you on the phone?"

"Ee-*yuck!*" Blake gagged, sneering at her. "I think I've seen enough of you to make me sick for three *weeks*."

Varsity scowled and flagged the middle finger. "Eat *this*, you prepubescent worm."

Then there are the girls who don't really care much for Blake.

I turned awkwardly from holding Tara's hand. "Okay, children. Nap time."

"Jeez, really. Come on," Tara urged. "Stop it."

"Yeah, we better stop," Blake chided mockingly to Varsity, "or I might end up bangin' you later..."

"You wish," Varsity snapped.

"...for your three-millionth boink," Blake finished.

We came across one house on Baker Avenue where a tragically naïve person left a bowl full of candy with a note: "Please take one." It was empty by the time we left.

The very next house was dimly lit and the porch was heavily decorated. A plastic skeleton sat poised in a chair on one side of the door, and a rickety scarecrow with a hideous demon mask was slouched on the other side. Our feet crackled on leaves scattered over the lawn as we approached. In the window, a porcelain jack-o'-lantern was flashing blue-red-green-orange-blue-red—

The scarecrow jumped to life!

With a monstrous cry, the form raised its hands and bounded forward. Tara and Varsity screeched at the top of their lungs as the figure sprang, scattering us over the yard. Varsity fell to the grass in subjection and the scarecrow doubled over in mumbled laughter. Another man was guffawing from the now-open front door.

"Son of a *major* one!" gasped Tara to the guy. "That scared the *blood* out of me!"

"*You're* scared?" laughed Varsity. "I almost ruined a thong!"

The guy under that demon mask and straw hat was chuckling himself into a fit. He introduced himself to us from underneath his mask as Gary and told us about his Halloween tradition, now in its fourth year. With my heart now out of my throat, I begrudgingly applauded the guy. His act captured the very essence of the night. The scarecrow spoke to us through his ugly demon mask for a few minutes, telling us we hadn't screamed half as loud as some groups tonight. He pointed to the door.

"We were thinking of dressing my buddy over there as a spider with a bungee cord around his waist and bouncing him down in front of kids in case they caught on to me."

"Yeah, that—that's great," Blake said, his tone biting with sarcasm.

"Oh, chill," Varsity puffed. "Just 'cause you got played."

Blake and Varsity descended into another exchange of insults, but I didn't hear a word, since a particular passing vehicle had captured my attention.

A red pickup truck with shiny silver trim and tinted windows drove slowly down Baker in front of us. I instantaneously shifted from laughter to desolate shock. The taillights blazed in a red glow as the driver paused in passing, watching us through that tinted glass. The truck then turned left on Winyah without signaling. I knew that truck, knew it like it belonged to my family. I even recognized a bumper sticker on the back. All night, I'd been on the subconscious lookout for a maroon Volvo. This new assault was real and terribly sudden.

Tara was first to notice my blank daze. A quick tug at my hand. "You all right?"

I stared at the taillights until they were around Wilson School. They seemed to disappear awful slowly to me. After we took Mounds and Almond Joys from the scarecrow and marched off, I spoke about the significance of what I had just seen. Blake had an easy remedy. He'd egg it if it came around again, as well as any Volvo within range. Even though I suspected Blake was not carrying any eggs for fear he might squish them again in his pocket, I told him, "Don't blow the dust, Blake."

They came right across the Wilson School grounds toward us. Three shapes appeared from the corner wall to my left, taking form when they paced through the spotlight glow on the basketball court. Their strides conveyed an intent that alarmed me from a distance. I stayed still, even when they jumped the chain-link fence and came into view. Then a street lamp revealed Joe Chiavetti.

I took a double take to the big kid on his right. Benton Crossey. He regarded me once, then moved his brown eyes quickly around us, as if surveying the odds. What was he doing now with Chiavetti?! Suddenly I wished I hadn't left his house in such haste that morning.

Maybe he was mad that I hadn't appreciated his hospitality or something. Guido Delisi walked beside Benton in his standard tagalong mode. Hidden beneath a Civil War soldier cap and a face darkened with soot, I suddenly felt completely stupid in my costume. Behind me, Blake made a funny noise. I stood on the pavement and felt my chest heaving. Joe's dark features sharpened as he kept the same swaggering pace to cross the street. I almost expected him to pull a knife. The situation looked bad enough, but to make matters worse, Tara stepped toward them.

"Joe," she called with sick apprehension, "don't be an ass!"

Joe managed the perfect insult. Almost indifferent to her presence, he continued right past Tara and up to me. I held stiff. Benton eyed me with a fixed concern as he strode up alongside.

"Don't worry, A'," he piped up first. "He just wants to talk to you."

"Not worried," I said, sounding like I meant it. "So who drives the pickup?"

Blake and Varsity moved out of the way as Chiavetti turned me around with a hand on my shoulder. I just let him. We walked a few yards away from the group. His cologne sucked.

"Joe, come on," I said in my coolest tone, hoping to invoke comradeship. "This is gettin' a bit melodramatic here, don'tcha think?"

Joe stopped and faced me, his arms crossed at his chest. Out of earshot from the rest, he chewed his lower lip and blinked his eyes almost sleepily.

"What's goin' on with you and Tara?" he demanded. A hand left his chest and he bit a nail. "That you the other night?"

I glanced at his black hair shining under the street lamp. It was shorter than that night on Prospect Street. I wondered if ever he remembered the encounter, how I'd helped him. I blinked.

"Well, you know, Joe—" I paused, stumped, scratched the dirt on my temple. "I was there this summer. It's not like I didn't see what happened with you guys. I wouldn't be stealing anyone."

"I just wanna know what you're doin' with Tara, that's all. Just answer me that question."

One house length back, Tara let out a sound before Varsity put a palm to her mouth. Suddenly I was embarrassed. Now I had to give an answer, not only to Joe, but to Tara. Benton rode in to rescue me.

"I knew this guy would find you tonight," he cut in, wrapping a friendly arm around Chiavetti's neck, "with or without me." He stared at Joe's ear. "I wanted to be there when you did. I'm on a mission, bro." Benton knuckled my arm. "A's my buddy. This kid's got more balls than you and I'll ever have." He laughed mockingly to me. "You believe this son of a lowlife? Wantin' to pound people for no reason? Least when I do it, I got an excuse." He let go and shook his head at Joe. "What's yours, huh? Oh, boo hoo, you can't hang around the park dishin' drugs to little kids now." I could hear Varsity laughing. Benton shoved Joe playfully. "Friggin' lowlifes you hang out with, Joe. Dealin' pot to my little brother's friends. How long I been tellin' you about that?"

Chiavetti put a hand to his chest and grimaced, his thin blond tail swishing as he shook his head like he didn't care. "*I* had nothin' to do with that."

"Don't gimme that, bro," Benton scoffed. "You all did." He pointed my way. "He clears them bums outta the park and you wanna destroy him for it?"

Joe squinted back at him. "What's chewin' your ass, moron? We agreed I wouldn't touch the kid."

Benton winked past Joe's shoulder at me. "I talked to him, A'. It's cool."

Chiavetti twisted a frown in his dark eyebrows at me and jerked a thumb back at Benton.

"Not that it's this dip's business," he jibed, "but no runnin' from me anymore." Joe paused, lowered his face to stare at my eyes in eerie Mafia-like fashion. "Cool?"

He stuck his fist out. It was as though a balloon had popped in my chest. I wondered if his father had anything to do with this. Reluctantly I rolled a fist and put it up. Joe's bony knuckles tapped mine. Oddly, we all moved off together.

Halloween Night was going to go on for me.

For a while, it almost appeared that we'd be hanging with these guys tonight, although Blake got a little uneasy when Varsity pointed him out to Joe from a distance and uttered a directive, using the word, "Runt." Varsity Carnoustie clarified the situation moments later when she simply left with them, drifting away in the night, disregarding us, drawn away by Benton, for whom she suddenly had the hots. Tara rolled her eyes at me in a melancholy fashion. Aside from maybe Donna Varano, most of her friends she could take or leave.

"Sucks that she left," Blake said afterwards, glancing back and fixing his wool cap. "I think I'll cry all the way back to her brothel." His eyes scanned the road. "Really I figured on bouncing her for fifteen minutes and leaving her for dead in a leaf pile."

"Blake," Tara professed tiredly, "even though she's not a very good one, she is my friend."

We trick-or-treated several more houses and my sack began to gratefully weigh me down. Tara stayed close to me now, not wanting to let my hand go. Turning right on Saunders Avenue, Blake checked the lonely surroundings and asked for my help with a huge tree branch by the side of the road. Though I refused, he gripped an end branch with his good hand and dragged the heavy limb. Bark and leaves scraped a din over the asphalt until its length spanned the width of the road, causing a substantial blockade. The large end, where the branch had broken off, was jagged with sharp dangerous spikes of wood. A fine mess we'd have been in had a car appeared around the corner. In the overactive scenario of my mind, I could envision this obstruction causing cop cars to swarm this part of town. I strode past Blake, leaving the branch blocking the road.

"I don't need any more trouble tonight, Blake," I seethed.

He ran up beside me and stormed, "What!"

"Somebody's gotta hold a mirror to you."

"What the *heck*! Don't make such a big deal."

I kept my eyes front and shook my head.

"This won't right the wrongs in your life, Blake. That's all I'm saying."

Blake looked hurt as we walked on. I wanted to say more but I thought he knew. I was watching out for myself as it was, paranoid, vexed by the systematic breakdown of my life as I knew it. Although I may have settled up with Joe, it was only a fragment to the problem, and it seemed like this calamity would never end. Would I have to go to court one day? Contempt! Juvenile hall or a five hundred dollar fine! It was staring me in the face, though some reach of my mind kept telling me they couldn't really do that to me. Yet if I talked and the cops arrested more kids, I'd be murdered. I felt my chest filling with thick air, my scalp tightening with chills, temples banging against my skin. For the first time in my life, I was feeling major stress, stored-up irritation from the entire week. Suddenly it was vitally obvious to me that Blake and I were venting anger in opposite directions. And here was Tara in the next minute, trying to soften the mood between us by telling us she never had so much fun.

I wanted to get away from Saunders Avenue before the huge branch stopped any cars. We turned onto North Chestnut near the tennis courts and I started thinking about my uncle's house, wondering if everyone was back from the costume party. I wanted to go home, to Dudley, to see if a cop car was stationed in front like promised, to see my room, to lie down in my bed. Then I felt Tara give my hand a squeeze and I stopped missing so much. Her legs were dark in the stockings under her white imitation fur coat and my eyes wandered to her neck, the soft creamy skin of which I wanted to pepper with kisses.

A tan Buick slowed beside us under a streetlight and down rolled the window. A man in dark-rimmed spectacles leaned his head out and asked for our help. I thought it was about the branch. I looked at him and saw his hair had been combed and plastered over his bald scalp like a giant black hand. Next to him sat a pink ballerina, about twelve or so, whose stare was bland and cold. The father's voice was squeaky, and when he spoke above the engine I couldn't believe at first what he was asking me.

"Have you seen a guy in a long"—he broke off and looked at the girl—"tan overcoat you said?" The girl nodded and he stuck his face at me again. "A long tan overcoat and a black mask?"

Tara later said my brow twitched and a baffled fear showed in my eyes.

"Why?" I asked.

The man got out of the car and motioned to the ballerina. He whispered with composed intent, "My daughter back there came home just now and told me some character showed himself to her." Tara gasped and the man seemed to feel the surge of her tone. He nodded along. "And if I find this guy—" He watched as Tara started walking carefully over to the Buick. "So you sure you haven't seen anything like this guy wandering these streets?" He held his hands up. "I know it's Halloween and there's all sorts of strange things walking around tonight, but—"

Blake and I checked each other and shook our heads in unison. The man wiped his brow in a hefty manner, an obvious indication that the attack on his daughter had charged him with rage.

"I don't want this happening to any other kids tonight," he said. He gestured back to the humming Buick, where Tara was now speaking through the window to the girl. "She's obviously upset, and my wife has called the police." He marked each word sharply. "I want this guy caught."

"Yeah." It was all I could say then. This was pretty blunt stuff to me, and I felt a weird honor just having him tell us. Then I thought of something.

"Where do you live?" I asked. "I mean, where did this happen?"

The man's angered condition had shortened his attention span. He'd now spotted a woman waiting for her dog to take a leak under a streetlight, and stalked over to ask her his question. I hoped he wouldn't scare her or anything, because the manner in which he walked to meet her was almost damning. The woman seemed baffled, then immediately attentive. I could hear him explaining the same story to her. Had she seen anything peculiar? Anyone fitting that kind of description? Basically a flasher. I shrunk inside as an old fear crept up my backbone.

I walked over to the light Buick and heard Tara sweetly invite the little girl out with us, though the girl declined the offer. Who could blame her? She even rebuffed Tara's offer of candy. I bent over, gripping my sack of cavity-hasteners like a book bag. Inside the Buick, the girl appeared shaken and annoyed, a little ballerina whose night had started on an innocent note and ended with a face covered in wary and disgusted confusion.

"Did the guy come after you?" I inquired.

"She doesn't want to talk," Tara whispered. Tara took me away gently. The idling Buick's engine seemed to speak of an unfinished pursuit, a frightening purpose. It was evident that we couldn't do much but get in the way as useless bystanders. With tired legs, we decided to make for Blake's house so he could sneak back in. Though I felt the anticipation of being alone with Tara, the image of my third-grade Halloween would not leave my mind. We walked on, scanning the streets with awed caution and speaking ironically of my article the week before. A queer dour feeling was rumbling in my chest, and my eyes beheld a hazy vision of the slowly moving asphalt.

We were blocks away from the rumbling Buick and its distraught driver still conversing with the woman when Blake halted us at the corner of a road called Maye Street.

"Hold it, Ash," he said abruptly. "I almost forgot. There's someone my mom knows who I want you to meet." Swarmed in black, his nose looked tiny and undefined, his teeth and eyes especially bright. "Actually, my mom wanted me to take you there." He smirked regrettably, his good hand clenching tighter to his pillowcase. "Well, that is, before being grounded."

Wordlessly curious, I followed him. Despite the mild air, a smoky smell drifted about the neighborhood, heralding a chimney fire nearby. A group of costumes walked an opposite path to the left of the street; one tall shape dressed as the Grim Reaper. Blake let them pass and angled his march over a lawn shrouded in plywood Halloween characters. Tara's hand was warm and moist now as I towed her along.

Whoever lived here enjoyed a brilliantly young heart. The whole scene blazed in color and light. A magnificent white and blue porch circled a beautiful Victorian home. Spider webs stretched across the beams, purple strobe lights blinking behind them. Plastic goblins hung from strings and blinked a lime green glow in the air. Cornstalks and a scarecrow (which we watched carefully) flanked the front door. Styrofoam gravestones rested in haphazard positions against the rails, and an array of enormous jack-o'-lanterns sat gleaming on every step. I immediately regretted that there is only one of these nights a year.

Blake pressed a finger to the doorbell light and deep chimes resounded inside the house. I felt very small standing in the midst of this huge animated porch. A stained glass moon with the silhouette of a broom-gliding witch hung from a suction cup in the large door window. I scrunched my eyes up from the strobe lights and saw a pleasant, smiling black man behind the hanging witch. He pushed open the door. *Monster Mash* floated softly out of the house.

"Trick-or-treat!" we chirped.

The man laughed gaily in the massive doorway, one in which three people could stand side-by-side.

"Happy Halloween," he called. "Come on in."

I glanced peculiarly around and followed the other two through the door.

From the left, a lady ambled into view, leaning on a cane, but she wasn't old. Favoring a hip, she waved shortly and had the same accepting glee on her face as the black man. The whole creative ambiance was warm and inviting, but I wondered why Blake's mother wanted me to meet her. I seemed to recognize her from somewhere. Blake took off his wool hat and barged in upon the woman. Behind him, I followed his lead, removing my soldier's cap in respect.

"Hey, Mrs. Leslie," Blake said.

The woman took her head back in surprise, laughing excitedly at Blake under his temporary skin tone. He recoiled as she pinched his cheek. She then stood back to gaze at us. A puff of straight red hair surrounded her pink and white face. Her eyes contained a light green sparkle, the color of early morning frost on a field of grass. Darks baggy sweats shrouded her body. In an awkward manner of haste, she apologized for her cane—she was in the middle of recovering from hip replacement surgery.

Mrs. Leslie folded her hands on the handle and asked us about our costumes, smiling when Tara tried to pamper words that would most carefully describe a showgirl.

"You're a pretty girl," the lady said. She pointed a finger back and forth between Blake and me. "And which of these two rogues is the lucky gentleman?"

Tara blushed, and didn't answer. While she squirmed, I studied her up and down. Girlfriend sounded more and more inviting.

"This is Tara, Mrs. Leslie," Blake introduced. Tara smiled back and shook the lady's hand. Better that Spencer took the initiative or I would have slipped and added, "the Curb Owl."

Turning on her bad hip, Mrs. Leslie and her male nurse led us into the dining room, where about thirty candles cast glows that danced on the walls. Decorative cutouts hung from orange and black streamers crisscrossing the room. A festoon of punch, cookies, cake, and other spaz-inducing treats sat on a long shiny oak table. Dracula's singing voice continued to bounce off the wooden walls. I had a turned admiration for Blake, bowled over by such a great find. Mrs. Leslie poured a glass of punch for each of us as we picked from the table and stuffed our faces with brownies, listening to the numbers of kids who'd already circled this table tonight.

Finally, in an awkwardly rehearsed fashion, Blake extended his hand with the bandaged thumb at me.

"Mrs. Leslie," he announced in a funny tone, "this is Ashley Munroe, the one who wrote the article." He shifted, allowing space to the woman.

I stopped chewing and my brow furled as this woman opened her mouth, joining her hands in that sanctimonious fashion.

"Ash," Blake told me, "this is the lady who called you."

Mrs. Leslie took a gentle if impulsive hold of my arm and led me past the enormous hall into her living room. The wooden floors squeaked noticeably under our steps. The woman had made a bit of a fuss over meeting me, grabbing my hands and telling me again how much she appreciated my courage. Mrs. Leslie then moved across the room with the help of her cane. Watching the back of her red head as she now led me, I quickly remembered her phone call, a lighthouse during that storm of threats. My article, she'd said, was the talk of the supermarket that morning.

We entered the living room and I found myself stepping into a bygone era. The oval oriental rug was old, flat, frail. Antique furniture appeared to be unusable. An ancient typewriter sat on a coffee table. Though the objects were of the past, someone obviously maintained them with loving care. I glanced back approvingly at the mustached black man in his whites. Resting above the mantle were China plates, candles, and the single object giving away the hint of anything near present-day—a school portrait of a soft-faced boy with blond hair in a Christopher Columbus cut. The portrait was the one thing in the room Mrs. Leslie touched.

Resting her cane at her waist, she lifted it off the mantle as gently as handling a Robin's egg.

"I'm very glad you're here," she said.

For a moment I was slightly thrown, thinking she was speaking to the picture. Then she looked at me.

"I'm glad you came because I want to share something with you. Blake's mother tells me you're still having trouble. Perhaps this might help out just a bit."

She faced the picture to me as if holding a baby. It obviously wasn't a 90's shot.

"This was my son," she said. "Larry was a senior at your school in 1979."

I felt the presence of Tara and Blake as they shifted behind me, could hear their feet creak the floor. There was something I couldn't quite yet place in Mrs. Leslie's light green eyes.

"He was in a car accident that year," she told me. "There were four in the car." I dropped my eyes to the old oriental, knowing what was coming. "The two in the front died. Larry was one."

A thunking of shoes on wood sounded on the porch and we could hear the light voices before the doorbell rang. The mustached nurse left the room. In a second, young girlie cheers of, "Trick-or-treat!" Despite the mood, the nurse managed to give a jolly greeting and invite them into the dining room. The big door creaked and a clamor arrived to the hallway.

While the mixed sounds of laughter, surprise, and *Monster Mash* in the next room distracted me, Mrs. Leslie turned her late son's senior portrait around. Even at a distance, I could see an old newspaper photo wedged in a crease on the back of the frame. The woman slipped the print out and handed it to me, and suddenly this whole thing just completely started to freak me out.

It was a snapshot of the actual car wreck. Within the wrinkles was a dark vehicle, mangled and bent in the middle as though the force of the crash had caused it to compress into itself. The windshield lay over the hood like a piece of plastic kitchen wrap, whitened over from shattering of the glass. I pictured a kid flying through it. Why would she keep *this*, I thought?

Mrs. Leslie put a hand on my arm. I kept blinking nervously, thrown by the forwardness.

"You know where they were coming from?" she asked me.

A small nervous laugh passed through my lips and I said curtly like any teenager, "No."

Her voice was matter-of-fact. "That Indian Park. Doing exactly what you wrote about in that story. The kid who drove the car was just like the one in your story. You, young fella, were very fortunate."

"Oh," I said in realization, "you mean Mindowaskin Park."

It suddenly came to me that this was why Mrs. Spencer wanted me here. Everyone in the room waited for me to faint or something, but I couldn't tell what Mrs. Leslie wanted. Was she angry with me? Her mouth was shut, but a tight smile curved her lips. When she patted my arm I realized her hand still rested on it.

"Someone had to put a stop to that," she said softly. "Maybe things would have been a little different for my Larry had someone like you been in school with him."

Back in the dining room, *Ghostbusters* began to play. Feet clogged in the hall and three girls, a bug, a raisin, and a bum, stuck their painted faces in the living room.

"Thanks!" they yelled in unison. "Bye!"

The black man saw them back through the huge front door. Just outside, the strobe lights blinked dizzily against the bats in the cotton webbing. I gestured to the porch.

"I like what you've done with your house, Mrs. Leslie." I cleared my throat, deciding to face an acknowledgment. "And I'm really sorry about your son."

Mrs. Leslie finally removed her hand from my arm. I uneasily handed the newspaper photo back to her. She placed it gently behind the picture frame, moved to the mantle, and set it back in its original place, where it would probably remain for another grievous chain of years.

"A parent never truly gets over the death of a child," she said to the picture. "It's the strongest bond you can ever have with someone."

Her head bobbed as she drew a breath. Oddly, when she turned back around, her face was vivid with forced joviality again, an amazing transformation. She fixed Blake with bright eyes and a clownish smile.

"Which is why *you*, young man, ought to get along better with your mother!"

Blake sort of dipped his head, grinning.

"By the way," he murmured. "You can't tell her that I was here tonight." He put his hands together. "Please? I'm supposed to be grounded."

Mrs. Leslie ran her free hand through her red hair and began moving with her cane back through the hallway, shaking a tired expression from her face.

"Kiddo," she told him motherly, "Stephanie is a single working parent. I myself know how tough a job that is. I just pray to God you never have to go through that yourself." She stopped beside him. "You're a teenager, you're supposed to have problems with adults. But Stephanie loves you very much. Your mother is not only your mother. She was a girl long before you came along, and now she's a woman who needs to be loved." Mrs. Leslie prodded Blake with her cane. "And you know what I'm talking about, Master Spencer."

Blake reddened. "Yes, ma'am."

"Don't concern yourself over how much she cares for this other guy, or how much she cares about you. Believe me, she cares about you. I know. I know how much a mother cares about her child. Stephanie wouldn't compromise you for the world." Mrs. Leslie held Blake's black chin in her hands and shook it for good measure. "Give her credit, son. She's doing the best she can. Don't squander your youth in bitterness and hatred. You'll never get it back. Never."

The black male nurse leaned against the banister and folded his arms. "That's right," he said. "Live life to the fullest, kids. Enjoy it before you have to go out into the real world." Against his white clothing, his dark neck and arms were muscular, though a warm gentle aura surrounded his face. Brown eyes darted over the three of us. "And take chances—or you'll regret not doing so."

Tara and I exchanged a stare when a yell sounded from outside.

Mrs. Leslie still held up a stern finger. "Not the kind of chance my son took, though."

Someone's voice was a bit loud for the neighborhood outside. I thought it was an impatient father. Tara leaned to look out the door. Suddenly she straightened, transfixed by what she was seeing. I neared the huge door and looked out on Maye Street.

One house over from where I stood, a stationary red pickup truck sat running. The silver trim glinted in the streetlight. A man in a shiny black theater mask stood just outside the open door in a tan overcoat. His hand gripping the top of the door, he continued to call out to a pair of girls making their way down the sidewalk. By the porch light, I could see the grisly awe in their frowns.

I pushed open the door and that black mask turned to spot me. From it I discovered myself frozen. Suddenly his attention was centered *here*. There was something I recognized in his voice.

"Go the f— back inside!" the mask hollered, as if he'd challenge me if I didn't.

Blake was suddenly beside me on that porch, observing the man's overcoat with concern.

"Who's that?" he amazingly kidded. "Varsity's male twin?"

The comfort of his gibe broke my trance and I started walking toward the man. A breeze hit my face and I didn't even blink from it. I kept remembering the eyes of that girl back in the Buick, and her father's demand: "*I want this guy caught.*" The rage I suffered wasn't savage as much as it was a feeling of vacancy, a smoky memory, something my mind had often touched. I moved briskly and soon felt my feet reach the solid hardness of the sidewalk. The man waited a couple seconds, then did what both disappointed and relieved me. He sank back in his truck, slamming the door. A tightness wrenched my body. Twisting back, my arms flew up.

"COPS!" I screamed in his hearing. "Call the cops!"

I looked back and forth from those on the porch to the truck right in front of me. The truck that had scoured my street and stalked me for days was now ripping its tires and propelling up Maye Street in the same manner the midnight blue sedan did eight Halloween nights before. I made a feeble effort to chase after it, on the chance I could see where this man intended to go—he turned right on North Chestnut. I ran back to the house, feeling sudden adrenaline igniting my body like a humming wire. The two little girls were taking slow confused steps to the next yard. I called out to them, telling them to stick around. They turned and kept walking further away down the street. I hadn't time to deal with them.

Tara was the only one left on the porch when I returned. I grabbed her hand and we rushed back into the house.

Inside, Blake was the one on the phone with the police, startling me because he was putting himself in tight jeopardy, since he wasn't even supposed to be out of the confines of 32 Colonial Avenue. He looked worriedly at me as the phone left his ear.

"Ash, here," he fumbled. "Talk to this guy."

The receiver had a stale smell. The ear was active with a voice speaking to another, specifics of the address. I guessed Blake had already given it. The officer on the line informed me that they had a patrol car in the area, called in by the man who had just accosted us on North Chestnut. Everyone stayed silent, listening to me tell the cop what just happened, or would have happened, to the two girls. I provided explicit details about the red truck, its tinted windows, the sticker on back, the make of which I thought was Ford. I was surprised when the officer cut off the call.

When I walked back in the hallway, the black man apologized for not coming out with me. Blake shook his head with an occasional laugh burst, and Tara was placing her bet that "that pig" hadn't gotten wind of last week's *Hi's Eye*. We all decided it was best to stay at Mrs. Leslie's for a few minutes in case the police needed us further.

Tara, Blake and I sat outside on the porch, each of us giving our own rambling astonished account when a call came in. Mrs. Leslie's voice sounded disturbed and unsure as she opened the huge door.

"Ashley?" she called. I turned and looked up at her. The woman's tone was excitable. She said, "The police are on the phone. They said they have the truck. They need you."

I was on my feet automatically. "To ID the guy?"

She shook her red-haired head no. I watched her for a second. A weird way to meet someone, I thought.

"Honey, they only have—" Her eyes moved over my head. I whipped around and saw what she was looking at. "Here they are," she said.

A Westfield police car was slowing brightly in front of the house. No one wanted to go but me. I kept hearing that guy curse at me, kept seeing his defiant demeanor. Something in his shout had convinced me that he wouldn't be remorseful tomorrow. I was compelled to go, but I wanted company. Tara and Blake finally decided to leave the candy sacks at the house and come with me in the patrol car.

I sat in the front passenger seat next to a middle-aged cop with close-cropped hair. He drove in an easy manner, asking what we saw, reassuring us that nothing bad was going to happen. We sat like small ignorant pupils, listening as the policeman told us how the driver had abandoned the truck by the side of a road with a flat tire not far from here. Suddenly I knew we were involved. We were three kids trapped into the affair, leaning on each other for support. I sat and watched the small computer under the dashboard. The car was warm and smelled like leather. Blake was trying to ask the cop what everything in the car was for, but he never got an answer. It was a quick ride that stopped with a left on Saunders Avenue, where we had just been, and there it was.

A hundred or so yards away, sharp beams of red light danced in a steady pattern on tree trunks and adjacent houses. Two patrol cars flanked the shiny red pickup that I'd seen driving by my house that week, and some cops were on foot circling around the vehicle. Blake's branch was angled in front of us, causing us to stop. His roadblock, I thought grimly.

The officer gestured ahead to the truck.

"There's no one there, but the hood's still hot," he reassured. I felt his voice aimed at my left ear. "Is that what you just saw?"

I felt the bursts of air through my throat and nodded.

He asked again, "Is it?"

I couldn't remove my eyes from the scene around the truck. "Yes—definitely."

The policeman put a radio to his lips and signaled to someone ahead at the pickup.

"He says it is. Definitely."

We left the car and stepped over the branch. Engines rumbled everywhere. The pickup's glossy silver trim shined from police flashlights. Those trademark tinted windows reflected the spinning red strobes. Here and there a tick sounded in the engine, a sign of recent activity. There was a gooey mess, like blue silly putty, around the flattened tire. Another policeman approached me and pointed to it easily.

"Whoever it was tried to fix the tire. He just gave up and ditched." The cop ran a hand over the back of his neck and rubbed. "He was in some hurry."

Even before he told us, I had already assessed the incredible. In the most magical turn of the night, the guy had run over the branch in a panic and split the right back tire on the rough end. On hearing of this, Tara and I threw a long gaze at Blake. I saw a relaxed pride in his bobbing grin that I'd never witnessed before. Suddenly I remembered getting angry with him for the act.

"You have his name?" Tara asked the policeman, her eyes suspending in wonder.

The man turned smugly to her in his dark suit. "We will shortly."

I stepped forward and stared blindly at the forlorn truck.

"That pickup's been circling by my house all week," I said, positive that the cop was listening. Sure enough, his voice was just behind me.

"Probably a kid in your school then," he told me.

I shook my head slowly, remembering. "I don't think so. He sounded older than that."

Another car's blazing headlights appeared around North Chestnut and stopped in front of the branch. The brights blinked off. I leaned to see it—the tan Buick. The jumpy father stood out and saw us. He held up a finger to someone in the car and came jogging over. He offered a hand.

"Are you the kids who called this in?"

One by one we nodded. He sighed as he shook our hands.

"Thank God." From that gesture I felt a sense of celebration in the weirdest of ideas—a capture.

Back inside the Buick, the girl was still too shy, or scared, to join us. She had changed from her ballerina outfit to jeans and a sweatshirt. When two policemen bent over to speak in the window to her, I felt a sense of satisfaction knowing that somewhere, some sad man was sweating the inevitable. Tonight his life was changed forever. Hiding would be fruitless. Soon he would be weeded out from his sequestered life and held accountable, not only to the Westfield Police, but to the four kids present whose lives he had lewdly encountered over the years. I was sure it was him.

I took another look at his flat tire, amazed by the irony. It had blown on the jagged edge of that huge branch.

The officer who had driven us over took our names as witnesses, and told us we were free to go. Just like that, we'd turned over this night and it was over. Despite our curiosity having yet to be extinguished, we were glad to leave.

We headed off toward Blake's, now faced with the daunting challenge of sneaking the boundless convict past his mother and back into the house. By now, the only way Blake's absence could have gone undetected is if a meteorite had leveled the house. Mrs. Spencer was a shrewd woman by detail, certainly not given to ignorance, for which Blake routinely and mistakenly discredited her; all of which made Blake's decision to try and sneak in through the basement window seem terribly stupid.

We ceased talking and held our tones to hushed sinister-like whispers when we reached his yard. Blake's plan was simple. We'd dip him onto the top of the TV set, where he'd find his footing and creep the rest of the way to safety. Even if Mrs. Spencer was waiting for Blake with a paddle, I was ready to stand up for him, stating valiantly that he played an influential role in the undoing of a major town nuisance, and had helped to exorcise demons for all three of us.

Carefully we began the endeavor. Tara and I held Blake's arms as he slid his sneakers through the opening in the swinging window. We were as quiet as candlelight, but then Blake's small frame began knocking a series of pings against the window and it caused me to hurry. Blake's legs disappeared and I tightened my grasp as the weight grew. Tara was a sport, holding faithfully without a grunt. The little crook's feet kicked the inside wall. Suddenly I remembered something. Damn! With all that had happened, we'd left our candy sacks back at

Mrs. Leslie's house! I cursed softly and glanced at Tara. She caught my eye, gave a soft giggle, and it all just fell apart. Blake's arms twisted violently out of my fingers and he sloped off into darkness.

BANG!

A loud crash filled the air, followed by sounds of tumbling, then silence engulfed us. Tara had a finger at her mouth, harrowing shock in her eyes. Immediately a light blinked brightness to the basement, revealing a sorrowfully dumb look on Blake's face. There he was, sitting sprawled with his hands on the orange rug and looking sadly toward the light. Their large 27-inch television set, which he'd toppled and sent crashing to the floor, lay next to him, shattered beyond repair. His tattered attire, black face, and panted breath would be all the proof Mrs. Spencer would need. Forget the explanation. Tara and I left him sitting on that carpet and ran off in shock, laughing our brains out.

It's odd how turmoil can bind us together as much as it tears us apart. I had this in mind as I walked Tara back through the center of town toward her house. She was surprised to find me cutting us across the playground section of Mindowaskin Park toward the lighted footbridge.

"What are we doing here?" she whispered, as though people were listening.

The area was empty of kids, of anybody. I looked over to the precinct, thinking about my visit earlier in the day, and our more recent adventure. The small bridge ahead looked beautiful, inviting now. I led Tara the Curb Owl by the hand and stopped her on the crest.

Live it and take chances or you'll regret not doing so —

I tilted my cap and fixed the hair on my brow, trying like hell to imagine the words she wrote to me in her letter. I needed them for guts. Automatically I put my hands to her small waist and moved her toward me, smelling her perfume and sliding my fingers together behind her jacket.

"Well," I finally answered, "this is probably the last place anyone would look for me tonight."

Tara's eyes softened as she moved them around my face. "You wanna head back home soon, I bet," she mumbled with slight regret. "Dirty face."

I leaned back from her face and shrugged. I was about to do it then, but her words set me back into the standard unease and innocence of squirming.

Tara's chilly hands suddenly crept around my neck, and they trembled. For the first time in front of me, she was timid, coy, though anxious. I can't quite remember whose face started toward the others'sfirst, but before I knew it, all sense left my body and I could only feel my mouth against hers. Tara's lips had an inviting warmth, then a wetness that stunned me. I started moving into the kiss, peeking at her closed eyes, the way her hair softly curved over her ear. She looked at peace. This was my Tara now, the one who had pulled me from school on Wednesday, stretching out her own neck to rescue mine. A tiny sound from her throat, an eyebrow twitched in contentment. I closed my eyes again, felt her hands leave my neck as her arms slid all the way around. It was like a song I had once heard. One kiss and I was a goner. For minutes we stood tightly on the arch, a Civil War soldier kissing a showgirl. It was quite an involved act, well overdue, lasting frighteningly long. We hugged each other so firmly I could feel the soft curve of her lower back, her chest moving against mine with breath.

When came the first chance to detach for air, I took it. I put my head against hers and looked at the pond.

"God," I panted, "I guess I really like you."

Tara backed her head out and stared me in the face.

"Wha-ho!" she suddenly joked. "A coming of age thing here! It's happened before, you know."

I couldn't really see well. Everything was a blur and I felt a stab of chills, like I could drop comfortably any second right on the bridge. My vision sharpened and I realized Tara had her forehead to mine, her face so close, her sparkly eyes lively and alluring. She looked different to me now, a new subtle shine to her expression. The lamppost behind me glinted beams off her eyes and softened her cheekbones. Tara kissed me again and I was caught between emotions. I either wanted her to slow down or pull me over to the grass. So this is what the Curb Owl kisses like, I thought. We pressed in even closer and each successive kiss was easier than the last, until it was an understood thing, something done with comfort and free will now. When we finally lifted our heads away, we were breathing funny. Tara paused.

"I've lost five pounds this month because of you," she told me out of the blue, tapping my nose.

I smiled and looked sheepishly down at her shirt collar, at the lustrous skin below her neck. I didn't know what she meant by that. Tara's shoulders bobbed in a fidgety shrug and I felt it in my arms. A slow smile peeled her teeth, the glamour of it swarming my vision.

"You are confusing me, sir." She kissed my cheek and brushed the back of my hair with her hand. The newness of it gave me the chills. "You know that?"

I relaxed suddenly, knowing she wanted verbal confirmation of my feelings. I swung her slightly side-to-side and we grinned at each other.

"*You* know what's going on here," I said. I planted another long one on her and she didn't ask me any more questions after that. A few tender moments later, we strolled off the bridge in the tightness of our holds and walked for Summit Avenue. There was more to be said, but it would get its chance in time. For now we just needed to take in the freshness of ourselves. The feeling was too ripe and pure for mere words. Just how could either of us have known, when we awoke this morning, that we'd be changed like this tonight? We never know at daybreak what the eventual nighttime path will tell us.

For the first time in our knowing, Tara and I kissed expressively good-bye at her back steps. I finally walked off with her watching me until I waved before turning on South Avenue. I jogged for the other side of town. It was late.

Sauntering calmly back through Mindowaskin Park, I found myself astounded to see someone ahead on the footbridge. Jerry Corcoran.

He was by himself, smoking a cigarette. Coors watched me walk up, not recognizing me until I bluntly stopped and leaned across from him on the other cement railing, folding my arms with a sigh. Tara's love moments before on that bridge was suddenly replaced by Coors's disdain. I remembered my costume, the cap shining over my eyes. He wasn't thrilled to see me.

"How's it goin' Coors?" I asked.

He took a rather slow time in saying anything.

"So that was you before with Tara Vovens?"

I nodded, hunching slightly from a breeze in the air. For certain, the coolness wasn't the only thing stirring me. I had no idea someone had watched us. My tingling endorphins from Tara's kisses had elevated my bravado and I strained my eyes to study his face.

"You mad at me, Coors?"

Coors's eyes were dull, dark. I remembered his noose and my name on his T-shirt yesterday, tried to dismiss it for the moment. He shrugged finally.

"What's done is done, y'know?" He finished his smoke and bobbed his head, eyeing me coldly. Flicking his butt over to the dark stream, he rested his hands behind him on the arch and just stared around. He wasn't looking at me anymore. In his rocky expression, I knew apologies and understanding would be short and difficult. I made a small attempt at a wave.

"See you around," I said as friendly as I could. He only nodded once, still without watching me.

I walked three paces down the bridge and started jogging through the park, my hustling pace increasing, not stopping until I reached the long stretch of Kimball Avenue. Coors's attitude had thrown me and I felt more and more free the further I left him behind. Listening for cars, wary of moving shapes, I crossed onto Harrison Avenue, observing with pleasant euphoria different Halloween decorations in windows, noticing every lighted jack-o'-lantern, their candles dancing within, dwindling down, soon to be snuffed out, as would be the glorious night. Trick-or-treaters no longer dotted the streets. I relaxed again, still relishing the sweet flavor of Tara's kiss swimming in my mouth. My blazer wasn't providing the needed warmth from the growing cold and I squeezed my hands in the light blue trousers' pockets, liking the smooth cushioned feeling, wishing and willing more warmth. A yard nearing me was dark but for a certain orange glow that became distinct as a bush drew out of my way. Another jack-o'-lantern stared at me from its beaming eyes. I decided to head over to Jenn Dolan's house on Birch Avenue to see Tyler. "She's havin' some people over tonight," he'd invited earlier that day. It seemed days ago.

I made my way along dark Parkview Avenue, past smashed pumpkins in the road when I became aware of a slight rumbling growing more distinct behind me. Instincts sharpened over the week compelled me to turn and look. At first I thought my eyes were playing a focus trick on me. I stopped, frozen in a twist, squinting back down the road.

A few house lengths down, a dark gleaming shape seemed to be moving. Or was it my paranoid imagination? A car was parked on the side of the road, parked far from—wait—*was* it moving? I squinted deeper. Very slowly, a street lamp beam trailed up the windshield and slid over the roof.

It was moving!

The driver saw my rigid stance alone on the road. The second I started to run, the headlights of a Volvo blinked on and high beams flashed in my face. A gripping fear seared my abdomen like a burn as I angled almost aimlessly across a front lawn. I couldn't yell or exclaim a thing; I was that scared. The Volvo rumbled toward me. I hopped over a line of bushes and the chase was on.

I dashed through to Cory Place, hearing the terrible intrusive sound of screeching wheels and doors slamming. Accustomed to zooming through properties, I raged across the street and up a driveway. Feet were behind me as I scaled a wooden fence. Adrenaline left for a second when I dropped to the next yard and felt the exhaustion wash through my muscles. Speed and movement my only allies, I started running again. The back yard was woody and I made my legs tear onward, wishing I wouldn't lead these guys so easily by sound and hoping no unseen obstacles would block my path. I bulled through to North Chestnut Street, checking back. Lumbering guys appeared out of the darkness from both sides of the house. Ahead was the beginning of Oak Avenue. I knew this terrain, giving me another ally. Their only chance, and a good one at that, considering the numbers, was cutting me off. I angled over a corner yard and dashed onto Oak. My pursuers began closing in, their voices and the sound of their running growing nearer. Thinking quickly, I veered left into the same yard as the night before and saw the second yard as dark as I remembered. Feet thudded in the pachysandra behind me as I leapt the weak white picket fence in one bound and landed on the grass, praying not to slip to a frightful fall. Even anticipating the pool cover, I barely detected it in the shady dimness. Bounding carefully to the side, I sailed over the sectioned pavement and cut to the right, offering no indication of the hidden indentation.

Behind me was the comforting sound of an enormous splash, a yell, then another plopping spray. I figured I had dropped at least two on the pool. The quickest way out of the yard at hand was to the right, plain by the light. My chest pained from panting, I went for the light and saw an opening back to North Chestnut Street.

Something living moved to block me.

A shadow hunched in my way between the two houses, a shape I discerned quickly. Shock ripped me like a hot flash. Jerry Corcoran! I was furious, and he wasn't big. I knew I could handle him. Coors kept himself steadied in an ape-like position, arms stiffly extended. I ran smacked right into him, taking him off his feet and barreled by, kicking his neck as I pulled my leg from his grasp. I flew on in a panic, feeling imaginary hands on my jacket collar. They wouldn't get me without a long haul. Bursting onto North Chestnut, I sprinted breathlessly down the long stretch, my throat burning from the sudden air as at least three pairs of feet pounded behind me. The grunts were haunting, like they wanted to yell at me but couldn't waste the effort to make words. Suddenly I realized that I had gained new advantages. They had abandoned the maroon Volvo, were smokers, and lacked the conditioning for an extended run. If my legs held out, and they should, they couldn't overtake me.

For the next half-minute it was a foot race, straight down North Chestnut Street, right past my uncle's house, finally across Mountain Avenue. I could've gone to my uncle's door, but it was most likely locked and the windows were dark. I could've yelled, but no sound would come from my lungs. I was in partial shock and in need of stopping for air. I sailed up Birch Avenue, almost home free. Two houses from the Dolan's I glanced back and jogged for a bit. The group behind me was just across Mountain, but it swelled as two wet jerks slogged their way up. The dry ones opened a last-ditch full sprint for me. I was amazed at their stamina. My legs felt like jelly, and I could hardly move them. The fight for survival held me in its clutches and I stumbled into another run. I could let them get this over with right here. End it. Sneakers hitting the pavement grew louder and I just about stopped to let this finally run its course. Then I decided to cut around to the Dolan's back yard. Brightness met my eyes. There was smoky haze and movement here.

Seated cross-legged, Tyler and Brennan were puffing tranquilly under the patio light. Music from a box radio was spilling in mellow fashion out onto the yard.

My brother saw my face and was instantly on his feet with a frown. Still running madly, I could hear the violent snapping of twigs behind me, branches being swiped hurriedly. I glanced mournfully at my brother. Only two of them out here. We'd be outnumbered. I ran right past them, gesturing a panicked thumb.

"IT'S TANNER!" I finally hollered. "GET OFF YOUR ASS AND KICK HIS!"

I coursed around to the front and could hear a number of yells, shouted curses, sneakers thumping around both sides of the house, still after me. Birch Avenue curved around like a J. All I could do was keep running, hoping to tire them out. My God, wouldn't this ever end?! I had dumped Corcoran on his ass, dropped two in a pool! They *had* to be close to the end!

"Tanner!!!" someone raged behind me.

I glanced back and decided to slow at last from what I was saw. I backpedaled at the astonishing turn of action. Around the bend of Birch, the group that was following me was now being followed by another—bigger guys, in bigger numbers.

I stopped—finally—and went to fold myself over a jeep's hood with a crash. Panting, I tilted my face back up. A sopping wet Lee Hackett was trying to grab hold of Dayle Tanner's jacket sleeve, calling out to him. Tanner, in all his purposeful insanity, still had his gaze fixed on me, his shag horizontal in the breeze he caused. Just as they all closed in, I focused past their shoulders, frowned teasingly, and pointed over Dayle's head. He grabbed me with a strong bony clutch and was about to lift me off the jeep's hood when I saw his brow twist in wonder. Another burnout screamed his name and Dayle turned. He didn't turn soon enough.

Large fingers and knuckles gripped his shirt at the shoulders and jerked him back hard to my right. Smack in front of me, every orifice in Dayle Tanner's face widened in unexpected horror as he was thrown like a wooden puppet to the grass. He very nearly maintained his footing until he tripped on the curb and crashed hard on his side, spinning completely over. The burnout rebounded, popping up like a coiled spring.

Suddenly he halted at the sight of John Kane.

Paul Miller, at whom Blake had fired a rocket just one dark night before, was standing next to Tyler, Brennan, and eight of their athletic friends. They all gathered around Lee, Coors, and three other wiry burnouts, overwhelming them in size, though tense, ready. These had been some of the "people" Tyler had told me about today. My brother was placed back to the side on which he rightfully belonged, with his crowd. A quick anticipation buffeted the air.

Six-foot-five John Kane had curly blond hair and a pug face like Candy's. He approached Dayle and stood tall in his football jacket with his burly arms crossed. I thought he'd issue a course utterance about his damaged house, but the first thing he said was this:

"I'll take on anyone here."

No one. The night remained silent but for panting and an occasional labored spit. Despite the chill, the burnouts were all reddened from exertion, covered only in worn jeans and T-shirts. There they were out in front of me now, as strange to me as the night was dark. I recognized two of them from when Dayle smacked me in the eye at school. One, a dark, gangly-built, greasy-faced mongrel had stuck a middle finger in my face. Now he stood slouched, sweating, and stuck in his stupor. This whole bunch knew only my name, and I hadn't a clue as to most of theirs, yet they had wasted their energies for days on me. Did one of them belong to that walkie-talkie? Their somber baleful eyes only blinked.

"Come on, guys," John incited mockingly. "Show each other how cool you are. Either way, any way, you end up lookin' stupid." Still they only watched him.

Impatiently, John now swung to the issue of his mother's house, initiating the sequence of events by cornering Dayle against the side of the jeep and taking his shirt again in his stubby fingers. I never imagined the sight of Tanner right next to me like this.

"Guess who's payin' for new siding?" John yelled. "Have fun last night?!" He stared at Dayle, who, incredibly to me, appeared frail and small.

Kane stepped backward, stretching Dayle's shirt as he looked around. The surrounding silence seemed like a dream fulfilled.

"Who else was there last night?!" John checked Lee and beat him down with his eyes, though Lee was just as tall. "You, wet boy! Hackett, you were there! You throw bottles at my house?!"

With his hair partially soaked and a ludicrous feather earring thinned-out from pool water, Lee opened his mouth to say something. John shoved Dayle against the jeep, dumping him on the hard metal. Tanner glared at me with miserably beaten contempt. Meanwhile, John walked over and stood formidably in Lee's face. Lee bobbed slightly but didn't move his feet, a tiny stubborn play of bravado that cost him.

John brought up an open palm and hit Hackett on the side of the jaw, sending the lanky frame staggering over the asphalt. Lee righted himself, his sorry earring swinging, turned away with his hands half-up in self-disgusted surrender.

A black Ford Taurus was making speed around the bend. It paused in front of the Dolan's until the driver saw the massed group in the road. At that it was upon us in two seconds.

"Jenn's parents called the cops," Tyler reported through strong panting. "This must be them."

John turned back from watching it, spat on the street, and nodded, eyes ablaze at Dayle.

"You're gettin' it for assault and battery now," he taunted in a glee.

Dayle creaked up and indicated me with a waved hand. His voice was gruff, like his throat needed clearing.

"I'll be cool if he doesn't press charges," he managed.

"He can do whatever he wants," John said in his ear. "You'll be cool 'cause I say you'll be cool, rathead."

I whipped my head to the approaching car and noticed the black Taurus was indeed an unmarked patrol car. I was watching all this happen from under the bill of my soldier's cap, which had somehow remained stuck on my head. Still panting, I crouched over with my hands shaking on my kneecaps, succumbing to sheer fatigue.

The same mustached policeman Blake and I had met at Franklin School the night before jumped out of the passenger door and shined a flashlight on everybody, demanding to know the circumstances. I was happy when he failed to recognize me. John had started to answer the cop when a regular white station car appeared with bright headlights from the other direction. Finally, I felt I could relax. The surrounding display of protection from my peers and the cops deterred any further violence as kids who had only moments before felt the conquest in their pursuit, stood around in a spent dreary state, rung out to silence.

Three policemen now took control, speaking loudly over the whirring of their engines. But during this, that brusque mustached cop, perhaps a bit anxious, dropped his flashlight next to the jeep, where it rolled under.

What happened next cut a slice in the tension.

As soon as the officer bent over to reach under and retrieve the flashlight, the instrument was held up to him by a hand appearing from under the jeep. The cop wasn't amused.

"Get up," he simply said, his patience long departed.

And from under the jeep crawled a seventh guy, a slack-looking burnout with long black bangs whom I recognized from the first night in the park. Out of his hiding spot, he jammed his hands in his jeans pockets and swung his hair with a quick insolent toss of his head. The cop shined a beam in his eyes.

"Son?"

"Yeah, Dad?"

One of his friends hissed, "Shut up!"

Too late. The policeman walked into the kid's face, raising the flashlight over his own shoulder as though about to plunge it in the kid's chest.

"You gettin' smart with me?!" he yelled. "Huh?! Are you gettin' smart?!"

The kid looked to the side and shrugged like a boy being reamed by a nasty teacher. "No."

The officer gestured back to his car.

"'Cause I'll put you in this car and drive you straight to jail or out in the countryside where I can get into your mind. Is that clear?!" He stared where his flashlight shined. "Is that clear?!"

"Yessir."

Jeez, he sure sounded awfully similar to the way he did one night before. The cops scribbled names on a pad and I was taken in the black car to sit next to another cop. I recognized this one well. Detective Falcone, the blond close-cropped man who'd visited our house what seemed a lifetime ago and suggested the exodus from Dudley Avenue. He watched me from the side and his eyes raked my costume. He didn't say anything about it, though he noticed my condition and asked me a few polite prods. Outside, last night's short-fuse cop continued to bear down with his temper, this time giving it to Dayle Tanner. I watched the events until Mr. Falcone put a hold of reassurance on my shoulder.

"They're not gonna bother you anymore, Ashley. We're takin' care of it." He jostled my shoulder and waited for me to look at him. "You got that? We're not gonna let 'em bother you again."

Even as I sat, I felt the air forcing from my lungs tiredly. I needed rest. Falcone got out, told me to stay where I was. While I slumped in the car, watching everything out the windshield, a police radio outside blared with something that caught my attention. I heard the crackle of "truck on Saunders."

I got out promptly, despite my spent state, and walked over to the portly officer whose radio I'd heard. Hair gel molded his dark side part, causing his hair to glisten under the street lamp. He looked at me absently. I swallowed and pointed to his waist. "Is that about the abandoned truck over on North Chestnut?"

Faces turned to me and the officer nodded. I licked my dry lips and sniffled. "I was there. I called it in." I spoke quickly, expectantly. "Mrs. Leslie's house? I was there. Have you caught the guy yet?"

He blinked petulantly. "We have a name." He didn't seem inclined to give it to me.

I pushed anyway. "I have to know. I was the one who called the guy in."

Tyler was at my side with kind of a vacant stare. It was like I didn't think he believed me or something. I turned to him.

"That flasher, Tyler? Remember?" I gulped back in recall. "He was around tonight. They got his truck."

Detective Falcone's eyes seemed to widen at me as he spoke, "No, not yet."

"What's his name?" Tyler asked.

Falcone's head was tilted up, his voice clear, proud, daring in the night.

"Daniel Wicks."

I noticed that the burners suddenly seemed to look at each other with this odd dread. But I didn't see my brother's troubled face until the cops started making talk like the issue was over. The police had gotten the names of everyone, and were busy escorting my pursuers into cars so that they could spend some thoughtful time at the precinct house until their parents picked them up.

Tyler Dakota Munroe stepped forward and held Falcone's arm as he passed. "Officer?" I was right next to him when he said to the ground, "That's The Landlord."

A crease appeared in the detective's forehead. He studied Tyler. "I'm sorry?"

Tyler turned and jimmied his hands stiffly in his pockets. His breath was visible in the chill.

"Danny—Wicks," he spoke out to the night. "He's the guy, The Landlord, the one you want my little brother to tell you was the supplier at Mindowaskin." None of the burnouts disputed my brother. Tyler jabbed a thumb at me, hitting me on the arm. "He never knew a thing about him." He sucked in air, then let it out slowly, moving his eyes reluctantly between officers. "But I do."

Falcone checked an officer who shrugged at him, then squinted over my brother, as though reading his soul.

"Would you stand by that?"

Tyler glanced at me, a small jolt of shame in his eyes. "I'll testify if I have to."

I released a hold of sustained breath and felt my shoulders sink.

"So *that's* why that guy's pickup kept passing our house!" I gasped to him. I stared at the pavement, realizing why I'd recognized the guy's voice. I remembered his prank phone calls.

Falcone had a confident quality about him, easy, like he could anticipate your next question. Taking short notice of my claim, he scratched his chin with his flashlight.

"You want to give us what you know, that's great," he said leisurely. "First we gotta catch this guy. He's still mopin' around somewhere." The detective backed up a step to turn and chuckle at the first cop. "Who knows?" he huffed. "Maybe we can get a stabbing pinned on this loon, too."

"Forget it."

Dayle's voice. Tanner, like a goat wandering into the wolves, took careful steps over in the quiet and fluttered a weary hand. His eyes were set differently now, humbled, cornered, yet thinking, discovering a sudden way out for himself.

"I'll rat him," he stated half to my brother. "Officer, that guy Danny was there when the kid from Roselle Park got hurt." I guessed stabbing was too severe a term for his mind to speak aloud.

Falcone's tone was one that still didn't like Tanner. He snapped quickly, as if to shut the shaggy kid up, "Well, if we catch up to him, we'll just let *him* tell us. You get back to where I told you. Now."

The burner shook his head, eyes to Falcone's waist. I'd never seen such a plaintive look on Dayle Tanner's face. The bully had been bullied and the shell had cracked.

"You don't have to wait for Danny to say anything," he mumbled.

Falcone was loud, barking. "How come?"

Weird how deep the silence after that. A hand left Dayle's jeans pocket and waved lazily twice.

"Because I was the one who did it. I laced the kid in the park." He looked up, tight-eyed, cautious. "M'I in trouble?" He peered around and shifted. "You guys were gonna find out from Danny anyway, I know it."

Nothing happened for a second, and then Falcone shifted a foot back and reached for his cuffs. I was so taken with the moment I backed over Tyler's foot and had to balance myself. The detective turned Dayle around until his face was over one of the kid's shoulders. Right in front of me, Tanner complied, watching out of the corner of his eye, avoiding the stares and drooping lips. Handcuffs snapped around the kid's wrists in back and his eyes met mine. I can't say the look he gave me then was friendly, but it wasn't demeaning either. Dayle's eyes were calm, relaxed, as if he knew what he was doing.

"It's cool, Munroe."

He jerked upright as Falcone straightened, loosening his hold on Dayle and taking his elbow. Dayle looked over at Tyler and sounded intrinsically normal now. A quick frown flinched in his face, like this was an everyday joke and he could handle it all.

"Munroe," he said to Tyler, "don't get involved. I can use this." He swiveled his head at Falcone as they began the walk to the car. "If I'm in trouble and I give you everything on Danny, I get leniency, right?"

Falcone nodded plainly.

"Probably. Depends on what your charge is, *if* there's a charge." He placed Tanner in the car and the kid squinted up at the officer, his braces glinting. Falcone's words softened the anxiety. "From what I know, the kid's all right. You also revealed this yourself. What we'll do is find out what this kid wants to do now. But what you're *definitely* going to do"—Falcone tilted his blond head and looked out at John Kane with a smirk—"you and some of your friends here, you're going to pool together some money and fix what you did to this young man's house." Now he gestured over to Tyler and me. "And what I'm sure you all did to *their* house. Understand me?"

Dayle eased into the back seat, like he'd been there before and it didn't faze him. I kept my eyes on him. He glanced at me just once. He still didn't like me, and never would, but at least the fire was gone.

The cops summoned two more vehicles from the precinct, and seven malnourished and dope-infested burnouts were seated rather complacently in back seats. No sirens blared, no red lights flashed, just bright headlights, the constant hum of engines, and the smell of exhaust making me sick. I turned at last and stumbled heavily toward Jenn Dolan's house. In a minute, Tyler appeared on my left, and big Brennan on my right. My brother put a hand on my cap and rolled my head playfully.

"You all right?"

I bumped an elbow lightly against him and told him how much I missed my bed. We walked in the house by way of the garage door. I took a last look at the blazing scene down the street, all the cars, the leaf piles glowing in headlights, the dozen or so neighbors who'd come out to watch the late night drama. I wanted to call Tara, to excite her with another twisted story. I wanted to dial my uncle's house, wake my parents and tell them everything that had happened tonight. I chose instead to let them all sleep. Whatever I'd tell them would sound the same under a lighter sky. Horribly, I now realized it was November, Halloween's candle had extinguished, and all I had left to do was go home. It was all right to go back home now.

11

I felt safe. The precinct cars had disappeared and the street was bare when I left the Dolan's. I had waited 'til everyone had gone so I could walk alone down Birch Avenue toward home. I could finally go back to my own bed. Tyler had offered to drive me in his Grand Am, but I had passed. I needed to walk completely alone, to think, to ultimately clear my head. When I reached soulful Sinclair Place, I stopped in the middle of the quiet road and took off my storied Union soldier cap, feeling the cool air breeze through my hair. This was where I stood, seven years ago tonight, when Daniel Wicks had first attacked my life.

Wicks would surrender himself the next morning, clueless that the cops would hold him for distributing to minors. I was to learn, from Detective Spera, that Wicks was also the guy he'd made mention of during our Halloween chat as the one living across from the high school and abetting students with weekend beer runs. Wicks was charged, witnessed by Dayle Tanner, and sentenced to at least ten years in prison. Through publicity, events tonight would deter any other potential derelict from further disquieting Halloween Night in Westfield.

Mindowaskin Park ceased serving as a sanctuary for the distribution of dope and alcohol, although I am sure that other spots took on the park's weary old role. Dayle escaped all criminal charges after he testified against Wicks, and personally apologized to Steven Durant. His bank account diminished somewhat in hospital fees, as he and his burnies collectively anted up to pay for damages inflicted on two properties. Though my parents had been covered, they did receive a gratuity in this manner.

I was eventually awarded a spot in the 1992 book edition of *Who's Who in High School USA*, and received write-ups in several local newspapers, as Blake had predicted. That December, the town presented me with a plaque for bravery in journalism and six businesses in town granted me scholarship money for college in years to come.

The school would swirl for a few days, then dwindle and return to its everyday routine. Kids had their own personal issues to help occupy their minds, and puppy love affairs, tests, homework assignments, fights with friends, dealings with teachers, college applications, and graduations to attend would consume our lives again.

Blake managed to escape from everything and everyone but his own mother. He had to pay for a new TV, and his mom slapped him with a month-long grounding, which she subsequently reduced to two mere weekends. Blake revealed his involvement in trapping The Flasher, on the grounds that he had to hold *something* up in defense. I don't think that's why his mother shortened his sentence, though. Aside from his mother's flaky waffling, Jim was the one to understand him, and convince her to ease up. I hoped like anything it would sweeten Blake's disposition. I also wished that Blake would somehow find his peace and direction in this one mad night, his lesson learned hard, even at the expense of innocent neighbors.

I left my pensive stance, dropped my cap back on my head, and began walking again down Sinclair. I could still smell Tara's perfume, the fruit-tangy scent that personified the Curb Angel. I couldn't wait to hear her voice again tomorrow, how it would go up an octave after I told her what had happened. I could still feel her kisses, the touch of her lips, the closeness of her face, the elated murmur in her throat, her eyes shut with lamplight on her cheeks, lashes laid softly against her skin. She had leaned against her back door long after we'd kissed goodnight, her head tilted to one side, a satisfied contentment coating her eyes.

The oval moon was sharp in the heavens, and away from the streetlights, offered a chalky blue glow to the mystic darkness. Surrounding stars shined through a tree now fully bare. Two houses past the intersection of Lawrence Avenue, I looked left.

In a large bay window close to the little street, a big jack-o'-lantern with a standard face of triangle eyes and square teeth gleamed its brilliant smile out to the night world. Just then, as if on cue, a lady in a white sweater approached it and lifted off the top, blowing the face dark. She then recapped it for the last time and left it as a shadow in the window. Gosh what a lonely sight.

My Halloween was coming to an end.

I walked on as I did again, feeling bigger than the night itself. The streets were finally safe.

Across the street a few houses back, I heard the squeak of a door. Hidden in the shadows, I turned around just in time to see Leah Hamilton step out onto her porch in jeans and a sweatshirt. Her chest heaved and she emitted an enormous burp that echoed in the silent neighborhood. The porch lamp gave sheen to her dark hair as she lit a cigarette, as though congratulating herself. She then sat on the top step, relaxing next to another lit jack-o'-lantern and blowing streams of white smoke that dispersed under the lamplight. Beside her, the pumpkin's eyes were inverted triangles, the mouth a perverse smile, like it knew something sinister. I almost thought at first that Leah was whispering to it, but was amazed when she leaned over the pumpkin— for she thought it her only company—and exhaled a slow stream of smoke that lit the air in front of the jack's sliced face. Strokes of beams flowed eerily from the eyes like a spooky effect in a horror movie. Leah sat back up proudly, as though content in her small skill. I stood behind a telephone pole and relished the taking in of such tranquillity. The cigarette glowed as she inhaled again while the face of the carved pumpkin continued to flicker in sharp light. Finally she, too, got up and bent over her jack-o'-lantern, leaned into the orange glowing fruit, and blew the candle out.

I waited 'til she was gone and smashed it.